THE
INTERROGATOR

Also by Andrew Williams

NON-FICTION

The Battle of the Atlantic

D-Day to Berlin

THE
INTERROGATOR

ANDREW WILLIAMS

JOHN MURRAY

First published in Great Britain in 2009 by John Murray (Publishers)
An Hachette UK Company

2

© Andrew Williams 2009

Many characters in this book existed although most of the events described are fictional.

A CIP catalogue record for this title is available from the British Library

Hardback ISBN 978-0-7195-2361-8
Paperback ISBN 978-0-7195-2371-7

Typeset in 11.5/14.75 New Caledonia by Servis Filmsetting Ltd, Stockport, Cheshire

Printed and bound by Clays Ltd, St Ives plc

John Murray policy is to use papers that are natural, renewable and recyclable products and made from wood grown in sustainable forests. The logging and manufacturing processes are expected to conform to the environmental regulations of the country of origin.

John Murray (Publishers)
338 Euston Road
London NW1 3BH

www.johnmurray.co.uk

For my parents

CONTENTS

PROLOGUE   1

PART ONE   9

March 1941   11

April 1941   35

May 1941   65

June 1941   109

PART TWO   183

July 1941   185

August 1941   261

September 1941   313

PART THREE   359

Historical Note on Codes   369

Note on Sources   371

PROLOGUE

Do not rescue people and take them along.
Do not worry about lifeboats . . . concern yourself
only with your own boat and the effort to achieve
the next success as quickly as possible. We must
be hard in this war.

**Standing Operational Order
No. 154, Befehlshaber der Unterseeboote, Admiral
Karl Dönitz**

2210 GMT
HMS *Culloden*
16 September 1940
55°20N, 22°30W

At nightfall the rhythm of the storm quickened and by the middle of the first watch the sea was surging knee-high across the quarter-deck. Sharp plumes of spray swept along the ship's sides into the darkness astern as she cut the top of one wave and raced to the bottom of the next. Douglas Lindsay – the *Culloden*'s first lieutenant – stepped into the shelter of the gun platform and hoisted himself clear of the tide foaming white towards him. He had made his way through the ship from bridge to quarterdeck and everything was secure, the lifelines rigged and the watch as vigilant as it could be on such a night. It was North Atlantic foul, and yet he was glad of the excuse to be on the upper deck, salt spray stinging his face and hands. On the bridge, the atmosphere was thick with failure, the captain restless and ill tempered.

Bent almost double, he stepped out from beneath the canopy on the port side into the wind. Spray rattled against his oilskins and he reached for a lifeline to steady himself. It whipped from his grasp. At the same moment he heard a noise above the storm that was quite foreign. It was a deep hollow boom like the sound of a heavy door slamming in a cathedral cloister. The ship shuddered and heeled violently, pitching Lindsay forward on to his hands and knees. Thin blue smoke was rising from the starboard side below the funnel, ragged chunks of steel falling through it like a fountain. The wireless mast, the bridge and fo'c'sle were toppling to starboard and above the wail of the Atlantic Lindsay could hear the screech of grinding metal. Someone at his shoulder was moaning, 'Please God no, please.' Then

3

it was over, over in a terrifying, bewildering instant. The entire fore-part of the ship had gone and with it close to two hundred men.

Through the spray and smoke, Lindsay could see the for'ard section drifting away, the dark outline of stem and bow uppermost, the bridge and most of the mess deck beneath the waves. A torpedo had torn the ship in two and men he knew well were struggling below against a dark torrent. He could see them there, a savage kaleidoscope of images, but he could do nothing to help them.

A seaman pushed roughly past, forcing him to look away. The deck trembled beneath his feet as the wreck of the stern pitched awkwardly, tumbling from wave to wave. Then a torch light flashed across his face.

'Thank God, sir . . .' The junior engineer, Jones, sounded close to tears. 'The captain's . . .' but his words were lost to the wind.

Lindsay ordered a headcount beneath the quarterdeck canopy. There were twenty-five seamen – the depth-charge party, the after-gun crew, engineer and stokers shivering in only their oily singlets and trousers.

'They'll miss us, sir,' one of them chattered, 'the other escorts, they'll miss us soon, won't they?.'

'Yes,' he said with as much conviction as he could manage. But their convoy and its escort ships were seven miles to the east and steaming away. The waves were twice the height of an ordinary house, rolling out of the darkness, their crests breaking into straggly white spindrift. The wreck was without power, the wireless and the lifeboats gone. Their best, their only hope was to cling to its heaving deck for as long as they were able. 'My first command,' and he almost laughed out loud.

Lindsay was twenty-four years old – tall, slim, with straw-blond hair, light-blue eyes, a soft voice and the faintest of Scottish accents. Before the war, he had considered a career in the quiet smoke-filled rooms of the Foreign Office. It might have suited him well – he was clever, articulate, close by disposition – but he had joined the volunteer reserve – the gentleman's navy. Many times in the last two years he had reflected ruefully on this choice – diplomats never died in war.

Shoulders hunched, spray driving hard against his face, he staggered as far for'ard with the engineer, Jones, as he dared. A little more than a third of the ship had gone, ripped apart at the break of the fo'c'sle. The sea was pounding the flat steel bulkhead of Number Two boiler room.

'It won't hold for long,' shouted Jones. As if to prove his point a huge wave thundered against it, forcing them to cower at the foot of the funnel, eyes stinging, salt spiking their throats.

Lindsay tugged at Jones's arm and pointed back along the deck. There was a rumble and seconds later a crack as a star shell burst over the sea to starboard and began to fall slowly back. Half a dozen seamen were gathered about the anti-aircraft gun, their faces turned intently upwards like Baptists at a Sabbath prayer meeting.

Chief Petty Officer Hyde was in command: 'No flares, sir, just twenty star shells.'

Lindsay glanced at his watch and was surprised to see that twenty minutes had passed since the explosion and it was almost half past ten. How long would the boiler room bulkhead hold? An hour, perhaps two, no more than two. 'One shell every six minutes, Chief.'

Hyde's face wrinkled in concentration as he counted: 'Two hours. Yes, sir.'

They made their way down dark companionways and passages, unfamiliar in the torchlight, intensely close, shuddering and bucking. The wreck's movement was sickening below and their mouths dry with fear that the bulkhead would collapse and catch them there.

'There's about three feet of water,' said Jones, his torch flashing about the boiler room. 'We're too late here. We'll have to shore up the engine room.' The atmosphere was thick with hot choking fumes and the sea rang in the boiler room like a temple bell. They stepped back through the watertight door and Lindsay watched as Jones and the stokers struggled in anxious silence to position a timber brace against the bulkhead. Wide-eyed, white, they flickered in and out of the torchlight like figures in an old film.

'It won't last long when the boiler room floods,' shouted Jones, the strain evident in his voice.

'You've done well,' said Lindsay with studied calm. They all needed some reassurance, some hope.

He left the engineer and returned to the quarterdeck where a second work party was trying to hoist depth charges over the side. They were

5

stacked in racks at the stern, a score or more of them, enough high explosive to scatter the wreck across the Atlantic. Another star shell burst on the starboard side casting a restless splinter of light. Number nine – it was almost eleven o'clock. The stokers were back on the upper deck, shivering uncontrollably, singlets clinging wet beneath their life jackets. None of them would survive longer than half an hour in the water, not at this latitude, even in September. He was on the point of ordering them below to search for clothes when there was a muffled shout from the lookout on the gun platform above. Jones raced up the ladder and was back in an instant: 'Flashing light to starboard, sir, perhaps two miles distance.' He was breathless with hope.

'Very good. Let's fire another then and quick about it,' said Lindsay as calmly as he could.

It was further twenty minutes before they could be sure, but as she pitched and rolled out of the darkness the seamen on the quarterdeck began to cheer. She was the dumpy little corvette HMS *Rosemary* from their escort group; there was no mistaking her open bridge and the sweep of her bow. Her Aldis lamp blinked madly at them.

'Signal from *Rosemary*, sir. She wants to get a line across to us and rig a bosun's chair.'

The wreck shuddered as a wave pounded against its makeshift bow, sending another drenching sheet of spray racing along the sides.

'Let's make sure we're ready to receive it, Chief,' shouted Lindsay.

The *Rosemary* turned to run on a parallel course and was lifted to the crest of a wave until she towered above them, her screws racing clear of the ocean. She was rolling unhappily, struggling to edge close enough to fire a line, the sea an unbridgeable broken white between them, the restless length of a rugby pitch. One pass, a second and then a third, and Lindsay knew it was impossible. Grim faces, sagging shoulders, the seamen about him were of the same mind. And at that moment, as if possessed by a contrary spirit, the wreck pitched forward with a vicious jolt, the sea sweeping along the deck to meet them.

'She's going,' shouted Jones desperately. No one needed to be told. Instead of rising with the next wave the *Culloden* was settling at a sickening angle, the sea boiling about its funnel.

'Signal to *Rosemary*, preparing to abandon ship,' shouted Lindsay. But the *Rosemary* was already hanging scramble nets down her sides.

Everyone was at the quarterdeck rail. To Lindsay's right was one of the stokers, eyes glazed, expression fixed, careless with the cold. It was too late to do anything for him.

'The *Rosemary*'s standing by.' He spoke as if to strangers, empty and distant. 'Stay with the Carley rafts and she will find you. Good luck.' And then, from somewhere, words he never thought he would hear, let alone have to say: 'Abandon ship.'

A few feet below him, the sea was surging white up the side, in constant terrifying motion. 'Go. Go now,' and with a great effort of will he stepped forward. The shock of the cold water left him breathless. He was struggling to keep his head clear, gasping, panicking. Swept to the crest of a wave, he could see the grey side of the corvette two hundred yards away and, close by, a Carley raft with men hanging round its sides. Heart pounding, he struck out towards it and welcoming hands pulled him in and on to a rope. At that moment, the wreck gave a deep groan and as the raft swung about he saw its stern rise from the sea to hang there, its screws glinting darkly.

'Swim, swim.'

They were too close. It would drag them under. There was a frenzy of splashing and the raft raced forward. Then with a blinding yellow-white flash, the sea lifted in a huge dome beneath them. Confused, only half-conscious, Lindsay let go of the raft. His eyes were stinging, his arms heavy as if he were swimming in treacle. The wreck had gone and the sea was on fire, shrouded in choking black smoke. A dark shape floated close by and he reached out to touch it. It half turned, a body, face burnt black, features unrecognisable, and he could taste its sickly smell. Through the smoke he glimpsed another seaman waving frantically. He was lost between waves for a moment but reappeared only feet away. His face was oily black and almost all his hair had gone.

'Where's the *Rosemary*?' Lindsay shouted, but the sailor was too frantic to listen or care. After a few seconds his head slumped forward on to his life vest. Lindsay tried to support him, to keep his mouth and nose clear of the water, but he felt weak and cold to his very core. 'I'm going to die,' he thought, and was surprised by how little it concerned him. He could see himself drifting on, pushed from wave to wave, held upright in the Atlantic by his life jacket, and he wondered if he had the strength to take it off.

And then someone was pulling at his arm and shouting, 'Give me your fucking hand.' More hands were pulling at him, lifting him up and over the side. And the last thing he remembered was his cheek against cold steel.

PART ONE

MARCH 1941

In the spring our U-boat war will begin at sea,
and they will notice that we have not been sleeping . . .
the year 1941 will be, I am convinced,
the historical year of a great European New Order.

Adolf Hitler Speech at Berlin Sports Hall 1941

1

The Admiralty's Operational Intelligence Centre
The Citadel
London

Mary Henderson woke to a splitting headache, her sheets damp with condensation and every muscle in her body stiff. It was morning but the room was as black as the grave. She lay there listening to the rumble of sleep. The Admiralty had squeezed three bunk beds – six women – into a narrow concrete corridor with no windows and no ventilation. Could it have been worse on a slaver? Mary wondered. Fumbling for her torch, she dived beneath the bedclothes and shone the light on the face of her watch. Seven o'clock. No time for breakfast – a small sacrifice – the canteen cooks boiled and battered the taste from everything they touched.

One of the bunks creaked threateningly. Mary surfaced, grabbed the bag at the bottom of her bed and swung her legs into the darkness. The bolt on the bathroom door slid into place with a satisfying clunk. She turned reluctantly to the mirror. Her sandy-green eyes were red-rimmed and weepy. Two days without sunlight had cast an unhealthy shadow on her white, even skin and her thick black shoulder-length hair fell in unruly curls about her face. Her girlfriends told her that she should make more effort with her appearance; she was pretty and, at twenty-six, too young for sensible shoes and badly cut tweed. Perhaps it was acceptable in the university libraries she used to frequent, but naval officers preferred a little glamour. Mary knew her friends were wrong. A spring frock from the collection at Adèle's might turn a head or two above ground but it would do nothing for her authority in the subterranean world of the Citadel.

Huge, featureless, it was a cruel brown block of concrete just a stone's throw from Trafalgar Square, Whitehall and Downing Street.

The Citadel was a little like a submarine with its squat tower on the Mall and its deck stretching aft to Horse Guards Parade, and rather like a submarine, it was larger below the surface than above. Mary had visited her uncle at the House of Commons the autumn before and he was the first to mention it to her. Hitler's bombers were pounding London by day and night and it had struck her as strange that a small army of workmen was busy throwing up a new building when so many were in need of repair. In the time it had taken to complete, she had abandoned her academic post at an Oxford college to become part of its secret life. Workmen were still crashing about the upper floors and there was the sharp smell of wet concrete in the corridors but the Navy's Operational Intelligence Centre had moved into its new home next to the Admiralty

By the time she felt presentable enough to leave the ladies' room it was almost half past seven. A couple of cross-looking Wrens were shivering in their dressing gowns in the dimly lit corridor. She gave them her sweetest smile. Room 41 was in the bowels of the building, down drab cream stairs and corridors, past the convoy wall-plot, the signals girls in Room 29 and the watch-keepers in 30. At its blue door, she paused to catch her breath, then turned the handle and stepped quickly inside.

'Good morning, Dr Henderson' – it was the duty officer, Lieutenant Freddie Wilmot. He liked to tease her with her academic title. 'Sleep well?'

'No.'

Wilmot frowned and shook his head in mock sympathy: 'Sorry to hear that but then I didn't sleep at all.'

'You'll be off duty in an hour – you'll be able to breathe again.'

Heavy pools of smoke swirled beneath the droplights like winter smog. The atmosphere was always impossibly thick in the Tracking Room. Everyone smoked – everyone but Mary. It had the stale smell of a room that was never empty. With the smoke, the half-light and the clatter of typewriters, at first her head had throbbed continually. But she was used to it now and perversely it helped to induce a strange, exhilarating mental clarity.

Mary Henderson was the first woman to be given a senior role in Naval Intelligence. Her crustier male colleagues had grumbled that the Submarine Tracking Room was no place for a 'female', an Oxford archaeologist. In her first weeks, they had made her feel as useful as a village bumpkin press-ganged into service on a man-of-war. What with the shrugs and snatched conversations, she had floundered in a sea of acronyms and potent initials: 'Put DDOD (H) on the distribution list'; 'don't forget DNOR and please be sure to ring the SOI. to FOS'. It seemed like a ritual designed to confuse the interloper in the clubhouse. She found it easier to nod and pretend, then secretly search the Citadel's telephone directory for clues. Her head of section, Rodger Winn, caught her with one on her knee, like a naughty schoolgirl with a crib sheet in an examination. But Winn was an outsider too, a clever lawyer with a twisted back and a limp. The Navy would have classified him as 'unfit' in peacetime but now the heavy duty of tracking the enemy's submarines in the Atlantic rested on his awkward shoulders.

Winn took Mary's education upon himself. Calling her into his office, he roughed out the structure of the Naval Intelligence Division on a blackboard. 'At the top, the Director or DNI, that's Admiral Godfrey in Room 39, entrance behind the statue of Captain Cook on the Mall. Under the Director, nineteen sections dealing with everything from the security of our own codes to propaganda and prisoners of war.' For more than an hour, he shuffled back and forth in front of the board, presenting the facts with the austere clarity of a High Court barrister. 'We'll only win the war at sea if we win it here in the Citadel first,' he told her.

The Citadel was the heartbeat of the Division, where threads from fifteen different sources – enemy signals, agents in the field, photographic reconnaissance – were carefully gathered. A thousand ships had been lost in 1940 and with them food, fuel, steel and ore. The country was under siege. The Germans held the coast from Norway to the Pyrenees and were busy establishing new bases for their U-boats. 'They're playing merry hell with our convoys. If we can't stop them, they'll cut our lifeline west to America and the Empire and we'll lose the war.' Winn was not a man to gild the lily.

Mary settled behind her desk and lifted a thick bundle of signals and reports from her in-tray. The first flimsy was from HMS *Wanderer* in the North Atlantic. At 0212 the destroyer had registered

15

a 'strong contact' with a submerged submarine on her echo detector. Two hours later and fifteen miles to the west, HMS *Vanoc* reported another. Was it the same U-boat on a north-westerly course? Perhaps the enemy was preparing a fresh pack attack on convoys south of Iceland. A timely warning would save ships and lives. Mary's task was to pursue the German U-boat as mercilessly on paper as a destroyer might at sea. It was careful work that called for a trained mind and the memory of an elephant. My sort of work, she thought with the self-conscious pride of a novice.

A few feet from her, Wilmot was dictating the night's 'headlines' to a typist and at the far end of the room, the plotters were clucking around a wall chart of the British coast. Room 41 was long and narrow, bursting with map tables and filing cabinets, too small for the fifteen people who would be weaving up and down it within the hour. It resembled a shabby newspaper office with its rows of plain wooden desks covered in copy paper, black Bakelite phones and typewriters. The main Atlantic plot was laid out on a large table in the centre of the room: a crazy collage of cardboard arrows, pinheads and criss-crossed cotton threads. At times the enemy's U-boats could be tracked with painful certainty – a distress call from a lone merchant ship or a convoy under attack – but at other times the plot was marked with what the section called 'Winn's Guess'.

'Good morning to all. A quiet night I hope?'

Rodger Winn had shuffled through the doorway, peaked cap in one hand, brown leather briefcase in the other. He blinked owlishly at the room for a moment, then began to struggle out of his service coat. The well-tailored uniform beneath was embroidered with the swirling gold sleeve-hoops of a commander in the volunteer reserve. He was in his late thirties, short, stocky, with powerful, restless shoulders, twinkling eyes and a good-humoured smile. Wilmot stepped forward with his clipboard to hover at his elbow: 'Good news, Rodger – Berlin has confirmed the loss of the *U-100*.'

'I heard that on the BBC,' replied Winn brusquely.

Mary bent a little closer to the signals on her desk in an effort to disguise an embarrassingly broad smirk.

'It's the only good news. I was trying to spare you the rest.'

'Don't.'

Wilmot led Winn to the plot and began to take him through the night's business. A tanker and three freighters had been sunk in the North Atlantic and four more ships damaged. 'But here the news is worse.' Wilmot's hand swept south across the table to a cluster of pin-heads off the coast of West Africa. 'Homebound convoy from Sierra Leone – SL.68. Six more ships sunk – three of them tankers – that's twelve ships in three days.'

Winn groaned and reached inside his jacket for his cigarettes. He shook one from the packet and lit it with a snap of his lighter: 'Any idea how many U-boats they've sent into African waters?'

'Perhaps three,' said Wilmot with a doubtful shrug of his shoulders. 'A French source in the naval dockyard at Lorient thinks one of them is the *U-112*. The crew was issued with warm-weather clothes.'

Winn half turned from the plot to blink over his glasses at Mary: 'Dr Henderson, what do we have in the index?'

Mary reached up to a small box on top of the battered filing cabinet beside her desk. She flicked through it, found the *112's* file card and handed it to Winn.

'Kapitän zur See Jürgen Mohr: a very capable commander,' he grunted. 'What's our source – can you check?' He paused to remove a thread of tobacco from his lip. 'The most senior U-boat officer still at sea. The darling of the newsreels. They've credited him with twenty five of our ships – perhaps after last night's attacks, a few more.'

Winn handed Mary the card: 'You'll need to update this.'

He turned back to lean over the plot, resting his weight on his hands. He had suffered from Polio as a boy and found it uncomfortable to stand unsupported for long. The pile of signals and reports on Mary's desk seemed to have mysteriously grown. She would have to work her way through it before the midday conference.

'He's winning, Mary. Winning.'

She looked up in surprise. Winn was gazing intently at a small portrait photograph on the wall above the plot table. It was of a thin, severe-looking man who sat primly upright, hands held tightly in front of him. He was wearing the rings and star of a German admiral and the Ritterkreuz – the Knight's Cross of the Iron Cross – hung at his throat. It was the face of the enemy, their particular enemy, the commander of the German U-boat arm:Karl Dönitz.

'Always a step ahead of us.' Winn drew heavily on the last of his cigarette, then squeezed it into an ashtray at the edge of the plot. 'A step ahead.'

Mary did not speak to Winn again that morning but she was conscious of his presence at the plot. He shuffled out of his office three, perhaps four times, to stand beside it, stroking his cheek thoughtfully, cigarette burning between his fingers. After an unpleasant lunch in the Admiralty canteen, she returned to her desk to find a note from him in her in-tray.

An interrogator from Section 11 visiting tomorrow at 1100. He says he has something for us. Talk to him.

Mary groaned and glanced resentfully at Winn's office but he was out. She pushed the note away. Who was this interrogator and what was so important that he could not send in a report like the rest of his Section?

2

MI5 Holding Centre
Camp 020
Ham Common
London

There was a sharp grating noise on the flagstones and the interrogator's head bobbed out of the light. He had lost patience. On the other side of the desk Helmut Lange hunched his shoulders. His right knee was trembling and his mouth was sticky dry. This time the blow drove him to the floor, a crushing tide of pain breaking through his body. The room was hot with confused, brilliant light. Something was dripping on to the stone in front of him.

'Get up. Get up.'

The words seemed to echo down a long tunnel. Then someone grabbed his arm tightly, pulling him to his feet.

'I know you're a spy, Leutnant Lange. Help me and you will help yourself.' Lange could feel the interrogator's breath on his cheek, smoky stale. He was an elderly man, softly spoken and with strangely sympathetic eyes, an army officer of some kind. His German was thickly accented. There were two more soldiers in the room, younger, harder.

'I'm a navy journalist,' Lange croaked, 'I've told you. It was my first war patrol.' His lips were salty with blood.

'The U-500 was going to land you in Scotland. Who were you to contact?'

Lange tried to shake his head. Shapes swirled before his eyes: highly polished shoes, well-creased trousers – someone was wearing gloves – crimson spots, there were drops of blood on his prison overalls. He felt guilty about the blood.

'You speak English,' said the interrogator.

'A little,' groaned Lange.

'And you've been trained to use a wireless transmitter.'

'No.'

'You're not the first, Herr Lange. We were expecting you. Another of Major Ritter's men. You were trained in Hamburg?' There was a note of quiet menace in the interrogator's voice.

'I was writing a feature piece,' said Lange. 'Why won't you believe me? Please, please ask the crew. Ask the commander, he'll tell you.'

'You're a fool not a hero, Herr Lange, and we're losing patience with you.' The interrogator paused, then added in almost a whisper: 'If you won't co-operate we'll take you to Cell Fourteen. The mortuary is opposite Cell Fourteen.'

Lange knew he couldn't stand any more, but how could he make them believe him? He had been in the room for hours, the same questions over and over, questions he could not answer. He knew nothing of U-boats or spies. It had been his first war patrol.

And then he was on his knees again, gasping for air, a deep throbbing pain in his side. He was going to be sick. One of the other men was shouting at him now: 'Cell Fourteen, Lange, Cell Fourteen . . . oh Christ he's . . .'

There was a bitter taste of bile in Lange's mouth. He retched again. His knees felt wet. The interrogator said something in English he could not understand. Then shadows began to move across the floor.

The door opened and he heard the sharp click of leather-soled shoes. Were they taking him to Cell Fourteen? He felt dizzy and he was shaking. There was a murmur in the room, his interrogator's voice raised sharply above the rest. They were arguing. Lange caught no more of their conversation than his name. It was important not to speak or move. He felt so tired, tired enough to fall asleep there on the floor.

For a moment, he thought he had been struck again. The room was full of painful light. But a soft voice he did not recognise said in perfect German,'You can get up now, Herr Leutnant.'

He was suddenly conscious that he was kneeling in a pool of vomit. There were five men in the room and they were all looking at him. He felt no better than a dog, broken and humiliated. He lifted a trembling hand to his swollen face. One of his eyes had closed.

'Let me help you.' It was the same calm, reassuring voice and instead of khaki this man was wearing the blue uniform of a naval officer. Lange began to cry quiet tears of shame. The naval officer reached down and hoisted him up on to unsteady legs.

'My name is Lieutenant Lindsay. I want you to come with me.'

Confused, Lange followed him out of the interrogation room and slowly, head bowed, along a dark corridor with cell doors to left and right. Footfalls echoed behind them and his heart beat faster. Perhaps it was a trick and they were going to drag him back. But at the end of the corridor, a guard opened the steel security gate and Lindsay led him down a short flight of steps into the rain. He stood in front of the cell block, cool drops falling gently on his face. Smoky London rain, he could taste it, smell it. To his right there was a large yellow-brick Victorian villa; opposite, a collection of Nissan huts and the perimeter wire. A wooden screen had been built a few yards beyond it to shield the camp from passers-by.

'Where is this place?'

'Do you smoke?' Lieutenant Lindsay offered him a silver cigarette case. Lange tried to take one but his hand was still shaking uncontrollably. 'Here.' Lindsay held a cigarette to his lips. The smoke made him giddy, numbing the pain in his face and sides.

Lindsay waved to a large black official-looking car that was parked in front of the house. It moved forward at once and a few seconds later pulled up in front of the cell block. The soldier behind the wheel stepped smartly out and opened the rear doors. Lange shuffled across the red leather seat, his trousers clinging unpleasantly to his knees.

'I'm sorry,' he muttered, conscious of the sickly-sweet smell.

The heater was on and the air was hot and stale. An opaque glass screen separated them from the driver and blinds were pulled down over the rear windows. It looked and felt like a funeral car. The engine turned again. Lange glanced across at the British officer sitting impassively beside him, and wiped his eyes with the back of his hand. He wanted to say, 'Thank you, thank you for saving me,' but the tight anxiety of the last four days was draining from him and his head began to nod forwards. He was just conscious of stammering, 'Where are we going?' but if there was an answer he did not hear it.

3

Room 41
The Citadel
London

It was a little after eleven and Mary Henderson had just begun to hack her way through a report from the Admiralty's technical branch when a shadow fell across her desk. She raised her eyes to its edge, to the doeskin sleeves and gold hoops of a reserve lieutenant.

'This is Dr Henderson.' Rodger Winn was standing at his side. 'Mary, I would like you to meet one of our colleagues from Section 11.'

The interrogator; she had forgotten all about him. She pushed her chair back and looked up at a curiously striking face, thin, with prominent cheek-bones and a nose that looked as if it had been broken on the rugby field. The lieutenant was at least six feet tall, upright, with wavy fair hair, youthful but for the dark shadows about his blue eyes.

'Douglas Lindsay.' He held her hand firmly in his for a moment.

Winn was fiddling impatiently with one of the pencils on Mary's desk, clearly itching to extricate himself: 'Lindsay's going to take you through some of the things he's wrung from the crew of the *U-500*. One of the prisoners – the engineer – claims they can dive deeper than we thought possible – below six hundred and fifty feet.'

Without waiting for a reply, Winn turned back to his little glass office, leaving Lindsay standing awkwardly at Mary's desk.

'I don't suppose Rodger offered you tea?'

'No but no thank you.'

She watched him struggle like an ungainly spider into a chair that was uncomfortably close to the desk. Glancing up in some confusion, he caught her smile.

22

'You're enjoying my discomfort, Dr Henderson,' he said in mock outrage, delivered with a twinkle in the primmest of prim west-of-Scotland accents. 'I'm glad to have been of some service.'

She laughed: 'Great service. Rodger seems impressed with your report.'

'It's not Rodger I need to impress,' he said with a weak smile. 'Our own submarine people refuse to believe us and if they don't, the Admiralty staff certainly won't.' He held her gaze for an uncomfortable, unblinking moment, then glanced down at his hands: 'Perhaps you're wondering why the Navy bothers with interrogators if it doesn't trust them to distinguish fact from fiction. I've asked myself the question every day for the last four months.'

'My brother works for Section 11 too.'

'Henderson?' Lindsay shook his head a little: 'How foolish of me – Lieutenant-Commander Henderson.'

Mary nodded. Her brother had joined Naval Intelligence a few weeks before the outbreak of war. Everyone in the family had been surprised. Their father was a gentleman farmer, prosperous, conservative, but with a keen armchair interest in the world. He was encouraged by Mary's mother to educate them well but with James it had been, a struggle. They were not close. He was only four years older than Mary but paternalistic, insufferably so, with conventional views on women and work. And yet, remarkably, he had mentioned her name to the Director's Assistant, Ian Fleming, and that had secured her the position in the Division.

Lindsay reached down to his briefcase and took out a red cardboard file marked 'U-500.' Placing it on the edge of Mary's desk, he opened it to reveal a sheaf of closely typed flimsies.

'The commander, Kapitänleutnant Fischer, was quite a decent sort, although his officers thought he was too familiar with the men – drank with them, enjoyed the same brothels, that sort of thing. There was a propaganda reporter on board but I haven't had a chance to question him yet. The other officers were Nazis, an ignorant bunch with no knowledge of history or literature. They were insulted when I asked them if they were religious . . .'

Mary leant forward as if to touch Lindsay's sleeve: 'Why were they insulted?'

'They are devout *Deutschgläubig* – German-believers. Their creed is pure blood, strong leadership – immeasurably superior to faith in a God they call a "Jewish Jehovah".'

'Do you ever meet prisoners who are just ordinary Christians?'

'Sometimes,' said Lindsay, glancing at his watch. 'I can tell you more, but perhaps some other time.'

It sounded a little like a brush-off. Mary flushed with embarrassment. She eased back into her chair, twisting her body towards the desk and away from him: 'I'm sorry, curiosity – it's just that the enemy is not much more than a name and number here.'

She glanced up at Lindsay and was surprised by his playful smile. 'No, I'm glad you're interested and I would be happy to talk to you about the prisoners in a little more detail, if you think it would be useful. There are a few sketchy observations here.' He rested his hand on the cardboard file. 'But this is just the crew of the U-500.'

Mary nodded: 'I can't get anything from my brother, he just grumbles about them.'

Lindsay frowned and was on the point of saying something but must have thought better of it. Instead he pulled out another file from his briefcase. This one was stamped in red, Very Secret'.

'These are SR reports, Speech Recordings taken in the last couple of weeks at our Interrogation Centre at Cockfosters.'

'You've been secretly recording the prisoners?' she asked.

'The interesting ones. It's a laborious process, you have to change recording discs every six minutes or so.'

'And they don't suspect?'

'They were warned not to say anything but they forget after a time. They can't help themselves, they're anxious so they talk. You know – 'What did he ask you?' Lindsay smiled a small tight-lipped smile: 'I'm just glad we don't have to beat it out of them.'

'Could you?'

'No.'

He began to leaf through the SR reports, drawing to her attention details of U-boat sailings, new commanders and ships attacked. It was routine intelligence, nothing that set Mary's blood racing, nothing that seemed 'Very Secret'. After a quarter of an hour he closed the file and slipped it back on the desk. One flimsy was still lying across his knees. Mary caught his eye again but this time he looked away. She watched him play with the edge of the paper, lifting it and letting it fall.

'Thank you, Lieutenant,' she said at last, 'I'll work my way through your file and . . .'

But Lindsay cut across her: 'There is one more thing.' He picked up the sheet on his knee. 'Commander Winn was rather cool about it,' he shifted awkwardly in his chair as if embarrassed at the recollection, 'but I think it's important. *Unser B-Dienst ist unterrichtet.* I'm sorry, do you speak German?'

'Not enough.'

'B-Dienst – the B-Service – is responsible for the Kriegsmarine's signals intelligence, code-breaking, that sort of thing.'

'I know.'

'We're under strict orders not to discuss signals and codes with the prisoners, but look at this.' Lindsay handed her the sheet of paper. It was the transcript of a conversation between three wireless operators. Prisoners 495 and 514 were from a U-boat sunk in January, but the third man was one of the wireless operators on the *U-500* – prisoner 530.

> *Prisoner 495: We heard on the radio that the convoy had*
>   *sailed on the 5th and was probably to the south of our area. It*
>   *is really amazing how well organised our 'B-Service' is, what*
>   *it seems to know.*
> *Prisoner 514: It was the same on my last U-boat.*
> *Prisoner 530: Our B-men know everything. They know when*
>   *the English convoys sail and when they arrive for sure.*
>   *They're very clever. They know how many ships are in the*
>   *convoy and the number of escort destroyers.*

Mary read it again and then for a third time. She could sense that Lindsay was watching her carefully and he wanted her to be impressed. She was impressed. A few short sentences but it might be something of real importance. Of course, it was just one prisoner and only a petty officer. Perhaps it was idle talk or a *ruse de guerre*.

Lindsay's chair screeched as he pulled it closer and their knees touched.

'You don't need to worry about people here, you know,' she said, blushing a little. 'They're all cleared to read this stuff.'

'It's just that I'm not sure Commander Winn wanted me to mention it to you.'

'No? Why?'

Lindsay brushed the question aside: 'You can see what this means.'

He was leaning forward, his blue eyes bright with excitement, almost childlike. Mary was conscious of how close he had pulled his chair, really too close. A tiny charge of excitement tingled from her neck to her toes. The proper thing would be to restore a businesslike distance but instead she pretended to study the transcript on her knee.

Beyond the edge of the paper she could see that his hands were squeezing the arms of his chair so hard his knuckles had turned white. He was a tightly coiled spring.

'You do see what this means,' he said again. 'Prisoner 530, Oberfunkmaat Zier – you see what this means?'

'What do you think it means?'

Lindsay leant back and took a deep breath: 'At least one of our codes has been broken.'

4

'**A**re you all right, sir?'

Lindsay opened his eyes and blinked at the blur of khaki by his side. It was one of the Citadel's guards, a tubby sergeant in a uniform at least a size too small for him.

'I'm fine, Sergeant, thank you.'

'Yes, sir.' With a sharp salute, the sergeant turned on his heels and began to march purposefully towards the gun emplacement beneath the centre span of Admiralty Arch. A work detail of Indian soldiers was filling sandbags in front of it, traffic passing to left and right, their strongpoint creeping up the white stone like a growth. Whitehall was still preparing for an invasion: there were trenches in St James's Park, rifle pits at the Palace. Across the Mall, a matronly-looking lady was bumping her pram up the steps at the bottom of Spring Gardens, a baby's gas mask swinging wildly from the canopy.

It was a glorious spring day. Lindsay was standing by the statue of Cook in front of the Admiralty, enjoying the bright warmth of the sun on his face. Exhilaration, he felt sheer bloody exhilaration and tense too, like an animal caught in the lights of a car at night. Reason and good sense were threatened. Mary Henderson had lit an unruly spark. She had the air of an academic bluestocking, dusty, a little neglected, but there was something reticent and thoughtful in her manner that he found very, very attractive. She was pretty in an unconventional way, with the most striking Slavic green eyes, complicated like jadeite. Quite different from her brother. Chalk and cheese.

Lindsay had spent his first awkward weeks as an interrogator shadowing James Henderson. It had been enlightening in a way. Henderson spoke barely intelligible German with a thick county accent and he bellowed it at the prisoners as if he was on a Prussian parade ground. Most were either baffled or openly contemptuous of him and not to be shaken from their belligerent silence. For his part, Henderson felt nothing short of hatred for them. Nor did he care very much for Lindsay. What would he think of Mary's invitation? It was as intriguing as it was unexpected. She had asked him to her brother's birthday celebration and he had surprised himself and said 'Yes'. Since the *Culloden*, he had avoided clubs and parties, and friends and family had given up trying to coax him out in the evenings. Perhaps Henderson's bash would be a new beginning, some sort of release.

The sun slipped behind cloud and Lindsay felt the sharp chill of a March breeze on his face. It was a little after one o'clock and he was expected at the Interrogation Centre – a dreary train journey through the north London suburbs to Cockfosters. He glanced over his shoulder at the entrance to the Admiralty, half hoping to find Mary in the traffic at the door, then he set off at a brisk pace along the Mall. In Trafalgar Square, a violinist, a refugee from Middle Europe, was playing Strauss for pennies from civil servants in their lunch break. Some soldiers in greatcoats were smoking and chatting close by, their eyes drawn as one to the legs of a passing shopgirl. The square had become a sad grey place, the fountains empty but for a few dirty puddles. Ugly brick shelters had been built on the north and west sides, their walls roughly plastered with air-raid instructions, and the east side was dominated by a huge soot-stained banner of a convoy sailing under the protection of the white ensign. London was changing, slipping into a dark pocket, a place of wire and rubble, ration cards and wailing sirens.

Beyond the square, smartly dressed women were beginning to gather on the steps of St Martin-in-the Fields for a service that was to be broadcast by the BBC to the Empire. Lindsay slipped through the crowd and on past the long, patient bus queues in Charing Cross Road. At Leicester Square, the concourse was heaving with shoppers, travellers with cardboard suitcases, blue and khaki uniforms. He joined the queue for the Piccadilly Line and was stepping through the ticket barrier when he heard someone call his name: 'Lieutenant Lindsay . . . sir.'

Turning, he saw the slight figure of a young naval officer pushing towards him. It was the *Culloden*'s engineer, Edward Jones, his thin freckled face pink with embarrassment.

'I'm sorry I shouted, sir,' he said anxiously, 'I was so pleased to see you. What a coincidence.'

They shook hands over the ticket barrier.

'Yes. Quite a coincidence,' said Lindsay quietly.

The last he had seen of Jones was on the ward of a Liverpool hospital five months before. In the days after the sinking they had said very little to each other. None of the survivors had talked much. A few had gone on drunken benders together in the city but Lindsay had turned inwards, ashamed and guilty, and there were the flashbacks. Every second, every word spoken on the ship that night picked over until it was raw. He felt responsible – he was the ship's first officer – he should have done more. Why was he alive when so many had perished? The question was always with him.

The doctors said it was a sort of battle fatigue and that it would pass – in time.

'How are you, Jones?'

'Fine, sir. I've been visiting a friend at the Admiralty. Spot of leave, my last for a while.' And he explained in his mellifluous Welsh way that he had become the engineering officer on a newly commissioned corvette that would begin convoy duties at the end of the month.

'Of course I would rather serve on a destroyer. Our little ship has this very awkward corkscrew motion. A glorified trawler. And you, sir?'

'I'm working for the Admiralty. With German prisoners,' said Lindsay almost apologetically.

'Oh, bad luck.' Jones coloured, aware that he had said something that might offend: 'Not that I want to suggest . . . but more comfortable.'

'Yes,' said Lindsay with a slight nod of the head. Of course it was more comfortable. They stood in awkward silence at the barrier as shoppers and servicemen bustled noisily past.

'Look, I'm sorry, Jones, but I must go,' said Lindsay at last, his voice a little strained.

Jones was clearly disappointed: 'I hope I haven't said . . .'

'No, no, of course not,' said Lindsay, cutting across him. 'I'm on my way to a meeting.' It was a lie and it sounded very like one too, but nothing had changed since the hospital. He could not speak of the *Culloden*, of the memories they shared, and what else was there? He held out his hand again and as Jones shook it they made proper eye contact for the first time. It was only for a moment but Lindsay recognised the deep weariness in the engineer's eyes.

Later, he found it difficult to shake the recollection of it from his thoughts. He stood at the edge of the Piccadilly Line platform and peered into the mouth of the tunnel, barely conscious of the passing minutes and the people who came to stand at his side. A distant speck of light began to rumble and flash towards him, almost imperceptibly at first, then it seemed to gather speed, faster, closer, faster, until it was disconcertingly close. It burst from the tunnel with a high-pitched scream that filled his mind with a familiar dull ache.

'HMS *Culloden*? It was last September. She was lost in one of their first group attacks. Some of the details were in the monthly bulletin. Cut clean in two.'

Rodger Winn pushed his chair back and reached for a cigarette. Mary was standing beside his desk with the *U-500* interrogation file in her hands. 'Lindsay was the first officer,' said Winn, 'and well, he . . .'

Winn leant forward and lifted a flimsy from the mountain of paper in front of him.

'Have you seen this?' he said, with the air of someone with more pressing matters to consider.

'What were you going to say about Lieutenant Lindsay?'

Winn blinked curiously at Mary, then looked away, but not before she had caught the suggestion of a sly smile.

'Did you notice his ribbon – the Distinguished Service Cross? Fleming says he picked it up on the night the ship was lost.'

Mary had not noticed.

Winn took off his thick black-rimmed spectacles and placed them carefully on the desk. Head bent, he rubbed his eyes wearily with his thumb and forefinger. 'Fleming has a high opinion of Lindsay,' he said from behind his hand, 'a natural interrogator, but he says the loss of the ship has hit him hard. You can see it in his face, can't you? He's a little over-zealous too. This business of our codes – the Director and Fleming agree with me – he needs to be careful not to overstep the mark.'

'I told him you'd think it was important and would want someone to look into it,' said Mary.

'Did you?' Winn looked up at her, his brow knotted in a deep frown. 'You're ready to make that judgement? Yes, it needs to be investigated but not by Lieutenant Lindsay. Interrogators are under strict orders not to question prisoners about their codes in case they give away too much of what we know already. The head of Section 11, Colonel Checkland, will be asked to send all that he has on this to Code Security here at the Admiralty. Of course, it's a possibility. They're hammering away at our codes but . . .' Winn held Mary's gaze for a moment, then said with careful emphasis, 'but we'll know if one of them has been broken soon enough, won't we, and from a rather more reliable source than Lindsay's prisoner?'

Mary nodded. Special intelligence. It was the secret key to their work in the Citadel, or promised to be. Only a small circle in Naval Intelligence – 'the indoctrinated' – knew of the source. Lindsay was outside the circle.

'Is there anything else?' Winn glanced down to the papers on his desk as if to indicate that he hoped there was not.

'Just that I've asked Lieutenant Lindsay to tell me a little more about the U-boat prisoners – morale, education, beliefs, that sort of thing. Is that all right?'

'Fleming tells me there's no better person.' There was a cautious note in his voice that surprised Mary.

'That's his job isn't it?'

Winn lifted his glasses very deliberately from the desk and slipped them back on. He stared at her intently, then he said: 'Yes, it is his job. But be very careful what you say to him about ours. You see, he's half German.'

The clock at the far end of Room 41 had stopped – one of the plotters was trying to coax it back to life – but Mary knew that it was at least ten. The cigarette smoke of the day hung eerily thick beneath the droplamps, softening the hard edges of the room. The plotters floated through it as if in a dream, distant and opaque. Mary's eyes were stinging with fatigue. She reached beneath the papers on her desk for her watch. Yes, it was a quarter past ten. There was just one thing more she wanted to do.

The duty officer, Lieutenant Geoff Childs, a dry but cheery soul, a peacetime geographer, was standing at the plot table: 'On your way?'

'Almost. Just a little housekeeping.'

She picked up her bag and walked down the room to one of the large grey filing cabinets that stood against the wall just beyond the plot.

Pulling open the top drawer, she began to flick through the tightly packed files of anti-submarine warfare bulletins. It was in the October report – homebound fast convoy attacked first on 15 September 1940 – thirty-six ships in nine columns with four Royal Navy escorts – a depressingly thick bundle listing the hulls and the cargoes lost; oil, grain, lead and lumber. A very brief paper had been attached to the main narrative:

Subject: Loss of HMS Culloden:
At about 2210/16 a torpedo struck the ship on the starboard side, probably in No. 1 Boiler Room. At once the ship began to list and then broke in two. This took place within a minute of the explosion. The wreck of the stern wallowed on an even keel until 1145/16, when the order was given to abandon ship. HMS Rosemary was on hand to rescue twelve of the crew.

It was signed by the 'senior surviving officer': Lieutenant Douglas Lindsay. Mary checked all the September and October reports but there was nothing more on the loss of the ship. It was puzzling. Everything was written up and circulated in the Navy, a small forest consumed every day. But two hundred men and a ship had been sunk and there were just five lines in the file. Why? She closed the drawer of the cabinet with a resounding thump.

Mary stepped out into a world of unexpected noise and light. A heavy rescue squad in blue boiler suits was marshalling at the entrance to the Admiralty and she could hear the clatter and whine of a fire engine in the Mall. The all-clear had just sounded and people were beginning to trickle from the surface shelters in Trafalgar Square. The sky flickered an angry orange and searchlights were hunting madly overhead, careering back and forth through the darkness. Above them, a cold white moon – a bomber's moon. A whirlwind of fire had rumbled and burst in the city, sweeping away warehouses, churches, homes, gouging great holes in streets and parks. And yet cocooned in her concrete world twenty feet below the ground, Mary had heard nothing, sensed nothing.

'It's the worst this year. They've got the Café de Paris.'

A naval officer she did not recognise was standing at her side. The Café de Paris: her brother had taken her to hear the West Indian Orchestra only two weeks before. It was expensive, smart and gay, one of the hottest nightspots in town and one of the safest. A waiter had told them the Café was untouchable.

'That's where this lot are going,' said the naval officer, nodding to the rescue squad; 'it's a mess.'

The windows were out and smoke and brick dust seemed to hang over Coventry Street like a fog. Was it curiosity, or a need to do 'something', or both? Mary was not sure why she chose to follow the rescue workers. The anti-aircraft guns were still thumping in Hyde Park and yet the street was full of people like her, the anxious and the nosy, fat men smoking cigars, women in evening dresses who looked for all the world as if they were queuing for a West End show. She walked slowly on, slipping through the dust fog like a shadow, her shoes crunching across a carpet of glass.

The ambulances were full and the stretcher parties had begun to lay the wounded and dying on the pavement in front of the Rialto Cinema. A foot, stocking torn and shoeless, poked rudely out from beneath a rough pile of the Café's tablecloths. A young woman was sobbing uncontrollably beside it, her face flecked with tiny splinters of glass. The Café was beneath the cinema, its entrance at the bottom of a long flight of steps, choked with rubble. A Dutch army officer was staggering up them with an elegantly dressed, grey-haired lady in his arms. She cried out in pain as he stumbled and Mary could see that her leg had been roughly set with a long-handled spoon from the Café's kitchens. Then they brought up an RAF officer on a stretcher, face ashen, thick trauma pad pressed to a hole in his head, and more stretchers and more walking wounded. Lonely figures wandered in the smoke haze, numb and uncertain. Mary recognised a clerical assistant from the Citadel, her pretty face streaked with tears, and she stepped out of the crowd to put a comforting arm around her.

'Have you seen Teddy?' Her voice was empty, distant.

'Sarah, isn't it?'

'Where's Teddy?'

A large Canadian nurse caught Mary's arm and pulled her roughly away from the steps: 'Mobile Aid Leicester Square.'

'Here—' and Mary wrapped her mackintosh about Sarah's bare shoulders. Then she led her by the hand through the press of spectators.

'There was a woman, naked, and bodies – bodies everywhere. An RAF officer was holding another woman and he kept saying, "mother's all right" but her head was practically . . .'

Mary stopped to fold Sarah tightly in her arms, to stroke her dusty hair: 'Shush. Let's not speak of it.' Sarah's slight frame began to heave with silent sobs. 'Where's Teddy?' she gasped again.

Two, three, four minutes, and they stood in the dark street hugging each other as ambulances, the walking wounded and the curious passed them by.

Teddy was waiting at the aid post in Leicester Square, his chin trembling with emotion: 'Thank God.' He wiped his eyes with the back of his hand and teardrops stained the dusty sleeve of his khaki uniform. Were they brother and sister or lovers? They left before Mary could find out, their heads bent together across the square. Sarah was still wearing Mary's old mac. At the aid post a weary Belgian doctor who had been in the Café told her that two bombs had crashed through the roof of the Rialto on to the dance floor. Only one had exploded but the carnage was terrible none the less. The Café was like the great ballroom of an ocean liner and its glittering mirrors had shattered into countless cutting, stabbing pieces.

Mary walked slowly home along Whitehall, mind and weary body oppressed by thoughts of the Café de Paris. The sky was still a flaming orange and strangely beautiful. But in the City – or was it further east in Stepney and Bow – firemen were fighting to save other streets, other families trapped in the rubble of their homes. Why was it like this? So many lives lost and so much pain. Nothing seemed to be beyond the reach of the Germans, nothing was sacred any more.

APRIL 1941

TOP SECRET
Interrogation on Enemy Signal Procedure:
. . . a firm rule must be maintained: prisoners
should never be interrogated on signals
procedure or questioned on the signals
they have made or received . . .

**Admiralty NID 11,
Notes on the Interrogation
of Prisoners of War 1939–45**

5

U-112
08°50N 15°30W
North Atlantic

'**A**laaaarm!'
It pierced the anxious silence like the cry of a man falling from a precipice. At once the dive bell began to tremble.

'Clear the bridge.'

Bodies dropping from the tower, heavy boots clattering over the deck plates, the lights swinging above the mess tables as every man sought his station in the boat.

'Herr Kap'tän. Destroyer.'

The first officer's face was white with shock, words tripping and tumbling from him: 'From nowhere . . . upon us . . . under a thousand metres . . .'

'Calm yourself. Down to a hundred.'

'Flood four and five.'

The control-room mechanics were already working the valve wheels, the sea rumbling into the tanks as the *U-112* began to dip sharply under. Seventy-six tight metres of steel from stern to bow. At least thirty seconds to clear the surface. Kapitän zur See Jürgen Mohr glanced at his watch and then towards the radio room:

'Well?'

The operator's face was half turned towards him, one hand pressed firmly to his headpiece, the other at the dial of the hydrophones: 'Contact closing fast. 050 degrees. Port bow.'

'Silent running, Chief.'

Young faces stiff and pale in the harsh light of the control room, bearded after a month at sea, their wide eyes turned to the depth-gauge needle dropping so slowly.

'Herr Kap'tän. Coming straight for us.' The voice of the radio operator was high-pitched and urgent. Seconds later and Mohr could hear her too, drawing ever closer, louder, closer, her screws swishing like wind in the Arctic. The young engineer at his side was gripping the skirt of the tower, his mouth a little open, his breath short and shaky.

'Engines full. Right full rudder. Deeper.'

The radio operator leant further forward to make himself heard: 'Herr Kap'tän. Depth charges.'

But he could hear the soft splash, splash, splash of the barrels as they broke the surface, rolling and sinking. And he followed the second hand round the face of his watch, 25, 30, 35 . . .

'Brace. Brace.'

A crewman was whimpering close by. As Mohr turned to look, a charge boomed beneath the boat, tossing the stern up and round in a corkscrew motion and he was thrown hard against the periscope housing. Deck plates lifted as a second detonated on the starboard side, then a third and the lights flickered and died . . . Someone was lying across Mohr's feet and he could feel a trickle of blood on his cheek. Some lights had shattered. The depth gauge had blown too. Another detonation, above them this time. A tin of some sort smacked against the skirt of the tower behind him. One of the men in the torpedo room for'ard was shouting something unintelligible, his voice shaking with fear.

'Steady. Steady there. Watch your depth, Chief.'

A swooshing of compressed air to the tanks and the 112's bow began to lift.

'Emergency lighting.'

'Herr Kap'tän.' The first officer, Gretschel, was holding his white commander's cap.

The faces of the control-room mechanics were turned towards him, anxious, expectant, trusting. They had been there together a dozen times.

'Depth?'

The second officer had taken his place for'ard by the gauge in the torpedo room: '180 metres . . .'

'Damage report, Chief?'

Everything was wet to the touch, oil and water working their way through valves, trickling down the pipes into the bilges, the deck plates treacherous underfoot, cracked battery cells, splintered wood, broken glass.

'Deeper. Take her deeper.'

Leutnant Koch's voice rang the length of the boat: '170 metres . . . 180 . . .'

'Where is she?'

The operator leant out of the radio room and shook his head: 'Nothing.'

But a moment later they could hear her reaching out for them with her Asdic detector, high-pitched, insistent, ping, ping, ping bouncing against the hull of the boat.

'Deeper still.'

'190 . . . 200 . . .'

'Contact closing, Herr Kap'tän . . .'

The thrashing of her screws again, attack speed, closer, closer, closer.

'Both engines full.'

'Depth charges dropped . . .'

A deep shudder ran through the boat as a charge detonated with an ear-splitting boom on the port bow. And then another, and another, and another, rolling the boat like a bath toy under a tap, throwing men against wheels and pipes and instruments and to the deck, and plunging them into darkness.

'Torches.'

Another barrage, charge after charge, the boat plunging down and round, a deep echo grumbling through the depths. Mohr could hear water cascading in a heavy stream from the periscope packing. His uniform was wet and the control room was filling with the sharp smell and taste of chlorine gas. Someone flashed a torch in his face: 'Herr Kap'tän, the starboard motor's gone completely.' It was the young engineer, Heine, his face contorted with stress and fear, 'And the port motor's damaged and the port diesel too.'

'Work on it and quickly.'

Then from the for'ard torpedo room: '210 metres . . . 220 . . .'

The boat was slipping away, the hull creaking and groaning under the pressure. And from somewhere near the stern, a wild knocking as if a giant sea creature was prising the *112* open like a shell. A sharp pop close by as another valve seal was blown open and then another and another and a fountain of water arching across the control room, twinkling in the torchlight. Mohr could hear water and diesel sloshing above the deck plates, and his ankles were wet.

'Get those valves tightened at once. Air to the tanks. Give her air.'

'Herr Kap'tän, there's too much water in the for'ard bilges.'

'230 metres . . .' The crew could hear the panic in Leutnant Koch's voice. Was this the end? If the *112* slipped much further it would be crushed under the pressure like an empty tin can. The stern and bow planes were in the surface position but the boat was still drifting to the ocean floor.

'Come on, give it air.'

'240 metres . . .'

They were deeper than the maximum dive depth now and still sinking. All heads for'ard of the control room were turned in Mohr's direction; the petty officers, the torpedo men and machinists, the radio operators and Braun the cook, so young, so frightened, breathless, silently pleading with him: 'What now, Kap'tän, what now?' And he knew there was only one thing he could do:

'Prepare to surface.'

The boat seemed to heave a sigh as compressed air rushed into the ballast tanks. Three, four, five seconds . . . a desperate stillness. It had barely moved.

'250 metres . . .'

Someone was muttering a prayer.

'Give it more, Chief. More.'

The boat's last gasp, a long steady hiss. And slowly, slowly its bow began to rise.

'240 Herr Kap'tän . . . 230 . . . 220 . . .'

A small cheer from the torpedo room.

'Silence.'

The *112* gathered speed, a giant steel bubble forcing its way to the surface.

That it should come to this after so long and on this most sensitive of missions. The British would be on them in minutes.

'Breathing apparatus. Prepare to abandon ship.'

Gretschel was standing beside him holding a *Tauchretter:* 'For you, Herr Kap'tän.'

'What will Admiral Dönitz say, Gretschel?'

'He'll be sure we did our best, Herr Kap'tän.' The first officer's voice shook a little with emotion.

The 112 broke the surface bow first and settled down by the stern, water surging from its deck. Cold fresh salt air he could taste swept through the boat like a wind as Gretschel flung open the tower hatch. It was almost midnight and clear, the sea quite still but for the dark silhouette of the destroyer closing fast on the port side, cutting a clean white wave at her bow.

'Enemy closing 055, a thousand metres, Herr Kap'tän.'

'Prepare the weighted bag.'

The secret papers and the cipher machine must go over the side at once. The 112 was sinking rapidly by the stern but he had to be sure.

'Out, out, out.'

In the worn, familiar faces at the foot of the tower the fear that even now that small ring of night sky above them might be snatched away, the boat sinking back, sealing them in their iron coffin. Mohr pushed his way through them to the radio room:

'Ready.'

'Yes, Herr Kap'tän.' The chief radio operator pointed to two bags on the small table in front of him: 'The Enigma ciphering machine in this one and the code books and mission orders in the other.'

'Come with me,' and he snatched up the bag with the mission orders. Climbing slowly through the darkness, the bag heavy at his chest, the sound of feet scuffling on the bridge above, and as his hand reached for the topmost rung a zing, zing, zing of bullets striking the tower. The destroyer was firing at them.

'Over the side.'

And the crew began dropping from the deck into the ocean.

'Scuttling charges set?'

'Yes, yes,' Heine shouted from below, panic ringing in his voice again.

'Open the strainer and get out.'

Another bullet pinged against the tower. The destroyer was close enough for Mohr to hear the slow rattle of her heavy machine gun. Her captain could have no idea of the prize he was going to drag from the Atlantic. The engineer was at his side:

'All right, you can join them.'

The little lights on the life vests of his men were rising and falling in the dark ocean, small groups clustered together, arms raised in supplication to the enemy. And the destroyer was edging closer, a beam of brilliant white light from a large lamp trained on the deck of the 112. Mohr picked up the bag at his feet, checked the seal and its weight – good enough – and with a great sideways sweep of his arm flung it over the lip of the tower into the darkness. A small phosphorescent splash and the bag and its secrets sank out of sight, dropping thousands of metres to the ocean floor. Mohr smiled ruefully. If only it were that simple, if only it could end there with the secret of their mission lost fathoms down where no one would find it. If only . . .

6

Interrogation Room 4
The Combined Services Detailed Interrogation Centre
Trent Park
Cockfosters

Lindsay looked up from his pad with a deliberate smile and reached for his cigarettes.

'Would you like another, Herr Leutnant?' he asked in German. He slid the packet across the shabby wooden table to Helmut Lange who pounced on it like a man possessed: 'Thank you.'

An angry-looking crack in his lip was making it uncomfortable to speak. About his right eye, the bruising was turning from ugly green to yellow and it wrinkled into a painful, mottled pattern when he smiled.

'Why do you think my . . .' Lindsay looked down at the packet of Players he was turning slowly in his hand, 'my colleague thought you were a spy?'

'I don't know. I'm a journalist, a navy journalist.'

Lindsay nodded.

'You believe me?' His face was broadcasting relief.

'Yes.'

It had been a mistake. They seemed to happen often. By some mysterious process the possibility that Leutnant zur See Lange was a spy became a probability the moment he was handed over to the Security Service – MI5. Spies had to be broken. Five had given the task to Major Cunningham, a prickly veteran of the Great War known for his 'robust' interrogation style.

'I think the man you call your colleague wanted to kill me', said Lange with feeling. 'I prayed to the Virgin Mary that it would stop. Then you came.'

'I just hope . . .' Lindsay sighed and held his hand reflectively to his lips for a moment, 'I just hope we can hold on to you, Herr Leutnant.'

The suggestion in his voice that this was by no means a foregone conclusion was not lost on Lange. Anxiety was written in thick lines across his brow: 'But you can send me to join the rest of the crew now.'

'First I must convince my colleague that I'm right about you and he's wrong.'

'I don't know any secrets. Speak to the crew of the 500 – they will tell you.' Lange was picking distractedly at the peeling varnish of the tabletop. He was a short man, muscular with close-cropped brown hair and a heavy shaving shadow that made him appear older than his twenty-three years. His round face was peculiarly expressive, almost guileless.

Lindsay opened the briefcase at his feet and took out a magazine with a photograph of a sinking ship on the cover. It was the German Navy's *Signal*: 'I read it as often as I can. Do you remember this one?' He pushed it across the table to Lange. 'There's a piece on page five about "the disintegrating poison of Jewry".'

Lange wriggled uncomfortably: 'That was written in Berlin.'

'I see. And are you worried about this Jewish "poison" too?'

'I'm a reporter, I write about the Navy,' said Lange defensively.

Lindsay stared at him for several seconds, the silence full of black-bird song. Shadows were dancing across the bare white walls of the interrogation room as the wind shook the branches of a large cedar growing close to the window. The officers of *U-500* had described Lange as good-natured, religious, an unlikely ideologue and a *Landratte* – uncomfortable at sea. He knew no more about U-boats than he needed for a morale-boosting feature piece. But Lindsay sensed that with a little coaxing he would talk freely and a clever, inquisitive prisoner could be put to good use.

'You're from Bavaria, aren't you?' he said at last. 'I can tell by your accent – Munich?'

'Yes, Munich.'

'And your father's a teacher.'

Lange shifted anxiously in his seat again. 'How did you know?'

'I've picked up a few things.'

'I've told you I don't know any secrets.'

'Yes, so you say.' Lindsay leant forward earnestly to look Lange in the eye: 'I believe you, really I do. But the other interrogator, the soldier, he doesn't, you see. You must help me convince him.'

7

By the time Lindsay had collected his papers, the prisoner had gone. Three hours' gentle probing and he knew Helmut Lange's life story. Only time would tell if it was worth the effort. He could still hear prisoner and guard clumping up what was once the private staircase to the top of the house. Trent Park was too grand and airy for anything as mean as a cell block. The chinoiserie and old masters had been replaced by camp chairs and wall charts but an air of bright elegance lingered yet. It was a strangely self-conscious air. The house was not what it seemed. The grand Palladian façade had been built only ten years before with eighteenth-century bricks salvaged from Devonshire House in Piccadilly; the portico was from Chesterfield House, the obelisks from Wrest Park: stones, stairs and statues, almost everything, had come from somewhere else. Trent Park had acquired its history. It fascinated Lindsay because it spoke eloquently to him of its creator: Sir Philip Sassoon – Eton and Oxford, Member of Parliament and Under-Secretary at the Air Ministry – the lisping, swarthy scion of Jewish merchant princes.

Sassoon was reputed to have lured anybody who was anyone in fashionable society to his home. The newspapers listed politicians, princes, even the King of a small country. Their cars had swept up the long drive and on to the forecourt where a Union flag was picked out in pink-and-white stone rescued from the old Westminster Bridge. But Sassoon was an outsider. No one Lindsay knew personally had been on the guest list but he often wondered if all that blue blood had whispered, 'Nice fellow but a little foreign.' Sassoon had died in the summer before the war and the Combined Services Detailed Interrogation Centre – CSDIC – had taken his home. Now young Nazis lived under his roof and strolled under escort through his gardens.

It was a little after four o'clock when Lindsay made his way down the grand oak staircase into the entrance hall. A low shaft of sunlight was pouring through the west-facing window, its smoky brightness shifting and swirling about the guards at the security desk.

'Lindsay, I've been looking for you.'

Lieutenant-Commander James Henderson was squeezing his broad frame through the half-closed porch door: 'May I have a word.' His voice bounced roughly about the elegant plaster ceiling and pillars: 'Let's walk.'

Lindsay followed him out of the hall and through the security fence on to the broad brick terrace at the east end of the house. They stopped by the gate to the swimming pool, once the heated height of luxury, empty now but for last autumn's curling leaves.

'I haven't wished you a happy birthday,' said Lindsay, offering Henderson his hand.

'You're coming tonight, aren't you?'

'Yes. Thank you.'

Henderson began to push at a loose piece of brick paving, edging it backwards and forwards with his shoe. He was an awkward-looking man, an inch or so shorter than Lindsay but broader and heavier, an East Anglian farmer even in his well-tailored blue uniform and an unlikely recruit to Naval Intelligence.

When he lifted his chin at last, there was a dark frown on his face and his lips were tightly pursed. There was clearly something difficult he wanted to say.

'Cards down, Lindsay, Colonel Checkland is cross because you went behind his back to the Citadel. It wasn't your place to speak to Winn about our codes.'

Lindsay almost smiled – Checkland was always cross with him. The Colonel was the head of Section 11 and had been for as long as anyone could remember. But Naval Intelligence was changing. Reserve officers twenty years his junior called the shots, clever amateurs with an academic contempt for rank and naval discipline – men like Rodger Winn and Ian Fleming. It was Ian Fleming who had found Lindsay his job as an interrogator and Checkland was certainly not going to forget that.

'The Colonel wants you to drop it,' said Henderson firmly. 'It was just idle talk, gossip. The right people at the Admiralty have looked into it and they're satisfied there is nothing to suggest any of our codes are compromised.'

'Did they interrogate my prisoner, Zier, the wireless operator?'

'Drop it. It's nothing. You've been here four months, you're good at your job but you're wrong about this, and there are important security issues at stake here.'

'Of course there are – the security of our codes,' said Lindsay crossly.

'I don't mean that.'

'What do you mean?'

'It's not important for you to know.'

Henderson paused to make eye contact and when he spoke his voice was cold:

'Do you think you know better than everyone else? Don't rub people up the wrong way. Look, we've taken a chance with you. Don't give us reasons to doubt you. The Director of Naval Intelligence has instructed interrogators not to question prisoners about codes. This is not for you. Leave it alone. Oh, and that's an order, an order from the Director.'

It was unambiguous, final, and it needled. Code and Cipher Security at the Admiralty had slammed the door shut without taking the trouble to interview Lindsay or Prisoner 530.

'It's a pity Colonel Checkland isn't prepared to back the judgement of his interrogators,' he said with a bitter shake of the head.

Henderson sighed pointedly. 'If you want to take it up with him in person, be my guest, but I would hate to see you have to go.'

Lindsay knew that was a lie. There was no love lost between them. But what was the point of brow-beating the messenger when in three hours' time he would be standing, glass in hand, at his party. Henderson must have read the resignation in his face. Touching his elbow, he began to propel him gently along the terrace in pursuit of the sunshine. A couple of well-dressed clerical assistants were perched on the stone balustrade at the far end, chatting animatedly beneath a vigorous lead statue of Hercules. He stopped well short of them and turned to face Lindsay. 'You're doing a good job, Douglas,' he cooed. 'Don't spoil it. Look, I need to be away. I promised Uncle I would be at his house by seven.' He hesitated, then said: 'I can't take you all the way – things to collect – but I'll drop you at the station.'

The Alvis roared up to the front of the house. Lindsay stepped through the security fence and flung his coat and case in the back. It was a five-minute run from Trent Park to the station at Cockfosters but in a little under two miles they would pass from open countryside into the grimy bustle of the city. Sassoon's great park was at the very outer edge of London: to the north, the woods and rolling hills of Hertfordshire, to the south, the steady creep of pebble-dashed sub-urbia. It was Hitler who had brought the city's march to a halt at the gates of Trent Park.

'Mary seems to have taken to you, old boy,' Henderson roared over his engine. They were batting between the limes that led in a long avenue to the gates, the sun yellow and blinding already.

'She's a lovely girl. I'm a little afraid of her – a bit of a scholar – the first in our family. Not sure I approve really. She was offered a Fellowship at Oxford, you know, but turned it down to join the Division.'

'I've only met her once,' said Lindsay. 'She wants to talk to me about the prisoners.'

'If you say so,' said Henderson sceptically. 'She has some academic friends, of course, but she doesn't invite them to parties. One of our neighbours in Suffolk took a shine to her but she frightened him away. Too bloody clever. I don't suppose you'll have that problem.'

The car scrunched to a halt between the puissant stone lions that flanked the gates to the Park, showering the guards with loose gravel. A cross-looking sergeant waved them on to the Cockfosters Road. Lindsay was struggling to think of something to say; for once, Henderson's imagination was faster than his car: 'She's quite religious, you know. Much better than me, goes to church every Sunday. Are you religious?'

'No.'

Pinstriped commuters brandishing copies of the *Evening Standard* were pouring out of the dull brick station. Heads turned as the car came roaring to a halt. Lindsay squeezed out of his seat and on to the pavement.

'See you later, old boy,' Henderson boomed.

Rattling through the gloom towards the city, Lindsay's thoughts turned again to Prisoner 530. It was typical of the Navy. If you stepped out of your box into someone else's you were jumped on. An interrogator with something to say about codes was trespassing and no one in the Admiralty was interested. Lindsay had listened to the disc they had cut and there was something in Oberfunkmaat Peter Zier's voice, a quiet assurance, that suggested he knew what he was talking about. It had been more than just a throwaway remark. Zier had refused to answer any questions about codes but the truth was there in his eyes, in the movement of his body and the little catch in his voice. A good interrogator had a sixth sense for when a prisoner was trying to hide something – Checkland had taught him that much.

'Excuse me. You shouldn't be reading that.'

A full-looking middle-aged woman in a heavy purple coat was leaning across the carriage towards him, her turkey neck and face flushed with indignation. She was pointing at the magazine that lay open on his lap.

'Did you hear me?'

Adolf Hitler was spread across the centre pages under the eighteen-point Gothic headline 'Die Mannschaft der Scharnhorst begrüssen den Führer'. The crew of the battleship *Scharnhorst* was cheering for dear life and the crooked cross flew proudly from the quarterdeck.

'That sort of thing is upsetting.' She was barking down the carriage now, demanding the attention of a dozen or so bored-looking passengers. Lindsay closed the magazine and reached for his briefcase.

'I'm obliged to read this.'

The woman twittered something about being more 'sensitive' but his thoughts were drifting away. He had rather sheepishly looked up the Henderson family in *Debrett*: traditional squirearchy with roots in the fifteenth century, a coat of arms and a short address in Suffolk. At the bottom of a half-page entry, Mary Victoria Hobhouse Henderson, born 1916, and a brother called James, born 1911. He tried to conjure a picture of Mary in his mind, her thick black loose-curled hair, the broad smile that scrunched and wrinkled her face, her sandy-green eyes. She had been sitting behind her desk in a ghastly tweed suit but she was tall, perhaps five foot seven, and appeared to have a good figure.

'Are you listening to me?'

The large purple woman was still blustering.

8

Lord North Street
Westminster

Ting. The ormolu clock on the mantelpiece at Mary's shoulder struck half past eight. The little panelled drawing room was thick with smoke and noise, a press of navy blue and bright evening silk. She could see her Uncle David's grey head bobbing towards the door, slipping from one outstretched hand to the next with all the effortless charm of the experienced politician. James Henderson had invited an odd assortment of naval officers, his club cronies and family friends from Suffolk. Mary recognised a good number of the men, but only one of the women. Her cousin Gillian was holding court in a corner of the room, shimmering seductively in a silver dress. She was some way through an anecdote that seemed neither interesting nor funny but her audience of junior officers was smiling devotedly none the less.

Mary was capable of party conversation too but it was sometimes a trial. A little charm, a little make-up, a dark green evening dress, and conversation never seemed to rise above the commonplace. Dr Henderson became just one of the girls. The more trouble she took with her appearance, the less she seemed to enjoy an evening. But she had made an effort for James's party.

It had been forward of her to ask Lindsay to the party, uncharacteristically so, and she flushed with embarrassment as she remembered the look of surprise on his face. But things moved quicker in war, they had to, and she had sensed that Lindsay was intriguingly different, a little intense but clever and funny.

'Your glass is empty, Miss Henderson, may I?'

A blotchy, thin-faced sub-lieutenant with a drunken stoop was brandishing a bottle at her.

'Just a little.'

He swayed forward and the neck of the bottle clinked sharply against Mary's glass.

'Forgive me. Bill Perkins. I'm with Commander Henderson at Cockfosters,' he bellowed above the party noise. Mary could smell cigarettes and her uncle's good Bordeaux on his breath.

'Wonderful party.' Perkins lifted his glass. 'Wonderful.'

She glanced impatiently at the open door and the dark hall beyond. Her uncle's housekeeper, Mrs Leigh, was taking a coat from someone in the shadows at the bottom of the stairs.

Perkins was fumbling in his jacket pocket: 'May I show you this? It's from *The Times* or perhaps the *Telegraph*.' There was something in the way Perkins unfolded the newspaper cutting that suggested it was a trusted substitute for conversation when imagination failed or drink rendered him incapable.

'Spare Dr Henderson, please.'

Lindsay was hovering at her shoulder with the dry smile she remembered so well from their first meeting. He looked younger out of uniform, handsome in charcoal grey, perhaps a little more Germanic.

'Oh it's you,' said Perkins coolly.

'Yes, me. Look, Commander Henderson asked me to find you. He'd like a word.'

'With me?' Perkins was surprised and pleased. He paused to empty the last of a bottle into his glass, then, without excusing himself, began to weave unsteadily across the room.

'Did my brother really want to talk to him?'

'No.'

'That was cruel.'

'I think your brother will cope, don't you?'

Mary tried to stop herself smiling. 'James doesn't like you very much.'

'Really?' Lindsay's voice and casual smile suggested that he cared not a fig.

'Let's see: "standoffish","arrogant","foreign".'

'How nice to feel welcome.'

'I'm sorry. I am direct. Don't you like people to be direct?'

'Wasn't that one of the words James used to describe me?' Lindsay reached over to the mantelpiece for a bottle Perkins had missed and poured a little red wine into both their glasses: '"standoffish","arrogant", you must judge for yourself. "Foreign"?' His head dropped a little wearily: 'You shouldn't be fooled by the west of Scotland in my voice, Dr Henderson. My mother tongue is German.'

'Yes. I know. Winn mentioned it.' She lifted the glass of wine to her lips for a moment but lowered it without drinking. 'Please don't call me Dr Henderson.'

Lindsay smiled and raised his glass in salute. 'I'm surprised your brother didn't tell you himself, he's very interested in my family.'

'Why don't you tell me?'

Lindsay placed his glass on the mantelpiece and reached inside his jacket for a calfskin wallet. From it, he took a small brown photograph, roughly torn at the edges, and handed it to Mary: 'Mother. The year my parents met.'

She was wearing a simple dress, hands resting demurely on the top of a high-backed chair. Younger than Mary, perhaps twenty, shorter too, with a pretty, round face and the same thick brown hair swept back into heavy curls. Her eyes were dark and round, and a little sad.

Lindsay's parents had met just before the last war. His father had visited Bremen to order something small but important for the family's engineering works. He met and fell in love with Edith Clausen. After a very Low Church wedding, the couple bought a large villa in the west end of Glasgow. A short time later Douglas Alexander Clausen Lindsay was born and then his brother Eric.

'We spoke German at home. Mother's went to church twice on Sunday. We were at school in Scotland at first, then, after some unpleasantness, I finished my education in Germany. That brought me very close to my family there.'

'Unpleasantness?'

Lindsay hesitated. 'I was a little too German when I was small. Some boys wanted to fight the Great War again in the playground – some teachers too.'

After leaving school, he had spent a year with his grandfather's company in Bremen trying to learn something about marine boilers and business. Then he went up to Cambridge to study history: 'Where I was Secretary of the Anglo-German Society.'

Mary laughed her short, breathless, rippling laugh: 'Clausen Lindsay, it has a certain ring.'

'So does Hobhouse Henderson.'

She raised an eyebrow archly: 'You've done some homework.'

'What else would you expect from an interrogator?'

'Do you still have close family in Germany?'

He did not answer but stared at her intently until she flushed a little and looked down: 'Sorry, a question too many.'

The hard core of the party was moving on to whisky and pink gin, the faint-hearted had begun to drift away. Perkins was now snoozing on an elegant but uncomfortably upright eighteenth-century settee. A gramophone had been spirited up from somewhere and James Henderson was bent over a pile of discs. Lindsay took a conspiratorial half step towards Mary.

'The Navy likes to keep officers with German connections away from intelligence, I expect you know that,' he said. 'They took a risk with me – I'm the only one with close family in . . .' he smiled his dry, tight-lipped smile, 'in the Fatherland.'

'You're a Scot and you've been decorated. Why should the Navy care?'

Only half in jest, Lindsay glanced at the people around them to be sure no one was listening: 'Security could have been more thorough.'

Without thinking, Mary placed her hand lightly on his sleeve: 'Tell me. I love secrets.'

'I have a cousin called Martin, Martin Schultze. And . . .' he paused for dramatic effect, 'he commands a U-boat. A successful one. I'm sure there's a file on his submarine in the Citadel.'

The gramophone began to crackle to the sound of Joe Crossman: 'I'll be glad when you're dead you rascal, you . . .' James Henderson was beaming at the room. Lindsay was laughing too.

'What's funny?'

'Your expression.'

His gaze followed the quiet sweep of the hand she lifted to her face in one graceful movement.

'Do you know about my ship?' he asked.

'There were a few lines in the bulletin.'

Lindsay looked down. He was turning the stem of his glass slowly in his hand. 'I used to wonder if it was Martin's submarine that fired the torpedoes . . .'

'That isn't very likely, is it?'

'All those ships lost in the autumn to a handful of U-boats – the odds were short enough to trouble me between two and three in the morning. I know now that it wasn't his boat.'

Lindsay slipped the photograph of his mother back in his wallet then took a silver cigarette case from his jacket. 'My grandfather gave me this. He served in the Imperial German Navy by the way. Would you like one?'

Mary declined.

He tapped the cigarette against the top of the case. 'At sea, the war's very simple. Boom: a torpedo bursts through the side of your ship and that's it. It's different in the Division, don't you think, face to face with the enemy?'

Mary thought of Rodger Winn at the plot table, gazing at his photograph of Dönitz like a monk before an icon. But that was academic interest. The fusty air of superiority in Room 40 sometimes reminded her of the Senior Common Room at her old college.

'You may find yourself on the opposite side of an interrogation table from your cousin one day,' she said with a smile.

'He would get the better of me, he always does . . .' Lindsay was about to say more but checked himself.

'Go on, please,' she said.

He lit his cigarette and drew a little anxiously on it. 'Would it shock you to know that I can't help feeling proud of Martin? We're close; he took me under his wing as a boy, he's a little older. People say we are very alike, not just in appearance but in temperament too. You know . . .'

He stopped abruptly and his face tightened into a frown. Mary's cousin Gillian was shimmering towards them, blonde and willowy and very elegant.

'This looks very intense,' she cooed. 'James has sent me over to remind you it's a party – his party. Gillian Neville, Lieutenant,' and she held out her hand.

'Lindsay.' His tone was only a polite degree above freezing. Gillian flushed an awkward pink. 'Sorry. I'm not welcome. James asked me . . .'

Mary lifted a gentle, caressing hand to her cousin's face: 'I know, darling, but we're quite happy chatting here. Tell James you're under fresh orders to sparkle somewhere else.'

'I was very rude,' said Lindsay when Gillian had left them.

'Yes. James was right about that.'

The little ormolu clock struck ten. The room was almost empty. Mrs Leigh was clinking glasses like an East End barmaid at closing time.

'You two coming with us,' I've got a table at the Havana, Denman Street.' James Henderson was advancing towards them coat in hand. 'It's got a good little coloured band. I was in two minds about asking you really, you've been such party poopers.'

'I'm sorry,' said Lindsay mechanically.

'No you're not. Well, are you coming?'

Lindsay looked at Mary who shook her head: 'I'd like to but I'm whacked.' The memory of the Café de Paris was very raw.

'Then I suppose that's a no from you too, Lindsay?'

'Well yes, I'm afraid it is, but I'll walk with you to the bottom of Haymarket.'

Lindsay joined the Havana party in the hall. Gillian Neville was bubbling conspicuously, her back turned resolutely towards him. Mrs Leigh helped him into his coat. The front door opened and the party began to drift on to the street. Lindsay turned to look for Mary.

'Here.'

Her cool fingers touched the back of his hand. She was standing at the bottom of the stairs, her skin very white in the flat shadow of the hall. 'I've written it down for you. If I'm not at home, Uncle's house-keeper will take a message. Sundays are good and some evenings.' She paused for just a second and then laughed: 'I feel sure you've got that maddening, slightly supercilious smile on your face.'

'And lunch-times?' he asked.

'Sometimes.'

He took half a step, reached for her hand and bent to brush it with his lips.

'Auf Wiedersehen. Ein süsses Schrecken geht durch mein Gebein,' he whispered.

Mary was still laughing as the door clicked behind him.

For once the city was still. It was a cool clear night, the sky sprinkled with blackout stars. The party shuffled along shuttered eighteenth-century streets towards Palace Yard and Parliament and Lindsay trailed self-consciously in its wake. The breeze was freshening from the west, gently rocking the flabby grey barrage balloons that clustered above Horse Guards like tethered elephants. As they crossed the Mall, James Henderson fell into step.

'Colonel Checkland rang me an hour ago with some extraordinary news. We've got that fellow Mohr.'

'Jürgen Mohr?'

'Is there more than one Mohr?'

'Yes.'

'Well it's the one I've heard of,' Henderson snapped. 'The bugger who sent a personal signal to Churchill in the first months of the war, directing him to the survivors of a ship he'd sunk. There was a great brouhaha in the Commons at the time. One of their heroes. The most senior naval officer we've bagged. The Colonel says the First Sea Lord's cock-a-hoop. HMS *White* picked up a contact off the African coast, pursued and depth-charged the *U-112* to the surface. She's on her way to Liverpool with the prisoners – expected in ten days. You're to meet her.'

'Fine.'

'Good.'

They walked on in silence.

Lindsay parted company with Henderson in the Haymarket and five minutes later he was climbing the stairs to his flat. His father had lent him the pied-à-terre the family firm rented in St James's Square. The apartment had been furnished by Lindsay's mother with austere 'Imperial' pieces she had rescued from his grandmother's home in Bremen. His father's men had worked a small miracle carrying them to the top of the house. They were a sentimental anchor for Lindsay's mother, a heavy dark echo of childhood and Germany. No one else liked them but no one was courageous enough to say so. The furniture made the small flat poky and uncomfortable, but it was rent-free and just a stone's throw from the Admiralty and Piccadilly Underground station.

Once inside, he felt his way through the thick blackness of the hall into his bedroom. A soft white light was pouring through the open curtains and he was able to move more freely. He took the little piece of paper from his pocket and smiled as he remembered the light touch of Mary's fingers: 'Abbey 1745'.

'Mary Henderson, Mary Henderson,' he chanted softly to himself, 'where will this take us?' And he eased himself on to his lumpy old bed, the telephone number held to the light from the window.

9

The Easter Sunday service at St John's was a dreary affair. Mary left before communion. Her uncle had invited two elderly colleagues from the Commons and their perjink wives to lunch. To the clink of silver and old china, they talked of defeat, of the losses in the Atlantic and the collapse of Yugoslavia, of thousands dying in the streets of Belgrade. As Mrs Leigh was clearing the plates the telephone rang in the hall. It was Lindsay.

'Rescue me,' she whispered into the handpiece.

He laughed: 'From what?'

'Please be quick.'

He arrived in Lord North Street between dessert and coffee. Mary left him on the doorstep and collected her coat and scarf before her uncle could draw them into conversation. A jeep from the Division's transport pool was parked a little way along the street, its engine still turning. Lindsay had spent the morning at Section 11's small office in nearby Sanctuary Buildings and was still in his uniform.

'Hyde Park?'

'Anywhere,' she said.

Bowling through the streets, the wind plucking at her scarf and hair, Mary's spirits began to lift. It was a warm blue afternoon, the sun was twinkling through the windshield and the plane trees in Park Lane were tipped with a promise of spring.

'I'm so glad you rang,' she shouted above the rattle of the engine.

'But surprised?'

'No. Why?'

'It's so soon after the party. But there were things I didn't have a chance to say.'

He turned into a street off the Bayswater Road and parked in front of the shell of a once handsome early Victorian terrace. A

60

muddy crater had cut the road in half. On the other side, Mary could see a house belonging to a friend of her mother's. Mrs Proctor kept a large pram in her hall full of papers and clothes and a strongbox of jewellery, just enough of her life to wheel to the shelter. But she was fortunate; until now her home had been spared.

They walked south-east across the park, away from the hum of traffic and the Serpentine with families and spooning couples ambling at its edge.

'Did Winn tell you?' Lindsay asked. 'Security has decided that none of our codes has been compromised, and there's nothing to worry about, nothing at all, it's just gossip.'

'No, he didn't tell me.'

'But you don't sound surprised.'

'No.'

'You know, they didn't investigate it properly,' he said with a little shake of the head. 'They didn't even speak to my prisoner, the wireless operator Zier.'

Mary said nothing.

The Royal Artillery had built a wire fence across the path to protect a battery of anti-aircraft guns and they were forced on to the grass, through the shaking daffodils.

'Did I give the impression at the party that I was suffering from a conflict of loyalties?' Lindsay asked suddenly.

'Your cousin Martin, the U-boat officer?'

'I want you to know, he despises Hitler.'

'He's fighting for him.'

'He's fighting for Germany.'

'It amounts to the same thing,' she said with slight irritation.

Lindsay shook his head: 'Really, no.'

She stopped walking and turned away from him a little, hands buried deep in her coat pockets, shoes and stockings wet with dew the April sun was too weak to burn away.

'This war, you know, I believe we're fighting a new darkness,' she said with quiet feeling. 'Something evil. Really evil.'

'Your brother said you were religious.'

She turned back sharply to look him in the eye: 'I haven't taken vows. But yes, I feel it's my Christian duty to do something, don't you?'

The question was flung like a gauntlet.

'Perhaps my cousin feels the same,' said Lindsay tartly. 'German bishops say it's a sin not to fight for the Volk.'

'My goodness, you do sound confused.'

'How patronising.'

They stared at each other for a frosty moment, then she reached across and touched his sleeve: 'Sorry, I didn't mean to say that.'

He smiled at her: 'I haven't forgotten – you like to be direct. But don't apologise, we're as bad as each other. And I'm rather protective of my cousin.'

Small white clouds were rolling east over the city now, their cold shadows scudding across the grass. They found the path again and walked on at a brisker pace. Lindsay asked Mary about her family and university and the years she had spent studying archaeology: 'I can't imagine you in a muddy hole.'

'I'll let you have my paper on Norse burial rites.'

He laughed. 'Background for the new dark age.'

Mary hesitated, then said, half in jest: 'My brother may have told you I'm an academic bluestocking. I deny it.'

'He said men were frightened of you, and now I understand why.'

'Don't tease me. James's friends are frightened of any woman who has something to say for herself but you must stick up for me. We're both outsiders, thrown into the same den of lions.'

'Then it is my duty to protect you.'

'Duty?' She looked at him steadily, chin slightly raised, daring him to catch and hold her eye. It was an unmistakable, thrilling challenge.

And he held her gaze: 'Duty? No. Not a duty.'

It was not until the following weekend that they were able to see each other again. By then the Germans had bombed the Admiralty, forcing daylight into dim, remote corridors, shaking even the sub-basement of the Citadel. Yugoslavia capitulated and Greece was on the point of doing the same. Lindsay took Mary to the Coconut Grove night club.

There was an expensive air of hysterical gaiety, with Society girls wrapped around young men in Savile Row suits. The Latin Orchestra was very fine but there was almost no room to dance. They sat at a table sipping martinis, upright and self-conscious and too far apart for conversation. Lindsay said something she took to be an invitation:

'Yes, if you like.'

'I didn't ask you to dance,' he shouted. 'We can't, can we, it's too crowded?'

He looked ill at ease, unhappy. 'What's the matter?' She reached across for his hand: 'Come and sit next to me.'

He squeezed in beside her, shoulder to shoulder, and she took his hand again, its palm a little rough and dry: 'Are you all right?'

'I haven't been to a place like this for a long time.'

'We can go?'

'No, no, it's fine.'

He smiled and raised her hand to his lips.

Later, she floated home, his arm around her, drunk with warm anticipation. They kissed in the blackout shadows at the end of Lord North Street, quiet, deliberate, intense kisses. And he pressed himself against her, breathed the scent of her hair and felt the weight of her head against his shoulder.

'I think I'm falling in love with you,' he whispered.

At last they broke apart and Lindsay held her hands tightly and bent to rest his forehead against hers: 'I'm not sure I'll be able to see you for a while.'

'Tired of me already?'

He laughed and kissed her forehead: 'I'm meeting prisoners in Liverpool, the crew of the *U-112* and then there are the interrogations.'

'Winn's very interested in the commander, Jürgen Mohr. He's quite a catch.'

'Perhaps it was your brother's idea to send me to Liverpool, to save his sister?'

'Perhaps he's right?'

MAY 1941

MOST SECRET
It is of the utmost importance that the loyalty and
integrity of any officer engaged in this work should be
beyond question and that their discretion should be of the
highest order. The closest enquiries should be made into
the political past and views of prospective interrogating
officers.

Admiralty NID 11
Notes on the Interrogation of
Prisoners of War, 1941

10

HMS White
Liverpool

It was 'the old *White*'s finest hour. She swept into Liverpool in a triumphant cloud of steam, decked in crew and bunting. Her captain, Lieutenant-Commander Jack Thompson, was enjoying the spectacle from his ship's open bridge. The brisk river breeze cut to the skin but he was too proud to care. He reached into his pocket and touched the rough edge of the signal paper.

From the First Sea Lord. The Prime Minister has asked me to pass on heartfelt congratulations to the captain and crew of HMS White. Keep up the good work.

The destroyer came to rest beneath the great brick bond warehouses of the Albert Dock and up and over went her ropes. There was already a disorderly murmur below, excited voices in the for'ard mess, whistling and singing, as if the ship were haunted by a mutinous ghost. The crew was preparing to celebrate ashore with beer at the Roebuck and dancing at the Grafton Ballroom.

'The local intelligence officer is here to talk about the transfer of the prisoners, sir.' The ship's first lieutenant was at Thompson's side. 'And some chaps from the press would like to take pictures.'

Thompson turned with a satisfied smile to the quay where the newspapermen had been joined by sailors and dockyard workers eager for a glimpse of the famous U-boat commander.

'Very good, Number One, I'll see the local IO in my cabin.'

The captain of the *White* was a deck officer of twenty years experience and it was his fixed view that only those who had seen service at sea were worthy of the King's commission. It was quite apparent to him that the plump, shiny-faced lieutenant who shuffled into his cabin a short time later had not.

'Lieutenant Cooper, sir.'

Thompson looked the intelligence officer up and down with barely concealed scorn. 'Please, sit down, Lieutenant,' he said briskly, 'It's rather cramped in here but no doubt you're used to that.'

Lieutenant Tim Cooper sank with some relief into the chair he had been offered: 'The news of the *U-112* cheered us up no end, sir.'

'Good.'

Thompson slid some closely typed sheets of paper across the table to him. It was a list of the prisoners, and a few general observations had been scribbled beside the names of the officers. 'I don't think there's anything of great interest there, but that's for you and your colleagues to judge, isn't it?'

'Has Mohr been co-operative, sir?'

Thompson stared pointedly at Cooper for a few seconds to indicate his displeasure, then said with careful emphasis: 'Captain Mohr, Lieutenant. Captain Mohr behaved in an exemplary manner and we treated him accordingly.'

A sheet of paper slipped unnoticed from Cooper's knees to the deck. He had the anxious air of someone with something on his broad chest but wisdom or fear got the better of him.

On the deck below, Kapitän zur See Jürgen Mohr could hear the stamp of soldiers' boots and the orders barked at his crew as they were led along the ship's side and down the gangway. He had been locked in the wardroom with the *White*'s silver trophies. The officers of *U-112* were standing stiffly before him.

'They will be coming for us in a minute.'

Mohr's voice was surprisingly high-pitched for such a tall man. He was too tall ever to be comfortable in a U-boat, lean, older-looking than his thirty–two years, his face weathered brown and creased.

'We've spoken often of the days to come,' he said with quiet authority, 'but I must remind you again. We still have a part to play in this war. Carry on fighting for your Fatherland.'

He had warned them time and again: be silent, be strong. They would be separated and questioned. It was vital they kept their discipline and the details of the mission locked tight. The British would work away at the smallest crack, prising it open until they knew all there was to know of the 112's mission.

There were voices in the passage and someone began to turn the handle of the wardroom door. Mohr got to his feet and picked up his white commander's cap: 'Remember, do your duty. Be vigilant. Victory is certain.'

11

It was still coppery bright when the sirens began to wail again, the last of the sun diffused in the warm haze of smoke rising from the city's smouldering streets. Within minutes, a ragged tide of humanity was surging along Lime Street: travellers with suitcases, servicemen with their girlfriends, the very old and the very young. No one panicked or protested. They moved with hunched, weary resignation. Lindsay stepped from the shelter of a doorway into the street and looked up to a skyline of broken brick pillars and roofless gables. Liverpool was being stripped to its core. The sirens began to die away. Lime Street was almost deserted now. He turned and followed the stragglers to the corner of Hanover Street where a patient queue was filing down steps into a large underground shelter. A stout old woman hobbled past him on swollen feet, a basket of food on one arm, a bundle of blankets beneath the other. It was going to be oppressively close inside the shelter. Lindsay lit a cigarette and walked a little way along the empty street. Beyond a telltale mound of brick and broken plaster he could just make out the domeless silhouette of the old Customs House. The city was black now and almost silent as if it were holding its breath.

He had been five hours late into Lime Street, the platforms lined with 'trekkers', the anxious and the homeless waiting for trains to carry them to the safety of draughty church halls in the suburbs. By the time Lindsay had fought his way out of the station it was after six o'clock. But he was pleased he had missed the *White*'s quayside welcome, the little triumph orchestrated for the newsreel cameras. The hacks would have been given their instructions. Mohr was certainly a catch. A celebrity commander never out of the papers, a holder of Germany's highest decoration – the Knight's Cross – famous for his dash and style, or what passed for it in the Reich.

From the west, the distant drone of approaching aircraft, slow and heavy. Searchlights began to sweep in sinister arcs above him and soon the horizon was peppered with the smoky flash of anti-aircraft shrapnel. He stood and watched as if in a dream. The first enemy flares were dripping on to the rooftops of the city, followed moments later by what sounded like a rattle of iron bedsteads thrown from a great height. There was a flash and a tongue of flame – incendiaries.

Then he heard someone shouting at him from across the street.

'What's the matter with you . . .?' The man's words were lost in a rising scream.

Lindsay instinctively hunched his shoulders. His feet were knocked from under him and his mouth was full of dirt. He looked up. A policeman was gesticulating wildly: 'Run you bloody fool.' Suddenly aware of the mad danger he had placed himself in, he covered the distance to the shelter at breakneck speed. He was just feet from the entrance when the ground rose, throwing him forwards against the sandbags. For a moment everything was a blur. Then someone was pulling his arm, dragging him down rubble-strewn steps towards the door.

'It's all right,' he shouted as he scrambled to his feet.

The door clanged shut behind him.

By the half lantern-light he could see a score or more of frightened faces. His rescuer was shouting something but it was impossible to hear above the scream and crump of bombs. He collapsed on to a bench and rested his chin in his hands. The air was thick with dust and the shelter shook and heaved, the explosions reverberating along its length like a blow on a tremendous kettledrum. The bedlam continued for eight or nine minutes then lifted almost at once. Nobody moved, but the darkness was full of whispering voices and the whimpering of small children.

'That's just the start – take my word for it . . .' Lindsay's rescuer had leant across and touched his knee. He looked as if he was in his fifties although it was difficult to tell because his round, amiable face was caked in dust.

'You were lucky, weren't cha?' he wheezed with a scouse accent you could cut with a knife. 'Feckin death wish . . .'

'You can stop that, George Barnes.' A blowsy-looking woman in a fake-fur wrap elbowed George so hard he nearly toppled off the bench: 'Just mind your language – there are ladies and children in here.'

The shelter smelt of piss. Some of the children were being settled under blankets on the floor; everyone else was preparing to make the best of the narrow benches for another night. Bundled and patched-up people, smart alecks and quiet ones, some knitting, some playing cards. The bombs were still falling. Like a storm on a distant shore, the low rumble of high explosives seemed to break and retreat. From time to time one fell close enough to send a shudder through the shelter and everyone held their breath and wondered where the next would fall. Then the weary murmur would begin again as if no one in the shelter wanted to be left with their thoughts for long. One of Lindsay's neighbours, the large woman with the sharp elbows, began to work her way through the streets that had been hit:

'Fountains Road, Chancel Street, Endborne Road and Newman Street. The shelter was destroyed in Newman Street and three small children from the same family were killed. My cousin Gertrude's husband was badly hurt on fire-watch down at the docks . . .'

A wizened old man swaddled in a khaki greatcoat many sizes too big for him leant across the shelter and spoke to Lindsay:

'My son's in the Navy. On a battleship.'

Lindsay nodded.

'Just a rating. Your ship an escort? We've got lots of 'em 'ere.'

'My old ship was a destroyer.'

'Did you sink one of their submarines?'

'No,' said Lindsay.

'Shame. I hate 'em you know, hate 'em. Don't you?'

'Who?'

'Who d'yer think? Germans. Nazis. Fuckin' hate 'em.' The old man spoke in staccato bursts as if he was in danger of being overwhelmed by his own anger. 'Look at this – women and children. It's murder. There's a German lives near us, his name's Fetteroll. Says he doesn't want to fight because his father's German. Don't understand why they haven't locked him up in that camp at Huyton with the other Krauts. Shoot the bastard.' The old man gave a short gasp. There were tears on his face. He wiped them away with the back of his hand. It was some time before he spoke again and then in little more than a whisper.

'Sorry. Things get on top of you don't they? You know, my wife . . .'

He left the sentence hanging there uncertainly and slumped back against the wall of the shelter, lost again in his coat and his misery.

Lindsay tried to think of Mary Henderson. He had seen her twice since the party, a few hours snatched from Naval Intelligence here and there. They had spoken with the same warm frankness, a frankness entirely natural to her but a little foreign to him. There had been other women before, drunken encounters of the sort familiar to most sailors, and two brittle affairs with 'nice' west-of-Scotland girls, but never a meeting of sympathetic minds. Mary was challenging, he loved her bright intelligence, her cool expectant eyes, her smile, her strange gasping laugh, and he loved the joy, the hope, he felt when he was with her. There was a sort of stillness, a grace, in Mary that was wholly captivating. Her world was built on sure foundations, faith its cornerstone, unshaken by war. He envied her a little and with her, his life seemed less empty.

The rude clatter of hobnailed boots on the steps dragged Lindsay back to the rumbling, shuddering world of the shelter. The door opened, the blackout curtain was brushed aside and a small boy in pyjamas and a coat was gently propelled across the threshold. He was followed by a burly fireman with a smoke-stained face: 'Room for one more? Found this little bugger in the street on his own.'

There was a good deal of clucking and fussing as the boy was settled with a blanket and a biscuit. Someone handed the fireman a canteen of water and he emptied it without pausing for breath.

'What's it like out there?' asked Lindsay's rescuer, George Barnes.

The fireman wiped his chin with a dusty sleeve: 'The city's on fire. Hell, that's what it's like, hell.' He seemed remarkably cheerful for one who had just escaped from the other side. 'Lewis's Store, Kelly's and Blackler's – a couple of the Navy's ships are on fire, I was on my way there . . .'

On an impulse, Lindsay got to his feet: 'I'll come with you.'

The fireman turned to look him up and down. 'Why? You'd best leave well alone.'

'I don't want to sit here. Let's go.' He pushed past the fireman to the door and stepped through it into a strange flickering half-light. The sky was the colour of a blood orange and smoke was rising thickly as far as the eye could see. He could feel the heat on his face and hands and small pieces of burnt paper swirled about him like leaves on an autumn day. A gas main had been hit and a jet of yellow flame was rising from the pavement like a geyser. At the end of the street, a four-storey building was burning fiercely and on the road in front, half buried by bricks and charred timber, a naked body, stiff and white. It was a sickening sight. Lindsay could not tear his eyes away. He took an uncertain step closer and relief began to wash through him: it was a dummy, just a shop's dummy.

The fireman was tugging at his arm: 'We'll have to go this way.' They set off down a side street at something close to a trot, their boots crunching across a carpet of broken glass and slate.

It was only a short distance to the river. Strand Street was a shambles. The front of a large warehouse had collapsed, spewing masonry across the road and exposing the blasted shell behind. A clanging ambulance was weaving uncertainly towards the quay where a thick pillar of acrid black smoke was rising from within the great brick walls of the outer dock. A short distance away, half a dozen exhausted firemen were standing round their engine waiting for instructions. Lindsay's companion roused them with an angry stream of four-letter words. High-explosive detonations flashed and rumbled down the river; people and history were being wrenched from the streets of the city.

Lindsay jumped up alongside the fire crew and the engine began to bump across the quayside cobbles. The inner dock was dark and strangely still but for orange light shimmering across the water. Then they passed between two towering warehouses and a world of noise and smoke and fire opened before them. It was as if they were being painted into some grisly medieval Day of Judgement. Firemen and sailors in smoke hoods were scurrying about with stirrup pumps and cutting tools, and pulling at the coils of hose that snaked around the dock. An auxiliary ship was listing badly, straining at its mooring ropes, its deck shrouded in a filthy choking cloud. Through the smoke Lindsay caught a ghostly glimpse of a second ship, an old-looking destroyer, its bows blackened and twisted.

'Get that fucking thing round the other side double quick.'

A Chief Petty Officer, his face and uniform black with oily smoke, was gesturing wildly across the dock. As the fire engine growled past, he jumped up beside Lindsay. 'Sorry, sir, didn't see you there. Brown, sir.'

'Is that your ship, Chief?' Lindsay pointed into the smoke.

'The old destroyer, sir, she's a mess, a fucking mess.' Brown's voice was trembling with emotion.

'Explosion's wrecked the whole for'ard part of the ship. The mess deck's a fucking shambles. We can't get on to it.' He paused, struggling to compose himself. 'There're lads trapped. Can't this fucking thing go any faster?'

'Is the Captain there?'

'No, sir, everyone was celebrating.'

There was no need to ask but Lindsay did: 'Your ship, she's the *White*?'

'Just back from Gibraltar. We sank one of their submarines. Funny, isn't it? We won't be sinking any more.'

The fire engine pulled up some thirty yards short of the *White* and the firemen were soon busy laying hoses and struggling into breathing hoods. Brown led Lindsay towards the stern of the ship. A dozen or so wounded sailors with haggard, sooty faces were limping back along the quay, hands on shoulders like something from the trenches of the Great War. By the warehouse wall there was another line: four or five pairs of highly polished run-ashore shoes protruding from a mound of blankets.

'I've got a bomb in this bucket, Chief.' A gangly-looking seaman, his face and uniform streaked with blood, was standing in front of them, his bucket at arm's length. An incendiary was fizzing like a firework in the bottom of it, a small bottle of white-hot metal.

'Bloody cover it in sand,' said Brown with exasperation.

They forced their way through the press of sailors at the bottom of the ship's gangway and up on to the deck. The swirling smoke tasted of fuel oil. Figures were drifting through it in ghostly motion, appearing and just as suddenly disappearing. Brown led Lindsay like a blind man across the ship to the starboard side where the smoke was a little thinner. A small party of sailors was gathered about a very young sub-lieutenant. He was clearly relieved to see Brown:

'Thank God. We need a whaler over the side, Chief.'

75

And he explained that half a dozen men had managed to slip down a rope into the dock but there were still more trapped below.

'The first lieutenant has given me this . . .' He coughed hard in an effort to disguise the emotion in his voice. 'Morphine. All right? You're to pass it through the scuttles.'

He thrust the box at a puzzled-looking Brown.

'Anything else, sir, you know, dressings and stuff?'

'No, Chief, that's not important now. Make sure they get the morphine. And get going, for God's sake.'

Brown and his party set off along the deck and were soon busy swinging one of the ship's boats over the side. Lindsay caught hold of the sub-lieutenant just as he was disappearing into the smoke. 'Can I help, Sub . . .'

'I don't know, sir. God, it's a mess. She was to have been fitted with a forward escape hatch – bit bloody late, isn't it?'

He stalked off without waiting for a reply. Lindsay stood at the rail, unsure what he should do. Smoky rain from the hoses on the quayside was pattering in heavy drops on to his uniform. He could hear Brown issuing orders to the boat crew aft. Then there was a blinding white flash and the sharp smell of cordite. He felt a hot rush of air like a desert wind and was thrown sideways as the ship shuddered. There had been another explosion for'ard. Pulling himself to his feet, he turned and staggered along the deck towards the stern.

The whaler was in the water but still alongside. It took just a moment for Lindsay to slip down the falls into her bow. An arc of water from the ship's hoses was cascading pink on to the burning deck and pouring smoky black down her side. The hull was hot to touch and the heat had shattered some of the starboard ports. They edged into the billowing smoke, the sailors resting at their oars, one hand for the boat, the other held firmly to nose and mouth. Lindsay's eyes were streaming so badly he could barely see the length of the whaler. Then he heard someone shouting, screaming with fear, and through the smoke frantic hands were waving from two of the mess-deck ports. One of the young sailors in the whaler began to whimper. The heat and smoke were almost unbearable. As they pulled closer to the open scuttles, they were showered with small fiery pieces of matting stripped from the deck above. There was another deep rumble inside the ship and for just a second the shouting, the pleading, stopped. By standing on one of the thwarts Lindsay was able to reach up with his hand to the porthole. An unseen, unknown man grasped it and held it tightly as if his life depended upon it.

'Morphine, we have some morphine for you,' Lindsay shouted, but he found it difficult to make himself understood. The whaler began to rock as more hands reached up.

'John, is that you, mate . . .?'

'Hang on in there, Taff, we're on our way . . .'

These were bonds forged over many months at sea, dangers, mess tables and hammocks shared. They were family. And as Lindsay stood there holding an unknown sailor's hand he thought of another crew, another ship, and of the desperate helplessness he had felt as she slipped into the darkness. Sleeping, waking, the memory was there, the same cold seconds, whistling sickly through his mind, the white faces contorted in a scream that would last for eternity.

'Sir, look . . .'

Through the smoke he could see shadowy figures on the quay, jumping, waving, and although it was impossible to hear what they were saying the panic in their voices was unmistakable.

'Get this morphine up . . .' he shouted.

They began to press small boxes of the drug into outstretched hands. At his side, Brown was shouting, 'For the wounded, mate . . .' and, 'Just in case.' Should he explain 'Just in case'? But it would be obvious soon enough, and he cursed the staff, cursed them for not fitting that escape hatch.

They began to slip away from the ship and there was a new note of despair in the voices of those they left inside her. Hope was leaving too. At their oars the sailors were grim-faced, heads bent, pulling hard. One of the older ratings in the stern was shaking. Then, above the roar of the fire, the grinding of aircraft engines very close and the rolling thunder of ack-ack.

Lindsay had just made the top of the steps when he was thrown to the ground by a tide of water from the dock. He lay there, face pressed to the wet cobbles, legs stretched helplessly behind him. Barely a second later and another explosion drenched him again. The third must have landed a little way up the quay because the ground heaved and he was showered with dirt and stones. Later he remembered being gripped by the blind, terrifying certainty that his legs would be blown off – they seemed so very far from his head and hands. But the fire storm swept over the dock in seconds and on into the city. Even before he raised his head, he could sense the injured close by. Slowly, painfully, he lifted himself to his knees. The shattered bodies of five – or was it six – men were lying just a few yards away like so much human wreckage.

'Oh God, no,' he muttered.

Bright red arterial blood rose in an arc from the ragged stump of a sailor's leg. The boy – he was no more than eighteen – was watching it in silent disbelief. Lindsay recognised his white-blond hair and delicate features – he had pulled one of the whaler's oars. People were running along the quay now and someone shouted to him, 'Give us a hand here.'

He stumbled forwards in a daze and a medical orderly thrust a large cotton pad into his hands: 'Hold it firmly against the stump.' Blood was seeping across the stones and into the dock. He pressed down hard and the young sailor screamed. Then he was conscious of grinding heavy metal and a deep hissing. He turned his head a little. Steam was rising in a cloud from the bows of His Majesty's destroyer *White* as she slipped slowly down, down to the bottom of the dock.

In his cell, a hundred yards along the quay, Kapitän Jürgen Mohr could hear frightened voices and the gonging of an ambulance bell. The explosions had crept closer and the last had shaken the walls and floor until the light flickered and died. He was sitting in impenetrable blackness, so black he felt he could touch it. And he could imagine he was in the control room of his U-boat again, surrounded by the pale, anxious faces of his men. But he felt calm, completely calm. Their lives were no longer in his hands. There were no orders he could give, he was powerless to shape events.

He heard raised voices in the corridor and someone hammered angrily on the cell door: 'Bastard.'

'Can I have some light in here?' he shouted back in English. But there was no answer.

Seconds later another explosion shook the building, throwing him from the bench to the stone-flagged floor. He picked himself up, gritty brick dust in his nose and throat.

Did his family know the *112* was lost? he wondered. Admiral Dönitz would be concerned that the British had managed to capture such a senior officer. But perhaps the senior officer would not last the night.

12

'You look exhausted, old boy.' Lieutenant Tim Cooper was slumped in the burgundy plush of the Exchange Hotel's bar, a plate of the chef's own sandwiches in front of him.

'Is this the best they can manage?' He peeled back the top of a damp triangle and carefully examined its contents: luncheon meat.

'I've had breakfast but . . .' He glanced hopefully at Lindsay who waved a careless hand at the plate. There was almost nothing in his appearance to suggest that a few hours before he had been squatting in smoke and blood beside a dying man. The hotel staff had worked a small miracle on his uniform and his shoes were polished to perfection. But there was a weary frown on his face and a more observant man than Cooper might have noticed the distant look in his eyes.

'It's been a bad night,' said Cooper mechanically, 'What a pounding Liverpool's taken.' He glanced at his watch, it was eleven o'clock. It had taken him two hours to make the short journey from the mess at Orrell Hey. Burning streets, flooded streets, streets choked with rubble and unexploded bombs. He had seen a parachute mine lying in the front garden of a neat little semi, huge and uninvited.

'The Central Library's still burning, and the GPO, and there's a steamer loaded with ammunition on fire in the Huskisson Dock. If that goes up, they'll hear it at the Admiralty,' he said. 'Did you hear about the *White*? The buggers managed to sink her. Thompson, her captain, was at the mess last night. Very tight. He climbed up on to the roof and stood there brandishing a pipe at them. Bombs dropping everywhere and there he was shouting, "Come on you buggers".'

Lindsay said nothing.

Transport for Mohr and the other prisoners from the *112* would be difficult to arrange but Cooper was hopeful of a train from Lime Street later in the day.

'It was sickening,' he said. 'You should have seen them together.'

'Who?'

'Thompson and Mohr – yesterday. You would have thought Thompson was entertaining Marlene Dietrich.'

'You don't like Commander Thompson,' said Lindsay drily.

'He doesn't like me, which is unforgivable. But he'll like you.' Cooper glanced down at the medal ribbon on Lindsay's uniform. 'But Mohr's a clever bugger. He spent time here as a boy. Must have run rings round Thompson.' He paused and began to examine his nails.

'Well, what is it?' asked Lindsay impatiently.

'I'm afraid I've bad news . . .'

'Bad news?' Lindsay gave a short humourless laugh.

'Yes. Thompson let Mohr talk to his men. He's had three weeks to prepare them for interrogation.'

'They didn't keep him from the crew?' asked Lindsay in disbelief. Lieutenant-Commander Thompson had broken the golden rule: isolate the commander.

'Sorry. I hope someone kicks his complacent backside for you,' said Cooper.

Lindsay lit a cigarette, and blew the yellow smoke at the bar-room ceiling. As it broke and curled, he could imagine the dancing shadows of the cedar on the walls of the interrogation room at the Park and hear the mocking whisper of its branches.

Standing on the quay above the wreck of HMS *White*, Kapitän Jürgen Mohr felt no satisfaction nor did he feel regret. It was one more act of war. *Das ist eben Schicksal.* Fate. The sinking of the *White*, the damage to city and port, these things happened in war. The country that inflicted the most pain and destruction would win.

'Get that lot into some sort of line.'

Mohr's men were shuffling out of a warehouse at the corner of the dock under the eye of a burly British sergeant.

'Don't any of you lot speak any English?' he shouted at them, 'Fall in now.'

'Can I help you, Sergeant?' Mohr's English was a little precise but perfect in every other respect.

'No you bloody can't. Keep away.' The sergeant pointed at two army trucks that were parked further along the quay. 'Corporal, take this one up there.'

Mohr shrugged. 'Suit yourself.'

'Suit yourself? Suit yourself my arse,' said the sergeant angrily, 'get a move on.'

Mohr picked his way through the rubble, the tangled hoses and bloody rags, the corporal stamping aggressively at his heels. They stopped beside one of the trucks and he leant against its bonnet to watch the sergeant pushing and prodding his crew into a ragged line. Smoke was still settling in a broad grey blanket over the river and its wharves. From time to time there was a deep dull rumble from the tightly ordered streets beyond the docks, where a demolition party was making the city 'safe'.

The crew had abandoned its line and Mohr was most of the way through his fifth cigarette by the time the small party of British officers arrived on the quay. They stopped to look down in silence at the black and twisted bridge of the *White*, fifteen feet of blasted steel breaking the oily water. Mohr recognised her captain and the fat lieutenant he had met the day before but not their companion, a tall, fair-haired officer. He dropped his cigarette, ground it beneath his shoe, then walked slowly towards Lieutenant-Commander Thompson.

'A cruel blow, Captain, really', he said, with as much sincerity as he could manage.

Thompson acknowledged him with a curt nod. He looked grey and careworn, his thoughts clearly somewhere close to the bottom of the dock. They stood there in foot-shuffling silence for a moment before Thompson said, almost as an afterthought: 'Yes, unfortunate.' A perfect piece of English understatement – Mohr just managed to suppress a smile. He listened as Thompson explained in an empty, colourless voice that the lieutenants at his side were arranging for the crew of the *112* to be transferred to a camp.

'I regret to say that an angry crowd has gathered at the gates of the dock. There are a lot of sailors' families in this city, but you will be quite safe with Lieutenants Cooper and Lindsay.'

Mohr smiled at him, 'I want to thank you again for your kindness, Captain.'

The fair-haired officer, the one Thompson had introduced as Lindsay, gave a short, humourless laugh. Thompson frowned and seemed on the point of rebuking him but changed his mind. There was something in his manner that suggested the two men had crossed swords already.

After another awkward silence Lieutenant Lindsay turned to him and said sharply in German, 'Herr Kapitän Mohr, there are some rules.'

'I was sure there would be,' Mohr replied in German. Then in English he said: 'But Commander Thompson doesn't speak German. It would be polite to speak English, Lieutenant.'

Lieutenant Lindsay stared at him coldly and Mohr was struck by the intense blue of his eyes. Then Lindsay said in German: 'You will be travelling to the station with your officers but your guards are under orders to prevent any talking.' He glanced at his watch, 'And we will be leaving in ten minutes.'

Mohr watched Lindsay and the others drift out of earshot. Something was niggling him, a faint but persistent echo. What was it? There was something about Lindsay that seemed inexplicably familiar.

After a few minutes, Thompson walked briskly away, his trophy prisoner no longer a concern. Lindsay and Cooper turned back to Mohr, deep in conversation. They had gone no more than a few steps when there was a blinding white flash. A savage growl seemed to roll up the Mersey towards them. Mohr threw himself face down on the rough cobbles. A chunk of steel plate clanged on to the quay close by and the sky was suddenly alive with the whistle and crash of shellfire.

'The ammunition ship.' Cooper was lying a few feet away. 'She must have been sent to every corner of the city.'

Mohr lifted his head a little and caught Lindsay's eye and in that instant, in the pandemonium, it came to him where he had seen the man before and he began to laugh, laugh out loud.

13

No mention was made in the BBC bulletin of the two thousand people killed or of the homes destroyed, no mention even of the city, although everyone knew the censor's 'port in the north-west' was Liverpool. In the Citadel the cost was carefully calculated, but in tons of food and fuel burnt, in ships sunk and berths damaged.

Mary had spoken to Lindsay on the telephone but he had not wanted to talk of Liverpool and by then the bombs were falling on London again. She had returned home very late one night to find Lord North Street closed and St John's Church in Smith Square burning like a torch. For more than an hour she had stood and watched the fire as if at the bedside of a dying friend, and reflected on the strange world she inhabited at the Citadel, where a church counted for so much less than a tanker.

The list of ships lost in the Atlantic was longer every week and yet the fog in which those in Room 41 had always worked was clearing a little. There were days when bold black track lines criss-crossed the main submarine plot with certainty and the enemy pinheads sported numbers like U-552 and U-96. And every day the mountain of signals on Mary's desk rose a little higher. The Citadel was a jealous master. She spoke to Lindsay on the telephone when she could but it was often after midnight and their conversations would peter out in weary frustrated silence.

At the time it had seemed like a coincidence but later, when she reflected on her exchange with Rodger Winn, she was not so sure. It was early afternoon on the day she had arranged to meet Lindsay after almost a fortnight apart. Winn had just returned from a meeting with the Director of Naval Intelligence and was talking to one of the watch-keepers in his office. Mary glanced up from the anti-submarine warfare bulletin she was reading and across at him. He caught her eye and smiled. A few minutes later the watch-keeper, Lieutenant Herbert, tapped her on the shoulder: 'Rodger says can you leave that for a moment, he'd like a word.'

She found Winn leaning back in his chair, hands behind his head. He sighed loudly as Mary stepped into the room.

'You look weary, Rodger.' She sat down opposite him. 'Perhaps you're pushing yourself a little too hard.' It was more familiar than she had ever been with Winn but his smile suggested he was touched by her concern.

'I am tired, Mary, tired of other people's stupidity. No, no, I don't mean you.'

'You're not about to give me a dressing-down?'

'No. Whatever for? You've really taken to this work – much more reliable than the chaps here.' He paused for a moment to light a cigarette, then said: 'How much do you know about Station X?'

'Almost nothing, except that we have a lot to thank them for. Frankly I've been too frightened to ask.'

'You know, the special intelligence we're getting now is just the tip of the iceberg,' said Winn. 'In the weeks to come it could alter the balance of the war at sea.'

Mary nodded.

Winn leant forward to cram the cigarette he had just lit into an ashtray already overflowing with butts. She could tell he was on edge. 'You're a member of a very small circle, Mary. And the members of the circle must guard its secret very closely . . .'

Mary flushed a little: 'I know that, Rodger.'

'Yes,' said Winn uncomfortably. 'This is difficult. I understand you're seeing Lieutenant Lindsay.'

Mary stared at him, confused for a moment and embarrassed. Then a hot tide of anger began to well up inside her and it was with difficulty that she managed to steady her voice: 'Who told you that?'

'The Director's Assistant. Fleming had it from your brother.'

'Yes, I'm seeing Douglas but I can't see what that has to do with you or him.'

'Can't you?' asked Winn coolly.

'No,' she lied.

'Of course you can.'

Mary was about to say something but Winn held up his hand.

'No. Let me finish. I probably shouldn't tell you this but the security people want to question you. Fleming has put them off. He told them I would speak to you instead.'

'Why? Is this to do with Douglas's family?'

'Yes. And also his interest in our codes. He's one of the few people fighting this war who's face to face with the enemy every day. The interrogators are under orders to avoid any reference to signals or codes. They could let something slip, a careless observation, a badly phrased question that reveals something about our signals or theirs. It's too risky – it could find its way to Berlin. Prisoners have their ways of passing on intelligence too. We know that.'

'I see.'

'So you will be careful what you say won't you?' said Winn.

'Of course,' she said crossly.

'Sorry,' said Winn – there was nothing in his voice to suggest that he meant it – 'but we need to be clear about these things.'

'And you are now?'

'Yes.'

'Then perhaps you'll excuse me.'

Winn shuffled awkwardly in his chair. Mary was struck again by the tired lines on his face, the tobacco-yellow tinge to his complexion, and in spite of herself she felt sorry for him. He was doing no more than his duty.

'It's fine, Rodger. I know how important security is.'

He blinked at her and smiled: 'I know you do.'

She was at the door of his office when, almost as an afterthought, he said: 'Funny, but he seems to have upset a few people, doesn't he?'

Mary turned to look at him sharply. 'Douglas? Who has he upset?'

'Well, what about your brother?'

It troubled Mary for the rest of the day. People were talking about her, asking, 'Can Mary be trusted?' It had never crossed her mind that she should speak of her work but Winn had gone out of his way to warn her against it and in a strange way that made a difference. She felt as if she was being drawn into a conspiracy to keep Lindsay at a distance. She was conscious that she was doing only half her job and she kept glancing furtively over at Winn's office to see if he was watching her. Winn was far too busy. He had probably forgotten their conversation already. But she felt an enormous sense of release when, at a little after seven, she stepped out of the Citadel into evening sunshine.

She had arranged to meet Lindsay beneath the lions in Trafalgar Square. He had booked a table at La Coquille just two minutes walk away in St Martin's Lane. It was only a few days after one of the heaviest raids Mary could remember and yet the square was bustling with West End theatre-goers. A group of young women in air-force blue was feeding the pigeons, joking, laughing, and a pavement artist was hanging his pictures on the railings outside St Martin-in-the-Fields.

'Hello you.'

Mary felt his lips upon her neck and she reached up to touch his hair. Lindsay turned her shoulders towards him, held both her hands and looked at her intently.

'I don't know if I've said it already, but you have the most beautiful eyes.'

'I think you've mentioned it, yes.'

'It's worth mentioning again. Shall we go?'

'Do we have to, Douglas? I don't feel very hungry.' She knew she did not want to spend the evening in a smoky restaurant.

'No, not if you don't want to.' He sounded rather disappointed. 'What would you prefer to do? It's too late for a show.'

'Then take me home.' The words seemed to slip from her. A thrilling impulse, not a thought, and she felt a little frightened.

Lindsay said nothing, but offered her his arm and they crossed the square.

'Have you missed me?' she asked.

'Yes. I've thought about you all the time.'

'Tell me about Liverpool?'

They walked slowly along Whitehall, past the Admiralty, Downing Street and the Treasury and Lindsay spoke of HMS *White* and the prisoners. The commander of the *112* had been at Trent Park for a week: 'Mohr's men call him "the Buddha". They respect him but they don't love him. He looks like every British boy's idea of an evil U-boat commander, black leather jacket, swarthy complexion – by no means the perfect Aryan man.'

She laughed. 'You mean like you.'

By the time they turned into Lord North Street the sky behind the broken silhouette of St John's was a rich blue. Mary took the key from her pocket. Her hand was shaking a little.

'Where's your . . .' Lindsay cleared his throat. 'Where's your uncle?' He was nervous too.

'In his constituency.'

The door clicked behind them. Before she could switch on the light he turned her towards him, held her face between his hands and kissed her, slowly at first and then quicker, harder, with trembling urgency. She was clinging to him but he pushed her gently away and his fingers were on her face then on her breasts, loosening her blouse.

'Where?' She took his hand and kissed it.

'This way.'

And fear was gone, and reason; there was only love and a wild excitement that just for a moment made her laugh out loud.

Later they lay together in silence, naked beneath a cotton sheet, her head resting on his chest. The steady beat of his heart made her smile. She was lying next to a man and that man had been inside her. Why had she let him make love to her? She was in love with him, she was sure of that. She had never been orthodox in her views about sex before marriage but it had happened tonight because, there in Trafalgar Square, she had wanted to draw him closer than any man had ever been to her, to give him a part of herself.

'What are you thinking?' he asked.

'Oh about you, about us.'

Her head slipped from his chest as he shuffled down the bed and on to his side to look into her eyes: 'I love you.'

'Thank goodness for that,' she said brusquely.

He laughed.

'Well, I wouldn't want to give myself to a man who didn't.' Lindsay smiled and stroked her face with his fingertips: 'I was under the impression you'd taken rather than given.'

Mary pushed at him playfully: 'Are you accusing me of being forward?'

'No, I'm grateful to you, and in love with you.' He reached beneath the sheet to caress her.

'Grateful?' She expected him to say something flippant but his face stiffened a little and he rolled on to his back.

'Grateful? Oh for bringing a little hope into my life, some love, yes some hope.'

'Was it so bleak?'

He gave a long sigh then swung his legs off the bed and stood up. She watched as he reached over to the bedside lamp and then he was lost in the darkness. A moment later she heard the clang of the shutter guard and thin white light poured into the room.

'Yes, it was bleak.' He padded back to the bed, sat on the end of it and reached under the sheet for one of her feet. 'I don't know. These things affect people differently but I've felt, well, angry, depressed, mostly guilty.'

Mary interrupted: 'Your ship? But you did more than your duty.'

He gave her foot a gentle squeeze. 'I didn't really, you know.'

'Of course you did. They don't give medals out for nothing.'

He snorted and shook his head vigorously. 'Yes they do. That was nothing. Nothing.'

Mary sat up and the sheet slipped from her as she moved down the bed towards him. She put her arms around him, pressing herself tightly against his back. They sat there in silence for a while, then she said: 'Will you tell me what happened?'

'No,' he said abruptly.

She felt a pang of disappointment and almost let go of him.

'Why won't you talk about it?'

He must have heard the disappointment in her voice because he turned to face her, leant forward and kissed her gently.

'I can't, Mary. Not yet. Not tonight.'

14

For three days Helmut Lange had watched the cedar's shadow creep around the walls of his room at Trent Park like a giant clock marking the hours between dawn and dusk. He had followed its shifting, twisted patterns as if they were a crazy reflection of his own thoughts: memories of his home in Munich, his father the teacher, his mother on her knees in church and his friends at the St Anna Gymnasium. Darker memories too, of his time at the front in Poland and those last desperate minutes aboard the *U-500*. There were no magazines or books, no distractions. The room was a blank canvas for memories, empty but for two roughly sprung camp beds with army-issue blankets and a bucket.

The other bed groaned as Leutnant August Heine rolled over to face him.

'Why are you smiling, Helmut?'

'Was I smiling?' asked Lange.

'You were smiling.'

Lange had silently cursed the British for holding him with a man called Heine who possessed not an ounce of poetry in his soul.

'If they don't want to interrogate us, why are they holding us?' Heine asked.

Lange shrugged. Heine was a typical northerner, reserved, perhaps a little shy, nineteen, slight, greasy brown as if the engine oil of the *U-112* was engrained in his skin. He seemed to have no interest in politics or religion, beer or women. He was an engineer – a small but essential cog – and U-boats were his chief, almost his only concern. At first his conversation had been limited even more by his commander's order to say nothing of the war and the *U-112*. Lange had formed the firm impression that Mohr was capable of inspiring a dread which the old Jewish prophets would have envied. But slowly, patiently, he had drawn Heine from his shell. The engineer had begun to talk freely of the *112*, of ships sunk and his commander's fame, and of the feature film that had been shot aboard. It was to the U-boat that Heine's thoughts turned again:

'Admiral Dönitz came to see us sail.'

'Yes,' said Lange as he hoisted himself up on to the edge of his bed. 'Cigarette?'

Heine reached across and took one from the packet. There were just three left.

'I was there too,' said Lange casually, 'there when you sailed.'

'You saw us leave Lorient?' Heine asked with boyish excitement. 'What a turnout.'

'Yes.'

The quay had been crowded with naval uniforms, the black great-coats of the senior officers at the head of the gangway. Lange remembered the *112*'s screws turning slowly in reverse, the shouts of 'Happy hunting', and the thump of the military band as it struck up the old favourite, 'Wir fahren gegen Engeland', the 'Sailing Against England' song. The music, the occasion, the spirit of the men on the narrow deck, flowers fastened to their olive-green fatigues – Lange had been full of pride and admiration.

'Have you met the Admiral?' Heine asked.

'Three or four times. The last time a few months ago. I took some photographs for a feature. He shook my hand and he remembered my name.'

Heine leant forward, eyes bright with excitement: 'Three or four times?'

'Four times, yes.'

'He visited our boat once and spoke to me. He's a personal friend of the commander.'

'Is he?' said Lange flatly. Almost everyone in the U-boat arm claimed Admiral Dönitz as a personal friend.

'The commander knows him very well.'

'Yes?' Lange struggled to suppress a yawn. His stomach was rumbling; it would be supper soon and perhaps the guards would bring news of his transfer to a proper camp. Heine was still speaking: '. . . at headquarters and before.'

Lange looked across at him: 'Herr Kapitän Mohr was at U-boat Headquarters?'

'Yes, for some time. He was . . .'

Lange stiffened and raised his hand with a jerk. The boredom and indifference that had fogged his mind for most of the last three days had been swept away in an instant. He knew little of U-boats, and no one had ever trusted him with a secret, but he was enough of a journalist to know that their conversation was dangerously close to one. Chit-chat was one thing but Heine was forgetting himself.

'I think we'd better talk of something else,' he said quietly.

Heine was pulling nervously at the cuff of his leather jacket, his face blotchy red, and when he spoke again it was in barely more than a whisper: 'I've been talking too much, haven't I? I'll say nothing more.'

'I think we should change the subject, yes. Tell me, have you ever visited Munich?'

'You won't say anything to Kapitän Mohr?' Heine's voice trembled a little: 'Please don't say anything.'

'No, no, don't worry,' said Lange. 'No one heard you except me and I can keep a secret.'

'I heard you,' the operator in the Map Room whispered under his breath as he lifted the heavy cutting head from the disc.

The Map Room occupied most of the first floor at Trent Park. It was not a room at all but a dozen rooms, each equipped with a recording table and a microphone amplifier. Room Three was at the dark end of the corridor. Lindsay opened the door and stepped quietly inside. The shutters were closed, the room harshly lit by a single naked ceiling bulb. It was little more than a cubicle, smoky and very close. Karl Jacob was sitting with his back to the door.

'You wanted to speak to me?'

Very deliberately, Jacob placed his headphones on the table in front of him then swung his heavy swivel chair about until he was facing Lindsay. He was an elderly man with a thin, thoughtful face, a neat grey beard and lamp-like glasses that made his light brown eyes appear enormous. He was dressed a little like a street musician in a shabby checked jacket and green flannel trousers. Once, he had been a doctor with a smart practice in Berlin – before his patients cared that he was Jewish.

'Yes, I have something for you, Lieutenant,' he said in heavily accented English.

A twelve-inch zinc disc was revolving slowly on the unit in front of him. Lindsay could see from the concentric rings of purple filings on its surface that almost five minutes of conversation had been recorded.

'Well?'

'It's your propaganda man. There's something he doesn't want you to hear.'

Jacob pushed back the steel cutting arm and lifted the disc gently from the turntable: 'Mohr was something at U-boat Headquarters.'

He handed the disc to Lindsay who placed it in a protective can that was lying open on the recording table. They had been listening to the crew of the 112 for nearly a week, until now, none of them had let anything slip.

'Thank you, Karl. Thank you very much.'

In the duty intelligence officer's room, Lindsay slipped the fragile disc on to a playback machine, settled behind the desk and picked up a broken set of headphones. He smiled as Lange's strong bass voice crackled in the single earpiece. Yes, Mohr had done a good job with his crew. Heine was very frightened. But he could use that fear.

15

The murmur of conversation and laughter stopped as Lindsay reached the half-open door of the old library. Colonel Philip Checkland was clearing his throat purposefully. Lindsay slipped sheepishly into the room.

'Good of you to join us,' said Checkland with clumsy sarcasm. 'I was just about to tell everyone about the *Bismarck*. Have you heard?'

'No, sir.'

The head of Section 11 was perched like a large grey thrush on the edge of a low desk, a heavy fifty-eight, soft brown eyes, jowls, crisp blue uniform. James Henderson was at his side and sitting in front of him were the other four interrogators and the section's Wrens. Lindsay slumped into a threadbare armchair beside them.

'The battleship *Bismarck* is out.' Checkland's voice shook a little with excitement. 'The latest report has her somewhere in the Denmark Strait. The *Prinz Eugen* is with her.'

One of the other interrogators, Samuels, caught Lindsay's eye and gave him a discreet smile.

'The *Prince of Wales* and the *Hood* are in pursuit.' Checkland coughed and waited for a response. There was none. 'Well now you're all here,' he said tetchily, 'the *U-112*. Annie, can you do the honours?'

The section's Chief Wren, Annie Sherlock, rustled about the room with the preliminary interrogation report. She dropped one with some force into Lindsay's lap and winked at him.

'The Admiralty's very interested in this one, shopping lists from the Tracking Room and the Anti-Submarine Warfare people,' said Checkland. 'Commander Henderson is going to take us through what we know already.'

Henderson gazed about the room for a moment as if waiting for an orchestra to strike up behind him. 'It will be obvious to all of you by now that the crew has been very well schooled,' he said at last. 'Kapitän Mohr was held in a room for a time with one of the stool pigeons, the Jewish refugee Mantel, but he rumbled that he was one of our stooges straight away. Frankly we've got bugger all so far. Graham, you've been working on the officers.'

Lieutenant Dick Graham coughed nervously, 'Yes, sir. The First Watch Officer – Gretschel – twenty-two, a Berliner, friendly.' He was clearly at a loss to think of anything more to say: 'Not married. Stubborn.'

'I think that proves my point,' said Henderson shortly. 'The little we know of them is on page four of the preliminary report, if you'd like to look.'

Lindsay turned to the page and glanced down it: Mohr, Gretschel and four more. The navigator, Obersteuermann Bruns, born in Zanzibar, aggressive, a fervent Nazi, silent on every subject but the inevitability of a German victory. The second officer, Koch, a prickly character too – a *Handelsschiffsoffizier* – an old merchant seaman. Then there were the younger officers – the engineer, Leutnant August Heine, and a midshipman called Bischoff who was on his maiden voyage and clearly knew nothing.

'The seamen are a little more talkative – the bosun's mate in particular. He's Brown's prisoner'– Henderson waved his report at a slight, owlish-looking man in his late twenties who was almost lost in a leather armchair. 'The 112 was operating with three more U-boats. They refuelled at Las Palmas in the Canaries and were to refuel again from a German tanker. Fourteen torpedoes in the body of the boat, six in sealed tubes on the upper deck. Details on page seven of the report. Samuels, you've been questioning the wireless operators.'

Reluctantly, Lieutenant Charlie Samuels got to his feet and began to stumble through his notes. Lindsay's thoughts began to drift about the foggy yellow room, settling for a moment on a clumsy mural of mermaids above the chimneypiece. But Samuels dragged them back: '. . . there is one thing that puzzles me. The wireless operators seem to speak a little English, although it's impossible to be sure how much because they are refusing to speak it to me.'

95

'Thank you, Samuels,' said Checkland without conviction. Lindsay raised a hand to catch his eye.

'You want to say something?'

'Yes, sir. Does Lieutenant Samuels have any thoughts about why the wireless operators speak a little English?'

'Well, is there a "why", Samuels?' asked Checkland.

'Not sure yet, sir. It may be nothing. A coincidence.'

'It would be useful to know how much they speak, sir.'

'Of course,' said Checkland shortly, 'and Samuels will do his best.'

The Colonel began to work his way through the Division's shopping list, matching interrogators with prisoners. The *112*'s engineers and torpedo men to Hadfield the section's technical expert, Charlie Samuels, to press on with the wireless operators Lieutenants Brown and Graham to finish the face-to-face interrogations with the rest of the crew. There was nothing for Lindsay.

'Right, thank you,' said Checkland. 'Let's hope we sink the *Bismarck*.'

Lindsay got to his feet and was about to say something when the Colonel raised a hand: 'Just a minute.'

Then he turned to speak to Henderson. Lindsay stood close by, head bent over the interrogation report. What did Checkland want with him? Things had been particularly frosty between them since his visit to Winn at the Citadel.

When the room was empty at last, the Colonel turned to him with a wry smile: 'All right Lindsay. Mohr.'

'Sir?'

'Jürgen Mohr. I want you to conduct the face-to-face interrogations.'

Lindsay groaned inwardly. He was being handed the poisoned chalice. 'Just Mohr, sir?'

'That's right. The Tracking Room wants something on the shift to the African coast. Any questions?'

Lindsay wanted to ask: 'Why me?' But he knew the answer. Checkland was going to take him down a peg or two. There was plenty Mohr could say, especially if he had spent time on the staff at U-boat Headquarters, but he was too careful and clever to say it. Better to work on the junior officers and other ranks. It was just a pity he would have to spend fruitless hours proving it.

'No. No questions, sir.'

Beyond the security fence, a warm evening breeze rippled the daffodil stalks on the lawn at the front of the house. Lindsay stopped to light a cigarette. The camp bus was parked on the forecourt close by and a group of confused-looking Luftwaffe prisoners was being shepherded down its steps into the house. He acknowledged the half-hearted salute from the guard at the gate and walked on round the east wing to the garden terrace. For once the stately sweep of lawn between house and lake was deserted. On the hillside above, the last of the sun was creeping up the obelisk Sassoon had erected to mark a visit by members of the royal family. As he watched its steady progress, someone stepped up to the balustrade beside him.

'The Colonel wants you to start on Mohr tomorrow.'

Henderson had followed him out on to the terrace. Lindsay turned to face him.

'Fine, tomorrow will be fine,' he said a little sharply.

Henderson raised his eyebrows and leant forward, an expression of concern on his face: 'Is something wrong, old boy?' The gentleman farmer had become the country parson but only for a moment: 'Is it Mohr? Don't you think you can handle him? We could ask your friend from MI5, Cunningham, Major Cunningham.'

Why did Henderson dislike him so much? Lindsay wondered, was it to do with his family? They were cast from different moulds but the suspicion he had sensed at their very first meeting had sharpened in recent weeks to something close to hostility. Perhaps it was because of Mary.

'Be my guest,' he said coolly.

'What do you mean?'

'Ask the Security Service to interrogate Mohr.'

Henderson sighed impatiently, 'Well, I would, Lindsay, but you see it's the Tracking Room. Winn wants you to do it.'

'Winn?'

'Yes, Winn.'

'The Colonel didn't say.'

'Of course he didn't. You weren't his choice but who can say no to the Tracking Room? Winn is hoping you can break him.' Henderson paused and smiled: 'But I can see that's cheered you up.'

Yes, it made a difference, Lindsay would not deny it. He must have made some sort of impression on Winn. Perhaps the Citadel was beginning to take Section 11 a little more seriously.

'Let me tell you something else,' said Henderson, 'although if you'd read the interrogation reports carefully I wouldn't have to.'

There was an unpleasantly smug note in his voice. 'It's in the notes. Mohr attacked a homebound convoy last September – HX.70.'

HX.70. Lindsay turned stiffly away to gaze across the lawn to the hillside. The entire obelisk was in shadow now. He felt cold, frozen, as if he had plunged into the Atlantic once more.

'Bit of bad luck,' said Henderson with a sly smile, 'That was the convoy the *Culloden* was escorting, wasn't it?'

Seven, eight, nine minutes passed and the sky deepened to a still blue. Lindsay did not acknowledge Henderson's complacent 'goodbye'. At sea, he had hated this hour, the convoy's ships black against the last of the light like targets at a fairground shy. Perhaps Mohr had enjoyed just that view of HX.70 through the UZO firing binoculars on the bridge of his boat. He noticed that the fingers holding his cigarette were shaking a little and he threw it down in disgust, grinding it into the brick with his foot.

The guards at the security desk in the entrance hall had logged Lieutenant Graham out but Brown was still in the house. No one in the mess had seen him but one of the duty Wrens in the office thought he might be with the RAF. Lindsay found him at the door of the old library, coat across his arm. He nodded coolly and was on the point of slipping past.

'May I have a word, Brown?'

He frowned and glanced deliberately at his watch: 'Can't it wait until the morning?'

'No. The *112* prisoner, Heine, I need something from him.'

Lieutenant Brown rolled his eyes upwards: 'Not now.'

Lindsay grabbed his arm and squeezed it very firmly: 'Yes, now.'

It was unfortunate that Brown and Graham were the designated interrogators. Lindsay did not care for either of them – the feeling was entirely mutual. Brown was a fussy little man with thin, wispy red hair and thick round glasses. Before the war, he had worked on *The Times* and someone in the Division had considered this a sufficient reference to recommend him to the Section. But Lindsay was amazed that a journalist could be so credulous – lazy too. He treated the Section like a bank with business conducted across a table in office hours only.

Brown shook his arm free: 'What's so important that it can't wait until the morning?'

'Heine has let something slip about Mohr. He spent time at U-boat Headquarters. I need to know what he knows.'

Brown snorted irritably and shook his head: 'It could take days to break Heine down.'

'If you're not prepared to do it, I will.'

Brown blinked at Lindsay uncertainly: 'The Colonel wants us to speak to Heine?'

'Yes, at once,' Lindsay lied.

The microphone amplifier room was hot and cramped with barely space for a chair between the equipment stacked high along its walls. At one end, a jack field connected the cells and interrogation rooms to the 'mapping' positions further down the corridor. Lindsay slipped into a chair behind the duty operator who handed him a set of headphones, then leant forward to push a plug home on his board. There was a rustle of paper and the sound of distant but heavy footsteps. Then Lindsay heard a door open and the prisoner was ushered into the room. Brown offered him a chair.

'Don't try to make friends,' Lindsay muttered.

Heine was the sort of German who would respond best to commands.

Brown cleared his throat: 'Just a few small things, Herr Leutnant. Some details to clear up . . .'

Yes, Heine had been a member of the *Marine-Hitler-Jugend*, the Wandervögel hiking club too. No, he would not describe the *112's* operational orders or give details of his commander's service history. After forty minutes, he was comfortable, still calm. Brown was no breaker. The interrogation was going nowhere.

Lindsay slipped off his headphones and got stiffly to his feet. Sometimes an interrogator needed the patience of Job but not with a prisoner like Heine.

'Truth in the shortest possible time.'

The duty operator turned to look at him inquiringly.

'Forget it,' said Lindsay as he stepped out into the corridor. Brown was going to hate him.

The interrogation rooms were on the same floor in the west wing of the house. A couple of bored-looking guards were posted at the door of Number Three. Lindsay stood between them for a few seconds, breathing deeply, then he reached for the handle and walked inside. A draught of cold air swept into the room with him, stirring the cigarette smoke above the table.

Brown glanced over his shoulder: 'What is it?'

Lindsay said nothing but pulled the door to with a heavy clunk and leant against it, arms folded. Brown was half out of his seat, a dark frown on his face: 'What on earth . . .'

'We're going to blow hot, blow cold,' said Lindsay calmly.

'What?'

'Just sit down.'

He looked across at Heine and said in German: 'Herr Leutnant, you are going to tell me everything you know about your commander – Kapitän zur See Jürgen Mohr.'

Heine shook his head slowly.

'Oh yes you are,' said Lindsay coldly. 'I know he was on the staff at U-boat Headquarters.'

Heine gave another nervous shake of the head.

'Don't deny it. I know. And I'm sure Kapitän Mohr would like to know how I know.'

Silence. Heine knew he was being threatened, but with what? Then his shoulders dropped and he crumpled over the table, his face in his hands.

'Not me.' His voice was shaking.

Unfolding his arms, Lindsay walked to the edge of the table and leant across it until he was only a foot from him:

'Look at me, Herr Leutnant. Look at me. It was you. You know it was.'

'I . . . please . . .' He was very frightened.

'Tell me and he will never know. But you must tell me, tell me now.'

Heine was hugging himself, rocking to and fro on his chair, close to tears.

'Herr Leutnant, tell me at once.'

It was an order.

'I can't . . .'

'Was Kapitän Mohr on Admiral Dönitz's staff?'

Heine said nothing but gave the slightest of nods.

Is that yes?'

'Yes.'

The break. It had been easy. Heine would answer their questions. Lindsay took a deep breath then glanced reluctantly across at Brown. His face was very pale, his jaws clenched tight with fury. Without losing eye contact, he pushed a scrap of paper across the table. Two words were written on it in pencil: 'You bastard.'

16

Brusque orders and the clump of heavy boots forced Jürgen Mohr from a satisfyingly deep sleep back to the close darkness of his room. Someone was rattling keys at the door, cursing loudly.

'Get your trousers on.'

A guard shone a torch in his face.

'The switch is in the corridor, to the right of the door,' said Mohr tartly.

Blinking sleepily in the light, he swung his legs off the bed and reached for his shirt and trousers. It was a little after midnight. His interrogator was hoping that in the stillness before morning the threats would seem more real. Mohr wondered whether it would be the uncertain Jew or that effete academic, Graham? Perhaps, this time, the lieutenant he had met in Liverpool. He smiled at the thought.

They led him down the back stairs and halfway along a dimly lit corridor on the first floor. The bare white walls of the interrogation room were lit by a single shadeless bulb, there was a plain wooden table with a metallic green ashtray at its edge and just one chair.

'The prisoner stands in front of the table,' said the sergeant, addressing a spotty youth in a private's uniform. 'Make sure he doesn't move.'

The door slammed shut and Mohr was alone with his guard. He walked slowly over to the barred window at the far end of the room.

'Come away from there,' said the soldier nervously, but Mohr ignored him.

Through a crack in the blackout shutters, he could see the moon, white and full and uncomfortably bright. He had been betrayed by just such a moon. The British escort ships had seen the silhouette of U-112 slip into the convoy. In four minutes, HMS *White* had been upon them, running over the top, pounding the boat, tossing men about like rag dolls, a blind pitiless barrage. The boat had surfaced for a moment then plunged hundreds of fathoms to join the enemy ships it had sent before it, a broken grey shell on the ocean floor.

'Herr Kapitän Mohr.' Lieutenant Lindsay was standing by the desk.

'Sorry, Lieutenant, I was dreaming. I often dream at this hour.'

Lindsay said nothing but sat down and took a notepad from the briefcase on his knee, opened it and began to write. For a full minute, the silence was broken only by the scratching of his pencil.

'Your crew has been very helpful,' he said at last in German. 'There are just a few small points to clear up, some biographical details.'

He glanced up from his notebook: 'You're thirty-two, single, from East Prussia – your family owns a small estate near Tapiau. Correct?'

Mohr stared down at the lieutenant impassively.

'You were educated in Germany and for a time in England too – Bristol. You joined the Reichsmarine in 1929 and served on the light cruiser *Karlsruhe*. You must have met Admiral Dönitz for the first time then?'

Mohr smiled.

Lindsay paused for a second and ran his forefinger down his note-book: 'You transferred to the U-boat arm a few months before Dönitz took command of it and saw active service in Spanish waters during the Civil War and at the beginning of this one. You've had a good war, haven't you – until now. The Knight's Cross from Hitler himself.'

'A good war,' said Mohr thoughtfully. 'Have you had a good war, Lieutenant?' He nodded at the ribbon on Lindsay's chest.

'How many ships have you sunk?'

'A lot.'

'And there was a dinner at the Reich Chancellery in your honour.'

'A bad dinner. The Führer is a vegetarian,' said Mohr with a shake of the head.

Lindsay smiled weakly, then, half turning to the door, shouted: 'Chair for the prisoner.'

A guard stumbled in and placed one in front of Mohr.

'How kind,' said Mohr drily, 'My reward?'

'For what?'

He shrugged. They were the table's width apart now, close enough for their knees to touch beneath it. Lindsay took a packet of cigarettes and a lighter from his pocket and pushed them across to him. Mohr took one, lit it and inhaled gratefully.

'Was Admiral Dönitz with you?'

Mohr directed a thick stream of smoke away from the table: 'At the Führer's dinner, you mean? Of course.'

Their eyes met for just a moment, but long enough for Mohr to register the shadows about Lindsay's eyes: 'You look tired, Lieutenant. You're working too late.'

'You know the Admiral well, don't you? Did you visit U-boat Headquarters often?'

Mohr gave a small smile and drew on his cigarette.

'Did you visit the Admiral at U-boat Headquarters?' This time there was a hard edge to Lindsay's voice.

'Let me ask you a question.' Mohr leant forward a little, his hands on the table. 'Where did you learn to speak German?'

Lindsay frowned and picked up his cigarettes. He took one out slowly, tapping it deliberately on the packet. 'I think you're forgetting yourself.'

Mohr laughed, shifting in his chair excitedly: 'How can I? I'm your prisoner. But what do you think – a game? The rules are simple. Answer my questions and I'll answer yours. Where did you learn to speak such perfect German?'

'University. What were your operational orders?' Lindsay snapped back at him.

'You know those – to sink British ships off the African coast.'

'And how did you plan to do it – your personal tactics?'

'That's your second question.'

Lindsay ignored him: 'You spent time ashore last year, where?'

Mohr felt a frisson of anxious excitement. Simple biographical details were unimportant, most of them were to be found in newspaper cuttings, but this was of a different order. It was an ambush.

'You haven't been very truthful,' he said with a deliberate shake of the head. 'You must have been to Germany many times . . .'

Lindsay cut across him again: 'Where were you last year, in France or Berlin?'

'Berlin.'

'No,' snapped Lindsay. 'You were in Paris and then at the Château Kernével in Lorient.'

He looked pointedly at his notes: 'A senior Staff officer, one of the six in charge of operations at U-boat Headquarters. You see, I know about your work.'

Mohr was concentrating on his smile but his face felt hot and his heart was beating uncomfortably fast. He had said nothing to his men about his time at headquarters but it was an open secret none the less. After all the preparation, the briefings, one or more of them had been weak.

'Let's not pretend,' said Lindsay sharply. 'It's your game, so tell me, what were your responsibilities at Kernével?'

Mohr shook his head reflectively: 'It was foolish of me to suggest it. We weren't going to play by rules, were we? You see, I know you didn't learn your German at a university.'

Lindsay's neck and cheeks were a little pink and for a second he glanced down at his notepad, When he looked up again his gaze was steady and dispassionate. Without taking his eyes off him, Mohr leant forward and said in a confidential whisper: 'I know a few of your, how did you put it, a few of your "biographical details".'

'Do you?' said Lindsay shortly, and he turned smartly towards the door. 'Guard. You can take the prisoner away.'

'Is this goodbye?' Mohr asked in English. 'Goodbye so soon?'

Lindsay gave a short hard laugh: 'Oh no, Kapitän Mohr. No.'

The corridor was empty, the house silent. A full five minutes passed before Lindsay pushed back his chair and got wearily to his feet.

He had summoned Mohr for a skirmish in the middle of the night, intent on securing his authority over him. Interrogation was a confidence trick. You had to use the five things you did know to tease the five you needed to know from a prisoner. But timing was everything and Lindsay had given away too much too soon. Mohr had wriggled free of his hook and he had been uncomfortably close to being caught himself.

He glanced down at his watch; it was half past one. The note on

Mohr for the Section could wait until the morning. It would need to be carefully worded. He collected his things, then made his way down the grand staircase into the entrance hall. Lieutenant Charlie Samuels was standing by the security desk, struggling into his coat. Short, pasty-white with tight black curly hair, Samuels was every inch the Ashkenazi Jew, quiet and formidably clever. He gave Lindsay a tired smile: 'Haven't you got a home to go to either?'

'I've just made an ass of myself with Mohr.'

'I'm sure it's no consolation but no one expects you to get anything from him.'

'You're right, that is no consolation,' said Lindsay. 'And you?'

Samuels pulled a face: 'Doing my rounds – the wireless operators. I mentioned them at the briefing, remember? I could see from your face that you didn't think it was a coincidence.'

'A coincidence?'

'They speak some English.'

Lindsay grabbed Samuels' forearm: 'Charlie, I'd forgotten. No, I don't think it can be.'

It was too improbable. Only prisoners like Mohr spoke English. None of the petty officers or ratings Lindsay had interrogated could manage more than a few broken phrases: 'What do you know of their histories?'

'Please let go of my arm, Douglas, you're torturing me.' Samuels gave him an aggrieved look. 'They're too frightened of Mohr to say anything. I don't even know how well they speak English.'

'Work on their histories, Charlie, find out when they joined the *U-112*. If you can't get it from them, try other members of the crew, they may have told a friend.'

'Only if you tell me why,' said Samuels.

Lindsay gave a tired shrug: 'They may have been brought together especially for this war patrol.'

'Why?'

'I don't know.'

There were only confused possibilities, questions. Samuels glanced wearily at his watch: 'I have to be here again in seven hours.' And taking Lindsay by the elbow, he led him into the fresh night air.

They passed through the security gate and began to walk up the gently curving drive towards the old stable block. Behind them the guards on the perimeter fence ambled heavy-footed from one pool of light to another. The house was shuttered tight as if closed for business at last. Lindsay could see from the clock in the little tower above the stables that it was almost at 2 a.m. No matter; he was tired but his mind was too busy to rest. He would borrow a jeep and make the slow journey home through the blackout.

At the stable gates he stopped and turned quickly to face Samuels:

'A bottle of whisky says they joined the 112 for this war patrol.'

'Don't touch the stuff,' said Samuels, wrinkling up his nose.

'But find out, Charlie. Find out. I know it's important.'

JUNE 1941

TOP SECRET 'C'

All intelligence sources have their peculiar merits and their peculiar blind spots; not one tells the whole story alone. Prisoner of War Intelligence is peculiarly strong in telling you what and how things are done by those who do them, while it illuminates the blind spots of other sources.

What men make good interrogators? . . . one would look first for a speculative mind unbound by preconceived notions and firmness of judgement in distinguishing means from ends.

Admiralty NID 11
Assessment of German Prisoner of
War Interrogation

17

Hatchett's Restaurant
Piccadilly
London

It was only eight o'clock but Hatchett's was in boisterous swing, the dance floor crowded with khaki and blue uniforms swaying to the hypnotic wail of Dennis Moonan's clarinet. In the smoky gloom at the back of the room, elderly waiters weaved between tables and men without partners sipped their drinks with studied nonchalance. At one table, tired, hungry and a little cross, sat Mary Henderson in her Citadel clothes, the only woman not on the dance floor. She lifted her watch to the light from the stage. Lindsay was twenty minutes late.

It was almost a fortnight since she had seen him last. They spoke on the telephone but short businesslike exchanges that left her feeling unloved. The grey war filled their waking moments, imprisoning them in their separate secret boxes. The 'Swingtet' took a bow and couples began to drift back cheerfully to their tables. As the floor cleared, Mary caught sight of Lindsay at the door. He was dressed in his charcoal grey suit and looked every bit as handsome in it as he had at her brother's party. She watched him gaze about the room before rising to wave. He saw her and smiled, then turned to speak to a short, dark-looking man in an ill-fitting brown suit who was standing at his shoulder.

'Darling, I'm so sorry I'm late, the car didn't arrive.' Lindsay turned to look at the man at his side, 'I've had to bring a friend.' He must have noticed her disappointment because he leant forward to kiss her forehead and stroke her cheek.

'Forgive me,' she said, turning to his companion. 'You must be one of Douglas's colleagues?'

The man smiled blankly at her.

'Speak slowly, darling, his English isn't very good,' said Lindsay.

'I'm sorry. You're one of Douglas's colleagues?'

Lindsay sat down and indicated to his companion that he should do the same. Then he leant closer, elbows on the table, and spoke quietly to him in German.

'I've told my friend here that I want to explain to you in English,' he said, turning back to her, 'but first, how are you? I've missed you.'

'Good. You're late, and I don't like sharing you with Hatchett's.'

'No, sorry. It wasn't to be for the whole evening. I rather think it will be now,' he said, glancing at his companion.

'Are you going to explain why?'

'We've been sightseeing and we saw *The Great Dictator* just round the corner in Haymarket. A jeep was supposed to take him back but it didn't show up.'

'Your friend works at Trent Park?'

'Works?' said Lindsay. 'No. He's a prisoner.'

Mary leant back in her chair.

'His name's Helmut. Helmut Lange.'

She glanced at Lange. He was watching the 'Swingtet' prepare for its next set, fingers drumming excitedly on the table.

'Herr Lange is very fond of jazz,' said Lindsay.

'Herr Lange, perhaps you will excuse us for a moment,' said Mary stiffly and she got to her feet. 'Douglas is going to dance with me.'

'What do you think you're doing bringing a prisoner here?' she asked crossly as they made their way to the dance floor. 'Does anyone know he's out?'

Lindsay squeezed her waist a little tighter. 'I didn't want to bring him but when the Military Police didn't show, it was that or leave you sitting here alone. And yes, we take prisoners out all the time. Lange's very grateful.'

'Yes, but you don't bring Germans to meet people like me.'

'Why ever not?'

Mary stopped and shook her hand free.

'Because, you idiot, I work at the Citadel.'

Lindsay took her hand and pushed her forward again: 'It's fine. Trust me. It's our secret. Lange doesn't even know your name.'

'I should go.'

They swayed about the crowded floor in silence. For a time, Mary was caught up in the music and the movement and the pressure of Lindsay's body against hers. When the dance ended she allowed him to lead her back to the table. Lange was on his feet applauding politely.

'Helmut thinks we make a handsome couple,' said Lindsay, smiling broadly.

At first Lange looked uncomfortable and spoke in little more than a whisper but no one seemed to care that he was speaking German. He was soon talking with boyish enthusiasm of his jazz heroes and of the visit he would make to New York when the war was over.

'I've just told him jazz is decadent and played by coloureds,' said Lindsay. Lange smiled weakly and said in faltering English: 'I like things that are decadent. I'm from the south.' Then they spoke of Lange's home in Munich, of the city's baroque churches, of skiing and hill-walking.

Mary felt a little more at ease too. Lange was very engaging and either commendably discreet or just plain incurious, for he made no effort to ask her anything about herself. Lindsay was soon too busy translating their conversation to play a full part himself.

'And did you enjoy *The Great Dictator*, Herr Lange?' Mary asked after a time.

Lange smiled thoughtfully, leant forward a little and in broken English said: 'We can laugh at the Führer in Germany but we don't because he is a good man.' Mary glanced at Lindsay. There was a small, enigmatic smile on his face, a restaurant smile, as if he was waiting to be served an interesting dish. He asked Lange a question in German, then said to Mary: 'He means "great" not "good". Hitler is a great man not a good one.'

'Is he a member of the Nazi Party?' she asked.

Lindsay shook his head but translated her question anyway and Lange's reply: 'He says all Germans love and admire their Führer.' Lindsay paused, then said: 'But he doesn't believe that. Propaganda is a bad habit, like biting your nails – not easy to stop once you've started.' He translated this too and Lange chuckled, rocking his chair backwards and forwards.

'He'd like to believe it, of course', Lindsay said to Mary, 'but he can't quite.'

And he explained that Lange had served as a despatch rider during the invasion of Poland in '39 but had hated the iconoclasm and easy brutality of the Army: 'He wanted to be a journalist so he volunteered for the Navy's propaganda service.'

Mary gave a short disbelieving laugh. 'He wanted to work for Goebbels. It was a career move?'

'Is that so strange?' asked Lindsay.

'What does he write in his pieces about the invasion of Poland and France and Yugoslavia and Greece?'

Lindsay clucked sceptically.

'Well?'

'Well, he'll only talk of the defence of the Fatherland. Why don't you ask him about his visit to a concentration camp?'

'He's been to one?'

'Yes, I have,' said Lange in English and his face twitched with irritation. 'You want your friend to interrogate me, Lieutenant?'

Lindsay shook his head and said in German: 'No, Helmut, but I told her you were a Christian and I think she'd like to hear you explain how a Christian justifies the camps. I'd like to know too.'

It was quite a time before Lange spoke again and when he did Mary sensed that he was struggling for the right words: 'Our priest at home was arrested and taken to a camp. They accused him of abusing children. It wasn't true. He spoke out against this racial purity. This is worrying but we are at war. When it's over, all this will stop, but until then we have a duty to protect the Fatherland.'

Mary held the edge of the table tightly as Lindsay translated Lange's words, a frown of concentration on her face, then she said: 'So your priest put God before his duty to the Nazi state?'

'Christians do not make revolution,' said Lange flatly.

Mary leant forward and, placing her hand on his, said quietly: 'Christians can't shelter behind their country's laws.' And she looked intently at him as Lindsay translated her words.

Lange shook his head slowly, then almost as an afterthought added, 'The Führer has done many good things.'

Mary sighed and sat back in her chair. No one spoke for a few seconds. The band was thumping out a sugary little love song and the dance floor was busier than ever. Then Lange leant across the table, took Mary's hand and squeezed it gently. 'You are right about some things, yes, I agree with some things,' he said hesitantly. 'Please understand; I think of these things too.'

She felt a little embarrassed: 'It's easy to preach in London.'

No more mention was made of the war, the Church or the Party and for the rest of the evening the conversation was warm and relaxed. At a little after ten, Lindsay announced that it was time to leave.

'Yes, but first Helmut must ask me to dance,' said Mary. Before Lindsay could begin to translate, Lange was on his feet. How strange, Mary thought as he guided her around the floor, she was in the arms of a Nazi propagandist and she liked him very much.

18

Lindsay woke at dawn the following morning after a restless night on a camp bed and as he lay there under the rough army blankets his first half-conscious thoughts were of Mary. He could see her sweeping round the dance floor, cat-green eyes bright with pleasure, more beautiful, more graceful in her sensible skirt than all those women who had made so much effort to please. He tried to cling to this warm, sleepy memory of her, caught up in the dance too, but it began to slip away. It was replaced by an image of Mohr's clever, confident smile, and it was this that finally drove him from his bed.

One hour and a greasy canteen breakfast later, Lindsay was perched on the balustrade of the Trent Park terrace, the sun warm on his back, in one hand a cigarette, in the other his 'bible' – the notes he used to prepare for an interrogation. It was always a little pantomime of sympathy, impatience, rage, and it needed to be structured carefully. So absorbed was he in this task that he did not hear the footsteps approaching from the front of the house.

'Enjoying the sunshine?' It was James Henderson. Lindsay turned to acknowledge him, slipping from the balustrade to his feet.

'Preparing for another crack at Jürgen Mohr.'

'Ah,' said Henderson a little sheepishly, 'I wanted to talk to you about Mohr.'

'Oh?'

'You won't be able to interrogate him today. He isn't here.'

Lindsay frowned: 'I have him in solitary.'

'No you don't.' Henderson was inspecting a crack in a broken flagstone. 'A car's waiting to take him to the Admiralty. The First Sea Lord, in his wisdom, has decided he wants to meet Mohr.'

'Does he think he can do a better job than me?'

Henderson shook his head. 'He wants to meet a famous U-boat commander.'

Lindsay gave a short, harsh laugh: 'I thought we were fighting a war.'

Henderson looked a little crestfallen; for once authority had let him down: 'Professional curiosity.'

Lindsay shook his head in disbelief. God save us from 'professional' officers and their fellowship of the sea, he thought. The captain of HMS *White* had been the same and they were still picking up the pieces.

'How's Sister Mary?' Henderson was anxious to change the subject.

'Fine, fine,' said Lindsay.

'You're still seeing each other then?'

Lindsay smiled. Henderson had done well to keep the disappointment from his voice: 'When we can, she's very busy.'

'Yes.'

For a while, they stood in silence. Lindsay wanted to say something for Mary's sake but could think of nothing. It was difficult to feel warm about a man who made no secret of his distaste for you.

'All right, I must get on,' said Henderson awkwardly.

'I'll follow you in.'

He left Henderson in the entrance hall and made his way into the west wing of the house. The naval interrogators had turned the old billiard room into an office and crammed it with files and ugly furniture. A couple of assistants were typing up SR transcripts. Lieutenant Charlie Samuels was the only one of the interrogators at his desk. Bent beneath an anglepoise lamp, he was scribbling frantically in what Lindsay took to be his interrogation bible.

'You're not going to believe this,' he said as he stepped up to Samuels' desk, 'Mohr is taking tea with the First Sea Lord.'

Samuels looked up at him, a smile on his thin, almost colourless lips.

'No, it's quite true,' said Lindsay, perching at its edge. He felt sure Samuels would share his disgust. But Samuels just looked at him then raised his eyebrows quizzically.

Lindsay was a little taken aback: 'Well?'

'How can you, of all people, complain if the First Sea Lord wants to make friends with a Nazi?'

Lindsay flushed with anger: 'I'm surprised to hear you say that, Charlie.'

'Why? You're not fussy about the company you keep,' said Samuels quietly.

'I make no apologies for being friendly with some of the prisoners – that's part of the job.'

Samuels looked down at his bible for a moment as if steadying himself, his hand covering his chin and mouth. When he looked up again Lindsay was struck by the sadness in his eyes.

'What's up?' he asked.

'Do you know what Checkland's written in the interrogation notes he's pulled together for the Director, for Admiral Godfrey?' Samuel's voice shook a little. 'I've scribbled some of it down here.' He pulled a scrap of paper from his bible and began to read from it:

Sight of Jew has adverse effect on mental attitude of prisoners . . . hardens resistance . . . mistake to employ interrogators of Jewish appearance . . . Germans have special instinct for slightest Jewish strain and this makes Jewish interrogators feel inferior.

He picked up his spectacles and peered at the paper as if through a magnifying glass. Satisfied there was nothing more, he said as calmly as he could: 'He is right about the prisoners but not about me. I hate most of them, despise them.' He paused for a moment then said: 'But Checkland would just say that proves I shouldn't be doing this job.'

Lindsay shook his head slowly. The Jew and the German, he thought, neither of us entirely trusted.

'You know, I loved Germany,' Samuels said suddenly. 'You understand, of course. I used to visit my grandfather in Berlin. He took me to the opera in Opernplatz – they burn books there now, and we haven't heard anything from him for three years.'

'My mother hasn't heard from her brothers.'

'It's different for us, and you of all the people here should know it,' said Samuels sharply.

'Yes, yes it is, of course it's different.'

Samuels pushed back his chair and stood up as if to indicate

that he had nothing more to say on the subject of his family. 'I
agree with you about the First Sea Lord; these U-boat commanders think quite enough of themselves as it is,' he said brusquely.
He picked up a file and thrust it at Lindsay: 'Look at this – you
wanted me to work on the wireless operators. The chief, the
Oberfunkmaat, served on at least two U-boats before the *U-112*.
I still don't know how good his English is – he's stubborn and
unfriendly. I haven't got anything concrete on the other one but
there is this SR transcript.' He pointed at the file in Lindsay's
hands. 'I've marked it up – page four. Our man's Prisoner 643,
Funkobergefreiter Heinz Brand.'

Lindsay turned the flimsy, closely typed pages of what was obviously a long, dull conversation between Prisoner 643, wireless operator Heinz Brand, and two others, until he found the snippet Samuels
had marked in bold red.

640: *Our landing craft will be able to land on the English coast
easily with the help of fog or a smokescreen.*
641: *I don't know how they'll get across.*
643: *I don't know what the Führer intends, but I'm sure it'll be
the right thing.*
641: *I'm surprised at how good our treatment is here, for
instance the treatment I had for my toothache.*
643: *In my diary I've put, 'Quantity and quality of food are
sufficient.' Actually it's better than it was on my old ship.*
640: *Before you joined the 112?*
643: *Yes.*

Samuels saw a quiet, hopeful smile appear on Lindsay's face. 'What
do you think, is that good enough for you?' he asked.

'It pays to feed the prisoners well,' said Lindsay with a short laugh
and he handed the file back to Samuels. 'So Brand was a wireless
operator on a ship before the *112*. It's something to work on. Do you
think you'll get more from him face to face?'

Samuels shrugged doubtfully: 'I'm going to try. Want to join
me? After all, Checkland thinks Aryan good looks make all the
difference.'

*

Interrogation Room Two was just like the others – white walls, simple table, hard chairs – stripped of anything that might distract from the unvarnished truth. The man standing before them was tall, an upright six foot two, nineteen, blond with a handsome good-humoured face. He was dressed in a dirty brown boiler suit and boots. Charlie Samuels had spent many hours trying to befriend Heinz Brand and the broad smile that greeted him suggested he had done a pretty good job.

'Are they looking after you, Heinz?' Samuels asked him in German. 'This lieutenant is my colleague.'

Brand saluted smartly. Lindsay did not look up from his bible.

'I have a few more questions for you, Heinz, just a few details I would like you to help me with,' said Samuels.

The 'few details' lasted for more than an hour. What did Brand know of the commander, how long had he been with the submarine, and what were the 112's orders? The same questions in German over and over again. Act One of the pantomime. Lindsay listened but said nothing. Brand was forced to stand at the edge of the table, shifting his weight uncomfortably from foot to foot. He said he was sorry but he was under orders not to say anything. His expression suggested that his regret was genuine, as if it was the height of bad manners to refuse to answer an enemy's questions.

'I know that before you joined the 112 you served on a ship. What was her name?' Samuels asked again in German. No reply.

'Your comrade Oberfunkmaat Henning speaks excellent English, so does the commander, and that's why you joined the U-boat. You were on a special mission. It was important that the wireless operators spoke English. Why?'

Brand shook his head. There was a long silence. Then Lindsay spoke and it was as if his patience snapped. Turning to Samuels, he said angrily in English: 'I'm sorry, Charlie, but you're wrong.'

Samuels looked down for a moment, then barely above a whisper: 'We can't be sure.'

'Wireless operators. English speakers. The two they landed last summer were the same. We can be sure.'

Lindsay glanced up at Brand who was anxiously biting his thumbnail. Their eyes met for a second and he shook his head a little.

Lindsay ignored him and said in a very audible whisper: 'He hasn't answered one straight question. He can't. He's a spy.'

'I don't want him to hang because we made a mistake,' said Samuels forcefully.

'We haven't,' said Lindsay. He stood up quickly and picked up his bible and cigarettes as if preparing to leave the room. 'Why are you concerned? He despises you, you said so yourself . . .'

Brand looked surprised, confused.

'. . . he's a Nazi. He hates Jews.'

'That's a lie,' said Brand in English. His voice trembled slightly with emotion; 'it's not true.'

Lindsay turned back to look him in the eye and when he spoke his voice was menacingly loud: 'Herr Brand, or whatever your real name is, you are very clever, very capable, but you are a Nazi and you're a spy. You have not been able to prove that you are not a spy. Lieutenant Samuels has had less experience than me . . .' Lindsay glanced down at Samuels and Brand followed his gaze. Samuels was gripping the edge of the table, a frown on his face. Lindsay ignored him: 'I know you are a spy, Herr Brand. You and your comrade were expected to send intelligence to Berlin on our convoys in and out of Freetown. You will be executed.' He turned towards the door but Samuels grabbed his arm: 'I think we'd better talk about this . . .'

They left Brand standing anxiously before the table. Neither of them spoke until they had made their way along the corridor and down the stairs into the mess.

'How long do you want to give him?'

'Twenty minutes,' said Samuels. 'Do you think that's enough?'

'Your call.' Lindsay flopped into an armchair and took a cigarette from the packet he had brought down from the interrogation room. 'You don't, do you, Charlie? I'll leave these with you, Brand will certainly need one.'

Samuels sat opposite him: 'You play the ruthless bastard well, Douglas, but was it necessary to bring up my Jewishness?'

Lindsay blew a long stream of smoke towards the mural of the god Mars over the fireplace.

'After what you'd said, it was on my mind. I could see he liked you, so it just came out. It worked, didn't it?' He paused for a moment to consider the next Act. 'Make him trust you too. Lay it on thick. Tell him I'm writing my report and you've got no more than a couple of hours to prove he's not a spy. Perhaps we'll be lucky with him and then perhaps I'll be lucky with Mohr. Perhaps.'

19

When Jürgen Mohr closed his eyes the broad oil-black calm that for a time marked a ship's end filled his mind. He opened them at once and gazed out of the window as the car ground past another parade of shops. The dreary soot-stained brick of north London seemed to stretch for miles.

'Not far to go, sir.' The young British officer in the front seat of the car had turned to look at him with a warm smile as if he had read Mohr's thoughts.

'Thank you, Lieutenant . . .' he could not remember his name. A cheery soul. His escort back from the Admiralty.

It was after five o'clock and the shops along the Seven Sisters Road were closing, queues forming at the bus stops. It would be the same in Berlin with shoppers pouring on to trams in the Kurfürstendamm, Alexanderplatz and the Unter den Linden. Mohr had spent a week's leave in the city at Christmas, walked its bustling streets alone, gazed into bright windows and tasted the cold clear air. He had enjoyed the bustle of ordinary life without feeling any need to be more than a spectator, and although he dined with friends more than once, it was in his own company that he was happiest. He had marked this growing sense of detachment in himself for some time and no doubt others had too. His family in the east grumbled that he never visited, hardly ever wrote, and it was many weeks since he had spoken and laughed with his friend Marianne. Marianne Rasch: her brother was lost on a U-boat in the first months of the war. She was younger and gayer, and always frustrated that he could not or would not show his feelings. But in war, no one could claim the right to a private life. By now Marianne would know he was a prisoner. She would know too that the *Bismarck* had been lost.

Mohr had been standing in the eighteenth-century hall where Nelson's captains had waited on the Lords of the Admiralty. When he was in London ten years earlier, he had walked down Whitehall to stop and stare through the white stone screen at the front, surprised by the modesty of the building. They had not permitted him to wear uniform to visit the First Sea Lord but had found him a dark suit that fitted well enough, and he felt honoured to be there. Then a member of Admiral Pound's Staff had told him ever so politely that they had sunk the *Bismarck*. The pride of the German Navy just so much broken flotsam and two thousand men lost.

The Staff officer led him in a trance up the staircase into the oak-panelled Boardroom to take tea with Admiral Pound. It was a very British affair. Sir Dudley made only a brief reference to the *Bismarck*, a shake of the head, regret for the loss of so much life, as if passing on condolences for the death of a respected friend. He asked many questions about U-boats and Admiral Dönitz but did not seem concerned when Mohr declined to answer them. It struck Mohr as strange that the man charged with protecting Great Britain's ships should take such a dispassionate interest in their destruction. Then Admiral Pound asked him to describe the sinking of his own U-boat and, judging it to be of little importance, he gave him a short, matter-of-fact account.

There at the Admiral's splendid table, polished to perfection, beneath those elegant oak pillars, he said nothing of the fear or the agony of waiting, the angry kaleidoscope of sights and sounds that was never far from the front of his mind. Even now, sliding about the car's leather seat, he could imagine the soft splash, splash of depth charges and the shriek of steel as the 112 shuddered and plunged towards destruction. 'Give it air, give it air,' he had shouted into the darkness, and they had managed to hold the boat. Then the thrash of propellers, the splash of more charges and detonations that rolled endlessly through the depths. And when the light was restored, grim faces, terrified faces, valves thrown to Open, water above the deck plates – they were too deep for the bilge pumps – and the boat slipping deeper still, its hull groaning and contracting under the pressure. That was the agony of waiting. They had all felt it – stiff and breathless, the air hot with the smell of oil and piss and battery gas. He had experienced it many times but the danger had always passed with a swish of retreating propellers.

'But my luck ran out,' he told Admiral Pound with an insincere little smile that the First Sea Lord returned. In the end he had forced the boat to the surface long enough to save the crew. At least he had saved the crew.

The car turned right off the Cockfosters Road and through the gates, and after a brief exchange between the driver and a guard it was soon bumping its way down the long carriageway to Trent Park. The warm sun was shining through the trees, dappling Mohr's suit and the red leather seat. He was still a prisoner and soon he would be interrogated again, and yet this was a sort of peace.

'We're back, sir,' said the young officer from the front.

The car turned left past the stable block and along the wire fence towards the front of the house.

Two thousand men dead. Admiral Dönitz had taught him that honour lay in duty and the harshest will to win. He had believed it to be the meaning in his life, his *Weltanschauung*. But in the silence of his prison room, he was beginning to wonder what would be left when the victory was won and the slogans no longer had meaning. Who would he be?

20

From the window of Interrogation Room Two, Lindsay watched the black Humber Snipe cruise slowly down the drive and come to a halt at the security gate. A sergeant stepped smartly up to the car, peered at the passengers, then turned and waved to his men. The gate opened and the car crept across the forecourt, where the union flag was picked out in pink and white stones.

'Mohr's back.'

There was the screech of a chair being pushed hurriedly away and a moment later he sensed Samuels at his shoulder.

'A nice suit. Do you think the Division found him that?'

Escort in tow, Mohr was led from the car and into the porch.

'I've got you what you want.'

Lindsay turned to look at him: 'Charlie?'

Samuels walked back to the table and picked up his bible: 'Poor Brand, quite a civilised German.' He flicked through his notes until he found the correct page then began to read:

Funkobergefreiter Heinz Brand. Born Hamburg 1922. Joined Kriegsmarine 1938. Trained wireless school Glückstadt, wireless intelligence Flensburg . . .

'Yes, yes,' Lindsay snapped, 'but what about the *U-112*?'

'All right, you were right,' sighed Samuels as if it were painful to admit. 'It was his first war patrol in a U-boat.'

Brand had served as a wireless operator on board an Atlantic raider called the *Pinguin* that preyed on British and Empire ships sailing outside the protection of a convoy. In January, he had transferred to the U-boat arm and a month later sailed out of Lorient on the *112*: 'And he confirmed that the other wireless operator, Henning, was a new boy too. That's the good news. The bad news – he wouldn't tell me why they joined the *112*.'

'Well done, Charlie, well done.'

Samuels looked at Lindsay as if he had taken leave of his senses: 'Where does this take us?'

Lindsay turned back to the window. A green bus was parked on the forecourt now and a motley collection of U-boat prisoners was empty-ing out of it. The guards were encouraging them none too gently down steps into the basement of the building, where they would be issued with soap and fresh clothes.

'This was the first war patrol south to African waters,' he muttered. His mind was racing with new questions and possibilities. Dönitz chose a senior Staff officer. August Heine had described him as 'one of the six'. Capable, experienced, Mohr was just the sort of commander you would want if you were going to try something new.

'The first south,' he said again for Samuels' benefit.

'But there were three other U-boats, and it doesn't explain why the wireless operators would need to speak English.'

'And Mohr speaks perfect English.'

Reaching into his jacket, Lindsay took out his cigarettes, tapped one gently on the top of his silver case and lit it. The tobacco hissed as he filled his lungs with the bitter smoke. He stood there, head bent a little, cigarette poised close to his lips, face wrinkled with concentration.

'Look, Douglas, let's . . .'

'No, Charlie, please, just . . .'

He raised a hand to silence him. The seconds slipped by. The answer was dancing like a shadow through his mind, tantalisingly close. It was something quite obvious. He closed his eyes – *English, English, the wireless operators speak English* – a constant beat in the darkness. And then it came to him: 'How bloody stupid of us. How stupid.'

'Well?' Samuels asked impatiently.

'Isn't it obvious? The wireless operators were reading our signals. Why else would they need to speak English?'

'Steady,' and as if to make his point Samuels reached out and placed his hand on Lindsay's arm. 'We don't know if the wireless opera-tors speak English well enough for that and even if they do, all our signals are in code. They would need to . . .' He stopped suddenly to scrutinise Lindsay's face, '. . . ah, I see. I see. Douglas, you're racing ahead of yourself.'

'No, Charlie, listen. There are other things . . .' Lindsay hesitated. It was neither the time nor the place to talk of his visit to Winn at the Citadel.

'This is not for us,' said Samuels with a profound shake of the head. 'If you think our codes have been broken you'd better take it up with Checkland.'

'He's an idiot.'

'I'm sure he speaks well of you too,' said Samuels quietly. 'Actually I agree with you but an interrogation room at Trent Park isn't the place to say so.'

Samuels picked up his bible and walked towards the door: 'Are you driving into Town?'

'Yes.'

'You can give me a lift. We'll talk in the car.'

He led Lindsay into the corridor and through the house to the main staircase. At the bottom, they turned into the entrance hall and walked towards the security desk. Behind it, the duty sergeant was on the telephone. Lindsay nodded and was halfway through the door when the sergeant put the receiver down with a bang.

'A message, sir.' He was addressing Samuels. 'Colonel Checkland's office on the telephone. The colonel would like to see you at once.'

Samuels groaned loudly and dropped his chin on to his chest: 'Perfect timing.'

Lindsay looked at him intently for a moment, then reached forward to touch his arm: 'A word.'

He led Samuels through the porch and across the forecourt to the perimeter fence. 'Look, don't mention codes to the Colonel.'

'What?' asked Samuels. He looked as if he could not quite believe what he had heard.

'Please. We need more time. You said yourself that there were too many unanswered questions.'

Samuels took out his handkerchief and held it to his mouth and nose. It was his little anxious ritual. Lindsay had observed him do the same in interrogations. A few seconds later he slipped the handkerchief back in his pocket with a weary sigh: 'I won't lie to him, Douglas.'

Lindsay clapped him on the arm: 'Just be economical with the truth, Charlie. We're on to something.'

21

It was after midnight when Mary finally turned into Lord North Street. Lindsay had been waiting on the steps beneath the shell of St John's Church for more than an hour. Time counted in cigarettes. An air raid warden had approached him and demanded to know what he was doing. He had asked himself the same question more than once. In the end his uniform was explanation enough for the warden.

Mary was almost at her uncle's door. 'Hey,' he whispered as loudly as he dared. She did not hear him. He walked down the church steps towards her: 'Mary, it's me.' His voice shook a little. She had unlocked the door and was on the point of stepping inside.

'Mary,' he said again.

'Douglas? What on earth's the matter?'

He skipped the last few yards until he was standing beside her. 'Nothing, nothing, don't worry.' Her hand was cold.

'Then why are you here?' She sounded very tired.

'Oh an impulse. Can we go in?'

She hesitated for a moment: 'My uncle may be here. Look, I'm very tired, Douglas.'

'I see,' he said shortly.

'No you don't,' she said and pulled him towards the door.

'No, really, I don't want to force myself upon you,' he said.

'Don't you? Then why are you here?'

In the hall, he helped her out of her jacket. She turned towards him, stroked his face with the back of her hand and then raised her chin a little, inviting him to kiss her, a quiet, tender kiss.

'I so wanted to see you,' he said. 'Last time with Lange, well . . .'

'I haven't quite forgiven you for that.' She turned and walked down the hall to the kitchen and Lindsay followed.

'I don't know where Uncle is.' She switched on the light and began reaching into cupboards for tea and cups.

Lindsay stood blinking by the door. He felt a little guilty: 'I'm sorry. I couldn't help myself. I wasn't sure you'd come home but I knew I'd feel better if I tried to see you.'

Mary turned towards him, cup in hand, and gave him a tired, sweet smile. 'I'm glad you came,' she said.

They sat at the kitchen table sipping tea and Lindsay asked her about Winn and the Tracking Room. She seemed distracted and answered only half heartedly. 'Let's not talk about work, I want to forget it,' she said.

'You're right. Sorry.'

'And stop saying sorry.' She got up and carried her cup to the sink. 'I want to go to bed.'

Her back was turned and there was nothing in her weary voice to indicate whether this was a dismissal or an invitation. Lindsay watched the graceful sweep of the hand she lifted to the nape of her neck – her coal black hair was tied in an unruly bun – hoping, willing her to turn to him with a smile. But instead she said sharply: 'Well?'

'Perhaps I should . . .'

'What?' And then she turned to look at him, an impish smile on her face.

He pushed back his chair, walked over to the sink and grabbed both her wrists.

'You witch,' he said, and kissed her, pushing her body hard against the sink.

She lifted her arms to his neck and she was laughing so much they had to stop. Lindsay began to laugh too.

'You tease.'

'I'm not. I want to go to bed.' She was looking at him intently with her twinkling green eyes, a small smile playing on her lips. 'And I want you to take me there.'

Lindsay leant forward and whispered: 'Like this?' His hands dropped to her hips and he began to lift her woollen skirt and slip. Her lips opened a little and he could hear her short shaky breaths, feel her arms tighten about his neck. And his hands slipped over the top of her stockings on to the soft warm skin of her thighs, and bending a little he lifted her from the ground.

'Still tired?' he whispered softly in her ear.

In reply she kissed his neck and whispered: 'Come on, carry me.'

Later he watched her sleeping beside him, curled into a ball, her hair loose about her shoulders and the pillow. And he wondered at their lovemaking, a little miracle of forgetfulness in which for such a short time there was only comfort, excitement, joy. But it was over and even there in the stillness of Mary's room, with her warm body pressed against his, restless thoughts forced their way to the front of his mind. Tomorrow he would interrogate Mohr again. He would be taking a risk, like a sapper pushing into dangerous ground.

He rolled from Mary on to his back and she whimpered a little, unconsciously pushing herself towards his warmth. Turning back to her, he swept a loose curl from her face then bent to kiss her cheek. Without opening her eyes she reached up to touch him and he caught her hand and kissed it.

'Can't you sleep?' she asked dreamily.

'No. Sorry.'

'Why are you always sorry?'

'Mother's Calvinism.'

She smiled, her eyes still closed: 'But you're of the elect?'

'No. A helpless reprobate.'

'I can help you.'

'You already have.'

She opened her eyes a little. 'Kiss me,' and he did, tenderly.

'Why can't you sleep? Are you thinking of the ship again?' she asked hesitantly.

'It's tomorrow. Tomorrow I will interrogate the commander of the *U-112*.'

Mary groaned.

'I know. I know. I'm sorry,' he said. 'But it's important.'

And he told her about the wireless operators, that it was no coincidence they spoke English, that they had both joined the *112* for its war patrol south, and that Mohr had been 'one of the six' senior Staff officers at U-boat Headquarters.

'I can't be absolutely sure but I think it's something to do with our codes . . .'

'Again,' said Mary sleepily. 'Haven't they ordered you not to get involved?'

He ignored the question: 'It's not proof they're reading our signals but it's evidence. Mohr was on the Staff. A word from him and I'd have the proof . . .'

'And if you don't get some sort of confirmation from Mohr that they're reading our signals?'

Lindsay pulled a face. They were lying side by side now and Mary was gazing at him intently, suddenly wakeful and serious. After a long silence she pushed herself up and the sheet slipped from her. He reached up to touch her breast: 'You're so very beautiful.'

'Douglas, you must leave this alone. You're going to get into terrible trouble.'

'You sound like your brother,' he said shortly.

'Perhaps he's right about this,' she said crossly.

Lindsay rolled away from her: 'He's an idiot.'

'He's my brother.'

'That is his only redeeming feature.'

'And is Rodger Winn an idiot too?'

Lindsay sighed loudly.

'He wanted you to interrogate Mohr, didn't he,' she said. 'But not codes, he doesn't want you to question him about our codes.'

Lindsay turned his head sharply to look at Mary: 'Did he tell you that?'

'Not in so many words, I just know and so do you. It's out of bounds. Leave it, Douglas. Promise me you will.'

'Of course I won't. I really can't understand this. Why is it so impossible?' he asked. 'My God. Doesn't anyone trust Section 11 or is it just me?'

Mary shook her head and said quietly. 'Please, please just leave it.'

Lindsay looked at her, slender and pretty, her dark hair unruly about her face, and he wanted to feel her close again. Reaching up, he pulled her down so that her head was resting on his chest and they lay there for a while without speaking. It was Mary who broke the silence:

'We should go away together.'

'Paris?'

'Very funny. Oxfordshire.'

'Ah. When the war's over I'll take you to Berlin.'

'If they win, someone might beat you to it.'

Lindsay laughed and reached beneath the sheet to gently caress her behind.

'Do you think Germans would be interested in this?'

'You are,' she said.

Mary slept there on his chest, a short restless sleep, until at a little before six, he slipped away. He stepped into Lord North Street with her sweet scent on his skin, her words troubling his thoughts.

22

None of the other interrogators were in the Trent Park office but the section's Wrens were busy at their typewriters under their diligent, vigilant chief. Lindsay's desk was beneath a window on the far side of the room so it was easy for Annie Sherlock to intercept him:

'A busy night, sir, working late?'

It was clear from her tone that she suspected him of something sinful. Sometimes Lindsay quite liked Annie. She was a formidable figure, a muscular five foot nine with calves shaped on the tennis court – her uniform always looked a size too small for her – dark hair and eyes, strong brown features. She could be funny, flirtatious, although Lindsay found her display a little intimidating, and she cared not a fig for rank.

'You were in great demand this morning, sir, everyone was asking for you.'

'Oh?'

'Commander Henderson seemed to have some idea where you might be;' this with a knowing smile.

'Did he?'

'He was anxious to talk to you. He said, "Ask Lieutenant Lindsay to find me before he does anything else".'

There was something in Chief Wren Sherlock's imperious manner that suggested Lindsay was in some sort of trouble.

'And Lieutenant Samuels wanted you too. He's left a note on your desk.'

'Thank you, Annie. Anything else?'

'Oh just more business. The survivors from the *Bismarck* are expected in the next couple of days.'

'Ah. Good,' he said distractedly. His mind was swirling with unpleasant thoughts. Checkland wanted to speak to him about Mohr, he was sure of it. Had Samuels said something? A note in

Samuels' big round hand was propped on his typewriter, marked rather too conspicuously, URGENT. Lindsay stood and read it by the window:

Checkland on warpath. Collared me and asked for reports on the wireless operators. Asked about you. Advise softly, softly with Mohr.

Mohr was lying on his camp bed staring at the low white ceiling when Lindsay stepped into the room. He made no effort to get up. Bright sunshine was pouring through the barred window, casting a long prison shadow on the bare floorboards. Some clothes and a couple of army blankets were neatly folded on a table, Mohr's boots were beneath it and there was a chair and a toilet bucket.

'Good morning, Kapitän Mohr,' Lindsay said briskly in German as if urging him to rise.

'What do you want, Lieutenant?'

'I would like to take you for a walk.'

'A walk?' Mohr raised himself on to an elbow and glanced at the window. 'I would tell you almost anything for the privilege,' he said and he looked as if he meant it.

Lindsay looked down pointedly at his boots. 'Well, let's go.'

He led Mohr past the guardroom and down the back stairs, pausing at the bottom to consider a discreet route. The hall was always busy and the security desk kept a register of the prisoners taken from the house.

'Are you lost? The entrance is this way.'

Lindsay turned to look at Mohr. He was pointing towards the long gallery, a dry smile on his face.

'No, there's another way out.'

The servants' corridor was to the right of the old dining room and at the end of it a door opened on to a covered walk that led round the west wing of the house.

Beyond the orangery and the icehouse, into the whispering beech-wood, and Lindsay began to breathe a little easier. Mohr caught up with him and the two men walked side by side along a rutted track – still thick with decaying autumn leaves – that climbed gently from the house. Mohr gazed up at the flickering canopy, smiling with pleasure.

Broken shafts of sunlight danced across his face, forcing him to close his eyes.

'Did you enjoy your job?' Lindsay asked him in German.

'Enjoy?'

'Submarine commander.'

'At first.'

'What did you enjoy?'

'The chase. Danger. Success.'

'And by the end?'

'It was my duty.'

They walked a little further in silence, then Lindsay said:

'You attacked a convoy last September, the fifteenth and sixteenth, do you remember?'

'I sank two ships on the first night – a small freighter and a tanker.'

'The tanker was the *Bordeaux*. Only a dozen men were rescued and most of them were badly burned.'

Mohr walked on in silence. There was nothing in his face to suggest that he felt any concern or remorse.

'I was with the convoy, one of the escorts,' said Lindsay with a nonchalance he did not feel.

Mohr glanced across and gave him a wan smile.

'Did you celebrate?' Lindsay asked.

'Perhaps, in a small way, I don't remember.'

The hill was a little steeper, the wood thinner. They were almost at the top when with a small cry of excitement Mohr stepped away from the path.

'These are good.'

He bent down beside the rotting, splintered stump of a tree and began to pull with both hands at the brown flat fungi clinging to its bark.

'What do you call this in English?'

'I haven't a clue. Don't poison yourself.'

'You have some more questions for me then?' Mohr half turned to look at Lindsay, his hands full of the fungi: 'You're wasting your time.'

'I'll be the judge of that.'

Mohr shrugged and turned back to the tree stump. 'Do you have a bag?' he asked.

'Why did you go back to sea, Herr Kapitän? You'd done enough. It wasn't a challenge any more, you were on the Staff, in a position of trust, responsibility. Safe . . .'

'It was my duty. My crew.'

Lindsay stepped from the track and walked to where Mohr was squatting by the rotten stump. Mohr looked up at him, then slowly got to his feet:

'Here, a present. You'll like it. Trust me,' and he leant forward a little, offering Lindsay the fungi.

'An important Staff officer returns to his boat . . .'

'Important?'

'. . . in the meantime the *112* has acquired two new wireless operators. Almost no one else has been replaced, only the wireless operators. And these two men speak English. Why?'

Mohr was standing only a few feet from Lindsay, the fungi still in his arms, his face set, expressionless, unblinking.

'I'll tell you then, shall I?' said Lindsay. He sounded much more assured than he felt.

'It was a special mission and it was important to have a senior commander, an experienced commander. Was it you or Dönitz who thought of the idea?'

Mohr was still looking at him, quite impassive, silent. Lindsay continued:

'It's only a detail. The plan was devised by the Staff. It was considered promising enough to justify sending one of Dönitz's most trusted officers back to sea, with all the risks that entailed – you might be taken prisoner . . .'

Mohr gave a small tight-lipped smile.

'. . . and you were given two of the Navy's best wireless operators – one from the merchant cruiser *Pinguin*. Did her captain make a fuss about losing one of his best men? I bet he did. But of course this was a special mission.'

Lindsay paused for a moment and, turning from Mohr, walked a few feet away, head bent in thought. He stopped to lean against the grey trunk of a beech tree and began prodding the carpet of leaves and husks with his shoe. He could sense that Mohr was watching him closely, waiting patiently, quite unruffled. It was warm, the sky a cloudless blue and almost nothing stirred in the wood; even the canopy above them was still.

'The thing is, Kapitän, I am worried, very worried,' and Lindsay turned to look at him again as if to offer proof of sincerity. 'You see, I haven't spoken to your wireless operators. My colleague, the Jewish one, he's spoken to them and he's convinced they're spies, that you were going to land them and they were to report on shipping in and out of Freetown.'

Mohr bent down and placed the fungi at his feet. When he lifted his head to look at Lindsay again there was a small but disconcerting smile on his face.

'I don't agree, in fact I'm convinced it's nonsense,' said Lindsay.

'Ha! Jews!' Mohr shook his head theatrically.

'You don't believe me? You don't think we make mistakes? What touching faith you have in us. We've hanged at least five men in the last six months. I'm certain one of them was innocent.'

'And I'm certain you did your best to save him.'

Lindsay ignored the scepticism in Mohr's voice: 'No. He could and should have proved his innocence. Things are not what they were. We're fighting for survival. You've taken tea with the First Sea Lord. I'm sure he was impressed, but if I shoot you, here, now, would he care? Of course not. The Red Cross would be told, "Shot while trying to escape." It's the same with your wireless operators. When people open their newspapers at breakfast they will read of two more spies hanged at Wandsworth Prison and they will say, "Thank God for our intelligence people".'

'And you want me to help you prove they're not spies by telling you what?' asked Mohr.

'I want you to tell me what they were doing.'

Mohr shook his head slowly as if incredulous that Lindsay should think him so naive.

'I know they're innocent, I know why they were there,' said Lindsay. 'You needed English-speaking wireless operators so you could intercept and decode our signals.'

Mohr glanced down and for just an instant Lindsay saw a heavy frown cloud his face, but the timbre of his voice when he spoke was as steady and confident as ever: 'That's what the Americans call a hunch. Not a good one. Not even your Jewish friend seems to believe you. Perhaps he doesn't trust you?'

'Don't you want to help your men?'

'Of course,' said Mohr with a short barking laugh. 'Of course, I understand. None of your comrades trust you.'

He was so pleased with himself that he did not notice he was trampling the fungi he had placed at the bottom of the rotten trunk. 'They don't trust you because they think you're German,' he said in English. 'That's it, isn't it? You're German.'

'No.'

They walked on in silence until they reached the crest of the hill where the ride forked west towards Sassoon's obelisk. Through the trees they could see the house below them and a small group of prisoners kicking a football about on the lawn by the lake.

'My men,' muttered Mohr.

Beyond the Park the quiet ordered streets of Cockfosters and Southgate were lost in a summer haze. At the edge of the wood Lindsay stopped. The other arm of the ride led down the hill across the old golf course to the lake; it would take them just twenty minutes to walk back to the house.

'How long have you been reading our signals for?' he asked Mohr suddenly.

'Are you still trying to break me?'

'How long have you been reading our signals for – more than six months, less?'

Mohr did not reply.

'More than six months?' said Lindsay forcefully. 'More or less?'

'You must have a low opinion of me.'

'Some of my colleagues are more direct. They might use other methods.'

Mohr laughed harshly: 'No walks in the park?'

'I am very, very serious. It would be better for you to answer. More or less?'

'I know . . .'

'More or less?'

'I know your cousin Martin . . .'

Lindsay tensed a little. So he knew; well, there was nothing more to say. He had been half expecting something of the sort. It was awkward but in a way it changed nothing. He was not going to persuade Mohr to talk to him. But he knew he was right, right about the codes, quite sure.

'There's a certain something, an expression you share. And Martin often spoke of a cousin in the Royal Navy reserve. You were close, weren't you?' There was a discreet but unmistakable look of satisfaction on Mohr's face: 'Martin laughed about it, a small joke. He would laugh now if he could see us here together. What a coincidence.'

Lindsay wondered if he should refuse to listen, but it was too late and he had to admit he was curious.

'We shared a mess for a time. The *U-bootwaffe* was very small before the war, as I'm sure you know. Martin is a good officer.'

Lindsay nodded.

'But you, Lieutenant, you could have been fighting alongside us.'

'No.'

Mohr smiled.

They walked on in silence again and were soon at the lake. It was lunch-time and small groups of uniformed Staff were talking and smoking on the north terrace. As they approached, Charlie Samuels stepped from the shadow beneath it and began scurrying across the lawn to meet them. 'I'm to take the commander back, Douglas. The Colonel is waiting for you in his office.' His forehead was wrinkled with anxiety.

'Fine,' said Lindsay airily. He was conscious that Mohr was following their exchange. He nodded curtly to him: 'Goodbye, Herr Kapitän.'

'Goodbye, Lieutenant. I hope we meet again soon.' Mohr turned to speak to Samuels, 'The Lieutenant and I have so much in common . . .' Samuels looked surprised. To Lindsay's great relief Mohr made no effort to explain.

'Good luck, Douglas,' said Samuels. Lindsay guessed that the words 'You'll need it' were on the tip of his tongue.

Checkland's office was on the first floor of the house, near the Map Room. A pretty Wren, very young, very well spoken, was keeping the door. She smiled warmly at Lindsay: 'Colonel Checkland is expecting you, sir, Would you wait just a minute?'

She slipped out from behind her desk, knocked gently and opened Checkland's door. Lindsay caught a glimpse of him at his desk before the door closed behind her. She reappeared a moment later, swinging her navy-blue hips, the room full of her perfume: 'The Colonel will see you now.'

Checkland was not alone. Henderson was standing by the fireplace. Lindsay stepped smartly into the room and stood to attention before the head bent over the desk. The door clicked behind him. Checkland carried on writing.

'Sit down, Lindsay.'

'Thank you, sir.'

Lindsay followed the steady course of his pen across the sheet of headed paper. He held it like a weapon. There were few personal touches in the room; some photographs of ships – presumably ones Checkland had served in – and the King, charts, the usual Service furniture and cream paint. He turned to look at Henderson who was gazing out of the window to the hill Lindsay had just climbed with Mohr, his face set hard, itching for a fight.

'Did you get my message this morning?' Checkland's head was still bent over his letter.

'Sir?'

Checkland looked up at him and very deliberately put down his pen.

'Don't play the idiot. James has spoken to Chief Wren Sherlock.'

Checkland's face was a little red but his voice was calm and measured. He had a certain easy authority and had been a fine interrogator in his day. The Germans had caught him spying before the Great War – bobbing about in the Baltic with pen and notebook. He knew what it was to be a prisoner.

'You were to find one of us at once.'

'I was going to find you, sir . . .'

'But not before you'd interrogated Mohr again.'

'No, sir.' There was no point in lying. 'I was hoping to speak to him yesterday but he was at the Admiralty . . .'

'You know of course that I've spoken to Samuels. You were under

142

strict orders not to question Mohr, not to question any of the prisoners about codes but that's what you've done.'

'Did Lieutenant Samuels tell you what he's dragged from the wireless operators?' Lindsay's voice was quiet and controlled too. It was one of the first things Checkland taught newcomers to his Section: never lose your temper because anger will cloud your judgement. 'We've proof that our codes have been broken.'

Henderson snorted sceptically. 'Proof, what proof?'

Checkland half raised a hand to silence him. 'Samuels did tell us they spoke English and that they were brought together for the 112's patrol to Freetown. That isn't proof our codes have been broken. Which code is broken, which cipher – one or all of them?'

Lindsay shook his head. 'That's what I was trying to wring from Mohr, sir.'

'Did you succeed?'

'No.'

Checkland gave a long, exasperated sigh. 'You have no proof but by questioning Mohr about codes you may have done a great deal of harm . . .'

'How much proof do you need, sir?' said Lindsay. 'They were . . .'

But Checkland cut across him sharply: 'What do you know of disguised indicators? Do you know anything about the sub-tractor system or onetime pads, reciphering tables and typex machines?'

Lindsay flushed a little. It was true, he knew very little about the mechanics of code making and breaking: 'I just know that . . .'

'You think you know that the Germans are into one or more of our codes. Yes, you've said.'

Checkland paused to consider his next words, then said with careful emphasis: 'You know, there are people who understand these things and they have better sources than us. You have put some of those sources at risk. You were instructed not to question the prisoners about codes and ciphers. You broke a direct order. You are a lieutenant in one small section of Naval Intelligence and yet you think you know better than the Director of the Division, his Staff, and me. It's a pity, Lindsay, you were a promising interrogator but with a little too much to prove . . .'

23

For once all the interrogators were in the office, swapping stories and smoking. Lieutenant Dick Graham was holding up a prophylactic the guards had taken from one of the prisoners. Lindsay tried to avoid catching his eye. He failed.

'You've come at the perfect time, Douglas. Tell me, what should I do with this? The girls won't give me a sensible answer.'

Lieutenant Graham's little audience giggled appreciatively.

'Would you like it?'

More laughter. Graham was a history don in Civvy Street, a greying thirty-six with pince-nez spectacles, a slight lisp and a taste for the bizarre. He was indulging it now, swinging the French letter like the pendulum of a clock.

'You're a member of the master race, of course, but I'm sure it will fit.'

It took Lindsay most of the afternoon to two-finger-type a presentable copy of his report. Two flimsy sheets. He sat back in his chair and stared at the lines above the ribbon:

To conclude: the U-112 was on a special mission to African waters under the command of one of Admiral Dönitz's most trusted officers. The mission required highly trained English-speaking wireless operators. Evidence and SR transcripts taken during the interrogation of other U-boat crews suggests the enemy is obtaining intelligence from wireless traffic. Kapitän zur See Mohr may have been using this intelligence to co-ordinate attacks on convoys in and out of Freetown. One or more of our codes has been broken.

Short and thin. But there were those little signs that meant so much to an experienced eye that never made it into a report. He wondered if he should have included a few:

. . . the prisoner Brand kept touching his lip . . .

. . . Kapitän zur See Mohr lost his composure when codes were mentioned and refused to make eye contact . . .

All this was evidence too but it counted for nothing because the Section's work was not respected in the Division. You had to have friends to put your case. He would send Winn a copy and Fleming too.

'How was it?' Charlie Samuels was standing beside his desk: 'You've been hammering that typewriter without mercy.'

Lindsay glanced beyond him into the body of the room: even Dick Graham was busy.

'I'm preparing my defence,' said Lindsay quietly.

'I thought you might be. Checkland wants to see me again,' Samuels looked at his watch, 'in ten minutes.'

His eyes were roving restlessly in every direction but Lindsay's, and he was nibbling a thumbnail like an anxious schoolboy summoned to his headmaster's study.

'Rest easy, Charlie, it's my fault, he knows that,' said Lindsay.

'Yes, well . . .' He sounded uncertain.

'Here.' Lindsay pulled the sheet from the typewriter and offered it to him: 'Read it, it might help.'

Samuels smiled weakly and shook his head: 'Not on your Nelly. Surrender followed by an abject apology. Section 11 suits me very well. I hate the sea, and I have family to look after in London.'

'You've never mentioned them.'

'You've never asked.'

It was true. Lindsay felt a little ashamed.

'Time up,' said Samuels. 'Wish me luck.'

Lindsay was still at his desk an hour later, his thoughts flitting from Mohr to Winn to Mary to Mohr. Rich golden light was streaming low through the south-facing windows, casting twisted shadows across the floor as the trees swayed in the gentlest of evening breezes. The office was empty but for the duty Wrens. The other interrogators were sipping pink gins in the mess. The late courier had taken Lindsay's report to the Admiralty and by now Checkland would have his copy too. He wanted to ring Mary but she would be at her desk in Room 41. Better to ring later and from the privacy of his home.

Turning to the window, he was struggling into his jacket when the door opened behind him. With strange certainty, he knew the person he least wanted to speak to had just stepped into the room.

'Lindsay, a word.' There was an ominously satisfied note in his voice.

'Here?' asked Lindsay, turning to face him.

Henderson looked at the Wrens; one was bent low over her desk, no doubt keen to impress with her industry, the other busy at a filing cabinet by the door.

'I say, would you mind leaving us alone? We'll answer the telephones.'

Lindsay settled into his chair and concentrated on appearing more relaxed than he felt. The last thing he wanted was another unpleasant encounter. The Wrens swept a few personal things into their bags and left without saying a word.

'You know why I'm here?'

Lindsay leant forward and shook a cigarette from the packet on his desk.

'Samuels is going. The Director is sending him to a POW camp in the north, an old racecourse. He can't do much harm there.'

Poor Samuels. Lindsay had the uncomfortable feeling he had presented Checkland with the excuse to get rid of him. He drew deeply on his cigarette, then said: 'Pleased?'

Henderson coloured a little: 'Not at all pleased. Two officers in the Section disciplined, intelligence sources put at risk . . .'

'Are you sending me to the races too?'

'I knew that first week you were shadowing me that we had made a mistake.' There was something like a triumphant 'told you so' in Henderson's voice.

Lindsay could not help smiling; he had begun to find the man's unrelenting hostility grimly amusing. It was an unfortunate smile. The expression on Henderson's face changed in an instant from complacent triumph to fury. He made a noise like a bull, half grunt, half moan, and slipped from the edge of the desk he was leaning against as if preparing to charge. Rough words tumbled from him instead: 'You're arrogant. You think your decoration allows you to behave just as you like. You're wrong. You see only a small part of the picture. I wish my sister . . .' He was struggling for something sufficiently insulting; '. . . you're an arrogant German bastard.'

'Finished, sir?' Leaning forward a little, Lindsay ground the butt of his cigarette into the ashtray. He did not feel anger, he felt contempt.

'And what was the Colonel's message, sir?'

24

Big Ben began to strike half past seven and before its closing chime Mary Henderson was on her feet and walking with brisk purpose through the park. Before her was the Citadel, forbidding even on a warm summer evening, a masterpiece of its kind, featureless and impartial. Inside it, the wheels of the machine were turning still, churning out an endless stream of paper. A cheery word to the guards at the Mall entrance then on into the Admiralty's cool marble hall. A group of crisply dressed Staff officers had just left the Director's office and were chatting noisily at his door. Mary slipped past, head bent, anxious to catch no one's eye.

'Dr Henderson . . .'

It was the Director's Assistant. She turned to greet him:

'Ian, how are you?'

Fleming reached for her hand, then kissed her warmly on both cheeks: 'Lovely, even in your customary academic dress, and do you know, I was just thinking of you.'

Mary raised her eyebrows sceptically. She had known Ian Fleming since childhood, an old family friend who had been at Eton for a time with her brother. But he was an adventurer – fine words had been followed more than once by a direct challenge to her virtue. A handsome thirty-three, Fleming was tall, immaculate, with wavy hair, tired close-set eyes, a strong jaw and a severe mouth that turned down a little disdainfully at the corners. She had always stoutly resisted his attempts to seduce her – that was why they were still on good terms.

'I've just left the Director. We were talking about your chap. Your name was mentioned too,' he said, squeezing her hand gently between both of his.

Mary coloured a little and slipped free: 'Why on earth . . .'

'It isn't a secret, is it? Don't academics take lovers?'

'Only sensitive ones.'

Fleming gave her a small dry smile: 'Have you spoken to him today?'

Mary shook her head.

'Then come with me.' He guided her by the elbow into a transept off the main corridor, then through a green baize door into a small office. 'You don't, do you?' he asked, waving a packet of Morland cigarettes at her. 'Very wise, they're rather strong,' and he gestured towards a chair in front of the desk. The room was thick with the smell of stale tobacco, well ordered, bright, unremarkable but for the view across Horse Guards to the Foreign Office and the garden of Number 10 Downing Street.

'You know I found Lindsay and introduced him to the Division . . .' Fleming settled into the chair beside her, his back to the door. 'Has he told you anything about his work?'

Mary shifted a little uncomfortably. 'Only what I need to know. Rodger asked him to brief me,' she said cautiously.

'Brief you?' He gave a short laugh, 'I see. And what have you told him about your work?'

'Only what he needs to know.'

Fleming's eyes narrowed as he scrutinised her face for a moment, then said: 'Section 11 wants rid of him. Colonel Checkland doesn't trust him and I suppose you know what your brother thinks?'

Mary frowned angrily and opened her mouth to speak but he held up his hand: '. . . the Colonel says he has a bee in his bonnet about our codes, that he asks dangerous questions. It hasn't gone down well here. He might give away more than he discovers. You know how careful we have to be. Has Lindsay discussed this fellow Mohr with you?'

'No,' she lied.

Fleming drew on his cigarette, the tip rasping and glowing, then he blew a sceptical stream of smoke at the ceiling: 'And his family?'

'What about them?'

He looked a little haughtily down his nose at her: 'The Director doesn't want to take any chances. He wants to send Lindsay back to sea. I'm going to try and persuade him not to. There are things a clever German speaker can do for me. But you should both be careful . . .'

She interrupted him crossly: 'Careful?'

'Yes, very, very careful,' he said firmly, 'and you most of all. You are one of the few who knows of special intelligence. Listen to me, it's good advice.'

Mary looked down at her hands, tightly balled in her lap. Were pieces of paper marked 'Very' or 'Most Secret' circulating in the Division, their pillow talk a subject for comment?

'Did we meet by chance?' she asked, and her voice shook a little.

'Yes. But I'm glad we did.' Fleming smiled and leant across to give her hand a gentle squeeze.

Mary stayed for only a couple of minutes more, to exchange a few strained pleasantries. Then Fleming's door clicked shut behind her and she stood outside it, breathing deeply. She was cross with him but crosser still with Lindsay. He was fighting his own little war, careless of orders and the opinions of others. And now their relationship was a security matter, their conversation a subject for speculation, what was private and special between them common currency. She shuddered at the thought. A phone began to ring in Fleming's office. It was almost eight o'clock and she was expected at her desk.

Slowly, with a distant smile for familiar faces, she made her way down brown lino-covered steps into the dim corridors of the Citadel, Fleming's 'careful' playing roughly through her mind. Outside Room 41, she hesitated then walked a few steps further to stand at a different door. It opened almost at once and a large bundle of files began to totter unsteadily out. Mary could see just enough short dark hair to be sure that one of the watch-keepers, Lieutenant Sutherland, was somewhere beneath them.

'Is that you, Dr Henderson?' There was a note of desperation in his voice. 'Are you coming in?'

'Yes, yes, I want to try . . .'

But Sutherland was concentrating too hard on his files to care what she wanted. And what did she want? It was a foolish notion – certainly not what Fleming meant by 'careful' – but it had taken hold of her in the corridor. She wanted to speak to Lindsay.

'Well, go on, take the door,' said Sutherland sharply.

Mary held it open for him then stepped inside.

Room 30 was a little larger than its neighbour across the corridor but just as smoky, with the same droplights and shabby office furniture. It had its own plot table too and on it a mad cat's cradle of thread and cardboard arrows tracked the enemy's small fleet of ships. A clerical assistant at the plot smiled warmly at Mary, another looked up from her desk for just a moment, but neither said anything to her. The room was unusually quiet. That was unfortunate. Personal telephone calls were strictly forbidden but at busy times no one noticed you, or wanted to be noticed.

In the far right-hand corner, an anonymous blue door led to the Teleprinter Room – the home of 'the secret ladies'. One of them, dumpy in brown lambswool and tweed, was standing over a teleprinter coiling a coded message around a spool. She was too lost in her world of printer's ribbon and tape to notice Mary enter and there appeared to be no one else in the room. At times, it was full of the harsh mind-numbing chatter of a dozen teleprinters sending and receiving signals. The ladies would hover about them like acolytes of a strange mechanical oracle, ready to rip, read, and distribute. To the right of the door, a long table was subdivided into six desks and on a shelf above there were a number of heavy black telephones. After just a moment's hesitation, Mary walked to the far end of the table, picked one up and placed it on the desk in front of her. The Admiralty switchboard connected her without question.

'Lindsay.' He sounded very weary.

'It's me.'

'Darling, I was hoping you'd ring.'

'Were you?'

'Is something the matter?'

'You're such a fool, Douglas. Why didn't you listen to me?'

'You know then? Thank you for your support,' he said frostily.

'Ian asked me what I know about your work and what I'd told you about mine.'

Lindsay said nothing.

'Well?' asked Mary.

'Well what?'

'Say sorry.'

'For what? No please don't answer that. Sorry. Satisfied?'

'No.'

The tense silence was filled by the brutal rhythm of a tele-printer.

'Where on earth are you?'

'Never mind. What's going to happen to you?'

Lindsay must have caught the note of anxiety in her voice because his tone softened too:

'I don't know. Your brother says I'll be sent somewhere I can't cause trouble.'

'Ian says we have to be careful and . . .'

There was a flash of tweed between desk and shelf – one of the ladies was on the move.

'I have to go, Douglas.'

A round and very stern face appeared above the telephone shelf: 'Miss Henderson, what are you doing?'

Mary cupped a defensive hand over the mouthpiece: 'Dr Henderson, if you please.'

It was time to insist on full academic dignity. She raised the phone: 'I'm sorry, Lieutenant, we can discuss this tomorrow. Please send me a note.'

And without waiting for a reply she put the receiver down.

The clerical assistant's face was pink with confusion: 'Dr Henderson, no one is supposed to make calls from . . .' And after a deep breath: 'I'll have to report this to the Officer of the Watch.'

Pushing her chair back smartly, Mary stood to face her. The clerical assistant was clearly younger than she looked – no more than twenty, with a minor public school voice, too finely cut.

'You must do as you see fit, Miss . . .?'

'Barnes.'

'. . . I was looking for a clerical assistant and the room was deserted.'

'But I was here —'

Mary broke in: 'Really, you must be more careful. I won't mention it this time, Miss Barnes.'

And with a short prayer for forgiveness, she stepped briskly from the room, across the next and into the corridor.

*

Later, at her desk in the Tracking Room, Mary began to regret her sharp words to Lindsay. It was a terrible waste, maddening. He was fumbling for the truth, breaking the rules, and now his reputation was clouded by failure and distrust. And she had let him stumble into this mess. He was paying the price for her silence.

25

The silence was broken only once. Lindsay snatched up the telephone, hoping to hear Mary's voice but it was his mother.

'Are you all right, Douglas?'

She spoke to him in English for the first time. They had always spoken German in the family. His father was working too hard, his brother had joined the Royal Air Force – 'Why don't you ever ring? I've heard nothing from the rest of the family but the papers say they've bombed Bremen.' And then there were tears. He was relieved when the call ended.

Rising from the couch, he drifted to the window of his little sitting room. It was half past eleven and St James's Square was deserted but for a couple kissing in the shadows, entirely caught up in each other. Everything seemed to be falling apart. He shook his head, disgusted with himself for being so full of self-pity. The spooning couple separated and Lindsay watched them amble along the pavement. A black Morris was parked against the kerb opposite and as they passed it he was surprised to see the glowing orange pinprick of a cigarette behind the wheel. He stepped away from the window and drew the heavy blackout curtains. After a moment's fumbling, he switched on the desk lamp and, reaching for a sheet of paper, wrote a brief note to Mary. If he delivered it now she would be able to read it in the morning, if not before.

The front door swung heavily to behind him and he stood on the pavement outside, catching his breath in the warm, still air. The city was humming restlessly even in the blackout and he could hear drunken voices outside the gentleman's club on the opposite side of the square. Close by, a car engine grunted. It was the Morris and peering closely at it, he could distinguish the silhouettes of two men. It pulled away quickly from the kerb as he approached. The driver seemed to glance furtively across at him before swinging the car into Charles II Street. Were they spivs conducting a little night-time business? If you knew the right person you could still buy anything in London.

The house in Lord North Street was close-shuttered. Slipping the envelope through the letterbox, Lindsay turned to wander slowly back, glancing over his shoulder in the hope that Mary would find it at once and call after him. He considered returning to ring the bell but it was after midnight and her uncle was probably at home. He spent a long hour brooding, walking he knew not where before turning almost reluctantly for home. On the doorstep, his keys slipped through his fingers. As he bent to pick them up, he glanced through the iron railings to his left. The black Morris was now parked between two other cars in the north-east corner of the square. The driver and his passenger were lost in shadow but Lindsay knew they were there and that they were watching him. The door clunked firmly shut and he turned to lean against the wall in the dark hall, his chest tight with anxiety. They were not black-market wide boys, they were Special Branch policemen, he was sure of it, perhaps the Security Service. He had been identified as a risk. Perhaps they had searched his apartment. He raced up the stairs, his head pounding, giddy with breathlessness. He would ring Fleming, and he picked up the phone, only to slam it back a few seconds later. Collapsing into a chair, he closed his eyes and tried to concentrate on breathing deeply. Two, three, four minutes passed and his pulse began to slow. He must keep calm. They were probably ordinary policemen carrying out some sort of surveillance operation that was nothing to do with him. Lighting a cigarette, he sat in the darkness and smoked it slowly down to the filter. This had happened before. Something in him snapped and he lost control. Foolish. Without bothering to look out of the window again, he walked through to the bedroom and flopped on to his lumpy old mattress.

That night, he had a dream. He was standing on the pavement below his apartment and the Morris was close by. The driver's window was open and an arm with a black tattoo of a fouled anchor was resting against the door. 'Who are you?' Lindsay shouted. There was no reply. He bent to look inside. A head lunged towards him and he recoiled in disgust. The man's face was no longer there, as if a giant hand had dashed it without mercy against a jagged rock. Tails of skin were clinging to the top of the skull and from one of these hung a tangled strand of auburn hair. And he knew the auburn hair belonged to a sailor from the *Culloden*. When he woke in the morning both his hands were hooked tightly around the frame of his bed. The Morris had gone.

26

The news came with the rations. The guard hammered on the door at half past seven and half an hour later he was back with the breakfast tray. Helmut Lange was dressed but lying on his camp bed, trying to ignore the tortured grunts of his room-mate who was busy jumping and stretching in nothing but a vest and pants. Obersteuermann Eduard Bruns considered it his duty as a good National Socialist to be fit and ready. 'Ready for what?' Lange had asked him on their first day together. Bruns had shrugged his muscular shoulders and then, after giving the question a little thought, replied: 'Victory.' He did not explain how he hoped to contribute to this behind the wire in a British prisoner-of-war camp and Lange knew better than to ask.

'Trent Park Hotel bed and breakfast,' the British corporal said cheerily as he placed the tray on the table. Some porridge, some toast and a tin mug of evil brown tea. 'Your last day, Fritz, your-last-day-here,' the corporal enunciated the words carefully, as if speaking to small children. 'New-hotel-tonight.'

Lange was glad to be moving at last. The formal interrogations had not troubled him because he had no secrets to betray, but Lieutenant Lindsay had taken him from the confines of his prison cell into the park and asked him very different questions, questions he was free but unable to answer. And at the club, the lieutenant's girlfriend had pressed him in a gentle way, too, about the concentration camps, the duty of the Church, and the Jews. Eyes fixed on the white ceiling of his room, Lange had prayed for guidance. In the still hours of the night, Bruns breathing heavily close by, his prayers had been answered and although he was afraid, he took comfort from the thought that he could shrink behind the wire.

At eleven o'clock the guards ordered them from the room, with keys jangling and doors opening the length of the corridor like a scene from the Last Judgement. A military lorry was parked just beyond the double fence at the front of the house and a group of twenty prisoners was standing in a line close by. Lange stepped forward to join them but the young British army officer in charge shouted something at the guards and one of them grabbed his sleeve: 'Not yet, Fritz.'

Bruns was at his side: 'They're our men from the *112*. They're separating the officers.'

The two of them stood in silence together on the forecourt and watched as the line of men was escorted through the wire and into the back of the lorry. As soon as the last man had scrambled inside it began to pull away and was replaced by a green military bus. All the officers of the *112* were assembled now, chatting and smoking in the sunshine. Lange recognised his first room-mate, the young engineer, August Heine. Then he heard voices in the outer hall and a thick-set British naval officer stepped through the door and held it open for Kapitän zur See Jürgen Mohr. The prisoners came smartly to attention. Mohr acknowledged their salute with a weak smile.

The British officer was speaking loudly in English. Lange watched them drift through the gate to the bus until a guard yelled something he took to be an order to follow. On an impulse, he began rooting about in his little bag for a pencil and, tearing the back off a cigarette packet, he wrote a short note.

Mohr was still talking to the British officer a little way from the bus. He half turned as Lange approached and looked him up and down: 'Yes?'

'Herr Kapitän, I was hoping to leave this note.'

He took the scrap of cardboard from his pocket and handed it to the officer who read it carefully, frowned, then placed it in his jacket pocket: 'All right. I'll make sure Lieutenant Lindsay sees it.'

Lange was on the bottom step of the bus when he felt a firm hand against his chest. It was Mohr and he was looking at him intently, his face set hard in a silent promise: Lange would be called to account for his note.

From the window of the interrogators' office Lindsay watched the military bus pull away. There were a few things he needed to rescue from his desk but no 'goodbyes' he wished to say. Well perhaps one, he thought, a fond farewell to Sassoon's ghost. It was difficult to take seriously because a small voice kept whispering, 'This is all a mistake.' Old notes, German newspapers, military handbooks – he swept them all into the large canvas bag he had once used for his rugby boots. It took just five minutes. He was trying to force the zip together when Charlie Samuels walked into the office.

'I've done that already,' he said, pointing to Lindsay's empty desk.

'I know. Sorry, Charlie.'

'Sufferance is the badge of all our tribe, Douglas. At least they had the good sense not to try and make a sailor of me.' Samuels lifted the plain cardboard file he was carrying with the satisfied air of someone preparing to hand over a fine present: 'I've something to show you.'

'What is it?'

'Not here,' he whispered conspiratorially. 'Come with me.'

He led Lindsay out into the servants' corridor and to the foot of the back stairs. Then, after checking that no one was about, he began to climb down quickly to the basement.

'This is very cloak-and-dagger, Charlie,' said Lindsay, behind him. 'I feel like Guy Fawkes.'

Samuels did not answer but turned right into a long low badly lit passage way, its walls lined with large cream tiles. Doors to left and right opened on to empty wine racks, boot and dairy rooms, a silver store and an archive, neglected and dusty. It was Lindsay's first time below stairs.

'In here,' said Samuels.

'Here' was a dingy barrel-vaulted cellar with whitewashed walls and terracotta floor tiles, lit by a single naked bulb. It was empty but for a rickety trestle table.

'All right,' Lindsay's voice bounced about the room, 'tell me.'

Samuels took a deep breath: 'My friend at Oxford sent me this. It will tell you all you need to know.' And he thrust a file at Lindsay in which there were four or five typed pages. The title in bold at the top of the first page was '**Administrative and Auxiliary Codes**'.

The Administrative Code was brought into force in 1934 and used unrecoded for routine signals . . .

Lindsay glanced down the page. There was a section entitled 'Naval Code', and on the next page, '**Long Subtractor System**' and '**Merchant Navy Code**'. Lindsay looked at Samuels and down again at the file.

'How on earth did you get this?'

'I've told you, a friend. It's a basic guide to the book codes we use. Be careful. My friend would be in very hot water for giving it to me.'

'A good friend,' said Lindsay.

'Yes,' said Samuels, 'someone else who likes to break rules.'

There was something in Samuels' voice that suggested his friend was a woman, perhaps an academic colleague and an old flame. Lindsay knew that the naval codes people had taken over one of the Oxford colleges and recruited some of the university's dons.

'You can read it later,' said Samuels, 'but for God's sake look after it. The most interesting stuff is on page four.' He leant forward to find the page and pointed to a paragraph near the bottom:

The enemy seems to have been able to keep track of British naval mobilisation at the beginning of the war and of our patrols in the North Atlantic and Home Waters. A copy of the Administrative Code may also have been captured when Norway fell in May 1940 . . .

'Charlie.' Lindsay's voice shook a little with excitement: 'The Germans broke one of our codes at the beginning of the war . . .'

'Perhaps two,' said Samuels.

'And the Admiralty knows. Then why . . .'

Samuels laughed and grabbed Lindsay's arm as if restraining a difficult patient: 'Steady, you need to read it. Our codes *may* have been broken. It seems the Germans salvaged some secret material from one of our submarines and captured more in Norway too. Anyway, they were changed as a precaution. We scrapped the Administrative and Auxiliary Codes last summer and brought in a new one, the Naval Code . . .'

'The Germans could have broken that too, Charlie.'

'It's history,' said Samuels, 'Read it. They changed the codes.'

'Do you think someone's deliberately trying to stop us? Trying to hide the truth?'

Samuels pulled a face: 'Honestly, Douglas, you're turning this into the plot of a penny dreadful.' He paused, then said with quiet deliberation: 'You know, there's a much simpler explanation.'

Lindsay turned sharply to look at him: 'All right, what do you . . .'

But someone in heavy military boots was approaching along the passage. Samuels raised his hand in warning.

'We should go,' he whispered, and he slipped through the half-open door. He must have surprised the owner of the boots because a frightened voice squealed: 'For Christ's sake,' and a second later, 'Oh sorry, sir'.

It was one of the guards, a red-headed corporal with a guilty expression on his face. They could rest easy. He was seeking a secret corner of his own for 'a crafty fag'.

'All right, Corporal,' said Samuels sharply and he brushed past him and began walking briskly back along the corridor. Lindsay followed a few feet behind. Neither of them spoke until they reached the top of the basement stairs, then, after checking that they were alone, Samuels pointed to the file in Lindsay's hand: 'History, Douglas, all right. Don't get my friend into trouble.'

'You said there was another, simpler explanation?'

Samuels thought for a moment, then shrugged: 'It was nothing. Forget it. Goodbye.' And he held out his hand. 'Perhaps we can keep in touch,' and there was something wistful in his voice.

'Yes,' said Lindsay as they shook hands, 'we must.'

27

The number 9 London bus was crowded and reeked of sweat and cheap perfume. Mary walked the last two stops. For once, she had made an effort to please and changed into a green summer dress that matched her eyes and showed her figure to great advantage.

Lindsay was waiting beneath a stone elephant at the corner of the Albert Memorial and had just lit a cigarette. When he saw her approaching, he put it out with his foot and dropped down the steps to meet her and wrap her in his arms. They stood for a minute in silence as concert folk drifted and chatted around them. Then Lindsay pushed her gently away and holding both her hands, looked her up and down: 'You're looking lovely.'

Mary was struck by the tired shadows about his eyes and she squeezed his hands and moved closer: 'I'm sorry, Douglas.'

'Don't be.'

'Have you spoken to Fleming?'

'No. Did he mention my report?'

Mary shook her head. Lindsay frowned and said after a moment's thought: 'I've learnt something more today.'

She tensed a little.

'No, all right,' he said quickly, 'I won't talk about it now.'

For a few seconds there was an awkward silence, then he pulled a scrap of cardboard from his pocket: 'Your brother sent me this. It's from Helmut Lange.'

She turned the piece of cigarette packet over to read the message, scribbled in a small neat hand.

Thank you for helping me. Please thank lovely lady. Sorry.

'He remembers "lovely lady",' said Lindsay with a broad smile, 'It must have worried your brother.'

'Why does he want to thank us?'

'I think he regards me as his rescuer. As for you, he's struggling with the old certainties – Fatherland and Führer – and you reminded him there are other choices.'

'I only met him for a few hours.'

Lindsay squeezed her arm playfully. 'And in those few hours . . . perhaps it was your eyes.'

Mary pulled a face at him. 'And the "Sorry"?'

'Ah, well in the end it didn't work.'

'Work?'

'He hasn't the courage to follow his conscience.'

'Did you want him to?'

'He might have been useful.'

'I thought you liked him.'

'I do.'

Lindsay began to propel Mary gently by the elbow towards the Royal Albert Hall.

'What are we going to hear?' she asked.

'I don't know.'

They bought a programme in the foyer: Elgar and Beethoven – the Fifth Symphony – Rachmaninov and Wagner. The hall was almost full already and a little too warm. The audience seemed younger, less grand than before the war, and judging by the faces and uniforms more international. They took their seats in the stalls and Lindsay reached across for her hand: 'I'm surprised about the Wagner, Hitler's so devoted to him.'

'Keep the war out of the concert hall,' said Mary with a smile.

But it was advice she failed miserably to follow. No matter how hard she tried, her thoughts broke free of the music, drifting from the hall to the war. She felt a little guilty, as if she was letting the orchestra down. Lindsay was shifting awkwardly in his seat beside her, clearly struggling to concentrate too. She felt sure his thoughts were full of interrogations and codes and the new piece of information he was bursting to share with her. Perhaps it was naïve but she hoped he would forget the whole thing. It was an obsession, dangerous for both of them.

Lindsay dropped Mary's hand. The Albert Hall was bursting with applause.

'Did you enjoy it?' he shouted across at her.

'Oh yes, especially the Wagner. What about you?'

'Oh yes, the Wagner.'

The chattering, cheerful audience swept them from the concert hall and on to the pavement. Most people were walking west towards Kensington High Street and the Underground, the sky in front of them yellow and orange, strewed with deep grey cloud. Blackout was at a little after eleven.

'We could have some supper,' said Lindsay.

'Where? No, it's all right, I don't feel very hungry.'

He turned her shoulders so she was facing him: 'Are you all right?'

'Yes. Fine, honestly.'

'Would you like to come back to my flat? I can make us something to eat.'

Mary hesitated. Fleming had said: 'Careful.' She wanted to be with Lindsay but perhaps it was better to wait until the dust he had kicked up had settled a little.

'Please.'

'I think . . .'

'Please.'

'Yes, all right,' she heard herself say.

Lindsay took her hand and led her from the concert crowd in search of a taxicab. They found one parked outside the American Ambassador's house in Princes Gate. It was a short journey round Hyde Park Corner into Piccadilly, the city drawing down its blinds, retreating into darkness. Mary stared silently out of the window, frustrated and surprised by her own weakness. The cab passed the sad shell of Wren's modest masterpiece, St James's Church, turned right into the Haymarket, then on into St James's Square, where it pulled up outside a tall smoky-black brick house in the south-east corner.

'My home,' said Lindsay almost apologetically.

'I'm sure it's very nice.'

'It's gloomy.'

At the top of the stairs, Lindsay opened the door and turned on the light to reveal burgundy walls and a heavy mahogany hall table.

'Mother's choice,' he explained.

Mary walked slowly around the small sitting room, picking up family photographs while Lindsay made them some tea.

'I spoke to my mother last night,' he shouted from the kitchen. 'She needed cheering up so I told her about you.'

'Why did she need cheering up?'

It was some time before he answered, but when he did:

'I told her I was in a little trouble. She was upset. She thinks I should keep my head down – she does.'

'And your father?'

'He's busy with the war effort: his company is turning out munitions now.'

Lindsay brought the tea into the room and they sat together on his mother's uncomfortable sofa.

'But my mother was pleased to hear about you.'

'I'm glad. Are you close to your mother?'

Lindsay began to laugh.

'Why are you laughing?' she asked.

'Does your question have something to do with Dr Freud?'

Mary laughed too: 'Well, you're clearly a troubled soul.'

'Perhaps,' he said quietly. He put down his cup and reached across for hers: 'The Navy, your brother, cups and a hard sofa – all very troubling . . .'

She let him pull her towards him and they kissed, slowly at first and then deeply, passionately. And after a time Lindsay led her through to his bedroom where they stood before the blue London night, kissing and caressing with growing urgency. Then he bent to lift her dress up and over her head, her hair falling loose about her shoulders. She stood there, self-conscious but trembling with excitement as he bent again to slip her pants down her thighs and then down her calves. And she could hear his breath sharp and short. Reaching under her hair, he pulled her head gently towards him. They kissed again, intense, wild kisses, until she broke free and pushed him away. And slowly, deliberately, she sat on the edge of the bed, and then she lay back on the bed, raising and parting her knees.

*

Later they lay quietly together, naked, wet with perspiration, her cheek against his chest. She could feel its easy rise and fall and the steady beat of his heart. And from time to time he leant forward to kiss and smell her hair.

'You're beautiful.'

Mary turned her head to kiss his chest, then said: 'I'm not but thank you.'

'Please allow me to be the judge.'

They were silent for a minute or so before Mary said: 'I don't want them to send you away, Douglas.'

'Oh you'll find somebody else,' he said breezily.

She raised herself quickly, a cross frown on her face: 'Why did you say that?'

'Sorry. A silly joke.'

She stared at him as if challenging him to say more.

'It's just that I love you,' he said, '. . . and I don't want you to leave me, and I suppose I wanted to hear you say you wouldn't.'

Mary bent again to kiss him passionately on the lips and his arms tightened about her. She lay there on top of him, her loose black curls falling to the pillow about his face, and she whispered: 'I won't, you goose.'

'Good.'

'I shouldn't have to tell you, but you doubt everything.'

'Myself most of all.'

'Why?'

'I don't know, Dr Henderson.'

She slipped off him and on to her back: 'If I were a medical doctor I might say, "You don't need to prove anything to anyone."'

She paused for a moment, then said: 'Perhaps it's something to do with your background, your family, and this whole codes thing is part of it now, isn't it? But you don't need to prove anything. You've already distinguished yourself.'

'Would you love me if I hadn't?'

'Honestly, Douglas . . .'

But Lindsay turned to place a finger on her lips: 'Please don't be cross with me. Look, I want to tell you about the *Culloden*.'

Mary reached across and with her thumb began to smooth the

deep frown that was wrinkling his brow. 'If you're sure you want to,' she said softly. Lindsay's face suggested he was anything but sure.

'You should know,' he sighed and he rolled on to his back again to stare into the mahogany darkness.

28

'She wasn't much of a ship. The bridge was open to everything the Atlantic could throw at us. No matter how careful you were, the sea found its way down the back of your neck into your oilskins and into your boots. I joined her at Portsmouth on the tenth of May 1940. I'd been told the captain was a Tartar but I was confident we would muddle along somehow. I was wrong.'

Lindsay turned to look at her: 'I need a cigarette.' He swung his legs off the bed and padded across the room to his jacket which had been carelessly thrown on a chair beneath the window. Mary watched him as he took a cigarette and lit it, his neck and chest flickering in the lighter flame. He settled beside her again, sitting upright against the bedhead.

'I remember Commander Cave's first words to me were, "More horsemeat from the universities?"' Pritchett Ernle-Erle-Cave; he considered himself to be among the nobility of the sea. His father was an admiral but the brains skipped a generation. After thirty years' service Cave was lucky to be the captain of a vintage destroyer. He cursed like a stoker. I think he must have been the rudest man in the Navy and unfathomably ignorant. The Admiralty dusted him off at the beginning of the war and gave him *Culloden*. I sensed in my first hours aboard that she was an unhappy ship.

'We missed Norway, Dunkirk and the fall of France. We muddled along that summer, escorting convoys in and out of the North-West Approaches. There was no hierarchy of misery at first. Cave treated everyone with equal contempt but then I did something very foolish. In an unguarded moment I mentioned my mother to one of the other officers. I don't know why, it was something I had learnt not to do at school. A couple of days later Cave walked into the wardroom beaming from ear to ear and asked if I would care to join him in the captain's cabin. He asked me about my family and was incensed when

I refused to answer. After that, he brought it up time and again, anything and everything to do with my family, Germany and the war.'

Lindsay paused for a moment to look down at Mary: 'But this isn't only my hard-luck story, Cave made it unpleasant for all the officers. You know he must have been a very lonely man.'

Mary reached for Lindsay's hand and gave it a gentle squeeze. In turn he lifted hers and, opening her fingers, kissed her palm tenderly.

'A lot of ships were lost in the summer but our convoys were fortunate. Merchant ships began to call us "the lucky *Culloden*". And then convoy HX.70. I can remember the face of our Canadian sub-lieutenant John Parker very clearly. We're leaving Liverpool, passing into the swept channel and Johnny's excited because he's met a nurse called Grace. There's a big grin on his face. He was nineteen, a lawyer preparing for the Toronto Bar.

'Four escort ships with Cave as senior captain in command of the group. We met the convoy north-west of Rockall Bank on September the fourteenth, some three hundred miles from home, a grey Atlantic sky and sea, the wind like a knife, nine columns of four ships five miles wide, all struggling to hold their station. Cave spoke to the Commodore of the convoy on the wireless and I remember the little-boy excitement in his face when he was told that five ships had been sunk the night before. With the convoy travelling at no more than six knots it was a racing certainty the enemy was still in contact. I swear it was the happiest any of us had seen him. His moment of glory had come, his chance to prove the Navy wrong after years of being passed over.

'All gun crews at action stations before sunset. I remember a thick white strip of moonlight rippling across the sea to the horizon and I could sense the enemy close by. Fear. Then at a little after eight o'clock it began. There was suddenly a small bright yellow light on the starboard side of the convoy. We weren't sure what it was at first and we were under Admiralty orders to maintain wireless silence for as long as possible. Cave tried to signal the other escorts with an Aldis lamp but there was no reply. Then one of the merchant ships hoisted a red lantern and . . .'

'A red lantern?' asked Mary.

'Torpedoed. And a few minutes later, there was an enormous explosion in the heart of the convoy: a tanker some two miles from us, a blazing mass of white flame, smoke rising in a huge column hundreds of feet into the sky. Then, on the far side of the convoy, another burst of flame and then another and another.

'As we approached the tanker, we could hear thump, thump, thump against the sides of the ship as if a giant sea creature was trying to batter a hole in our hull. Cave shouted, "Go and see what that is, Number One." The ship slowed and I made my way down to the fo'c'sle. The sea was heaving with timber, heavy wooden pit props. Then one of the crew shouted, 'Over there, sir, look', and there was a collection of little red lights dancing on the water, tossed towards us by the swell. We must have passed within a couple of hundred yards of them. I couldn't see their faces but I could hear them: 'Help, help, please God help . . .'

Lindsay reached over to the bedside table and lit another cigarette, smoke curling to the ceiling. Mary felt suddenly tense and cold and conscious that it was late, the still time between two and three o'clock when the night is at its darkest. In the silence she wrapped the sheet more tightly about herself. Lindsay did not look at her, but after a couple of minutes he began to speak again, quickly, harshly: 'But I can't blame Cave for leaving them, the convoy was under attack. We threw Carley rafts and promises, "We'll be back." But we didn't go back. And then we were closing on the tanker. The sea was calmer about her, heavy with a sticky blanket of oil, and in places it was on fire. The ship was burning from stem to stern, the bridge just a twisted shell. We weren't that close but I could feel the heat and hear the whoosh and roar of the flames, and the smoke was a billowing, choking black mountain even against the night sky. The convoy scattered. The Commodore must have despaired of the escorts and with good reason, never mind the enemy; we hadn't even managed to make contact with each other. Honestly, it was a shambles, really a total shambles.

'I'd returned to the bridge to find Cave in an impotent rage, cursing the other escorts and his own crew. It was a little after eleven, and I remember thinking, "Oh God another four or five hours of this." Of course, we know now it was one of Dönitz's first pack attacks and there were four, perhaps five, U-boats chasing in and out of the convoy.

They were all there, the *U-boothelden* – Otto Kretschmer, Prien, Mohr . . .'

'Mohr?' said Mary with surprise. 'Mohr attacked the convoy? When did you find out?'

But Lindsay ignored her question: 'We zigzagged to and fro for more than an hour, firing round after round of star shell over the sea in the hope of catching sight of a U-boat but we didn't see anything, we didn't hear anything. The Asdic detector was useless, just an empty echo . . .'

'They were on the surface,' said Mary.

'And it was quite obvious to me that we were wasting our time. By now we'd fallen five or six miles behind the convoy. I drew this to Cave's attention and he exploded. I was forgetting my place, he said, I was questioning his judgement, thirty years' experience he said. The U-boats were forgotten, I was now the enemy. It was a very unpleasant scene. My God, he'd more important things to worry about than me, but it was panic, he'd lost control. We weren't "lucky *Culloden*" any more. Then there was a terrific flash on the port bow, followed by another column of fire and smoke and that put an end to his diatribe. It was obvious even to Cave that we were searching in the wrong place. We went chasing over to the burning tanker, the men still at their stations, cold, tired, frightened. As we approached, we could see by the light of the flames another ship close by, a large freighter with her deck and cargo lights burning. She was listing heavily to port. We put scramble nets over our sides with a couple of burly ratings at the bottom to help survivors aboard but we didn't find any one – just empty life jackets. I remember a small explosion somewhere deep inside the freighter, a sound like breaking glass; it blew the hatches off and there was a shower of wet ash from the funnel. The sea was in the engine room. The lifeboats were out there somewhere but Cave was anxious to rejoin what was left of the convoy. It was almost three o'clock and the sea was rough and getting rougher. By then we felt helpless and rather ashamed. Cave had a face like thunder. He used to glare at you from under dark bushy eyebrows. I remember glancing about the bridge that night and everyone was concentrating hard on the horizon, desperate not to catch his eye. For a moment I was barely able to contain myself, I had this mad, mad urge to laugh out loud.

'We overhauled the main body of the convoy and the other escorts just before dawn. The Commodore's ship was among them but he had no more idea than we did how many ships had been lost in the night. One of the other destroyers had picked up two hundred survivors, some of them in bad shape, and Cave gave her permission to leave us and make best speed to Londonderry. He sent the other escorts to round up stragglers and we were left with the rump. I shouldn't think our presence was very reassuring.

'The men were allowed to stand down from action stations, stand down before they fell down, weary and demoralised. I managed to snatch a couple of hours' sleep too. Some stragglers joined us during the day but the glass was falling, sea state eight and worsening and we were soon struggling to keep our little convoy together. I don't think Cave took any rest, he was running on adrenalin, a little unhinged.

'Then at about eight o'clock that evening we did pick up a firm contact. Ping, ping, ping: imagine, Asdic contact at last,' "Echo bearing one-sixty." I remember the operator bouncing with excitement. He lost contact in the wake of a merchant ship but just for a few seconds. Bugger the convoy, Cave was determined to hunt and sink his U-boat.'

Lindsay sighed and reached down to stroke Mary's hair: 'By then the wind was almost storm force and we were ploughing into a head sea. The ship dragged her old bones to the top of a wave then raced down into the trough, before struggling to rise again. After ten minutes of this sort of pounding the submarine disappeared. We were disappointed, of course. A chance to redeem ourselves had slipped away. I remember Cave bullying the Asdic operators with threats and imprecations. The sub-lieutenant, Parker, felt sorry for them, he was a sensitive chap – more "university horsemeat" – and he said very tentatively: "Perhaps the submarine has surfaced, sir?" Of course it had, it was taking advantage of darkness and the weather to make its getaway. But Cave was furious again, furious. Was Parker trying to undermine his authority? Did anyone else want to pass an opinion? And he gave orders for another Asdic sweep. The temperature on the bridge dropped an uncomfortable couple of degrees but Cave didn't care because he found a strange comfort in bullying his officers.

'Imagine our situation. We'd left the convoy again, God knows if it was safe, we were trying to echo-find a submarine that was almost certainly on the surface and we were travelling at barely six knots on an almost straight course. The U-boat was out there somewhere in the darkness. We were asking for trouble. I remember glancing across at Parker and he caught my eye and nodded, or rather twitched, meaningfully at Cave. And I thought, "Oh God, he wants me to say something." Reasonable you might think – I was the first lieutenant. "What's the point?" I asked myself. My opinion would be neither sought nor welcomed, far from it, and so to my eternal shame I kept quiet. In fact I managed to shake my head a little at Parker and he rolled his eyes upwards, no doubt in complete exasperation. And so it happened.

'Half an hour later I was visiting the quarterdeck watch when a torpedo hit us on the starboard side. I was thrown to the deck and something must have hit me because the doctors found a jagged cut on my back . . .'

'The scar,' said Mary. She was still holding his hand and she gave it an affectionate squeeze.

'Then a terrible grinding noise and – well – it was terrifying. The whole bloody forepart of the ship was listing to starboard, toppling into the sea. Just seconds, that's all, it happened in seconds, no time for anyone to escape. And there it was drifting away from us on its side – the wind shrieking around it and . . .'

'Darling, please, you're hurting me,' said Mary.

'I'm sorry.'

He let go of her hand, took a slow deep breath then reached for his cigarettes, but he did not light one, he just held the packet.

'Most of the crew was in that part of the ship, almost two hundred men. There was nothing we could do, nothing. Cave, Parker, all of them lost. No survivors. I didn't see the forepart sink, we were fighting to keep what was left afloat.

'What were you thinking?'

'I tried to be busy and to keep the others busy. I don't think I thought, "I'm going to die", not while the wreck was afloat. But it was obvious that the boiler-room bulkhead was beginning to buckle and that we wouldn't last until the morning. I remember holding on to the edge of a Carley raft, and I remember the deep cold and others close by – we were between the hulk and the corvette, *Rosemary*.'

Lindsay paused, then said: 'I'm not entirely sure what happened next . . .'

He took out a crushed-looking cigarette and tapped it on the back of the packet. Then he lit it and by the lighter flame Mary could see that his hand was trembling, although his face was composed and quite calm.

'There are only impressions, snippets of memory. There may have been an explosion inside the wreck that detonated some of our depth charges. There was fire on the water and I tried to swim away but couldn't and it caught my sleeve, it was sticky, and I held it under. And I remember panicking because I couldn't see the corvette through the smoke. For a moment I couldn't see anything, anyone, and then as the smoke drifted I saw a man close by, and I tried to reach him. I'm not a strong swimmer but I tried to hold his head up. And at that time I knew I was going to die in that smoke and fire. And then the next thing I remember is someone pulling at me. One of the *Rosemary's* officers told me later that I was as black as a Negro when they fished me out. I was clinging to another member of the crew – Baker – but he died almost as soon as he reached the deck. In the end they pulled fifteen of us from the sea alive and of those, three died aboard the *Rosemary.*'

Lindsay leant over to the bedside table to put his cigarette out and then turned and shuffled down the bed until he was lying under the sheet again. Mary touched his chest. It was cold and she moved closer to share the warmth of her body. His eyes were closed. She bent forward to kiss him tenderly.

'Darling,' she whispered. And she stroked his cheek.

'I'm sorry. You didn't need to know all that.'

'Don't be sorry, I'm glad you told me.'

He smiled wearily: 'Do you understand?'

'Understand?'

'You've seen the official report. For once there wasn't a Board of Inquiry. I gave my version but the Admiralty wasn't interested. One senior officer said to me, "Unlucky name *Culloden,* you know", as if that explained everything. Ironic don't you think? For a time we were the lucky ship. Fleming told me there was some private criticism of Cave but the Admiralty buried it, saved his posthumous reputation.

So there are just those few meaningless lines in the report. In my judgement he was responsible, not just for the sinking of his own ship but for most of those we lost from the convoy – fifteen in all. Sheer bloody incompetence. And the other officer who was to blame, well he was decorated.'

'Douglas, no.'

'I share responsibility, of course I do,' he said in a flat voice. 'Remember the look Parker gave me on the bridge, pleading with me, "Say something, Number One, the ship's in danger." And I shook my head, too frightened to speak my mind. I know I am to blame.

'The Admiralty wanted to hand out medals and it wanted photographs and newspaper copy, something to deflect public attention from the losses, and I was one of the chosen. Someone decided I'd shown the necessary presence of mind on the wreck – enough to justify a Distinguished Service Cross. And to my eternal shame I accepted it. Here . . .'

Lindsay opened the drawer of the bedside table. The decoration seemed to draw the thin light from the window, swinging silver at the bottom of its ribbon.

'A silver cross.'

He put it back on the bedside table.

'Some time after the sinking, I was asked to identify the body of a sailor washed up on a beach in Ireland, naked, torn, four weeks in the water. And I recognised the man, at least, I recognised his red hair. Short, good-humoured George Hyde, married with a daughter. And I cried for him.'

Lindsay's voice cracked with emotion but when Mary tried to kiss him, he stopped her, taking her face in his hands.

'No sympathy. I've told you all this so you know. I have a duty to Parker and the others to speak my mind. I don't just follow orders any more.'

Mary leant forward again and this time he did not stop her. She kissed him long and tenderly and stroked his hair, pressing herself tightly against him. She felt so sorry for him, she wanted to say, 'Don't blame yourself, what could you do?', but she knew it would sound trite. What could she say? His judgement was clouded by mad destructive guilt. It was the root of his troubles, Mohr, the codes, as if he needed to expiate what had happened to the *Culloden*. She knew she should end this nonsense. It was just that she had given her word to people she respected, people who trusted her and, yes, she would be breaking orders – breaking the law.

'What are you thinking?'

'You said you'd found out more about our codes?'

Lindsay looked at her closely: 'Do you really want to know?'

He told her of his conversation with Samuels and the note he had been given on British codes: 'Our codes have been broken before. It played a major part last summer when we lost so many ships . . .'

There was an almost indecent note of satisfaction in his voice.

'Who is this friend of Samuel's?'

'Why do you want to know?'

'He should know better.'

Lindsay pulled away from her a little: 'We're on the same side, remember? Perhaps Charlie's friend felt we were on to something.'

'Does Samuels think so?' she snapped.

'No. But if they've been broken once . . .'

'Leave this, Douglas. You're wrong. Believe me.'

'. . . they may very well have broken them again.'

'Didn't you hear me? You're wrong. I know you're wrong.'

He was staring at her, trying to gauge her expression, collecting his own thoughts. She wondered if he was angry. But when he spoke his voice was quite calm.

'What do you know?'

Mary took a long deep breath. This was a betrayal, no matter the reason, the person.

'I know our codes are secure. Naval Cipher One was changed after Norway and the Germans haven't broken Cipher Two,' she said quietly.

'You know?'

'Yes. I know.'

Lindsay lay there in silence for a moment, then rolled away from Mary and off the bed. She watched him walk across the room and take his dressing gown from the hook on the door.

'Where are you going?' She pulled the sheet a little higher, suddenly conscious of her nakedness beneath it. He was standing with his back to the window.

'I'm not going anywhere.'

'Come back to bed then.' She knew he wouldn't.

'How do you know, why are you so sure?'

It was impossibly hard to answer, and she thought for a moment of Lindsay stepping over the side of the *Culloden* into the storm. She curled into a tight anxious ball beneath the sheet.

'Well?'

'There are some things I know that you don't,' she said at last. 'Of course there are.'

Lindsay said nothing. She couldn't see his face in the darkness.

'I tried to tell you.'

'Tell me what? You didn't try very hard,' he said coldly.

'I couldn't tell you, Douglas.'

'You couldn't?'

'No.'

'But you've changed your mind.'

'Yes. Because I love you and this obsession with our codes is dangerous – it's damaging you.'

'I see.'

Seconds slipped by and she watched him stiff and silent against the window as he pressed the last pieces into place. And she was afraid and full of regret and wanted to deflect his thoughts: 'Come back to bed, please come back to bed.'

'We're reading their signals, aren't we? Aren't we?'

It tumbled out of her: 'Yes.'

And for a moment the room itself seemed to be alive and physical like an animal breathing heavily, its heart thumping in the darkness. She spoke quickly and nervously as if to hold it at bay: 'Our code people at Bletchley Park – Station X – have broken their Enigma ciphers – everything, well almost everything. We can decipher and read their signals, sometimes only hours after they're sent. Dönitz's orders, the reports the submarines sent to headquarters – the fuel they need, the ships they've attacked, course and position. When the wife of the engineer on *U-552* had her baby we were among the first

177

to know. Do you see? If our codes had been broken we would know, believe me.'

And now Lindsay was moving away from her to the door and the room filled with blinding light.

'That was cruel,' she said.

'No more than you deserve.' He clearly meant it. She heard him drawing the blackout curtains.

'Have you a dressing gown I can borrow?'

'No. Yes, there's another one on the back of the door.'

Then she heard him leave the room. She opened her eyes and glanced at her watch on the bedside table: it was four o'clock. She felt weary and very weak at the prospect of the questions, the conversation to come. Slipping from the bed, she walked quickly to the door and wrapped herself in Lindsay's dressing gown. It was a burgundy colour like the flock wallpaper in the hall and she wondered if it was a gift from his mother. Lindsay was in the kitchen, she could hear the kettle and the chink of china being loaded on to a tray. He had turned the lights on in the sitting room. 'That must be where he wants me,' she thought.

On the couch, feet curled beneath her, Lindsay's dressing gown pulled comfortingly tight, she waited in tired silence. It was such a long night, a mini melodrama, like one of the baroque mysteries her mother enjoyed, drawing people's motives and the threads of their lives together. Stories that always seemed to end so neatly.

'Tea? I haven't any milk.'

Lindsay put the tray on an occasional table and knelt beside it. As she watched him there, bone china cup in hand, ancient green dressing gown, tousled blond hair, she felt a pang of love and longing, a need to be close to him again. She wanted to lean forward and touch him, but before she could move he turned to offer her the cup. How small and fragile it looked in his hand.

'Thank you.'

He did not look up but turned to the tray to pour another. She knew what he must be thinking.

'I'm sorry, Douglas, but I couldn't tell you about the Enigma ciphers. We've been told to say nothing to anyone, to husbands, to lovers, to anyone.'

178

'Does Checkland know?' He sounded tired and low. He had finished pouring a cup of tea for himself but was still kneeling at the table with his back to her.

'Checkland? I don't know,' she said. 'Probably. Yes he does.'

'And your brother?'

'Perhaps.'

Lindsay's cup and saucer rattled a little as he lifted them from the tray. With what seemed like a great effort he stood up and made his way to one of the armchairs on the other side of the table. Only when he had settled in it did he look up at Mary.

'What an idiot you must think me, all of you.'

'Darling, of course not.'

'No one considered telling me, I suppose. Why? I couldn't be trusted?' He felt wounded and was making little effort to disguise it.

'Douglas, I don't know how or why Checkland and my brother know – perhaps they guessed . . .'

'Samuels,' said Lindsay breaking in, 'I think Samuels must have.'

'But most people in the Division don't know,' she said. 'Rodger Winn told me most of the government don't know, so, you can't really . . .'

Lindsay was shaking his head in disbelief.

'Aren't you listening to me?' she asked exasperatedly.

He raised his head to look at her, and his expression was stiff, almost hostile. 'I'm still a bloody idiot. God, I was so sure.'

'Douglas, please.'

'I suppose I understand why no one else told me. Of course it's of the first importance, but you, you . . .'

He did not finish and he did not need to because Mary knew what he was thinking and she flushed hot with embarrassment.

'I was told to say nothing.'

'Yes, yes, husbands and lovers, you explained.'

'But you don't believe me or you blame me . . .'

'. . . for allowing me to make an idiot of myself? Of course not, I applaud your discretion,' he said bitterly.

'You know now and it could cost me my job, who knows, my liberty too.'

Lindsay put down his cup, got to his feet and walked over to the fireplace, cursing quietly under his breath: 'Such a bloody idiot.'

179

'Please, Douglas, come here, please.' She wanted to end this hateful talk of secrets and codes but his back was resolutely turned towards her. He seemed to have forgotten the love, the intimacy they had shared only hours before, brushed it aside. When she spoke again her voice trembled:

'Please, Douglas, I'm sorry but I . . .'

She stopped abruptly in an effort to control her feelings. Her chest felt tight with frustration and disappointment and exhaustion. And Lindsay must have sensed that she was close to tears because he was at her side, his arm about her.

'I'm sorry, I'm sorry, what else could you do?' he whispered as he stroked her hair. And he lifted her chin and brushed away a silent tear with his lips.

It must have rained in the night because a fine mist was rising from the roofs, the sun blindingly bright on the wet grey slate. It was after nine o'clock but Sunday quiet. Standing at the sitting-room window, Lindsay could hear the bells of Westminster Abbey calling, an insistent but comforting round from treble to tenor. He had slipped out of bed without waking Mary, gently lifting her arm from his chest, and he had watched as she curled into the warmth they had shared, tracing with love the curve of her breasts and hips beneath the thick cotton sheet. Her face was white with exhaustion, worn down by the emotional battering of the night and long hours at the Citadel. 'God, I love you,' he had whispered, 'I love you so much.' But now, standing there at the window, gazing out to the world beyond the bedroom, he felt empty and useless, as if someone had kicked the stuffing from him. And yes, he loved Mary very deeply, but no matter the words and kisses of reassurance, he could not quite forgive her. She had been part of a conspiracy to hide the truth from him. He knew it was foolish to think so but he could not help it. Yes, orders, a secret of the first importance, but Mary had watched him throw away his position, behave like an idiot. She had told him about the Enigma ciphers only when the damage had been done.

He walked across the room to his dark galley kitchen, picked up his cigarettes and lighter, then, returning to the window, lit one and exhaled, a comforting stream of smoke. He had noticed he was smoking more, forty or even fifty a day, but he could think more clearly with a cigarette in his hand. And in its reflective haze it was easier to admit that the emptiness he felt was not just disappointment that Mary had hidden the truth from him. He wanted to be right. He had been so certain the Navy's codes were compromised, so sure that he was doing something useful, something that would help to wipe the slate clean. And now that hope was gone.

PART TWO

JULY 1941

LANGE Helmut   Leutnant z S (PK)

PW No 86993
Br. of Service   Navy
Date of Capture   24-2-41
Nationality   German
Date of Birth   8 Aug. 21
Weight   170
Hair   Brown
Chin   Flabby
Mouth   Large
Height   5′ 9″
Complexion   Fresh
Eyes   Brown
Teeth   Regular
Scars   Appendix
Languages   German and a little English
Religion   Roman Catholic
Remarks   Amiable

29

Number One Officers' POW Camp
Stapley
Lancashire

It was the *112*'s burly navigator who came for Lange. Bruns's meaty shoulders filled the door-frame. His tone was polite and easy but his restless body churlishly insistent: would Leutnant Lange be good enough to present himself to the Ältestenrat.

Heavy drops were tapping at the casement windows and the broad terrace beneath them was deserted but for a sentry standing dripping at the wire. It had rained for a few hours on every one of the six days he had been here and the football pitch between the inner and outer fences was a quagmire. Above the house the broken woodland and bracken slopes were unseasonably green even for a Lakeland summer.

Lange slipped a letter he was writing into the pages of the book he had borrowed from the camp library.

'What are you reading, Herr Leutnant?' Bruns was making an effort to be amiable.

'*Great Expectations*. Charles Dickens. I want to improve my English.'

'Why? After the war everyone will speak German.'

Lange glanced up at him to be sure he was serious then he picked up the book and, pushing his chair away from the table, stepped across to his bed to slip it under the pillow.

'You're lucky,' said Bruns enviously. 'This is a nice room.'

Yes, Lange did count himself fortunate. It was bright with a high ceiling, lemon-yellow wallpaper and old pine floorboards. Everything was in good order. There were five low camp beds, a table and five collapsible chairs. His bed was in a corner between a fireplace of royal blue tiles and an oak dresser with a vanity mirror, the glass cracked and spotted with rust. In the opposite corner was a makeshift wardrobe on which five cardboard suitcases were neatly stacked.

Camp Number One for German officers. On their first night, they had leapt from a lorry on to a loose stone carriageway in front of an imposing Edwardian mansion. A cool breeze was shaking the tops of the tall pines beyond the wire, and by the low moon they could see the valley falling away from them, its slopes roughly chequered with drystone walls. The guards had hurried them into a panelled entrance hall with large mullioned windows, then up a fine carved oak staircase to bed.

A few days later, Lange had found an old newspaper in the common room in which their prison camp was described as 'the U-boat Hotel'. The paper's correspondent grumbled about the library and the grand piano in the old billiard room, that some of the rooms had log fires and the Germans were permitted to read newspapers and listen to the BBC. A Member of Parliament had promised to raise the matter with the War Office. But for all that its walls were panelled and papered and its windows lead-paned, it was a prison much like any other: two hundred men behind two security fences and a belt of barbed wire, roll calls, lights-out, camp searches and the discipline of their own Ältestenrat.

'Are you ready, Herr Leutnant?'

'Yes.'

Lange followed Bruns out of the room without closing the door behind him. He was expecting the Ältestenrat to call him and he had tried to prepare himself. Mohr's hand planted firmly against his chest pressed upon him still, as did the recollection of those hard little wrinkles at the corners of his mouth, the contemptuous stare. On Day One Lange had heard that Mohr had joined 'the council of the eldest'. It was the correct order of things. The council was made up of the three most senior officers and Mohr was now the most senior. On Day Two he learnt that there was to be an investigation. The Ältestenrat would gather intelligence on British interrogation techniques and some officers would be asked to give evidence. By the following day the camp knew it would be about much more.

Lange had been preparing the camp's daily news digest when the second officer of his own U-boat, the 500, had fluttered into the room like a coal-black crow. Schmidt was a thick-set youth with metallic blue eyes and bad skin, beneath which beat a heart full of National Socialist zeal. He perched on the edge of his bed and lit a cigarette:

'Anything in the British papers about our armies?'

The whole camp was hungry for news. It was three weeks since the start of the invasion of the Soviet Union and pride and confidence were high. But Lange had found nothing of importance.

'Well, I have some news for you,' Schmidt had whispered smugly, 'but not for the digest.'

There was a rumour that someone in the camp was giving intelligence to the British.

'The Ältestenrat is sure he's a naval officer. Can you imagine what will happen if it is true?' Schmidt had laughed, a grating and mirthless laugh.

Bruns led him down the corridor and up the narrow wooden back staircase to a bedroom under the eaves.

'Wait here, please.'

It was small but comfortable with just two camp beds, necessary furniture and a fine view of the valley below. The camp's senior officers had elected for the privacy of the servants' quarters at the top of the house. Lange sat at the desk beneath the window and tried to look at ease. The waiting, the wild thoughts, the tight little knot in the pit of the stomach were so familiar; if anything, the anxiety was more acute than it had been when he was questioned by the British. To be interrogated and judged by your comrades and perhaps found wanting, such a thing was unthinkable. He could hear Bruns speaking in a low voice to someone in the corridor.

On his fourth day in the camp the *U-112*'s engineer had found him in the exercise yard. Lange was watching a muddy game of football, a wet mist beading his wool jacket. Then August Heine had touched his elbow.

'May I speak to you, Helmut?' His voice was strained and unhappy.

It was the first time they had spoken since they had been held together at Trent Park. Heine had behaved rather boorishly since then, cutting him dead more than once.

'Is something the matter?' Lange had asked coldly. It was plain enough that there was from the alarm in the engineer's chestnut eyes.

'Please, I must talk to you.'

Then he had turned and walked away and Lange had followed, edging along the wire towards the house in silence. After casting about to be sure there was no one close by, Heine stopped beneath a dripping oak and began fumbling for a cigarette.

'Well?' Lange asked impatiently. Heine was making him feel nervous, twitching and turning like a ferret in a cage.

'Do you think he knows?' His face was drawn and pale with misery.

'Who?'

'The Kapitän.'

'Knows what?'

'About me.'

Heavy drops of rain pattered through the canopy above, seeping into Lange's jacket and running like tears down Heine's face. It smelled of autumn already. Lange remembered wondering if the engineer was suffering from barbed-wire sickness. There was talk of men breaking after only weeks. The cell's four walls, the grunts and moans of other prisoners in the night, footsteps, bright lights and the anguish of failure that chip-chipped away at the spirit.

'Have you seen the doctor?'

'Why?' Heine had stared for a few puzzled seconds at Lange, then brushed the question aside: 'They asked me about the Kapitän, his time at headquarters. The British asked me. They heard us speaking together.'

'But you told them nothing?'

'No,' said Heine quickly. His tortured face said 'yes'. That such a dedicated man, proud of his small part in the Reich's great enterprise, should be so very, very afraid. As Lange sat there in the bedroom at the top of the house, the memory of it made him feel tired and stale.

'Say nothing. I will say nothing. Say only that you did your duty;' that was the advice he had given Heine – and a reassuring squeeze.

*

Bruns was at the door again and behind him a Luftwaffe lieutenant Lange did not recognise, his shoulders square and hard.

'This way,' and Bruns stepped back to allow Lange past.

There were three rooms on the corridor and the smallest belonged to Kapitän zur See Jürgen Mohr. He was the only prisoner who was not obliged to share. Bruns tapped gently at his door.

'Yes, come in.' Mohr spoke with the quiet assurance of those who are used to being obeyed without question. He was sitting at a table, with the light from the only window behind him, and on the bed to his right was Fischer, the commander of the *U-500*. A Luftwaffe major he knew to be Brand was standing a little apart at the window, a cigarette smoking in his hand. Lange took two short strides to the table and snapped smartly to attention.

'Sit down, Leutnant Lange.'

Mohr nodded at the low chair opposite him. As well as being smaller than the others, his room was also a little more impersonal. There were three or four books beside Mohr's bed and a small, unframed picture of a young woman with indecently large eyes and a bright smile. Lange was surprised to see it there.

Mohr's face was as stiff and empty as a plaster saint's. Kapitänleutnant Fischer says your war patrol with him was your first?

'Yes, Herr Kapitän.'

'But you have carried out other reporting assignments?'

'Yes, Herr Kapitän.'

Lange wondered if his composure sounded exaggerated. The chair felt small and hard. He was struggling to sit upright.

He watched as Mohr leant across the table with his chin in his right hand and his eyes cast down in thought. His hairline was receding a little and he was greying at the temples. The bed squeaked as Fischer adjusted his weight and at the window there was a burst of blackbird song. It had stopped raining and the sun was twinkling through the small leaded panes. After an uncomfortable silence Mohr raised his head a little and stared at him. His eyes were an impenetrable brown and there was the faintest of smiles on his lips – it was not a pleasant one.

'Tell me about your assignments.'

What was there to tell? Christmas with the U-boat heroes, submarines in and submarines out, in the Channel with the *Schnellboote* and photographs and interviews with Admiral Dönitz.

'You spoke to the Admiral at headquarters?'

Lange looked down at his hands. His fingers felt hot and thick and awkward. It was a simple question simply put and not a muscle had moved in Mohr's face but he knew at once, and with a certainty that chilled him to the marrow, why he was being asked it. He swallowed hard:

'U-boat Headquarters, yes.'

He could feel Mohr's eyes on him and thoughts and fears crowded one upon another.

'You look a little uncomfortable, Lange.'

With an effort he looked up at Mohr: 'No, Herr Kapitän, thank you.'

'You should be.'

He tried to concentrate on a crack in one of the leaded panes behind Mohr's left shoulder. The Luftwaffe major was still at the window, an expression of barely disguised contempt on his heavy face.

'Yes, you have met Admiral Dönitz.' Mohr glanced down at a sheet of paper on the table in front of him,' 'three or four times.' He stared at Lange for a moment, then, turning to the paper again, he ran his finger halfway down: 'The last time was a few months ago and he recognised you and shook your hand. Is that correct?'

It was correct and Kapitän zur See Jürgen Mohr knew it was correct. August Heine had obviously remembered their conversation well. Of course he would remember it clearly – it was the afternoon he had made his mistake. There had been only four cigarettes left in Lange's packet and he had been decent enough to give the greasy little bastard one. Was Heine trying to protect himself? He was terrified of Mohr. Had he told him everything? This time he had been interrogated by someone he was required to answer. Perhaps he had panicked and thrown someone else to the Ältestenrat?

'Is that correct, Lange?' Mohr's high-pitched voice was cool and steady and full of quiet menace.

'Yes. Yes, Herr Kapitän.'

'What was in the note you wrote to the British lieutenant –

Lieutenant Lindsay?' The question was rattled out with a speed that demanded an instant answer.

'I . . . I thanked him for his kindness, Herr Kapitän,' Lange stammered. 'He saved my life.'

'Every word, I want every word?'

'It was in English, something like thank you for helping me and please say "thank you" to your girlfriend.'

'His girlfriend?'

'Yes.'

And then another question and another, more questions, relentless like a dark cat's-paw ruffling the ocean on a summer day with the promise of a change for the worse. Lange had said nothing to Lindsay he should regret. And yet he felt guilty. He must be guilty. It was in the room with him. He could see it in Mohr's suspicious eyes and feel it in the aggressive silence of the others. Guilty of befriending an enemy.

Lange was sitting on the edge of his bed staring at his worn brown leather shoes when his old commander, Fischer, found him later. The 'interview' with the Ältestenrat had lasted an hour and ended with a promise of more questions to come. It had left him drained and careless and desperate to be alone. It was late evening now and his room-mates were downstairs, either in the library or the old billiard room. Perhaps they were listening to the news digest he had prepared for that day or at the piano singing hearty U-boat songs. Night was drawing in quickly with the next front approaching from the west and the room was falling into shadow. Fischer did not switch on the light.

'You're a fool.'

Lange sprang to his feet and turned smartly towards him. The commander of the *U-500* was a little taller and a little older, with a heavy, baggy face high in colour and the small moist blood-shot eyes of a drinker. He was wearing a worn loose-fitting brown suit that reeked of stale cigarette smoke. In the four weeks Lange had spent with the crew of the *500* he had seen Fischer drunk and incapable more than once. He had also seen and admired his cool leadership under fire. Fischer was rough but fair.

'Do you know what will happen to anyone who has given intelligence to the enemy?'

Lange was surprised by the note of concern in his voice. He turned and gently pulled the door to, then nodded to indicate that Lange should join him on the bed.

'I like you, Lange, or I used to. But you've been fraternising with the enemy – Kapitän Mohr thinks you are guilty of much more. Look, I want to help you. Perhaps you were tricked by this British interrogator into giving something away. It is an easy mistake, they are very clever.'

Fischer paused, then began slapping the pockets of his jacket: 'Shit. Do you have one?'

Lange offered him a cigarette. He lit it, then planted it in the corner of his mouth. 'Kapitän Mohr wants to know if you were tricked. He must know. There is a secret of the first importance to the Reich that he has to protect. Telling him the truth is the best way of proving your loyalty now.'

'I told Herr Kapitän Mohr everything we spoke of. There was nothing more.'

Fischer flicked his cigarette into the corner of the room in exasperation. 'Look, Lange, believe me, I am doing you a favour. There are some ruthless cunts in this camp who would welcome a chance to prove their loyalty to the Führer in any way the Ältestenrat asks them to. The British won't protect you, they don't care. Mohr thinks you're hiding something from him – if you are, then tell him at once before he forces it from you. Understand?'

Fischer stared at Lange until he met his gaze with a slight nod: 'Believe me, Lange, that is good advice. Tell him everything.'

30

2nd Unterseebootsflotille
Keroman Base
Lorient

The security barrier lifted at last and the black Citroen lurched forward, its engine roaring impatiently as the driver searched for the gears. Deep ruts had been cut in the loose gravel track and the car bumped awkwardly across the construction site, a cloud of summer dust in its wake. Smoke was billowing from a vast rectangular trench a few metres from the track and drifting lazily across the hot white sky. Men and machines were busy at its edge, tearing at the ground as if intent on cutting a rough finger of land from the rest of Lorient. The driver of the Citroen braked hard for a column of French labourers who showed no inclination to step aside. Handkerchief pressed to nose and mouth, Leutnant Erich Radke gazed impatiently from the back seat at their sullen faces and through them to where the Reich's engineers were marking out the ground for a vast new U-boat bunker.

'Shit. I'm going to be too late, Albert! It's almost two o'clock.'

Albert leant insistently on the horn and one of the German engineers looked up and shouted across at the Frenchmen. Reluctantly, they started to drift from the track and the Citroen began to creep through the gears again.

Beyond the dockyard gate, it turned left on to the quayside cobbles just as the band was striking up the 'Sailing Against England' song. The U-boats were moored in front of the new cathedral bunker, the tip of its concrete Gothic arch just visible above the makeshift offices and workshops that had been thrown up around the military dock. A crowd of well-wishers, secretaries with flowers, comrades in naval uniforms and soldiers from the local barracks, was gathering on the quay. Snatching his camera from the seat beside him, Radke jumped from the car, his smart leather-soled shoes slipping a little on the cobbles.

Two boats were alongside with their crews in orderly lines on the deck aft. The screws of the one closest to Radke were already churning deliberately through the oily water. As it swung gently away from the wall the crowd began to cheer and shout, 'Good luck', 'Happy hunting', and the military band struck up 'We Sail Against England' again.

Radke struggled to control his emotions. He was to have sailed with the U-330 but at the last minute Admiral Dönitz had refused to release him from his Staff duties. A pity: the commander of the 330 was only twenty thousand tons from a Knight's Cross and everyone had expected him to sink enough to secure it on this war patrol. Kapitänleutnant Martin Schultze was known to be outspoken and his views on the Nazis had brought him to the attention of the Gestapo, but that had only served to cement his reputation. Radke had visited the 330 in the echoing gloom of the cathedral bunker the previous evening, as the last of the fresh food was being stowed, and had drunk a farewell glass of champagne. Schultze and his officers had been in excellent spirits, laughing, joking, and there was much talk of how the U-boat would win the war for Germany. It was refreshing because everyone at headquarters had been a little downcast since the loss of the U-112 in the spring, and anxious too – the capture of Kapitän Mohr was a grave blow. But Radke had been able to give Schultze and his men the latest figures – almost four hundred enemy ships sunk in the first half of the year. England was finished. Finished.

Someone touched his elbow. It was Siegmann, one of the other young officers on the Staff.

'Wish you were going with them?' he asked with a smile.

'Of course. Don't you?'

Siegmann gave a non-committal shrug.

There was a general murmur of excitement from the crowd and they shuffled to the edge of the quay to get a better view of the U-330. One of the boat's officers was carrying out a formal headcount and a camera crew was filming him for the newsreel. Before it could finish there was a tremendous cheer as the commander began to make his way down the gangway.

'There's Schultze,' Siegmann shouted.

The commander was wearing his white cap and a black leather jacket, tall, fair, youthful, an almost beardless thin face. He must have said something to the camera crew because it instantly scuttled up the gangway to the quay. The crowd watched him climb the ladder on the outside of the tower to the bridge as the ropes were released fore and aft.

As the 330 slipped past, Radke could see that the symbol of the lion rampant on the conning tower had been repainted. An order from the bridge and the crew began to fall out, some disappearing inside the steel body of the boat, most lingering on the cigarette deck, talking and waving, enjoying the light and the air.

A woman on the other side of the security fence at the end of the pier was screaming hysterically. Siegmann nudged Radke: 'Listen to that. A broken heart.'

The 'lion boat' was clear of the dock now and swinging slowly about. For a moment it was lost in a cloud of exhaust fumes as it switched from battery to diesel engines, then it began to follow the wake of the first U-boat out into the river, gathering speed towards the fortress at the harbour entrance, the passage to the west and the wide Atlantic.

31

It was more than an angry impulse. It was a kind of madness. There it was, at the same time and in the same space, in the north-east corner of St James's Square. Lindsay needed to touch the cold body of the car and speak to its driver before it disappeared again. It was real. It was parked there. The engine growled as the driver let out the clutch and the car began to pull away. Both driver and passenger were wearing soft fedoras like tinsel-town gangsters. It began to pick up speed, preparing to turn into Charles II Street or Pall Mall. A well-polished Morris Eight. The front door banged to behind him. He was running. A woman screamed and he cannoned into someone on the pavement. He could hear the car straining as the driver changed up another gear. Then the radiator grille was rushing towards him.

'Stop, stop.'

There was a screech of brakes and another high-pitched scream and the car kangarooed and coughed to a halt. It was two feet away, shiny black and chrome, just as he had seen it in his dream. He leant forward to touch its bonnet. The driver's mouth was hanging open in almost a parody of amazement. He was ugly but he did have a face – dark, unshaven with heavy jowls – and he was dressed in a police suit, brown and badly cut. A cigarette was burning between his yellow fingers. His friend was thinner, taller, with the crumpled greyness of a long sleepless night. They were both staring at Lindsay. Morning traffic was passing round the square to the right and left of the car.

'What the hell do you think you're doing?' An elderly man in an expensive suit – perhaps a Jermyn Street tailor – was glaring at Lindsay from the pavement close by. He had his hand at the elbow of a woman who was brushing dust from her skirt. 'You could have been killed,' he shouted. 'You should have been killed.'

Lindsay ignored him and began walking round the car to the driver's door.

'Can we talk?'

He bent his face close to the glass. The driver's eyes were fixed on the buildings on the south side of the square.

'Here beautiful,' and he tapped lightly on the glass.

Slowly the driver wound down his window and flicked his cigarette end into the distance.

'Whatcha want?' He was a Londoner and his voice was cool and belligerent.

'Who are you? Special Branch?'

'What are you talking about?' He laughed and glanced across at his friend who smiled and shook his head. 'Mad Scottish cunt.'

'You're right, I am,' and reaching into the car, Lindsay grabbed the driver by the throat and shook him hard. 'Now stop pretending, you halfwit, and tell me.'

The door on the other side swung open and the passenger got out.

'Leave it, all right? We don't want trouble', the driver croaked. 'I'm sorry I called you a cunt. I'm even sorry I called you Scottish.'

The other man was beside him now, a hand on Lindsay's arm: 'Let him go.'

To make his point more directly he punched Lindsay hard and he punched him expertly, a hammer blow to the kidney that drove him to one knee, gasping for air. Just to be quite sure, he hit him again in the face. And as far as he was concerned, that was the end of the matter. He did not wait for Lindsay to rise but began walking round the front of the car to the passenger side. Then someone beyond Lindsay's bent shoulders caught the man's attention: 'Hello, Officer.'

A policeman was walking towards them.

'Are you all right, sir?'

'Yes, fine.' Lindsay tried to straighten his back. 'Fine. Thank you.'

'You don't look it.' The policeman was itching to reach for his notebook. 'Did this car hit you, sir?'

'No.'

'This man ran out in front of us, Officer.' The driver was on his best behaviour.

'My mistake,' said Lindsay. 'I thought I recognised him.'

An apology, a simple explanation and a few frosty pleasantries. The driver straightened his tie and winked as he pulled away. Lindsay stood and watched the Morris brake at the bottom of the square, then turn right into Pall Mall. There was the unpleasant, salty taste of blood in his mouth. He touched his bottom lip and winced.

'All right now, sir?'

'Yes, thank you, Officer. Thank you so much.'

Of course, it was not the way a naval interrogator should behave. But he was not an interrogator any more. He was a reserve lieutenant in search of a role. Would anyone notice if he did not present himself for duty? Perhaps his Special Branch minders in the Morris would notify their master. But the red mist had lifted and he knew he would go. What else was there to do?

Fleming had found him a temporary job in the Director's personal office and was trying to keep him busy with little errands to various parts of the Admiralty. He was writing short radio scripts for the 'black section' too. Lurid tales of orgies in the flotilla messes, a well-known captain with the clap, champagne bottles commandeered by the thousand – everything and anything that might appeal to the inner *Schweinhund* of the German seaman. There was talk of a posting abroad to Gibraltar or North Africa, talk of a mission to capture an enemy E-boat or intelligence papers from a weather station. Talk.

No one in Room 39 expected Lindsay to be there long enough to need a desk of his own. After two weeks he was still camping across the corridor in the office used by the uniformed messengers and those waiting to see the Director. The Admiral ignored him and his personal staff were indifferent too – sometimes downright hostile. It was a question of trust. The 'unpleasantness' at Trent Park seemed to cling like stale cigarette smoke.

Only Fleming acknowledged him as he slipped into the room. The Director's Assistant was standing by the west-facing windows that looked towards Horse Guards and the Foreign Office. Lindsay wanted to talk to him about his confrontation, to ask him if he knew why he was being followed, but not in front of the others.

'I've a job for you tonight. A pick-up. All right?' Fleming sounded out of sorts.

Lindsay was hoping to meet Mary that evening. She was only corridors and stairs away from him but it was harder to meet than it had ever been. He had seen her only once since the night at his flat. Once in St James's Park when they had met for lunch. The more he struggled to fill his day, the busier she seemed to be. She did not say why she was busy and he knew better than to ask.

'Of course Ian, where is the pick-up?'

Fleming leant across an empty desk and ground his cigarette into an ashtray.

'What have you done to your lip?'

'A little accident.'

'I see. Come and see me later. I'll have the details for you then.' And he walked over to his own desk by the Director's green baize door and sat down. Conversation closed.

It was dusk when the taxi dropped Lindsay beside a heap of smoke-blackened bricks on the Commercial Road.

'You'll have to walk the rest – second right.'

He felt he was paying for his freedom. The cab driver was a Jonah who took a perverse pleasure in the misery of others and there were tales aplenty to tell. They had driven along East End streets shattered, and some abandoned, after pitiless months of bombing. Almost a third of Stepney's houses were damaged, the driver said, no water, no power, and rich trippers from the West End who wanted to see 'the other half' sheltering in tunnels and beneath railway arches.

'Are you a tripper?'

It was a respectable question. What else would bring a smart fare in an expensive suit into this broken landscape at dusk?

If he had been able to, Lindsay would have said that he ran errands for a man called Fleming who liked dark corners and that this was just one more. It always seemed to be harder than it needed to be. The Director's Assistant had asked him to meet 'a friend' from the Security Service, MI5. What Fleming's friend was offering, and why he was offering it in the East End at dusk, he would not say. When pressed, he was evasive and then he was sharp. It was ludicrously cloak-and-dagger and it made Lindsay uneasy.

A little way up the road small groups of men and women were emptying out of a pub and trickling home past half-boarded shops, their windows taped and streaked with grime and pigeon shit. Sad, damaged people in a sad, damaged place. A couple of painted girls in summer frocks tottered uncertainly towards Lindsay, their arms draped about each other for support. They stopped and gave him a bleary look then, one of them – a frowzy blonde – swayed closer and blew him a gin-soaked kiss.

'Do you like me?'

'Oh, very much.'

'Nasty lip. Who've you been kissing then?'

They cackled wildly. Lindsay slipped past them, picking his way through the bricks that had tumbled on to the pavement. They shouted at his back. He kept his eyes firmly to the front.

Number 350 was a sooty three-storey building with a shop front on the ground floor. Its windows were empty and the counter, too, but its shelves were coated in a generous layer of dust. No coupons needed. The front door was sloughing off its paint in large green flakes. Loose sheets of the *Daily Mirror* rustled on the step as a bus swept past in a cloud of fumes. It was not the sort of place the Director of Naval Intelligence would visit in person. Lindsay checked the address he had scribbled on the paper – yes, it was Number 350.

A sour-looking middle-aged man in an ill-fitting navy-blue pin-striped suit answered the door: 'Papers?'

He was Security Service muscle, tall and square with small ears shrivelled and scarred in a rugby scrum.

Lindsay gave him his papers. If he had been asked, he would have handed over his wallet and the keys to his flat too.

'This way, sir.'

The gatekeeper led him along a dingy corridor to the back of the house, damp nicotine-stained paper peeling from the walls, then up an uncarpeted stair case to the first floor. There were several doors on the narrow landing – his guide slipped through the nearest one. Seconds later he was back: 'You can go in, sir.'

He stood aside to reveal a small dark room lit only by the low circle of light from an anglepoise lamp. The lamp stood on a plain wooden table in the centre of the room. A silver-haired man in a dark suit sat behind the table and a single empty chair had been placed in the light in front of it. A second man, younger, solid, was standing in shadow against the wall.

'Please identify yourself.'

Lindsay took a step into the room and handed his papers to the man at the table: 'Lindsay, Lieutenant Douglas Lindsay.'

The door clunked to behind him.

'My name is Colonel Gilbert.'

His voice was smoky and hard. He glanced at Lindsay's papers, then leant back in his chair and spread his large hands on the empty table in front of him. He was in his late fifties with a worn, angular face, his hair was white but his eyebrows were bushy black and he had sharp little blue eyes.

'You've come to pick up a package?'

'Yes.'

'It will be here soon. Sit down, Lieutenant. Cigarette?'

The Colonel slipped a cigarette case from his jacket pocket and offered it to Lindsay. He took one and Gilbert lit it with a snap of his lighter.

'I'm sorry we've dragged you out here. The shop used to belong to Russian anarchists. It's ours now.'

'Do you have many customers?'

'Some. The bottom end of the market.'

Gilbert stared at Lindsay for an uncomfortable, unblinking few seconds, then said: 'You've family in Germany, haven't you, Lieutenant?'

Lindsay drew deeply on his cigarette, then blew the smoke in a steady stream towards the ceiling. He was conscious of the Colonel's creature, the younger man, close to his shoulder.

'Is there a package?' he asked quietly. 'And if there is, will you give it to me?'

'In good time,' said Gilbert coolly. 'Tell me about your cousin Martin. Are you close?'

Lindsay closed his eyes for a second, a forced smile on his face.

He opened them again and said: 'Lindsay. Lieutenant, Royal Navy. JX 634378.'

'I have the authority to talk to you, you know. Commander Fleming sent you to me.'

'To collect a package.'

'Do you have something to hide?'

'Are those your men outside my home?'

'A prisoner called Lange sent you a note. He wanted to thank you, didn't he – why?'

Lindsay stretched forward and pressed the end of his cigarette into the tabletop. The stub lay there looking almost obscene beside the small black ring it had burnt in the varnish.

'If you don't have what I want, I'll leave.'

Gilbert brushed the stub on to the floor with the back of his hand and leant across the table, his hair a strange yellow-white in the light of the anglepoise: 'Is there something you're not prepared to tell us?'

'Lots of things, Colonel,' said Lindsay quietly. 'Perhaps – if there is a package – you will make sure it reaches Commander Fleming.' And he pushed back his chair as if to rise. Tight little frown lines had appeared on Gilbert's face. Slowly, deliberately, he looked over Lindsay's shoulder at his large silent companion and nodded his head.

Almost unconsciously, Lindsay stiffened, braced for a blow from behind.

'Don't worry, Lieutenant. This is just a chat.' Gilbert must have seen him flinch. There was a supercilious little smile on his face.

'No unpleasantness,' then, as if an afterthought, 'for now.'

The door opened behind Lindsay and light from the landing crept across the floor and under the table. Lindsay turned his back on Gilbert and walked towards it.

'Goodbye, Lieutenant. We will be seeing each other again, I'm sure. Oh, and there is a delivery – pick it up on the way out, would you.'

Lindsay did not reply but brushed past the thug at the door and began to thump down the wooden stairs. The angry rhythm of his feet echoed through the shop. *Verdammter Mist!* He gripped the banister and muttered it to himself. What a mess.

It took him more than an hour to walk home. He was glad of the time and the cool air and the darkness of the blackout, its emptiness and anonymity. It felt unfamiliar, as if he was walking through a New World city, roughly planned, a vast building site of half-finished streets, the sidewalks criss-crossed in the moonlight by broken shadows. At the Tower of London he was stopped by a policeman who wanted to know his business at that hour. More than once he looked back to see if he was being followed, without expecting to see anyone. And slowly the anger he felt, with Gilbert, with Fleming, with Checkland, with the Navy, was replaced by a sadness that glowed deeper, like the wooden heart of a fire.

The apartment in St James's Square was empty. He had given Mary a key but she never used it and there was nothing to suggest there had been uninvited visitors. Lindsay flung MI5's parting gift – a large manila envelope – on to the couch and walked over to the mahogany sideboard to pour himself a whisky. Before he could reach it the telephone on the desk by the window began to jangle. It was nearly one o'clock in the morning, late even for Mary to call.

'Douglas?'

His father's voice was strained with anxiety.

'Are you all right?'

'I'm fine.'

'The police were here to speak to your mother. I'm afraid she's in a bit of a state. They want to know about our family.'

Two of Glasgow's finest had presented themselves at the engineering works and accompanied his father home. They wanted photographs of the Clausen family, their ages, occupations, correspondence and last contact details.

'They were especially interested in Martin. They knew a good deal about him already.' There was a cautious note in his father's voice and Lindsay wondered if it had occurred to him too, that someone might be eavesdropping. His mother had told them she had heard nothing from her nephew for two years but that was not enough to satisfy them. They had wanted to know if anyone in the family was in contact with Martin.

'They asked about you in particular, Douglas.'

'Yes.'

'They were a little unpleasant to your mother.'

'How unpleasant?'

His father did not answer.

'How unpleasant?'

'Very unpleasant. But I will speak to the Chief Constable about it tomorrow.'

There was some concern about 'Mrs Lindsay's status', they said. 'Nazi connections', they said. She was a 'low-risk Category C' alien but that might change and they had spoken of new restrictions.

'The wee buggers had the nerve to talk of internment.' His father's voice shook with emotion. 'I pointed out that our sons were fighting for their country.'

'They threatened her?'

'In so many words. Honestly, Douglas, we are beginning to behave like the Nazis.' His father had asked the policemen to leave at once and they went without protest.

Lindsay did his best to be calm and reassuring, to talk of 'misunderstandings' and 'silly mistakes', but there was no mistake. When his father hung up he lit a cigarette and sat at the desk with his glass. He had heard that the Security Service interrogators at Camp 020 called it 'the game'. One old player had told him that ends always justified means in war. His rules permitted everything but the rack and the thumbscrew and perhaps there would be a time when those would be necessary too. And in such a game your friends could sometimes become enemies.

The little carriage clock on the chimneypiece struck two. He got wearily to his feet, took off his jacket and draped it over the couch. It slipped down the back on to the envelope he had been given at Five's little shop. It was addressed to Room 39 and stamped MOST SECRET. Lindsay picked it up, rubbing the rough paper between his fingers. Then, on an impulse, he reached over to the desk for a paperknife and slit it open with ruthless precision. There were two sheets of foolscap inside. The first was a cover page with a circulation list that included DNI – the Director of Naval Intelligence. Subject: 'A Breach of Security in the Division'. He turned to the second page.

1. *The following extracts are from a letter sent by a German prisoner at Number One Officer's Camp. The prisoner, Captain Mohr, is well known in his own country and has achieved some notoriety in this. In the early months of the war he sent a signal to the First Lord of the Admiralty with the position of survivors from a ship his U-boat had sunk. He is the most senior Kriegsmarine officer in our hands and a possible source of important intelligence.*

2. *The letter was sent on 12th July 1941 and is addressed via the usual channels to a Marianne Rasch. From its tone and content it can be assumed that Miss Rasch is intimate with Captain Mohr.*

3. *It contains the following passage:*

'By an extraordinary coincidence I have had the unexpected pleasure of conversing at length with a cousin of my old comrade Schultze. Do you remember Schultze? His cousin is an interesting young man who shares many of our ideas. He entertained one of our officers at a jazz club and introduced him to his girlfriend. My meetings with him made me even more convinced that this war between Germans and Anglo-Saxons is some sort of madness. It will be over soon, I am sure. In the meantime, please write to Schultze and let him know his cousin prospers, although he looks tired and must be working too hard.'

Lindsay gave a short humourless laugh. It was impossible not to admire the audacity of the man. He closed his eyes for a moment and rumpled his fingers through his hair. Mohr had the instinctive cunning of the true hunter. It had let him down only once and he had become a prisoner but now it was serving him well.

4. *Further investigation with the co-operation of ADNI and personnel in NID sections 8, 10 and 11 has revealed the identity of Schultze to be that of a U-boat commander, Lieutenant-Commander Martin Schultze. His cousin has been identified as Lieutenant DAC Lindsay RNVR Until recently Lieutenant Lindsay has been serving as*

an interrogator at C.S.D.I.C. and he was responsible for questioning Captain Mohr. Although something of his family background was known to the relevant sections in the Division, this close connection to the German Navy was not, nor his apparent sympathy with 'Nazi ideas'. It is the opinion of this officer that further inquiries should be carried out at once to prevent any risk of a damaging breach of security and that the Security Service should be asked to investigate.

The report was signed by a Major Macfarlane of Military Counter-Intelligence Western Command. At the bottom, someone else – perhaps Gilbert of MI5 – had scrawled in pencil: *Concur. Recommend removal of officer at once and immediate follow-up.*

Lindsay slipped the report back into the envelope. He wondered if Colonel Gilbert had expected him to read it. Perhaps the report was part of the game too? It must stop, stop at once. This spiral of suspicion was not malicious, it was cold policy, but his mother and Mary were in danger of being caught up in it too. He dropped the envelope on the couch and walked over to the window, stepping carefully behind the heavy blackout drapes. His lip was throbbing.

The black Morris was parked in the north-east corner of the square again. It was too dark to see behind the wheel but he felt sure the same ugly driver was there. He was too tired to care any more. His file could be stamped 'Security Risk' and sent to the Admiralty Registry for burial.

32

Number One Officers' POW Camp
Stapley,
Lancashire

A shaft of soft light was pouring through a crack in the shutters on to the yellow wallpaper above Lange's head. It was close to five o'clock. He had woken with an anxious start. His skin was damp and cold and the pulse in his neck throbbed. He pulled the rough blankets to his chin, wrapping them like a cocoon about his body. His room-mates were still sleeping, he could hear the steady rise and fall of their breathing. He could hear voices in the corridor too and a floorboard creaked close to the door. Someone was rattling the handle. Lange knew with stiff cold certainty, in a frozen second, that something was very wrong. Heads at the door, light striking a steel bed-end and the first harsh whisper.

'Schmidt. Are you ready?'

Schmidt was ready. He was in the bed closest to the light from the door and as he pushed his blankets away Lange could see that he was dressed in the shirt and trousers of the evening before. Everyone in the room was stirring now.

'Who's there?' It was Bischoff from the bed beneath the window.

'Shut up. Shut up and stay where you are,' someone whispered harshly.

'Schmidt. Lange. Come with us.'

He could not move. They were going to hurt him. But if he lay with his head on the pillow he would be safe. They would leave him if he said nothing, if he did not move a muscle.

'Come on, Lange.' It was the first officer of the *U-500*, Dietrich. 'Help him, Schmidt.'

Schmidt took two steps across the room and grabbed Lange's blankets.

'Get up,' and he jerked them roughly from the bed. 'Get up.'

He was lying on the bed in only his shorts. 'Sweet Mary, help me.' His lips moved as he chanted the prayer silently. 'Sweet Mary, help me.' Schmidt bent down and shook him roughly by the shoulder.

'What's the matter with you? Bruns, help him.'

But Lange swung his legs from the bed and reached for his shirt.

'And quick about it,' Dietrich hissed. 'The rest of you – back to sleep. This is none of your business.'

There were five men in the corridor. Oberleutnant zur See Dietrich was in command. A nasty piece, short, heavily built, ideologically pure, twenty-three. He had made his contempt for Lange crystal clear in the weeks they spent together aboard the 500.

'May I speak to Kapitän Mohr?'

Someone shoved Lange from behind.

'Shut up.'

Where are you taking me?'

Bruns held him by the arm: 'This way.'

They followed Dietrich quickly and quietly down the corridor and on to the landing above the hall. A Luftwaffe lieutenant Lange did not recognise was acting as lookout at the top of the stairs. He nodded curtly to Dietrich to indicate that it was safe to continue. The British guard posted in the vestibule at night must have left the house already.

Down the stairs at the double and across the inner hall with Bruns's grip bruising his arm. He was breathless with anxiety and his knees were shaking so hard he was sure he would collapse. At the end of the long corridor another Luftwaffe officer stepped out of the shadows to signal that the coast was clear and they hurried on into the West wing of the house.

On the right of the dark passage the kitchen and the servants' hall, the prisoners' washroom on the left. Dietrich led them to the kitchen door. He was reaching for the handle when it opened from the inside. Someone shoved Lange hard from behind and he stumbled through the door. Bright light was reflecting off the cream tiles that covered the walls from floor to ceiling and it took a few seconds to adjust. The kitchen was crowded. He was shocked to see the faces of some twenty men turned towards him, cold and silent. The ones he recognised he knew to be good National Socialists. The large wooden table the cooks used for food preparation had been pushed back against the wall and in its place was a single wooden chair. Sitting on the chair was a white-faced and crumpled August Heine, his eyes wild with fear. Lange looked away.

They had chosen well. The kitchen was perfect. Twenty-five foot square with a cold stone floor, one door and no windows looking on to the rest of the camp. There was a large Edwardian range to the left of the door and on the opposite wall shelves of copper moulds and pots and pans. Some ugly-looking meat hooks hung from a thick bar that ran just below the ceiling. Lange's arrival had interrupted some sort of public interrogation – or humiliation. The second officer of *U-112*, Koch, was bending low over Heine, his face an intimidating scarlet, one hand gripping the back of the chair. But it was Dietrich who took command, his voice echoing in the tiled kitchen: 'This swine has betrayed his captain and his comrades. He has betrayed his Führer and his Fatherland.'

For a few terrifying seconds Lange was sure he was the one – they were accusing him of treason. But Dietrich took two very deliberate steps towards the chair and sweet relief washed through him and another prayer: 'Thank you Lord, thank you, thank you Lord.'

There was an ugly air of expectation in the kitchen and hard, hard faces. The line of Dietrich's jaw was tight and there was a hollow look in his eyes. He was slowly clenching and unclenching the fingers of his right hand. Then he lashed out at Heine, hard, with the flat of his hand, and the noise was sickening. Heine reached up to brush his red cheek with trembling fingers, his mouth a little open, his eyes full of shock and puzzlement. A small balding Luftwaffe officer with the sharp features of a rat leant forward to shout in a high-pitched voice: 'You deserve that, you bastard.'

There were embarrassed coughs and the shuffling of feet, but from some a murmur of approval.

'This is a copy of the evidence collected by the Ältestenrat.' Dietrich held a yellow file above his head to be sure they could all see it. 'This swine volunteered important information to the British that could compromise our U-boat comrades at sea. He has . . .'

'No.' Heine's voice cracked with emotion. 'No, never.'

'Shut up or you will get the same again.'

'He has been examined and the evidence is clear. Now he will confess in front of you all.'

Tears were rolling down Heine's face and his mouth and chin were trembling uncontrollably. And yet Lange could see a certain glassy determination in his eyes too. Heine was going to fight. His comrades, his captain, the U-boat arm, these were his life.

'Please, I told the English nothing.'

'We have proof,' Dietrich shouted, the colour rising in his face. 'Proof, here. Your own words and a witness,' and he flapped the yellow file in front of Heine's face.

'Confess.'

Heine shook his head: 'I'm innocent.' He shuffled round the chair to look at the men standing on either side of him. 'Please. I've said nothing.'

His words bounced emptily about the kitchen. No one spoke. Then Dietrich turned to look at someone standing close to Lange.

Bruns was wearing gloves. Heine must have noticed too. He shook his head and groaned: 'No, please.'

And Lange was trembling. Was this what the Ältestenrat wanted? He wanted to shout, to scream: 'No. Stop. Stop now.' The words were there, on the tip of his tongue, but his mouth was sticky with fear. It was impossible to make a sound. He stood transfixed and helpless. The first blow sent Heine crashing to the floor. For a moment he was lost behind arms and legs as he was pulled upright. Then a second blow and a third blow. And the kitchen was silent but for the clatter of the chair and the shuffle of feet and the low groans of the man prostrate on the floor.

Heine was still conscious when they hauled him upright again. There was a deep cut in his lip and spots of blood on the front of his nightshirt. His right eye was puffy and closing and his cheek blue and swollen. The pride and courage in his eyes had gone. And Lange's face was wet with tears. He knew, yes he knew, the pain, the humiliation, and the memory of Lindsay helping him from a pool of vomit. What sort of patriots were these? How could this happen? But he was guilty too, guilty, yes. And more than just a silent witness – a sort of Judas.

Someone was holding a thick rope with a noose knotted at the end.

Koch was tightening it, squeezing, squeezing the air from Heine. He was writhing, thrashing on the chair. It toppled sideways again but this time no one helped him to his feet. They were kicking him, grunting and cursing, and Lange could hear the scuffing of boots on the stone floor.

'Stop. Don't kill him.'

It was Dietrich. He pushed impatiently through the shoulders that had closed over Heine's body: 'Get him up. He must sign.'

The rope was still hanging obscenely from Heine's neck. Someone pressed a pen into his hand. Grazed, dirty fingers closed around it and letter by painful letter he wrote his name in the yellow file. Did he know what he was doing? Did any of them know what they were doing?

Dietrich held up the sheet of paper in triumph. Everything was in order. Justice must always be seen to be done.

'The swine . . .'

And Heine's confession was met with a chorus of abuse.

'We should hang the bastard.'

'No, the bastard should hang himself. He would if he were any sort of man.'

And someone yanked the rope beneath Heine's chin, dragging his head from his chest.

'There's a meat hook in here. String the bastard up from the ceiling.'

The rope cut deeper. Heine's lips were drawn tightly over his teeth and he gasped and whooped for air, his hands tearing at the noose. And in his tortured face there was a desperate plea for help. He seemed fleetingly to look at Lange, beseeching him, begging, 'Please, please.'

'Stop it. Stop it.' The words came to Lange at last, breathless and shaking with tears. 'Let me help him.'

But someone was holding him down, twisting his arm behind his back. It was his room-mate, Schmidt.

'Shut up,' Dietrich barked and he pushed his face close to Lange's. 'Why do you want to help a traitor?'

They were all looking at him now, angry that anyone should dare to challenge their justice with a show of pity.

'Why? You of all people.' Lange could feel Dietrich's hot stale tobacco breath on his cheek. His blue eyes were mad with anger, the pupils fully dilated. Slowly, he reached up and pinched Lange's left cheek between his thumb and forefinger, digging his nails in hard until he gasped with pain.

'You're lucky it's him,' Dietrich hissed.

'I just, I . . .' Lange could not speak. The words had gone again. The window was closing.

'Take him back. We don't need him any more.'

It was Bruns who took hold of his arm. 'Come on.'

And Lange wanted to go with him, to escape, to run, to hide, 'Go, go now,' the words screaming, echoing through his mind. But he could not move. He could not move. Guilt was tearing at him, guilt and a helpless paralysing fear of what would happen when he was gone.

'Come now,' Bruns almost pulled him off his feet.

'And not a word,' Dietrich glared at him. 'Not a word to anyone, do you hear?'

There was silence in the kitchen, a cold complicit silence as they watched Bruns bundle Lange to the door. Then a low despairing moan and Lange turned quickly to look at Heine. The rope was slack and he was rocking to and fro, his face in his hands. Dietrich was standing over him again with the end of the rope in his hands.

'If you're a man you'll do it. Do it now.'

Then the kitchen door swung firmly shut and Lange was in the dark passage.

Later, he lay with his face on his pillow, chinks of light forcing their way through his closed fingers. He was alone. Soon the bell would ring for roll call and he would have to go down to the terrace. His room-mates were there already. Dietrich would be there, Schmidt, Bruns and the others. He would have to look them in the eye. Twisted faces, he could see them now, the fury and the relish with which they had set about their task, the pleasure. Nineteen. Heine was only nineteen. All he had ever wanted was to be an engineer, an oily rag for his country. Why, why, why? Was it their collective humiliation, their way of coping with the helplessness and shame of being prisoners? They needed to prove their loyalty and dedication to duty even at the expense of their own. Yes, they were all to blame. But as he lay there on his bed Lange knew he would never escape the conviction that he was most to blame. It was the yellow file. He could see it in Dietrich's hands. He could see it in front of Heine's bruised face. And the engineer was holding a pen in trembling fingers to make his confession. The yellow file. Lange wondered if he would ever be clean again.

33

The car was waiting for Mary at the bottom of the church steps with its engine running.

'Prayers for victory?' he asked as she slipped into the seat beside him.

'Yes.'

'Wonderful.' And he pressed his foot to the floor.

Her uncle was watching from the top of the steps with a concerned look on his face, the church emptying around him.

The Austin smelt of oil and cigarette smoke and was stuffy even with all the windows open. There was an alarming screech as Lindsay worked his way through the gears. It would take them a little less than two hours to reach Oxford. It was a perfect summer Sunday and a hamper and ice bucket were balanced carefully on the back seat. Mary was relishing the prospect of a few precious hours away from the grind and the grime of London.

But the journey began awkwardly. Lindsay looked more tired, more careworn than she had ever seen him but he was short with her when she said so. They seemed to have lost some of their old easy familiarity. He made little effort to answer her questions and conversation began to peter out between Marble Arch and Notting Hill Gate. She was relieved of the obligation when, on the outskirts of west London, he was able to open up the throttle and the wind began to whip through the car. With the sun blinking through the windscreen and the throb of the engine, she was asleep before they reached High Wycombe.

They parked on the Woodstock Road in Oxford and Mary took him into her old college.

'This is for bluestockings, isn't it?' he asked provocatively.

'For clever and free-thinking women, you mean.'

An old scout recognised her as they were ambling round the main quad and they were obliged to listen to her litany of woes about rationing at high table and civil servants in the university buildings. It seemed to Mary that Oxford had changed very little; it was quieter perhaps but still timeless and mellow in the summer sunshine. Lindsay was thinking the same:

'Someone must have missed Oxford off the Luftwaffe's map.'

'You sound sorry.'

'No,' he said thoughtfully, 'no, I'm glad.'

'Perhaps it represents something greater.'

He gave a short laugh: 'A corner of civilisation? Do you think Warsaw or the East End of London knows? Anyway, there's time yet.'

'Gosh, what good company you are.'

He put his arm around her waist and squeezed it: 'Sorry.'

It was the first time he had touched her that day.

They walked into broad St Giles past the memorial for those of the city who had fallen in the Great War, to St John's College and on towards the neo-Gothic buildings of Balliol. And Mary told him something of the history of the Scottish college and of its founders John Balliol and his wife the Lady Dervorguilla. When John died in 1268 his heart was cut from his chest, embalmed and kept close by his widow. It was buried beside her at last at the abbey she built in his memory. 'Sweetheart Abbey not far from Dumfries.'

'I'll take you,' said Lindsay.

'Who knows, by the time this war's over you may not love me.'

'I will love you,' and he turned to face her. 'But you'll be tired of me. I'll have exhausted your patience.'

He lifted her chin and she allowed his lips to brush her cheek before turning away.

'Perhaps,' she said, breaking free.

They walked back to the car for the hamper, then on past the gaudy High Church brick of Keble College to the University Parks. Here the war was making its mark. The railings were reduced to a few broken inches and the park to the south of the path had been turned over to allotments. Sunday gardeners were bent over their strips like the lay brothers of a medieval college. They found a peaceful spot beneath the shade of a sweet chestnut, a stone's throw from the River

Cherwell. Lindsay had done well: a bottle of Bordeaux, duck, pickled herring, some cheese and fresh bread – even a bar of American chocolate.

'How on earth . . .'

'Good intelligence. For you, guvnor, a shillin',' he said in a Scots-cockney accent.

'You ruthless spiv.'

'I know how to please a lady,' and he smiled warmly at her. 'Pass me the corkscrew.'

He opened the bottle, then began arranging knives and glasses and food on the rug.

'Is this a little indecent?' she asked, rolling down her church stockings.

'Wonderfully indecent.'

After they had eaten, they lay on the blanket soaking in the lazy heat of the day. It was humid and still, with not a breath of wind to stir the broadleaf canopy above. A college bell was tolling in the distance, and closer, excited voices and the solid clunk of bat on leather ball, laughter from the river and the splash of a punt pole inexpertly handled. And in such a place, on such a day, the battle in the Atlantic was no more than an abstraction. Eyes closed, empty of all but feeling, sun on muscle and skin, a trickle of perspiration on her throat and the grass brushing the back of her legs. She was surprised and almost sorry when he touched her again, a loving caress with the back of his hand lightly against her arm.

'May I tell you something?'

'Of course.'

'The Security Service – Five – tried to question me and I think I'm being followed.'

She sat up, turning to look at him: 'Followed? Why?'

He shrugged: 'Kapitän Mohr is chasing me.'

He told her of his visit to the shop on the Commercial Road, of Mohr's letter with its pointed reference to his cousin, of the telephone conversation with his father and the black Morris he kept seeing in St James's Square.

'I tried to talk to the driver but all I got for my trouble was a thick lip.'

Mary reached across to stroke his cheek but he took her hand and kissed it.

'I can't believe this, Douglas. This is terrible.' Her voice trembled a little. 'And Ian Fleming is involved too. Have you spoken to anyone else in the Division?'

'I haven't been into the Admiralty since all this blew up. The Director sent word he didn't want to see me. They've got the report, of course.'

'It's bloody. It's . . .' She took a deep breath and tried to be calm but tears and resentment were welling inside her.

'I'm sorry, Mary, I didn't want to spoil the day. It will sort itself out. A cousin in the Kriegsmarine is not a capital offence,' he gave a harsh laugh, 'yet.' He paused for a moment, then said: 'It's my mother I'm concerned about, and you. Sooner or later they will speak to you.'

'Let them,' she snapped crossly. Then she reached up with both hands and pulled his head down to kiss him hard. After a while, they broke apart and lay quietly side by side. The sun was lost behind a mass of blue-grey cloud and the air heavy now with the promise of thunder.

'You should leave the Division,' she said.

'And go back to sea? I can't.'

'You may have to leave. Perhaps I should too.'

Lindsay raised himself to his elbow abruptly: 'Because of me? No. No. They won't let you and it would be madness anyway.'

There was a white flash in the west and seconds later the crack and rumble of thunder. Mary got slowly to her feet and began to brush the grass from her frock. By the time they reached the park gates heavy raindrops were spotting their clothes and rolling down their faces. Lindsay swung the hamper on to his back.

'Can you run?'

'Of course but I'd rather walk.'

He smiled and brushed a strand of wet hair from her face: 'As you wish.'

Another sharp flash and almost at once the thunder. People began hurrying past under macs and umbrellas and the Sunday papers. Mary's dress was clinging thickly to her skin and her hair hung in rat's tails about her face. At the end of Keble Road she stopped to balance on Lindsay's arm and empty water from a shoe. Looking up, she saw he was blinking madly as the rain ran down his forehead into his eyes.

'What on earth . . .' and he pulled a face at her. She began to laugh. And for a time she could not stop, short breathless infectious laughter. He hugged her and she made him dance a little circle as the rain fell in a drenching sheet in the empty road.

They drove the steamy car through the city in search of a tea-room and found one close to the station. Its sympathetic owner showed them to a table close to a heater, then served tea and a biscuit. Lindsay held her hand across the table:

'Thank you for today. I feel calmer. You know sometimes I worry I'm imagining those men in the car outside my home. They are there but perhaps they have nothing to do with Special Branch. They may be thieves going quietly about their business. Am I going mad?'

She smiled and gave his hand a squeeze: 'Stark raving.'

He laughed and rolled his fingers over his bottom lip like a halfwit.

But in the car on the way home, silent except for the rhythm of the road, she wondered if he was right – was he a prisoner of his own imagination? In their secret world of possibilities and lies, wild thoughts would perhaps come easily to a fevered mind. They reached St James's Square at dusk and there was no sign of a black Morris Eight or men in soft hats and raincoats.

'Will you come in? I'll drive you home later,' he said tentatively. 'If you have to go, I mean.'

She did not feel able to refuse.

There was a letter from the Admiralty waiting for him in the hall.

'It's from Fleming. The Director wants to see me first thing tomorrow.'

'Good. You can sort things out.'

'And he's sent a cutting from today's *Sunday Times*.'

It fluttered to the floor and he picked it up without glancing at it and put it in his jacket pocket. 'I'll read it later.'

In the apartment, he drew the blackout curtains, then switched on the sitting-room lights while Mary made some tea. She was loading his mother's bone china on to a tray when he shouted through to the kitchen:

'Hey, come here.'

He was standing at his desk holding the newspaper cutting beneath the lamp. It was only a short piece, no more than the length of his index finger.

'Listen to this:

A prisoner is reported to have committed suicide at a camp for enemy officers in the North Country. Camp guards found the body of the nineteen-year-old U-boat officer hanging from a pipe in the wash-room last Tuesday. The camp for captured German naval and flying officers is known locally as 'the U-boat Hotel' because the prisoners enjoy special privileges. An MP who recently visited it described the rooms as 'luxurious' and claimed the prisoners were better fed than his own constituents. Military Police officers are still interviewing prisoners but are understood to be satisfied that the dead man took his own life.'

'And that's it,' he said, looking up at her.

'Why has he sent you that?'

He turned slowly away from her and drew back a curtain to look down into the square.

'I don't know. Perhaps because I interrogated him.'

'Who?'

'The dead man, of course.'

He held his fist to his mouth, tapping his lip thoughtfully with his knuckles, and when he turned to her again his eyes were their brightest blue: 'Do you think this is something to do with Mohr?'

She slammed the tray on the table so hard that a cup jumped on to the rug: 'Would that make you happy?'

'Yes,' he said and there was the old smile again, dry, a little supercilious, 'I'm afraid it would.'

34

The Director of Naval Intelligence was in no hurry to see Lindsay the following morning. He was directed to a hard wooden chair next to the kettles and milk bottles in the messengers' room and left to slide up and down it for an hour. The whispers, the grim faces and sideways glances suggested it was common knowledge that he was in for a 'roasting'. No secret travelled faster.

He was shown into Room 39 at the Admiralty a little before nine. A meeting of Section heads had just broken up and a small group of officers was chatting and smoking around the large marble fireplace. There was no sign of Fleming and he stood there for a moment unsure whether to wait or knock at the Director's door.

'Sit down, Lindsay.'

It was Commander Drake, the Admiral's slow-moving, easy-tempered doorkeeper, except that this morning he sounded uncharacteristically brusque.

'Admiral Godfrey will be with you shortly.'

Lindsay took a chair by the baize partition in the corner of the room and watched the traffic come and go. After a few minutes the door to his right opened and Ian Fleming came out holding an Admiralty docket. He nodded curtly: 'Step inside, Lieutenant.'

Rear-Admiral John Godfrey was sitting at his large mahogany desk. He did not speak, he did not smile, not a muscle in his face moved as Lindsay walked smartly across the carpet to pre-sent himself in front of it. He was a distinguished-looking man, fifty-three, severe, with a lantern jaw, thin lips and the bright eyes of a hawk. They did not leave Lindsay's face. Fleming took up a position on his right, his arm resting on the black marble mantelpiece behind the Admiral's desk. He looked as if he was at a funeral. When the Director spoke at last his voice was clipped and cool:

'Do you want us to win this war, Lindsay?'

'Yes, sir. I am a . . .'

'"Yes" or "No" will suffice.'

'Yes, sir.'

'Then it is hard to understand your behaviour. You put our codes at risk, disobeyed a direct order from a senior officer and you have been hiding your family's connections to the Nazis.'

'The Kriegsmarine, sir.'

'Don't fence with me,' he barked. 'If it weren't for Commander Fleming you would be shovelling coal on a trawler somewhere between Rockall and St John's.'

'Yes, sir.'

The Admiral leant back in his chair and picked up a thin cardboard file marked 'EYES ONLY' in red.

'You've seen this, haven't you?' He waved it lazily at Lindsay. 'Commander Fleming says you opened it, although you didn't have the authority.'

'Yes, sir, but I was sure Commander Fleming wanted me to read it.'

'So you know that both Military Counter-Intelligence and MI5 recommend your immediate transfer from the Division.'

He glared at Lindsay for a few seconds, then tossed the file back on to the desk.

'Can you give me a good reason why I shouldn't transfer you?'

Lindsay hesitated. His heart was bumping furiously.

'Well?'

'I am good at my job, sir.'

'You haven't proved that,' he snapped.

'No, sir.'

'Thank goodness, humility at last.'

The Admiral looked at him closely, hard wrinkles about his eyes. Someone was giving orders on the parade ground below his window. A clock ticked lamely on the mantelpiece.

'All right, sit down.'

And he pointed to the leather library chairs on the other side of his desk. Picking up the file again, he took out a closely typed sheet of foolscap.

'This is the transcript of Mohr's letter in full.' He pushed it across his shiny black desk. 'Read it.'

It was in German, unremarkable but for the references to Lindsay's cousin and the evening at the jazz club with Mary and Lange. Mohr asked his friend to reassure his family that he was in good health and he wrote of shared memories, of days sailing on the Wannsee in Berlin, of walks and dinners. At the end of the letter he had added a few awkward words of love, dry and conventional, nothing that would offer comfort to a lonely sweetheart. Lindsay slid the paper back across the Admiral's desk.

'The jazz club, sir.' He took a deep breath before continuing. 'Dr Henderson left as soon as she was aware I was with a prisoner.'

Godfrey shook his head: 'That isn't important now. Why do you think he made such pointed reference to you? He knew we'd read the letter.'

Lindsay shrugged: 'He knew it would cause trouble, sir. I think he believes it's his duty to carry on fighting any way he can.'

The Admiral said nothing but reached across his desk for a silver cigarette box which he offered to Lindsay and Fleming.

'Is there anything else about the letter that strikes you as strange?'

Lindsay took a cigarette, smelling it, then rolling it thoughtfully between his fingers: 'Perhaps one thing, sir. It's clumsy, badly written for an educated man.'

The Director of Naval Intelligence smiled. It was a tough little smile but it was the first that Lindsay had seen since marching into his office.

'Yes, badly written and let me show you why.'

He opened the file again and withdrew a small square of light blue paper; on it were the dots and dashes of a signal in Morse code.

'Look at Mohr's letter again. Look at the first letter of each word in the opening and final paragraphs. Words that begin with letters from A to H are dots and words from L to Z dashes. Words that begin with letters from I to K indicate spaces. Here.'

Godfrey handed the signal paper to Lindsay: 'It says: *Two Wabos at fifty. Security problem. Position known but mission safe.* And that's it. With the exception of his swipe at you, the letter was written to conceal this message – that's why it reads so badly. It's not the first time U-boat prisoners have used this code. No doubt Miss Rasch has been instructed to forward everything Mohr sends to Dönitz's headquarters.'

Lindsay pulled hard on his cigarette, savouring the hot sharp taste of the Admiral's tobacco. Smoke curled about the paper on his knee, smudging Mohr's secret dots and dashes. *Wabos* was just U-boat German for *Wasserbomben* or depth charges. The *U-112* was sunk by two depth charges exploding fifty metres from its hull. But the rest of the message was harder to disentangle.

'Well, you've spoken to Mohr?'

The Admiral's voice suggested he wanted to hear something that would justify the time and trouble he was taking with a junior lieutenant.

Lindsay frowned: 'If Mohr was expecting us to read this, why did he risk a secret message?'

It was Fleming who replied: 'He knew we would censor the references to you. If you look carefully you can see he has not used any of the words in that part of the letter in his message. He's a clever chap. He may have wanted to embarrass you, yes, but he also wanted to disguise his real purpose – the coded message.'

'Well, sir . . .' Lindsay leant forward to extinguish his cigarette.

'"Position known" I think he means his own position. You see I asked him about his time at U-boat Headquarters.'

'You also asked him about codes,' said Godfrey coolly.

'Yes sir.' Lindsay half turned to look at Fleming: 'And the cutting you sent me? Does the dead man have anything to do with this?'

Fleming glanced across at Godfrey. The Admiral was watching Lindsay with the fixed gaze of a sleek cat in a garden full of birds.

'It's possible,' said Fleming cautiously. 'Was the *U-112*'s engineer one of your prisoners?'

'Heine?'

'You're surprised?'

'Yes.' Lindsay nodded. Yes, he was surprised. Heine was a practical man with the patience and dogged determination of a born engineer, not the sort to take his own life.

'It was Heine who told me that Mohr served as one of the six Staff officers responsible for all day-to-day operations in the Atlantic. A sensitive role. Heine was terrified his comrades would find out.' Lindsay could picture his pinched, swarthy face across the table, fear in his brown eyes. He had played with that fear to extract all he could from the engineer.

'But I don't think he told us enough to kill him.'

'The Military Police think he committed suicide – they may be right,' Godfrey replied. The note of scepticism in his voice suggested he believed quite the opposite. 'Heine was either beaten or involved in a fight before he died. His face was very badly bruised.'

He pushed back his chair and walked across the room to the window. Filthy slate-grey cloud was scudding across the sky above the Foreign Office, sweeping gusts of rain into Horse Guards and tossing the barrage balloons about their moorings.

'I don't care about the engineer,' said Godfrey. 'But if he was murdered I want to know why. Are we missing something? What does Mohr mean when he says his "mission" is safe?'

He turned sharply to look at Lindsay, a silhouette against the window: 'Commander Fleming thinks you might be useful.'

Every nerve in Lindsay's body was tingling, every muscle taut as if he was reaching for something almost within his grasp, at the very tips of his fingers: 'Yes, sir. I think I can help.'

Fleming raised a quizzical eyebrow and Lindsay wondered if he had sounded too confident.

'Good.'

The Admiral walked back to his desk but remained standing, his hands resting on the back of the chair.

'I've spoken to Colonel Checkland and for now you will be answering directly to me.'

'Yes, sir. And the Security Service? They've been watching my home.'

'I don't know what you're talking about, Lindsay, do you, Ian?'

Fleming shook his head.

'Oh and Lindsay, don't make any more mistakes. Clear?' It was a cool, crisp dismissal. Godfrey leant over his desk and opened another file.

The moment the door clicked gently shut, the Director's gaze lifted to his Assistant: 'You had better be right.'

'He isn't a spy, sir . . .' Fleming frowned and leant forward a little to brush a speck of ash from his trousers.

'But?' Godfrey detected an uneasiness in his voice.

'I think he's a little damaged. The business with the *Culloden* . . .'

'Enough to impair his judgement?'

'I don't think so.'

'We're taking a big risk. If Five don't think we should trust him, I don't think we can entirely.'

'There's a fellow at Stapley Camp called Duncan. Another Scot. Military Intelligence. Solid. Colonel Gilbert's instructed him to keep a close eye on Lindsay.'

'All right, Ian.' Godfrey picked up a silver paper knife from his desk and waved the point lazily at Fleming: 'And in the meantime, let's hope he's as sharp as he thinks he is.'

35

. . . I will take heed to my ways that I offend not in my tongue. I will keep my mouth as it were with a bridle while the ungodly is in my sight . . .

The priest's voice was strong and musical for one so bent by age. He had followed the little cortege with unsteady step to the north-east corner of Stapley churchyard and was standing beside a freshly dug mound of earth. Gathered about him was a score of blue and khaki uniforms and beneath the canopy of a yew tree close by, an honour guard of military policemen in their red caps.

. . . I held my tongue and spake nothing: I kept silence, yea, even from good words but it was pain and grief to me . . .

It was a perfect summer's day and the old and the very young from Stapley village and the neighbouring farms were at the drystone wall of the churchyard to witness the spectacle. The Germans were in their full service blue and hanging from the throat of their commanding officer was the red, white and black ribbon of the Knight's Cross of the Iron Cross. Someone recognised him from the paper as the ruthless Nazi responsible for sinking more than twenty British ships.

Deliver me from all mine offences and make me not a rebuke unto the foolish . . .

Kapitän zur See Jürgen Mohr glanced at the Prayer Book in the shaking hands of the clergyman, then down to the coffin at his feet, draped in the white ensign of the Royal Navy. It was a pity the British would not permit them to use their own battle flag. Still, they had agreed to bury August Heine with full military honours. He would have been gratified to know that his commander and comrades were going to these lengths after such an unseemly end. It was three weeks since they had cut him down from the washroom pipe, tired weeks of questions and recriminations. The Military Police had been unpleasant but reassuringly incompetent.

The priest finished the psalm and handed the Prayer Book to a village youth in a grubby surplice, then took a step back from the grave and nodded to the camp commander. Major Ronald Benson cleared his throat – German was a trial: 'I would like to express my deep sadness and regret at the passing of a brave young man, a sadness we all feel at Number One Stapley. We stand here – British and German side by side – united in mourning for Leutnant Heine, and together we remember his family in our prayers.'

Benson paused to look across at Mohr: 'I would like to invite Leutnant Heine's commanding officer to say a few words.'

Mohr had prepared his few words, a short speech about loyalty, the comradeship of the boat, honour, but standing at the grave, his shoes heavy with earth, those sentiments seemed trite and careless. He wanted to turn and walk away, to be alone. And yet what else was there? He had brought his own officers from the *U-112*; Fischer was there with his men and there were one or two others, fifteen prisoners altogether. They were all looking at him, expecting him to say something in praise of Heine's life and to make sense of his death. Dietrich was standing at his right hand, his head bowed in a pretence of prayer, and beside him Schmidt, the curly-haired second officer of the *500*. To their right, he could see Bruns, his own navigator. These were the men to speak of sacrifice and loyalty, their faith in Germany unshakable, ruthless in its service.

When he spoke, his voice was as strong as it should be: 'Men of the U-boat arm. Our comrade, Leutnant Heine, has fallen and is to be buried here in foreign soil. He was no less a casualty of this war than his brothers who have died at sea. His heart was always that of a true German, loyal to his Fatherland and to his Führer. We honour his sacrifice and we salute him now, confident that the victory he desired above all will come soon.'

And those empty, meaningless words were all Mohr could think of to say. Fortunately, he was relieved of any further obligation by Major Benson, who had clearly heard quite enough about a German victory.

'All right, get on with it, Vicar.'

Four British soldiers stepped smartly forward to carefully fold the white ensign, then they took up positions on either side of the grave.

Man that is born of woman hath but a short time to live, and is full of misery . . .

The plain pine coffin began to disappear a few gentle inches at a time. It seemed to Mohr that no one was greatly affected, there were no tears. Those who might have cried over the body of August Heine did not even know he was dead.

Thou knowest, Lord, the secrets of our hearts . . .

It was a shame the British were not able to find a Lutheran pastor but he did not object to the words of the English Prayer Book. The dead man would not have understood them in any case. The coffin reached the bottom of the muddy trench and the soldiers stood to attention, the ropes still taut in their hands. Benson gave the order and the guard of honour stepped forward with rifles at the ready. Gunfire rang out around the churchyard and a baby by the wall began to wail; a second ragged volley followed, and then a third and sharp cordite smoke drifted across the grave. Mohr could taste it in his mouth. He bent to pick up a handful of earth.

. . . earth to earth, ashes to ashes, dust to dust . . .

It rattled and bounced on the coffin lid. The others stepped forward in their turn, hands stained by the earth from the grave: Gretschel, the *112*'s first officer, Koch and Bruns and young Bischoff, the midshipman, then Fischer and his men. The last to reach for a handful of soil was the propaganda reporter, Helmut Lange. Mohr watched him standing there, squeezing it hard in his fist, forcing the dirt through his fingers. He hovered at the muddy lip of the grave, his face frozen in some sort of trance. And the seconds began to slip away. Major Benson cleared his throat pointedly and the priest laid a hand on Lange's arm. He shook it free. Was Lange losing his mind? It was too late for the dead man's mercy.

'Come on there.'

The old priest tried to comfort him again. Someone coughed

uneasily, heads were down and Mohr could sense the men closest to him shuffling from one foot to another. Lange was embarrassing them all.

'Leutnant Lange.' Mohr spoke his name firmly.

Lange looked up at last and slowly turned his head towards them. And Mohr could see that his dark eyes were cloudy and distant, his cheeks stained with tears. So there was someone there to weep after all. Then Lange shuddered a little and closed his eyes. And when he opened them again it was plain to Mohr that he was with them once more. It was the face of a different man, no longer frozen but alive. And it was full of contempt and fear and loathing.

Lange's fistful of earth clattered on to the coffin lid with disturbing force. There were astonished gasps from those watching at the churchyard wall. Mohr stepped forward at once and took him firmly by the arm:

'Leutnant Lange. Please.' And he turned to whisper to Fischer: 'Hold him.'

Major Benson nodded anxiously to the priest.

. . . for that it hath pleased thee to deliver this our brother out of the miseries of this sinful world . . .

And it was over in minutes. The priest closed his prayer book and stood back from the grave. Mohr breathed a sigh of relief. Perhaps that was an end to the matter and they could bury the truth with Heine in this quiet country churchyard. He would have to speak to the propaganda reporter again. Lange had made an exhibition of himself and that was dangerous. Fischer was leading him away.

'Kapitän Mohr, if you and your men would make your way to the truck.' Benson was beside him with the soldiers of the honour guard. It was an end to the brotherhood of arms.

'Certainly, Major.'

A couple of squaddies were resting on spades beneath the east window of the church, their sleeves rolled up ready. With the last of the mourners they would begin shovelling and scraping the earth back into the grave, beating it down hard with their spades. At their feet was a simple wooden cross with Heine's full name and rank painted carefully in black Gothic script. For a time it would look strange among the grey lichen-covered stones but Heine's name would be lost within ten Lakeland winters and the cross would rot and fall within ten more.

The old priest was waiting at the gate to shake Mohr's hand and say a few words. Major Benson and his men were standing a little beyond it at the tailgate of the covered lorry that would take them back to the camp. Most of his men were already inside but he was in no hurry join them. Young faces bobbed up at the wall to peer at him and giggle but Mohr did not mind; it was refreshing, he felt a sort of freedom in the churchyard. A car horn sounded a short distance away. A military Humber was edging on to the muddy verge to pass a tractor which a farmer had parked carelessly in the lane.

'I'm sorry about your young lieutenant.' The priest's handshake was limp and cold, his face a liverish white, the ghostly colour of a U-boat engineer after weeks without natural light. 'He was so far from home.'

'Yes.'

'I understand from Major Benson that you don't have your own pastor at the camp, Captain.'

'No.'

The Humber roared, its wheels spinning wildly, throwing soggy divots across the road.

'I would be prepared to take a service from time to time – in English, I'm afraid, I speak very little German.'

The passenger door flew open and a naval officer climbed awkwardly out. He spoke briefly to the driver then began walking by the church wall towards them. His face was lost beneath the shadow of his peaked cap but Mohr recognised him at once.

'Thank you. I will speak to my men.'

He turned from the priest and walked through the gate to the truck. Helping hands reached down to pull him into the back and the guards lifted the tailgate and pushed the pins into place. He was a prisoner again. They sat in silence, shoulder to shoulder on the benches, studying their shoes, listening to the English voices a few feet away.

'. . . Yes, Lieutenant Lindsay, we were expecting to see you yesterday.'

There was no warmth in Benson's voice.

'I'm sorry I missed the funeral.'

'Shall we meet in an hour with the camp IO, Lieutenant Duncan – he's a Scotsman too by the way.'

'Thank you. I would like to begin at once . . .'

There was a grinding roar and the lorry began to shudder. The driver engaged the clutch and it rattled forward a few feet. Mohr leant across the body of the truck. There was at least one other person who recognised that soft Scottish voice. Lange was sitting at the end of the bench opposite. He seemed to have made himself very small in the shadows. His knee was bouncing anxiously, his hands restless; his face was turned away but Mohr could see that he was biting his lip. Mohr turned back to the mouth of the truck. Through an evil cloud of exhaust, he watched as Lindsay picked his way between the headstones. The soldiers were bent over their spades, dark patches of perspiration on their shirts, and most of the conical mound of earth above the grave had already gone. Lindsay stood and watched them for a few seconds, then bent to pick up something at his feet. It was the wooden cross. He turned it over to read the inscription.

The engine roared again and the truck lurched forward, throwing Mohr against his neighbour. He reached up for a canopy pole to steady himself. When he looked again Lindsay was staring back at him, the cross still in his hands. The truck was gathering speed and in a matter of seconds the churchyard was lost from view, but those troubling few seconds were in Mohr's thoughts for the rest of the day.

The camp commander's office was in the old lodge at the entrance to the park, a comfortable distance from the enemy. Lindsay was shown up to a dingy little waiting room on the first floor. An orderly was leaving with the remains of the Major's lunch and he left the door ajar. Benson was grumbling volubly.

'. . . it's disruptive and quite unnecessary, but I've been ordered to do all I can for him.'

The Major's secretary gave Lindsay an embarrassed smile and slipped out from behind her desk to knock at his door.

Benson was a tall, heavily built man in his early forties with a florid complexion and glassy limpid eyes. He was a drinker. Lindsay noticed his hand tremble a little when he stepped forward to shake it. Beside him was the camp's intelligence officer.

'Lieutenant Duncan will be able to help you with the details of the case,' said Benson, waving airily at the files on his desk. 'It's not often Naval Intelligence gets involved in this sort of matter.' The frostiness in his very military voice suggested that this was altogether a good thing.

Duncan greeted him with a warmer smile. They sat at Benson's desk and he ordered some coffee.

It was a 'tragic' but 'straightforward' business, he said. He had seen it happen before. Some men just fell apart behind the wire and Heine was the type.

Lindsay raised his eyebrows: 'Really?'

'The senior German officers had been watching him for some time. He was very highly strung.'

Duncan shifted uncomfortably in his chair.

'The Military Police found nothing suspicious,' said Benson, 'and I don't expect you to.'

The clinking of cups at the door signalled the arrival of coffee. Lindsay glanced over at Duncan. He was in his early thirties, stocky, with bad skin and curly black hair. He reminded Lindsay of the senior foreman at his father's works in Glasgow. There was something in his watchful silence and tight body language that suggested he did not see eye to eye with the commander of the camp.

'I expect you would like to see how we found him?'

Benson reached for an envelope and drew out a bundle of photographs. He waited until his secretary had left the office, then handed them to Lindsay: 'Not pretty.'

Heine was dangling from the pipe like a broken carnival puppet. His face was swollen and twisted, his tongue lolling thick and blue from his mouth. His feet were only inches from the washroom floor and in the corner of the photograph there was an upturned chair. His arms hung freely at his sides. It was an undignified way to depart this earth.

'He killed himself a little before morning roll call when the washroom was sure to be empty and his body was discovered almost as soon as it was over.'

'And the police think he took his own life?'

'Yes.'

'And you agree?'

'Of course. There was no evidence to suggest his arms and legs had been tied at any point. His neck wasn't broken – the poor fellow strangled himself.'

Benson pulled a face: 'A ghastly way to go; his mind must have been completely unhinged.'

Duncan gave a pointed little cough. Lindsay turned to look at him.

'There were the bruises on his face and body, sir.'

His tone was measured, his accent reassuringly familiar, like a Glaswegian bank manager, the sort your grandmother might trust with her life savings.

'He received those injuries in a fight with one of the other prisoners,' said Benson, addressing Lindsay only. He was clearly irritated. He was the sort of man who expected life to tick like a clock, each little cog in the mechanism turning beautifully on to the next in a predictable well-ordered movement. And the camp was his empire – he was going to guard its reputation jealously. 'You will find the details of the fight in the statements here.' He laid his hand on the files in front of him. 'Duncan will take you through them.'

He pushed his chair back suddenly and got to his feet. There were other things he wanted to attend to in the camp, he explained. Lindsay wondered if he needed a drink.

Lieutenant Duncan breathed a sigh of relief as the door closed behind him.

'You're the intelligence officer. What do you think?' Lindsay asked at once.

Duncan looked at him cautiously: 'I don't know if he took his own life but I don't think he got those bruises in a fight. I can't prove anything because none of the prisoners will talk to me – not even the friendly ones. A fellow called Schmidt – he was with the 500 – came forward to say he got into an argument with Heine. Mohr brought him to us. But neither of them would tell us what it was about.'

'And the police?'

'Why spend time on a dead German? Aren't we trying to kill them by the thousands?'

'Is that your view too?'

'No. I helped cut him down.'

Lindsay nodded in acknowledgement, then asked, after a moment's thought: 'Don't you have a trustee, an informer inside the camp, one of the prisoners?'

'No. It's very tight.'

Rising from his chair Lindsay walked slowly over to the window. They were changing the guard at the gate and along the perimeter wire. An elderly-looking sergeant was barking aggressively at his men, every bristling inch the parade-ground martinet. It was the Army at its most senseless. And it seemed to Lindsay that the wire and the guard offered no sort of challenge to a resourceful prisoner intent on escape, but where was there to run to here?

'Do you think he was murdered?' Duncan asked.

'Do you?'

'I don't know. But I am sure they are all lying about the fight.'

'Mohr?'

'Oh, he just said it was regrettable . . .'

'No. What do you think of him?'

'Major Benson is impressed.' There was a barely disguised note of contempt in Duncan's voice.

'And you?'

Duncan shrugged: 'I think he knows how to get what he wants. The Ältestenrat runs this place.'

'The Ältestenrat?'

'The council of the eldest – the three senior prisoners.'

Lindsay turned away from the window and walked back to the desk. 'I'd better look at the statement Mohr gave the investigating officers and the other ones they collected too.'

It took a little under an hour to read them all. Lieutenant Duncan returned at four o'clock with tea and a few damp biscuits. The military investigators had taken statements from all the officers of the *U-112*, Heine's room-mates and one or two prisoners who were known to have been on good terms with the dead man. No one was very forthcoming. There was the suggestion more than once that Heine was struggling with captivity and close to breaking. The second officer of the *112*, Schmidt, repeated that he had had an argument with Heine and it had 'boiled over'. He refused to give any more details. The first officer of the 112, Gretschel, said he had barely spoken to Heine since arriving at the camp and he knew nothing of a fight, but he would remember him as a good and dedicated comrade. 'This sentiment was expressed with a great deal of feeling,' the investigator had noted. Mohr's statement was cooler. Heine was 'young', Heine was 'highly strung', Heine was 'close to cracking' before he became a prisoner. And Mohr implied that he had nursed him through two fraught war patrols that had shredded the young engineer's nerves and then the trauma of the sinking. He said he had not been surprised to learn that Heine had picked a fight with another prisoner.

Lindsay flicked through the statements again, then tossed them back on Benson's desk. 'With the exception of Gretschel, there isn't much warmth in these, is there? And I don't recognise Heine.' He picked up his cigarettes and leant forward to offer them to Duncan.

'Do you know a man called Lange? Leutnant zur See Helmut Lange?'

36

It was stifling in the theatre and the three little maids were wilting in the heat. Mary slipped in and out of the first Act. With a supreme effort she dragged herself back for the second, ramrod straight, eyes fixed on the stage. Tears of make-up were rolling down poor Nanky Poo's cheeks. The large man in the seat to her left smelt like a wet dog and she could feel the perspiration on her own face and neck. Her dress was clinging uncomfortably to her back and thighs. On her right, James Henderson was drumming his fingers and tapping his feet with something very like girlish glee. He had insisted on taking Mary out for the evening. Rationing was making a good dinner in London almost impossible, he said, and he had proposed *The Mikado* at the Savoy Theatre instead. Anxious to avoid anything but the most casual conversation, she had agreed. It was months since she had spent any time in her brother's company or wanted to, but tonight he was on his best behaviour. During the interval they spoke of the land girls on their father's farm and of a nurse James was chasing who had coal-black hair and a winsome smile, of Rommel in the Western Desert and the bloody, inexorable advance eastwards into Russia. He did not mention Lindsay and she was careful not to present him with an opportunity to do so.

At the final curtain they emptied gratefully into the Strand, breathing drunken lungfuls of evening air. James took Mary's arm and marched her without ceremony across the road towards Covent Garden. Supper at a quiet club, he explained, and a chance to talk properly. Resistance was useless because there was plainly something he was burning to tell her: Mary was sure it was going to be something unpleasant. It came in the end with coffee. The club was almost empty but James bent his head a little closer. A choking cloud of his cigar smoke swirled about the table.

'You know I saw Fleming yesterday and he mentioned your visit to Hatchett's. He learnt of it from a letter, I think?'

Mary raised her eyebrows in a show of surprise.

'Please don't deny it. You were there with a German prisoner.'

'I have no intention of denying it,' she said coolly.

He leant even closer, an angry frown on his face: 'Don't you understand the risk you were taking? A woman in your position at the Citadel. Special Branch have spoken to me about you and Lindsay. Special Branch. You should show a little more loyalty, you know.'

'Loyalty?'

'To the Division, to Winn, to me. I helped you into that job.' His voice was full of hushed resentment.

For a moment Mary could think of nothing to say. She stared at him, her mouth open in astonishment. Then with cold fury: 'You pompous idiot.'

She dumped her napkin on the table and got quickly to her feet.

'I don't blame you, I blame your bloody boyfriend,' James stuttered. 'I got into a devil of a lot of trouble over that note the prisoner gave me for him. Should have gone to Security. You see, he doesn't understand . . .'

His last words were lost in a shower of water. Mary had picked up a glass and emptied its contents over him. She heard with satisfaction his sharp intake of breath and the hiss of his cigar.

'Leave Douglas alone. Do you hear? Leave us both alone.'

Then she turned her back on him and without glancing at the astonished faces to left and right, she walked swiftly from the club. She did not stop walking until she reached Lord North Street. Fumbling for her keys, she could not help smiling at the recollection of her brother goldfishing, a wet strand of hair across his forehead and a dark green patch on his shirt and uniform shoulders. She would feel guilty and apologise in time, in a few weeks or perhaps months.

But it was with more than a little trepidation that she settled at her desk in Room 41 the following morning. She did not expect it to be the last she would hear of Hatchett's. Winn was going to have his say too. At the top of her in-tray, as always, were the urgent strips torn from the teleprinter run by the secret ladies, the traffic from

239

Station X with its snapshot of U-boats in the Atlantic, the intelligence picture ever clearer.

And in these flimsy decrypts the fear of a change for the worse with a new coded number each week as yet another U-boat finished its work-up and set out on war patrol for the first time. The talk at the Tracking Room plot table was of a doubling of Dönitz's fleet within months, a hundred U-boats operational by Christmas.

It was a little after ten when Geoff Childs touched her shoulder lightly.

'Rodger would like to see you.'

She glanced past him towards Winn's glass box. He was staring at her intently and she looked away and up into the thin brown face of Childs who frowned by way of a discreet warning.

'Sit down, Mary.'

Winn was polishing his round spectacles with his handkerchief. He sounded friendly but businesslike, his jaw set, his lips tight with purpose. The nervous strain of the Atlantic battle was always written deeply in his face. His desk was covered in flimsy signal papers and well-ordered files but Mary knew it would be empty by the end of the day whenever that proved to be.

'I want you to run a special check on the route of a ship outward bound to Freetown and from there to Egypt. They want me to authorise her detachment from the convoy.'

The ship was the *Imperial Star* and she was travelling in a well-protected convoy with aircraft parts and carrying some specialist fitters. But she was an old White Star liner capable of more than fifteen knots and the convoy was travelling at half that speed. The Ministry of Shipping was anxious to give her her head, to let her break free and sail alone, unescorted.

'This is the fourth time they've asked me,' he said, waving a blue message paper at her, 'four times in four days. But I don't feel comfortable about it. The hunting has been good for them in African waters and two of the larger Type IX U-boats sailed from Lorient a fortnight ago. They may be somewhere close to Freetown. I want you to check. Go through what we have. Go through it very carefully.'

Winn leant forward to pick up his cigarettes, took one and lit it with a frustrated snap of his lighter.

'And one thing more.' His voice was no longer businesslike but severe.

A slow anxious charge tingled down Mary's spine.

'What on earth did you think you were playing at? I was this close to having you transferred,' he said and there was only an inch between his thumb and forefinger.

'I . . . I left at once,' she stammered.

Winn stared at her for a moment, cool, unblinking, appraising. And then with his eyes steady upon her face: 'Does he know?'

'Does who know what?'

'Don't play games with me, Dr Henderson,' he said coldly.

'I am not, Commander Winn. I want to hear you ask me properly.' And her voice was hard and defiant.

'Does Lieutenant Lindsay know we're reading the enemy's signals? Have you told him?'

'You know he's working for the Director, Admiral Godfrey. He's back in the fold.'

'Have you told him?'

'No.' And Mary shook her head crossly. 'No, of course not.'

Winn studied her face carefully for a few seconds more, then lifted his cigarette to his lips: 'Good.'

Later, as she leant over the plot table with her notepad, she wondered at her own cool mendacity. It was wrong, the Bible said so, and yet with alacrity she was becoming a hardened and practised liar. Was it Lindsay or was it the secret world they both inhabited, with its half truths and deceits, that was scratching at her old certainties? She was not a natural rule-breaker and she felt uncomfortable lying to Winn but it had been shockingly easy and it was shocking, too, that it pricked her conscience only a little. But she would need to be careful, very careful.

There was nothing on the Atlantic plot to indicate an immediate threat to the *Imperial Star*. Homebound SL 76 was attacked on 29 and 30 June by at least two submarines and ships were lost. The U-123 sank another off the African coast four days later. But there had been almost no recorded activity or signals traffic for a fortnight. The black U-boat pinheads were concentrated in the

North Atlantic. Mary checked the files for reports of sailings from the French coast and examined the special intelligence for anything that might indicate an imminent threat. The *Imperial Star* did not appear to be in danger. It was impossible to be entirely sure, even with the benefit of the Germans' own signals, but perhaps this time Winn was being a little too cautious. It was the middle of the afternoon before she was ready to tell him so. He stomped out of his office to stand at the edge of the plot and she slipped out from behind her desk to join him.

'And you've checked everything?' he asked.

'I could ring the Naval Section at Bletchley Park – with your permission, of course. They may have something more on the two larger U-boats that sailed a fortnight ago.'

'No. That's fine. We've done enough already. I'll tell Admiral Godfrey I have no objections. The Ministry can release the *Imperial Star* from the convoy and route her separately.'

Winn turned away from her to lean over the plot: 'And I hope to God we're right.'

She spent the rest of the day bent over the latest batch of signals, weather reports from outbound U-boats, convoy sightings, damage reports, a constant flow of small pieces, some to be discarded, some to be fitted into the picture of the battle. At a little before seven Commander Hall from the Trade Division was back to confer at the plot table, then at eight the Director and his entourage. Was Dönitz moving his U-boats westwards? Was he supplying them at sea? And what size of fleet would attack convoys to Russia? Godfrey wanted answers to all these questions and more.

But by ten the smoke was beginning to settle beneath the drop lamps once more. Mary was clearing her desk mechanically, her eyes stinging and wet with fatigue. The plotters would be busy with signal bearings throughout the night and the secret ladies would ghost in and out with their pieces of teleprinter paper. In the morning a fine layer of smoke would still be hanging there like mist on the sea's face in winter. A day that never seemed to end would begin again. For now, the bridge was the night duty officer's. Freddie Wilmot was in Winn's office with someone from anti-submarine warfare. Mary could hear their laughter and Wilmot's excited voice. A moment later he came out clutching a teleprinter signal.

'We've bagged the *U-330*,' and he shook the paper at Mary. 'Dönitz has been trying to make contact for days and now Berlin has confirmed it.'

'Good. When and where?'

'An aircraft from Coastal Command caught the boat on the surface and managed to depth-charge her as she was crash-diving. The pilot reported oil and debris but this is confirmation. No survivors.'

Wilmot walked over to the U-boat file index by the plot table and took out the 330's card.

'Rodger wants to check its history. Berlin called it "the lion boat", claims it sank fourteen ships.'

Mary nodded politely. The loss of an enemy vessel in the Atlantic was always good news but not the sort she wanted to celebrate. Some of the boys took a different view, especially when the boat had a history. Wilmot took his card back to Winn and Mary picked up her bag and walked over to the coat rail by the door. She was struggling into her mac when Winn's office door opened again.

'Rodger would like to see you before you go,' said Wilmot breezily.

Winn was perched on the edge of his desk, the U-boat file card on his knee, a cigarette burning between his fingers.

'Wilmot told you about the 330?'

'Yes. Good news.'

'Yes.'

Winn flicked ash off his cigarette then squeezed it into an ashtray. 'It was a successful boat, an experienced commander.'

He slipped to his feet and walked round the desk to his chair but remained standing.

'Do you know the name of the 330's commander?' he asked.

'No, but I can check.'

'No need. I have it here,' and he lifted the file card. 'Schultze.'

The name rang a distant uneasy bell but Mary was not able to say why. 'You can tell Lieutenant Lindsay,' said Winn coolly.

A cold shudder passed through her body. The penny had dropped and how foolish not to remember. Schultze was Lindsay's cousin

'Martin'. She looked down for a moment, confused and a lump formed in her throat. She felt strangely guilty.

'Thank you, Rodger.'

'Tell him I'm sorry.'

'Yes. Yes, I will.'

She turned slowly to leave but at the door stopped and looked back at him: 'Is this news we're supposed to celebrate?'

He lifted his eyes from his desk and stared at her, his gaze intense and unblinking as ever.

'Yes, we should celebrate.'

37

HMS Imperial Star
16°42N/25°29W
North Atlantic

It was a breathless heat, insufferably close even at six o'clock. The captain had given permission for passengers to sleep on the promenade deck and some had already staked a claim to a few feet of polished boards with bags and blankets and the life vests they would use for a pillow. At dusk the blackout would be enforced, deadlights dropped over ports, gangways to the deck sealed, and those who retired to their stifling cabins would be condemned to hours of restless torment. Tempers were fraying. The captain had barked at a lady passenger who insisted on complaining to him in person about the children playing hide-and-seek on deck. A couple of soldiers had come to blows very publicly and were sweltering under guard in the brig.

On the bridge, Third Officer Hall wiped his brow with a damp handkerchief, then reached for the glass of cold water the steward was offering him on a tray. There were grey hulls as far as the eye could see: the *Imperial Star* was ship number four in column number three, limping south at the speed of the slowest tramp in the convoy. Hall was an old blue-water sailor with twenty years' experience and keeping station between ships was a kind of special purgatory which the tropical heat was making even more unbearable. He envied the escorts their freedom – a destroyer was cutting an impressive bow wave half a mile to port – at least they had the run of the convoy. It was the single topic of serious conversation in the officers' dining saloon. Was the ship safer in this protected box of sea? For his part, Hall was firmly of the view that she should be given her head; her twin screws were capable of sixteen knots and speed, surely, was her best protection. The captain had not expressed a view but the crew – even the engine-room stokers – were able to sense his frustration. They had all seen ships sunk in convoy and the recollection of it was sharp and cold even now on the sunlit bridge.

'They're still playing Vera Lynn in the lounge. I've begged the steward to let me throw the record over the side.' It was Murray, the Chief Officer, a Glaswegian, short, thick-set, a White Star officer for more than thirty years. He had conducted a general round of the ship, starting with the ancient naval gun on the foredeck. Everything was as it should be; the ladies dressing for dinner, white-coated stewards serving in the bar, the Army playing bridge, in one of the saloons, in another the RAF flirting with some of the nurses who were with the ship all the way to the Middle East. The watch was in place and at a little before dusk the men would be ordered to stand to the guns. But for now at least there was a hushed, somnolent quality to the *Imperial Star*, the hum of the engines, the gentle whooshing of a calm sea along her sides.

The duty wireless operator was hovering at Murray's side with a small square of signal paper in his hand: 'From the Commodore of the convoy, sir.'

The Chief Officer took the signal, glanced at it and handed it to Hall: 'Deal with it, would you?'

The code and cipher books were held under lock and key in the purser's cabin. It took Hall just fifteen minutes to decode the signal and when he returned to the bridge it was in triumph: 'Is the captain in his cabin? Admiralty orders. We are to finish the journey alone at the best speed we can make.'

His fingers were drumming excitedly on the polished brass telegraph as if he were itching to push it forward from slow through half to full speed ahead.

'We are to alter course at sunset. Should cut at least a week off the voyage.'

'If we get there,' said Murray coolly.

Later, something of the same thought could be read in the faces of the passengers crowding the rail as the sun dipped behind the convoy. At eight bells the *Imperial Star* turned out of the column and her decks began to tremble as she gathered speed to the south and the dark horizon, churning a white fan of water in her wake. Third Officer Hall could almost feel the ship stretching as if waking from sleep. The watch changed as always, the ladies still dressed for dinner, the sheets were turned down in the first-class cabins and drinks served in the bar. But there was a new urgency and a new purpose to every action. And the atmosphere in the passenger saloons crackled like an old wireless, the conversation hushed and anxious. For once the top of the old gramophone was closed, the scratched seventy-eight of Vera Lynn's 'Yours' lying on its torn green sleeve beside it.

38

The Military Police hut was cold and damp and smelt of diesel. Its rough walls were little more than a shelter from the Lakeland weather. But it was well placed at the edge of the woodland in front of Stapley Hall, secure between the belts of wire, quiet and hidden from the watchful eyes of the Ältestenrat. Lindsay began with the officers of the *U-112*, the Nazi roughnecks, Bruns and Koch, as sullen and aggressively silent as they had been at Trent Park. The first officer, Gretschel, decent but clever and disciplined, was not to be tempted into unguarded confidences. He was restless, uncomfortable, playing with his cigarettes, and there was a slight contraction of his pupils when he was asked about the bruises on Heine's face, but he refused to do more than repeat the statement he had given the Military Police. And the young midshipman, Bischoff, was grim and fixed-jawed, afraid lest he forget his well-rehearsed lines:

'I only spoke to Leutnant Heine a couple of times in the days before he died. He was very upset, he hated being a prisoner. Footsteps, lights, a banging door, almost anything seemed to set him off.'

Lindsay asked Bischoff about the bruises but he refused to say any more or look him in the eye. Bischoff could be broken in time and in a different place. His relief when the guard came to take him away was almost tangible. Lindsay stepped outside the hut with a cigarette to watch the soldiers shepherd him along the fence. He had given the sergeant instructions to observe Bischoff closely when he joined the other prisoners. It was Bruns who found him first, placing a reassuring arm about his shoulders – at least that was how the gesture appeared to the sergeant from the other side of the wire.

The other naval officers presented the same story. Heine's death was a surprise. How could it have happened? The commander of the 500, Fischer, said he should have done more to help the dead man come to terms with being a prisoner. Richter, his engineer, felt keenly responsible. He knew Heine's mindset and how it was tormented by the loss of the *112*.

'He was ill. A sort of combat sickness and haunted by the thought that he had failed.'

'Failed?' Lindsay had asked.

'He thought he could have done more to save the boat.'

All the prisoners were lying. He had expected them to. After two tobacco-fuelled days gently probing, Lindsay was left with the overwhelming impression of evasion and fear. Lieutenant Duncan sat in on the first day's interrogations. His German was not strong enough to follow the interviews closely but he was a canny judge and he could sense the prisoners' fear too. At the end of the second day, he visited Lindsay again: 'He was murdered, wasn't he?'

'Perhaps.'

'You haven't seen Mohr yet?'

'No.'

Lindsay pulled the door of the hut to and stepped out from beneath the shade of the surrounding trees into the evening sunshine. He stood there soaking it in through every pore, a light breeze ruffling his hair.

'I'll see Lange and Schmidt and Mohr tomorrow. I want to talk to them in the washroom where he died.'

Duncan raised his eyebrows: 'Why?'

'Why use the washroom or why those three prisoners?'

'Both.'

Lindsay shrugged. He had resisted the temptation to speak to Lange first in order to protect him but he was still the best hope for some sort of insight into the whole business. And Schmidt had admitted responsibility for the bruises to Lange's face. His story about a fight was clearly a lie – that made him vulnerable. But Lange, Schmidt, the sad sordid death of Heine, they were the levers, the means by which to prise open the end that was Jürgen Mohr.

'Instinct, just a feeling,' Lindsay said. 'And perhaps the set will help with the performance.'

'It's just down the corridor from the prisoners' kitchen so it'll be difficult to secure,' Duncan sounded sceptical. 'They will all have to use Washroom B. I don't think Major Benson will be happy.'

They began crunching down the gravel carriageway towards the officers' mess. Lindsay would have preferred to stretch out on his bed with a book in the room he had taken above the village pub but he was making an effort to be friendly with the camp's officers. Duncan was good company, if a little nosy, but some of the others were boorish in a regular military way. He had already spent an uncomfortable evening deflecting questions about his business at the camp and the DSC ribbon on his uniform jacket.

'You know, none of the prisoners seemed surprised to see you,' said Duncan. 'Didn't that strike you as strange? They were told the investigation was over, now that we've buried Heine.'

'Mohr knows we're interested in him. They were expecting me or someone like me.'

The orderly behind the mess bar mixed Lindsay a pink gin and then another. He was considering a third when a sergeant approached him with a message. Someone from the Navy called Dr Henderson had phoned and asked him to ring back at once.

'Is there a phone I can use here?' he asked Duncan.

'I'll show you,' and he ground his cigarette stub into an ashtray.

But Major Benson had seen them from the door and was making his way quickly towards them.

'No, please. Let me buy you one,' he said with a warmth Lindsay thought owed more to the prospect of the drink than to the pleasure of his company.

'I see you've picked up some bad habits in the Navy,' he said, pointing to Lindsay's glass.

They sat at a table close to the mess's only window, from where there was a view across the broken woodland to the rough sheep pastures of the valley below.

'So, it's been a fruitless visit.' There was something close to a sneer in Benson's voice. Lindsay glanced at Duncan who pulled an apologetic face.

'No, sir.'

Benson ignored him: 'The Military Police did their job pretty well.'

'Yes, sir.'

The camp commandant wanted to know how much longer

Lindsay expected to be there. What did Naval Intelligence hope to find? Kapitän Mohr was a fine man and they understood each other well. Another drink? His hand shook a little as he raised his glass to his lips. And then he was back on the beaches at Dunkirk, lost among the abandoned lorries, the choking oil-black smoke, the helpless and the dying. And the Navy should have done better. Another?

By the time Lindsay was able to excuse himself, night had crept up the valley to the camp. He had missed supper and was now quite drunk. A corporal ran him down the road to the village pub. It was only as he was undressing in the little bedroom under the eaves that he remembered the message to ring Mary but it was too late and it was as much as he could do to collapse into bed.

He slept badly and woke with a start at three o'clock, his sheets clammy and cold. And when he closed his eyes again he slipped back into the confused grey half-world of the ship. Mary was there too. She was standing on the quarterdeck, the sea washing about her bare legs. And she was shouting something; he could hear the panic in her voice, but the wind whipped the words from him. Then she began pointing frantically over the side and he turned to the rail and looked down. August Heine was looking back at him, eyes wide and bloodshot, his blue face bloated and shining, the rope-marks raw and angry about his neck.

At six o'clock he got up to smoke a cigarette by the window. A thin drizzle of mist was hanging halfway up the valley sides, the sun still low and yellow above the eastern hills. A tractor roared down the road with a weatherbeaten farmer at the wheel, his collies perched precariously on either side. In a few hours he would interview Mohr. There was nothing he could accuse him of, no questions Mohr would be prepared to answer, but he would be required to stand in front of the table and he would know that the pursuit was beginning once again. Lindsay looked down into the village street and smiled quietly with something close to pleasure at the thought.

Lieutenant Duncan sat shivering behind his desk in only his shirt and trousers. His tiny office was only a few steps from the mess where he had taken a skinful the night before, a damp, cold shoebox of a room with flaking plaster walls. His thick head was not improved at six o'clock in the morning by the stiff rattle of his old typewriter. He ripped the page from the restraining bar and read it through:

> . . . *Lindsay intends to question Lieutenant Lange and Captain Mohr today and has made it clear he would like to conduct both interrogations on his own. He is particularly interested in the propaganda reporter's, position in the camp. I believe he is the German officer you referred to in your briefing.*

Duncan paused. He quite liked Lindsay. A little reserved, perhaps, a bit prickly about his past and his family but he seemed straight enough. What had the man done to warrant such close scrutiny? He reached for his mug of tea – it was cold already.

> . . . *he will not be drawn into debate about the war and Germany. Nor is he prepared to say why a Naval Intelligence officer should be so interested in the death of a prisoner* . . .

The Security Service had demanded that he thrash out this report himself. There were to be no copies and he was to keep his watching brief on Lindsay secret from Major Benson. Duncan had met Gilbert from Five once, and for twenty minutes only, but it had been long enough to convince him that the Colonel was a ruthless bastard – cool in a very Eton, Oxford and the Guards sort of way and comfortable in his half-world of secrets and lies.

> . . . *as yet there is no evidence to suggest Lindsay is communicating with the prisoners on any subject other than the death of Heine and other related intelligence matters but to be present at all times would arouse suspicion. It is possible notes have been exchanged in my absence. The prisoners are searched after leaving interrogations. We have conducted a thorough search of Lieutenant Lindsay's room and belongings but have found nothing* . . .

'Despatch.'

The office door opened with a stiff military jerk and a burly-looking military policeman stepped across the threshold.

'Get this off at once, Corporal.'

39

At one end of the rectangular washroom there were two rows of handbasins with cracked and stained mirrors above; the shower cubicles and latrines were at the other end. Heine's pipe ran across the ceiling between the two, cast iron, six inches in diameter and painted a muddy green. Lindsay had the table and chairs placed beneath it.

'Sit down, Helmut.'

Leutnant Lange looked crumpled and grey and anxious.

'Here?' He glanced up at the pipe.

'Yes. Here.'

Lindsay pushed a packet of cigarettes across the table to him: 'Help yourself.'

He waited as Lange took one, lit it and drew in a comforting lungful of smoke.

'You look tired, Helmut. 'You know why I'm here, of course. You knew Leutnant Heine well . . .'

'Not well.' He wriggled his shoulders uncomfortably.

'You shared a room at the interrogation centre, you knew him better than most. Tell me what you know.'

'He was depressed. He hated being a prisoner. He was sure he'd failed his comrades and his commander. No one could talk to him.'

It was the same short story in choppy insincere sentences and they were contradicted even as they were spoken by Lange's restless body language.

Lindsay stared at him, slowly turning his lighter over and over in his right hand, trying to catch and hold his eye. He failed.

'Do you think they would hang you from this pipe if you told me the truth?'

Lange looked up for a second: 'I . . . I . . .'

Then he changed his mind and hunched forward over the table, his hands twisting in his lap.

'You know I'll protect you.'

The propaganda reporter made a noise in his throat that was something between a grunt and a hollow laugh, rather like the neighing of an asthmatic horse.

Lindsay picked up his cigarettes and shook one from the packet. He was on the point of lighting it when his hand stopped and he lifted his head to look at Lange again: 'Why did you tell Kapitän Mohr that I had taken you to a jazz club? It made things very difficult for me.'

'I . . . I'm sorry.' Lange was looking at him now and there was a very pained expression on his open face. 'I know I shouldn't have.'

'It was unfortunate.'

'I'm sorry, Lieutenant, really I am.'

Lindsay shook his head, 'All right, we're friends. Forget it.'

Neither of them spoke and their eyes met for a moment before Lange looked down in embarrassment. Then he took a deep breath: 'Perhaps he did kill himself – in the end. Perhaps. But it was murder.'

Lange closed his eyes for a moment and rubbed his lips with the back of a shaking hand. A tap was dripping into a cistern close by, drip, drip, drip, the echo bouncing off the hard wet walls of the washroom.

'Senseless bloody murder. He was found guilty of treason by the Council of Honour, you see.'

'The Council of Honour?'

'Yes.'

He had to drag the words out of himself, his body rocking to and fro on the chair. 'The Ältestenrat discovered he'd given information to the enemy.'

'To me?'

'Yes.'

The pipes above them clanked as they flooded with hot water.

'And the bruises?'

'He was interrogated.' Lange sighed – his breath long and shaky – then covered his face with his hands like a child hiding from an angry parent.

'You were there?'

He nodded without moving his hands from his face.

'And others?' Lindsay's voice was barely more than a whisper.

And he nodded again.

'Who?'

Lange dropped his hands and there were tears on his face: 'It was my fault.'

'Who beat him?'

'I . . . I can't say.'

'Schmidt?'

'I . . . can't . . .'

'Did Mohr know about it?'

'God forgive me. It was my fault,' and he threw his head back and groaned long and loud, until the walls and pipes beat it back hollow and despairing. Lindsay got up and walked round the table to put a comforting hand on his shoulder. Lange reached up to touch it: 'Thank you.'

Almost a minute passed before Lindsay spoke again, his hand still on Lange's shoulder: 'Did Mohr authorise this Council of Honour?'

'No,' Lange shouted the word. 'No . . . I don't know, I can't say.' He placed his elbows on the table and pushed himself upright, then wiped his eyes with the back of his hand. 'They don't trust me you see. If I say anything more I will be a dead man.'

'I've told you, we'll protect you. Isn't it your duty? Your duty to all I know you believe in – that you still hold dear.'

Lange's body stiffened and he shrugged Lindsay's hand from his shoulder.

'Don't talk to me of my duty, of my faith,' and his words rasped like grinding metal. 'Don't. You don't care if I live or die.'

The silence filled again with the clanking of the pipes. Lindsay stepped away and walked round the table to look down at him. Lange lifted his chin a little, his jaw firmly set, his eyes almost lost beneath a heavy frown: 'Heine means nothing to you, does he?'

'If he was murdered, yes he does.'

'I don't know if he was murdered. I have nothing more to say.'

Lindsay pulled out the chair, its legs grating harshly across the stone floor, and leant on the back of it to look at him across the table:

'All right Helmut. You decide. You said it was your fault. Think about it. We'll leave it – for now.'

256

Then he half turned to shout at the door. A moment later Lieutenant Duncan came in with the guard, peaked cap neatly tucked under his arm. He stood at the table and watched as Lange was led from the washroom.

'Any joy?'

'Some.'

'I've been asked to deliver this,' and he pulled a small grey envelope from his pocket. 'The office received it this morning, something from your lot.'

Lindsay took it and tore open the sleeve.

'I think Schmidt will be a waste of time,' he said. 'I'll see Mohr next.'

It was written in the camp secretary's fine hand:

A Dr Henderson rang from the Admiralty. She wanted to speak to you in person but I said you would be busy all morning. She said she had sad news. Your cousin's ship has been sunk and there are no survivors. Your family has been informed. Major Benson has asked me to pass on his condolences.

A. B. P.

Lindsay stared at it blankly for a few seconds. What was he supposed to feel? For a time they had done everything together, like brothers. It was Martin who had taught him to sail and Martin who had introduced him to his first girlfriend. They shared the same dark sense of humour, the same shoe size, the same taste in music, and they had enjoyed taking risks together. And now he was dead, lost in the Atlantic like thousands of others. And he could feel only a deep grey emptiness like the ocean itself. God. What was left but pain and loss?

'Is something the matter?' It was Duncan.

'Yes.'

Lindsay glanced up, then handed him the note. Duncan looked at it carefully and when he had read it he folded it gently in two:

'I'm sorry.' He cleared his throat nervously: 'It's a war crime, a bloody war crime.'

'What?'

'The U-boats. The attack on our merchant ships.'

Lindsay felt an urge to laugh. Instead he looked away, an angry knot in his stomach. Shafts of sunlight were streaming through a high window on to the wall at the end of the washroom, bleaching the colour from the blue-grey tiles. And then the room was plunged into shadow again.

'Shall I tell them to take Mohr back?'

'No. I'll see him now.'

'Are you surprised to see me, Mohr?'

Kapitän zur See Jürgen Mohr raised his dark eyebrows and his lips twitched in a small smile: 'No. I've been looking forward to talking to you again, Lieutenant.'

He was standing in front of the table. The guard had removed the other chair. 'But couldn't we have met somewhere pleasanter than the shithouse?'

Lindsay glanced up at the pipe above their heads and Mohr followed his eyes: 'Terrible,' and he shook his head a little. 'And it was terrible news about the 330. No survivors. Oh, you're surprised? You shouldn't be. Your BBC has been gloating about the sinking for nearly twenty-four hours.'

Lindsay stared at him coldly. 'Isn't the BBC propaganda?'

'We sort the truth from the fiction,' he said with a smile. 'The 330 was a fine boat. You should be proud of Schultze. He died with honour for his Führer and Fatherland – they all did.'

'Honour?' Lindsay almost spat the word at him. Leaning forward to the table, he flipped open the brown cardboard file that was lying in front of him, then slid it towards Mohr. 'And was this for Führer and Fatherland too?'

Mohr glanced down at the swollen blue face of Heine, his tongue hanging obscenely from his mouth.

'No. Take a good look, Herr Kapitän,' Lindsay snapped.

Without taking his eyes off him, Mohr reached across the table for the picture, lifted it deliberately and looked at it again. And for a fleeting moment his expression changed as he struggled to maintain his composure, his weathered face cut by lines of pain and regret.

'Poor man.'

In an effort to disguise his feelings he casually tossed the picture back on to the table, sending it spinning towards Lindsay.

'The sinking of our boat. The humiliation. And prison drives men to terrible things.'

'Spare me the lies. You pushed him very hard, didn't you?'

'Pushed him?'

'You interrogated him. You interrogated a number of the prisoners. The evening with the PK man at the jazz café – remember?'

Mohr smiled: 'Leutnant Lange is fond of the story, he tells it to everyone.'

Lindsay lifted his hand and rested it on the thick file in front of him: 'I've spoken to the other U-boat officers and I know the Ältestenrat wanted to know what they'd said to us. You were looking for someone who gave away just a little too much and you thought you'd found him – Heine. But this . . .'

He pushed the picture back across the table: 'You authorised this senseless killing, this murder.'

'Is this going to go on much longer? Perhaps I can have a chair?' There was an impatient, contemptuous note in Mohr's voice and he turned to look at the guard who was standing stiffly to attention at the far wall.

'A chair, please,' he shouted in English. The soldier did not move a muscle.

'Well?'

The guard just stared back at him belligerently.

'You're a prisoner, Mohr,' said Lindsay coolly. 'Remember?'

Mohr flinched as if the words had stung him between the shoulders and he turned quickly to face Lindsay, his boots squeaking sharply on the stone floor. Was it the affront to his dignity? Something inside him seemed to snap. 'You're the murderer, Lieutenant. You drove him to it.'

Mohr didn't shout or thump the table, his voice was only a little louder but his face was livid and blotchy red and there were anxious scratch marks on his throat, a sort of wildness in his eyes. The quiet military veneer had cracked for the first time.

'You interrogated Heine, you threatened him. He told me you were going to tell me he was a traitor. He was a vulnerable prisoner. His mind was clouded – he was sure he'd betrayed his U-boat comrades and his country. He could not live with the guilt and he took his own life. So you put the rope around his neck, Lieutenant, you did – not me.'

Mohr looked down at the photograph still lying in the middle of the table between them and his shoulders seemed to drop a little as if the anger was draining from him. When he spoke again his voice was cool and reflective: 'Heine was a casualty of your war.'

And he lifted his head to make firm eye contact with Lindsay: 'Our war. The dirty little war we're fighting.'

Their dirty war. The thought beat long after Mohr had been led away. It was beating in the mess over lunch and in the camp commandant's office as Lindsay said goodbye to smug, self-satisfied Benson. It was beating in his head now as the jeep swung him backwards and forwards along country lanes to the station. Was it dirtier than the one being fought in the Atlantic? Perhaps Mohr had become the demon he was fighting inside himself. But it was the same war, it was cold, it was ruthless, and to the victor the spoils – there were always casualties.

AUGUST 1941

TOP SECRET:
Characteristics of an Interrogator
A breaker is born and not made. Perhaps the first-class
breaker has yet to be born. Perhaps he has yet to be
recruited from the concentration camps, where he has
suffered for years, where, above all he has watched and
learnt in bitterness every move in the game.
**Lieut.-Col. Robin Stephens, Commandant of MI5's
Camp 020,
The Interrogation of Spies, 1940–47**

Top Secret 'C'
The security of a source is worth more than any product
or by-product, however spectacular.
**Admiralty NID 11
Assessment of German Prisoner of War
Interrogation, 1945**

40

U-115
06°54S/07°35W
South Atlantic

The last of the sun was settling into the ocean behind the ship, painting her high funnel and masts an eerie tropical orange. She was an old liner of more than twelve thousand tons, perhaps a troopship, zigzagging defensively in 40-degree turns. Hartmann adjusted the focus on the bridge's firing binoculars: 'Careless.'

Her deadlights were not pulled down over the ports and she was twinkling provocatively at the *115*.

'Have the crew eaten?'

'Yes, Herr Kaleu.'

'Good. She'll turn south-westerly and cross our course within the hour.'

The sea was building, a summer gale forecast. He would attack from the surface, the dark grey hull of the U-boat lost in the restless night.

The *U-115* had found her at a little before ten that morning. Her smoke was drifting in a long tail across the ragged tops of the ocean at the very edge of the horizon. A large ship, and where Kapitänleutnant Paul Hartmann expected to find her.

'Full ahead both engines. Course two-one-zero.'

The deck beneath Hartmann's feet had trembled, the diesels hammering their battle song as the U-boat plunged forwards at attack speed, its bow rising in fine clouds of spray that swept across the foredeck and into the faces of the men atop the tower. Urgent, incessant, beating the length of the boat, from the crew quarters aft to the forward torpedo room, and every man's heart beat with the engines, faster and faster and faster, an end to the poor hunting, an end to idle days of African sunshine. And the excitement had been plain in the faces of the watch and of the men squinting at the horizon from the rail of the gun platform, older than their years, weathered and lined by the sea and the tropical sun, their beards flecked white with salt. It was Hartmann's first patrol as their commander but they knew of his record, that he had served with one of the great U-boat heroes – with Kapitän Mohr.

He had followed the wisp of grey smoke through the bridge's firing binoculars until his eyes began to water and late in the afternoon he sent a signal to U-boat Headquarters:

TARGET LOCATED GRID SQUARE FF 71. IN PURSUIT. NO ESCORT. COURSE SOUTH WEST. FOURTEEN KNOTS.

And headquarters had replied:

AT THEM. ATTACK THEM. SINK THEM.

He had smiled quietly to himself because he knew it must have been written by the Admiral. It was pure Dönitz.

'Tubes one and three ready?'

'Tubes one and three ready, Herr Kaleu.'

'She's turned. Steering 200 degrees, approximately twelve knots.'

Yes, she was a big ship, close to 20,000 tons, roughly camouflaged in grey, deck guns fore and aft and a watch searching the dark surface of the sea for an enemy bow wave.

'Take her hull down.'

The order was repeated to the control room below and as the waist tanks of the submarine flooded the sea swept up the foredeck until only the tower was breaking the waves. They would catch the ship just before she turned again, broadside on, in – he glanced at his watch – perhaps six minutes.

'Half engines.'

He could sense the intense excitement of the men about him, as they turned stiffly through the points of the compass, their glasses hunting the darkness for escort ships. He bent to the voice tube:

'Stand by tubes one and three.'

In the 'cave' for'ard, the torpedo men would be clutching their stopwatches, ready to count out the seconds from release to impact. Anything between a thousand and three hundred metres would do. She was edging into the spider lines of Hartmann's firing sight now, rising and falling gracefully in the swell, her bow cutting a crisp white wave. And as he followed her stately progress the heavy night cloud parted, catching her in silhouette against a bright sickle moon.

'Twelve hundred metres.'

He could see sailors moving about her foredeck. There was a small yellow flash of light – one of them must have lit a cigarette.

'A thousand metres.'

He heard a sharp intake of breath at his side and his heart leapt into his throat. Was she beginning to turn?

'Steady, steady, there's still time.'

Final bearing check, final distance check, and with his eyes still on the target he reached for the firing handle and pressed down with the full weight of his body.

'Tube one: fire!'

The first torpedo was on its way.

'Ready tube three: fire!'

And the second in its wake. Steel fish they called them for'ard, seven metres long, contact detonation and enough explosive to blow a hole in the side of the ship a bus could drive through.

'Hard rudder right.'

The 115 began to turn sharply away but Hartmann's eyes didn't leave the ship.

'Two minutes. One minute. Thirty seconds. Twenty seconds. Ten.'

Had he made a mistake? No. A hard little explosion, a column of white smoke and water rising like a glorious fountain up her side and cheering, he could hear the men cheering in the control room below. Thank God. Then the second torpedo burst through her plates and almost at once she began to heel to starboard. It was a small miracle. Twenty thousand tons of steel and wood brought to a standstill in seconds. The first torpedo must have struck her amidships in the hold – he could see the ragged hole in her side – and the second in or close to the engine room. A cold inexorable tide of water surging into her hull: the ship was surely doomed. He lifted his head from the glasses and leant over the tower hatch.

'Has she given her name yet?'

'No, Herr Kaleu.' It was his first officer, Werner. 'Will she need a third?'

'No, she's finished. Let's take the boat a little closer and pick up her captain if we can.'

'Perhaps we've bagged a regiment of British soldiers with two torpedoes.'

'Perhaps.'

The sea was still building, the weather turning for the worse and with the ship listing heavily, swinging out and filling the lifeboats would be no easy task. But he could see the first of them slipping slowly down her side. There was the urgent ring of boots on the tower ladder behind him and he turned to find the chief wireless operator climbing on to the bridge, his signal board in hand.

'Well, Weber?'

'The liner's sent a distress signal, Herr Kaleu. SSS. 06.54° south, 7.35° west. She's the *Imperial Star*. Lloyd's lists her as 18, 480 tons, built in 1913.'

'Damn them.'

If the British picked up 'SSS' they would know the ship had been torpedoed and would assume the enemy submarine was still close by.

'All right. Ready tube two. Let's send her on her way.'

41

It clattered off a printer in Room 29 at the Citadel with the rest of the rip-and-read, no more, no less significant to the secret ladies than any of the other signals. It dropped into the duty officer's tray in the tough hours of the middle watch between three and four o'clock, when the brain swirls like sea mist. And Lieutenant Freddie Wilmot considered it for a minute or two before leaning over the plot table to press a shiny new black pin into the Atlantic. Another ship lost – eight were reported that night – but a definite fix on the *U-115*. Then he clipped the piece of flimsy signal paper to his board and moved on.

And it was still on his board when Mary Henderson stepped through the door of the Tracking Room at a little after seven that morning. Winn's hat and coat were already hanging on a hook and she turned to look at his office. He was bent over his desk, his back towards her, smoke curling through his fingers, preoccupied with the night's traffic. A grey and bleary-eyed Wilmot was talking to one of the Wren plotters in front of the German grid map that hung on the wall at the far end of the room. The U-boat gave its position in signals at sea as a lettered and numbered square on the map. Somehow – Mary was not sure how or when – the Division had acquired its own copy. Two of the clerical assistants were perched on the edge of their desks enjoying a few precious minutes of calm and conversation that was nothing to do with convoys or casualties or the deadlines of the day. It would be another hour before the first visitor, before the ringing of the telephones and the clatter of the typewriters and teleprinters reached its customary infernal pitch. Time enough for breakfast. Mary glanced guiltily at her desk where a bundle of signals and reports was sitting at the top of the in-tray. But her stomach was urging her in a most unladylike manner, much to the sly amusement of the clerical assistants.

'The needs of the flesh, Dr Henderson.'

'Yes I'm sure you're quite an authority, Joan,' she replied. 'If Commander Winn asks, I'll be back at my desk in twenty minutes.'

The queue at the Admiralty canteen was painfully slow and Mary was obliged to bolt her too thinly buttered toast and abandon her tea, although its hard tannic taste was with her until lunch-time. The frantic dash back to the Citadel and through the traffic in its narrow corridors left her feeling a little nauseous. Winn was standing by her desk, his head bent in concentration, shoulders hunched, arms tightly folded, a brooding presence. She had seen him like that a hundred times and yet she sensed there was something wrong today. He was wrestling with some great emotion, anger or perhaps pain. And there was a strange hush in the room, the plotters whispering at the back wall, the trilling of a single telephone. Wilmot was perched on a desk close by, anxiously biting the quick of a nail. He shook his head a little as Mary approached the desk and cast a warning glance at Winn's back. But Winn heard the squeak of her shoes on the linoleum floor:

'You were at breakfast . . .' He did not turn to face her '. . . and Lieutenant Wilmot was keeping it to himself.'

'But Rodger . . .'

Winn waved a hand to silence him: 'The Germans have sunk the *Imperial Star*.' He took two stiff steps towards the plot and pointed to the little pin with *U-115* on its head just off the coast of West Africa: 'Here.'

The *Imperial Star*. Mary felt a tight lump in her throat. She covered her mouth with her hand and for a moment she was sure she was going to be sick. Those poor people. Oh God: 'I'm . . . sorry . . . its my fault . . .'

That was all she could stammer, a few words of regret, but she knew if she tried to say more she would be lost. The rest, the questions, the explanations, the excuses caught in her throat, choking inarticulate guilt. She licked a salty drop from her lip then quickly wiped the rest from her face with the back of her hand.

'Sorry . . .'

But Winn's hand was at her elbow now: 'Come with me. Can you arrange some tea, Freddie?'

And she allowed him to guide her gently from the plot and round the desks into his office.

'What an exhibition. I'm sorry, Rodger,' she said after a moment.

'No need to apologise. It hurts. But remember, it was my decision in the end.' He shook a cigarette from a packet and lit it with an angry snap of his lighter.

'How can you do this job without the comfort of tobacco?'

'But you asked me to check her course . . .'

'And you did and there was nothing to suggest she was going to be in any danger,' he said firmly. 'Here,' and he pushed the flimsy signal paper he had rescued from Wilmot's board across the table to her. Special decrypt message from Station X, number 206/T85.

TOP SECRET U
CX/MSS/T18/206
TOO 08/2130Z/08/41 ZZZ

SUNK IMPERIAL STAR. TOTAL 18, 500 TONS. GRID
SQUARE FF 71. SURVIVORS IN BOATS. COURSE NORTH
WEST.

It was an immediate priority – ZZZ – signal from U-boat to head-quarters where no doubt it was a source of much rejoicing.

'And is there . . .' Mary's voice cracked a little, '. . . is there any news of the survivors?'

Winn shook his head then picked up a piece of paper from the desk in front of him: 'Two or three families, fifty nurses, some RAF mechanics – specialists – thirty or so, 250 Army and Navy personnel, more than three hundred crew members with the ship's gunners, and the cargo – aircraft parts and some ammunition. The RAF at Ascension is searching the area . . .'

He hesitated and glanced down at his desk as if to prepare Mary for distressing news and she felt the tight lump rise into her throat again.

'I'm afraid no one picked up her distress signal and it was some time before they began the search . . . The weather was pretty bad. But they're still looking . . .'

Mary's hand was at her mouth, her bottom lip was trembling. She let her hand drop to her skirt and digging her nails into the brown wool she pinched her thigh until her eyes watered with the pain.

'Are you all right?' Winn asked.

'Yes.'

'We made the right decision with the intelligence we had on U-boat movements at the time. It's not the first mistake we've made, Mary, and it won't be the last . . . still . . .'

Pulling his small black-framed glasses from his face he placed them carefully on the desk, closed his eyes and pinched the bridge of his nose thoughtfully. The smoke from his cigarette was curling up lazily from a glass ashtray and over the desk like a burnt offering before a temple Buddha. Mary sat and watched him lost in thought and the noise of telephones and raised voices in the Tracking Room filled the little office.

'You know, we've had this sort of coincidence before and we've always dismissed it as cruel luck . . .' His eyes were still closed, his face crumpled in a frown. 'And perhaps it is, but I think we need to investigate this a little more . . .' He reached for the last of his cigarettes.

'The *Imperial Star* left the convoy on 31 July on her own course and was making good progress, travelling at something like fifteen knots. She maintained total wireless silence. The *U-115* – the only enemy submarine south of the equator as far as we know – sank her six days later. Now the U-boat would not have had the fuel to follow her at that sort of speed for long, it must have come upon her almost at once. Imagine, many thousands of square miles of ocean – what sort of odds would you get on that happening? Unless . . .'

He picked up his glasses and slid them back on his nose with his forefinger.

'Unless of course the U-boat knew where to find her . . .'

Mary leant forward, her right hand gripping the edge of his desk: 'Do you believe that?'

'I don't believe anything until we've checked all we have on the *U-115*'s movements and been through the special intelligence for July and August. And we must speak to the Naval Section at Bletchley.'

Slowly, deliberately, he ground the last of his cigarette in the ashtray. The restless hum of activity from the Tracking Room washed into his office again. It was after eight and Hall from Trade would be with them soon. At nine there was the telephone conference with the Staff at Western Approaches in Liverpool.

'We're looking for anything that might suggest U-boat Headquarters knew the *Imperial Star* was leaving the convoy on an independent course. Then see if you can find a list of ships travelling alone that have been attacked by the enemy. Anything in the last three months that strikes you as strange.'

Mary was a little irritated by Winn's cool, detached tone, as if it was some sort of academic exercise. So many lives were at stake, like those poor people in the *Imperial Star*'s boats. But she knew she was excited too. It reminded her of how she had once felt in a muddy hole in Wiltshire when, after crawling down a tunnel, her torch had flashed round a stone chamber hidden for thousands of years.

'Please be discreet.' Winn must have read the excitement in her face. 'Perhaps it was an appalling twist of fate, just the worst sort of coincidence, so we don't want to cause a general panic – not yet anyway.'

Her lips twitched with amusement, a provocative little smile she was sure he would not be able to resist.

'I know why you're smiling: you're thinking of Lieutenant Lindsay.'

'Yes.'

'Don't. This must stay inside the Citadel. If our codes are compromised then he may be able to help us but it's too soon to say.'

'And Mohr?'

'Well, he isn't begging to tell his story, is he?'

There was a polite knock at the office door. It was Freddie Wilmot with some tea. A large, ruddy, genial-looking regular was standing behind him – Commander Dick Hall of the Trade Division.

'One of the clerical assistants can help you, Mary. Hawkins seems bright enough. I'm sorry about the tea. I expect it's cold by now anyway,' and he shot Wilmot an unfriendly look.

Mary got to her feet and was on the point of turning to leave when he leant forward a little and said in a confidential voice: 'And you? Are you all right? You've been working very hard . . .'

It was a little late and a little clumsy but well meant and Mary smiled warmly at him: 'No harder than anyone else. I'm fine now, Rodger, really.'

'Good.'

Mary left him to the business of the day, U-boats gathering for a pack attack, a convoy sailing into danger, the battle fought hour by hour in the Atlantic, and as she watched him at the plot with Hall she felt something close to gratitude, even affection. She felt embarrassed too, cross with herself for losing control of her feelings. Own up to the loss, yes, acknowledge some responsibility, yes, but fight on, fight on. If she was not able to keep a cool head in the face of adversity she was no use to anyone. This was her life now, her mission.

'All right, Hawkins. I want every signal sent by U-boat Headquarters since the beginning of May.'

'Dr Henderson?'

'And I want them now.'

At a little after midday the Germans broadcast a crowing report on the sinking of 'a troopship' called *Imperial Star*. There was no mention of the survivors. Winn sent Geoff Childs to tell her.

'*Schrecklichkeit.*'

'What do you mean, Geoff?'

'A terror sinking, don't you think? Beastly Huns – it was the same in the First War – only the uniforms have changed.'

By then Mary had worked her way through two days of decrypted signals and found nothing. But Joan Hawkins was busy collecting more and Trade was pulling together a list of the independently routed ships sunk that summer. Then at six o'clock in the evening Winn came to see her with news that a lifeboat had been found more than two hundred miles from the last known position of the ship.

'Thirty-eight people, four women and two children.'

'And do they think there's a chance of finding more?'

Winn shook his head. They stood in silence for a few seconds, unable to look each other in the eye, then he gave a wry smile:

'Oh and I forgot to tell you, the Ministry of Shipping have complained to the Director. The minister wants to know why such an important ship was permitted to sail alone, unescorted, beyond the protection of a convoy.'

There was nothing to report at seven o'clock and nothing at eight and by nine Mary was convinced she must have missed something and would have to begin again. Joan Hawkins's slight shoulders were bent over a desk, her head resting in her hands, her hair an unruly curtain in front of her face.

'Go home, Joan.'

She looked up at Mary and the loose brown curls fell away to reveal a pretty elfin face and dark eyes, rheumy with fatigue and the smoke that hung in a pall over the room.

'We'll begin again tomorrow. Leave that with me.' Mary nodded to the file of signal flimsies between her elbows. 'And thank you, Joan.'

By ten o'clock she was reading the broken sentences on the signal paper as if through the bottom of a bottle, the convoy numbers distant and opaque. After staring blankly at a signal for five minutes she resolved to finish the file in front of her and go to bed. The rest – there were four more on Hawkins's desk – would have to wait until the morning. She smoothed the folds from her skirt, then, getting to her feet, raised herself on tiptoe and stretched her arms above her head, enjoying the sense of feeling flowing slowly back into her body.

'You need some help.' Rodger Winn was closing the door of his office. 'I'll ask Scholey and Childs to join you tomorrow.'

He walked over to the coat rack and lifted his mac from a hook: 'Bletchley are looking into this for us. It will be a day or so before we hear anything.'

Winn left and she settled to her last batch of signals for the day. But she had read only a couple when, with a small pointed cough, he announced that he was back and standing at her shoulder.

'You made me jump.'

'I'm sorry but I thought you'd like to know Lieutenant Lindsay is looking for you. I found him in the corridor.' There was a studied coolness in his voice that left her in no doubt of his disapproval. 'It would be better if you went to him. You'll find him at the entrance to the Admiralty.'

'I see.'

'Good night then,' and after nodding to the night duty officer he shuffled out of the room.

Lindsay was waiting for her in the Mall, his shoulder against the peeling grey-green trunk of a plane tree, an evil-smelling cigarette between his fingers. It was a pleasant evening, the sky a deep indigo and in the gentlest of breezes the late summer scent of cedar and pine. And for just a moment – the taxis racing under Admiralty Arch, a theatre party laughing on the steps beneath the Duke of York – it was possible to forget the *Imperial Star* and the concrete walls of the Citadel where it always felt like winter.

'Kiss me.'

'You found me.' He flicked his cigarette into the gutter then wrapped his arms around her.

'Winn told me you were here,' she said a short time later, her head resting against his shoulder.

'Yes. He caught me in the corridor outside the Tracking Room. It was after ten so I'd assumed he'd left. He wasn't pleased to see me.'

'I'm sorry about your cousin. I know you were very close.'

She felt his body tense.

'Yes.'

'How is your mother?'

'Of course, she's upset too.'

To pre-empt more questions he bent his head to kiss her.

'I haven't seen you for ten days,' he said when they broke apart at last.

'I've been counting too. Did you get anything from Mohr?'

He shook his head: 'But I have something to work on.' And he told her of the bruises on Heine's face and the Court of Honour, of the fear he could sense in the camp at Stapley and of how carefully those he had spoken to had been schooled.

Then he took both Mary's hands and rested his forehead against hers: 'Will you come to my flat tonight?'

'I can't. I'm sorry. I do want to.'

He lifted his head sharply away from hers: 'But not enough.'

'I have to stay . . .'

'But I'm only five minutes walk from this place,' he said incredulously. 'For God's sake, we haven't seen each other for ten days. You don't need to sleep in the library too?'

She took half a step back and lifting a hand to her hair, ran her fingers slowly through it, tired and frustrated by his anger.

'Please?'

'I do need to sleep, Douglas. You don't understand there's something very important I have to do . . . a ship, the *Imperial Star* . . .'

She could not say more because a choking tide of sadness and regret began to well up from deep inside her, shaking her body, and it was so hard to contain. She turned quickly away from him to the Mall and gave a quiet little sob. But he must have heard her or seen her shoulders crumple.

'Darling, I'm sorry,' and he was behind her, holding her, kissing her hair and it was impossible, she knew she would surrender, and her chest began to heave with sobs that caught and trembled in her throat. Gently, he turned her to him and she pressed her cheek against his blue uniform jacket.

'Sorry,' she muttered. 'That's the second time today.'

And she told him about the *Imperial Star*, of six hundred men, women and children lost at sea. And he kissed the tears from her cheeks and wiped the corner of her eyes with his forefinger, then he kissed her neck and the palm of her right hand: 'I love you.'

'That's why I have to stay,' she said. 'I feel responsible.'

'It wasn't your fault. Of course it wasn't.'

'Perhaps it doesn't make sense but I feel responsible and I want to do my best to make sure it doesn't happen again. If our . . .'

She cursed herself for being so stupid.

'If our?'

'Never mind, it's something I'm working on but I don't want to talk about it now.'

Lindsay raised a knowing eyebrow: 'I see. And does this "thing" you are working on have anything to do with our codes?'

'I don't want to talk about it, Douglas, please don't press me.'

He must have recognised the weary note, the pleading in her voice, because he gave her hand a comforting squeeze: 'All right, but does this "thing" explain why Winn was so unwelcoming?'

'Perhaps,' she said with a shrug.

He frowned but only for a moment: 'Come here,' and he pulled her tightly to himself again and they stood in silence beneath the rustling canopy of the plane. From time to time a blackout taxi crept past in search of a fare and a night bus rattled under Admiralty Arch into

Trafalgar Square but the city seemed strangely empty and still. Mary was in danger of falling asleep on Linday's shoulder when after many minutes he spoke again: 'Will you tell me? Not now but later.'

'Why?' she asked, taken aback.

'You know why.'

She groaned wearily, 'Please.'

'Well?'

'. . . there is nothing to tell. Look, I have to go,' and she pulled away from him.

She was not going to be bullied and was too tired to think it through clearly. There was nothing yet to justify another breach of Winn's trust.

42

I t was Geoff Childs who turned up the signal and the ship. He had
set about the files with the relish of a natural archivist until two
fruitless days blunted even his determination and patience. But at a
little after two o'clock on the Saturday afternoon he let out a mighty
whoop of triumph that rang round the Tracking Room and the
corridor too. All heads swung towards him and for a moment there
was a stunned silence. He was half rising from his desk, still bent over
the slip of paper.

'It'd better be good, Geoff.'

He turned to look at Mary: 'I think it is.'

Lieutenant Childs was older than his thirty years, with a reputation
for being something of a dry stick, but he had taken off his glasses and
his eyes were shining with boyish enthusiasm.

'It's an old signal, sent from U-boat Headquarters to the *U-201*
on the sixth of May,' and he stepped out from behind his desk and
handed it to her:

1849/6/5 ACCORDING TO SAILING SCHEDULE SHIP
WILL BE IN GRID AK22 EAST BOUND AFTERNOON OF 7/5

'They must have got that sort of intelligence from our signals.'

His voice was husky with excitement and Mary felt guilty that she
was too tired and jaded to share it. A single scrap of rip-and-read was
not conclusive proof that the Navy's codes were compromised; the
intelligence could have come from a German spy or from a captured
document. And the reference to the 'shipping schedule' seemed a
little neat:

'Would U-boat Headquarters betray its source in a signal?'

Childs frowned, irritated by the scepticism in her voice: 'It's entirely
possible. The Germans believe Enigma is the cipher that cannot be
broken. Dönitz has no inkling we're reading his signals. Of course

that sort of intelligence should be need-to-know only but from time to time his people will make mistakes.'

Childs leant over his desk to check the Trade Division's report on shipping movements for the day: 'According to our records, the *Clan Innes* was at 60°45 North and 33°02 West at a little before four on the afternoon of the seventh of May – that would put her in grid square AK22.'

'All right, anything else sent on the seventh or eighth?'

Childs picked up a shabby brown cardboard file and shook it at her: 'If you want to know, help me look.'

And it was Mary who found the next signal. She held it in her right hand and the paper trembled as a tingle of excitement passed through her whole body. Childs was right; he had found something, something very important. For a few days in May, U-boat Headquarters had been very careless. It was an update on the progress of the freighter, *Clan Innes*:

1440/7/5 B REPORT. SHIP IN GRID AL14 ATTACK WITHOUT FURTHER ORDERS.

It left little room for doubt about the source – the B-Dienst. The Kriegsmarine's signals intelligence service was intercepting and reading British wireless traffic. She passed the signal to Childs who looked at it and at once began bouncing in his chair with a smile like a Cheshire cat on his face.

'What happened to the ship, Geoff?'

'Sunk the same day, the seventh of May.' He opened the Trade Division file on the desk in front of him and flicked through the reports until he found the one he was looking for. 'Here we are, *Clan Innes*, lost with all hands, 145 men. Bastards.'

He glanced at Mary: 'Sorry.'

'Don't be.'

And there was more in the file. The same two days in May yielded three signals with intelligence on a homebound convoy that was sourced to 'B-Reports':

1805/6/5 B REPORT. EASTBOUND CONVOY HX 121. GRID AL22. COURSE SOUTH SOUTH EAST. EIGHT KNOTS.

And the following afternoon another position report and an injunction:

1445 /7/5 B REPORT. CONVOY HX. 121. GRID AM13.
PRESS HOME ATTACK.

But it was the last signal sent to the U-boats pursuing HX121 that was the most thrilling – and disturbing:

AT 0230 TODAY ADMIRALTY ISSUED WARNING OF A
U-BOAT IN GRID AM13

Five small pieces of paper in total, five small pieces out of the hundreds of signals sent to Merchant and Royal Navy ships every day that suggested some at least were being read by the Germans. But they were the only five in the many files of decrypted messages they had read, and with so few in so many weeks it was impossible to tell if one code or many had been compromised.

'What a bloody mess' said Childs. Why didn't someone pick up on this before? And it's not the first time the Germans have penetrated our codes, is it?'

Mary could not help a half-smile as she thought of Lindsay.

'I don't think we've got much to smile about.'

'No,' she said with a defensive shake of the head, 'no, we haven't. I think it's time to show this to Rodger, don't you?'

But Winn was not in his office and he had left word with one of the clerical assistants that he would not be back until late in the evening.

'Look at us,' Childs said at his door, 'like children waiting to show teacher their treasure.'

The pleasure Mary felt at their discovery was blunted by the delivery of more files from the Registry. Hawkins dropped them on her desk with a sly smile, as if to say, 'so you think you've finished, do you?' Amidst the smoke, the trilling telephones, the soporific murmur of voices, her thoughts began to drift from the dry sentences of the signals to Lindsay, the joy she felt in his arms, intense and shameless, a warm wistful haze of memories. She had promised to make up for their last unsatisfactory meeting and he had promised with a mischievous smile to hold her to it. They were to rendezvous in front of

Victoria Station at eight o'clock that evening and have dinner at a restaurant close by. But now she would meet him only to excuse herself and he would be cross and would want to know why. The thought troubled her for the rest of the afternoon and was still hanging over her when she left the Citadel to keep her appointment.

They met at a newspaper stand on the filthy concourse, steam and soot belching from the engines beyond the barrier, the station ringing with the shrill whistles of the guards on the platforms, raised voices and the heavy slam of carriage doors. She let him kiss her, a long, tender, conscienceless kiss that only ended when the grumpy newspaper seller began barracking them for spoiling his trade. They shuffled on a few feet without protest and kissed again. Then she told him that their evening was going to have to end in the noise and squalor of the station, in the company of bored commuters and rowdy squaddies.

'Aren't you disappointed?'

He laughed and squeezed her tightly: 'You're cross with me for not putting up a fight but would it do any good to protest?'

'You have to care enough to try.'

'I do care. Of course I do. Do you have to go back right away? May I walk you back?'

They left the station and crossed the road into Victoria Street and on past the rubble and dust of what had once been a tidy row of shop fronts. It was a strange sight. The blast had demolished the shops at random, leaving those that remained like broken teeth in the mouth of a pensioner. They walked quickly and in silence. Lindsay was lost in thoughts he did not want to share. When they reached the piazza in front of Westminster Cathedral Mary shook her arm free. 'Have you been inside?'

'No.'

'I want to light a candle.'

He looked at her, then rolled his eyes up to the striped campanile. 'I thought you needed to be at your desk.'

'It won't take long,' and she set off towards the front of the cathedral.

She was not sure he would follow until his hand fell upon hers as she pulled the handle of the heavy door. A late Mass had just finished and the dark Byzantine interior was rich with the sweet perfume of incense. Beneath the baldacchino, the servers were clearing candles and cloths from the high altar. And for a moment the smoky gloom, the low lights reminded her of the Tracking Room and those who served with monastic discipline at its table.

Lindsay bent forward to whisper in her ear: 'Popery. My Mother wouldn't approve.'

She turned her head to glare at him and began walking down the aisle towards the Lady Chapel, her shoes clicking on the bare stone. The chapel was empty but for an old woman in a heavy threadbare coat mechanically working her way along her rosary. It seemed brighter than the rest of the cathedral, a bank of votive candles burning before the altar, the gold ceiling shimmering with light which reflected off the glass tesserae depicting Christ in majesty upon the tree of life.

'Why are you lighting a candle?'

'Oh, for those people lost with the *Imperial Star*.'

She leant forward to place it at the back of the stand and gasped as a flame caught her wrist.

'Let me,' and he took it and pressed the wax home. Then he lifted her hand and turned it over and was on the point of kissing her wrist when she pulled it away: 'Not here.'

'Sorry.'

They stood in silence for a minute, mesmerised by the flickering light, then, with his eyes still fixed on the candles, Lindsay said: 'Why do you need to talk to Winn again this evening?'

She did not reply but concentrated on the small yellow flame of her candle.

'If it's about our codes, I think you should tell me.' His voice was calm but insistent, even steely.

'Not now,' she whispered sharply, 'this is neither the time nor the place.'

'Is there a time and a place?'

'No. I don't know.' Why was he pressing her? Hadn't she risked enough already? 'For goodness sake, Douglas, we're in a church. I didn't come in here to be interrogated.' She turned quickly from him and began striding back along the aisle, careless of the noise she was making, the rough echo of her footsteps resonating through the cathedral. A young priest in a cassock stopped to watch her pass, his hands on his hips in a show of disapproval.

Lindsay caught up with her in the piazza. 'Look, sorry, but you know what this means . . . how much I've risked already.'

'Just find me a cab, would you?'

He stopped suddenly to look at her, hoping she would turn back, but she walked briskly on and this time he did not follow her. A taxicab was crawling down Victoria Street and she hailed it from the kerb. At once she regretted her haste and turned to look for him. He was gone.

'Where to, dear?'

'Oh no,' and she pressed her hands to her temples and cursed herself for handling him so badly.

'The Admiralty.'

It was too late and she was left with the frustration and the bitter disappointment and the doubt. When would they talk again or touch?

Winn was standing at his office door. As soon as he saw Mary he called to her: 'Come in, I've got something to show you', and for once his cool barrister voice betrayed his excitement.

'You've seen Geoff Childs then?' she asked flatly.

'Childs? No,' and he waved a dismissive hand, showering ash from the cigarette he was holding on to the desk of his secretary.

'So no one's told you? We've found something important.'

'All right, you tell me,' and he stood aside to let her into his office.

Lieutenant Childs slipped back into the Tracking Room as she was beginning her brief. He had enjoyed what only he could describe as a 'satisfactory' canteen supper. Unlocking his desk drawer, he took out the decrypts and presented them to Winn with the hushed reverence of a wise man before the manger. Winn dragged his anglepoise over and switched it on with a purposeful click, then began reading and shuffling the little pieces of paper in its light.

'B-Reports,' he muttered after a minute and glanced up at Mary, then across at Childs.

'There isn't much doubt, is there?'

He looked at the flimsies again then with an exasperated grunt tossed one back towards them: 'My favourite: "Admiralty issued warning of a U-boat". That's us, here, the Tracking Room. What a mess.'

Reaching for his cigarettes, he lit one, then said:

'And I have news too. I've been at Bletchley and the Naval Section there has done some analysis of the *Bismarck* operation. There are some indications that the enemy was able to follow the British hunt for the battleship.'

Winn picked up a file from his desk and removed a report stamped 'Most Secret': 'There's a long list of German signals here that seem to draw on our own. Here, for instance, sent on the twenty-fifth of May:

ENEMY AIRCRAFT OF SQUADRON ZB6 REPORTED TO PLYMOUTH AT 1405: AM IN CONTACT WITH ENEMY BATTLESHIP.

'I'm going to ring the Director tonight. He knows about Bletchley's work but he'll want to know about yours too. The maddening thing is our Code Security people at Section 10 were given some of this stuff a fortnight ago. Sheer bloody incompetence.'

Winn sighed and eased himself back in his chair: 'It isn't clear how far this goes. The enemy will be working on all our codes and ciphers, the question is, which ones has he broken – one, perhaps two or more? And how can we be sure?'

Mary looked at her hands, neatly folded in her lap, and the angry mark on her wrist, still smarting from the candle burn. And she wondered for a fanciful moment if it was a sort of punishment, a stinging reminder: Lindsay, the codes, the *Imperial Star* and all those ships setting out in ignorance across the Atlantic.

'Marvellous. They're reading ours and we're reading theirs,' said Childs with a small dispassionate smile.

Winn gave him a disapproving look: 'We don't know how many of our signals they're reading yet but one is too many. One signal sank the *Imperial Star*.'

Childs wriggled uncomfortably.

'All right, I've a call to make to the Director,' and Winn picked up the green phone on his desk. 'Go to bed. And thank you.'

They both got up and Childs moved towards the door but Mary hovered at the edge of his desk: 'There's Jürgen Mohr, of course.'

Winn did not bat an eyelid but kept dialling. Only when he had finished did he look up at her, his face impassive, the receiver to his ear: 'I hadn't forgotten.'

It was nearly midnight when Mary left the Citadel. As the Admiralty's doors swung open into Spring Gardens she touched the tightly folded square of paper in her pocket. Fine summer rain was beading her brown wool jacket. Her wrist was throbbing lightly. A strange comfort. She set off across the Mall and did not stop walking until her finger was on the bell of Lindsay's apartment. She felt purposeful but calm, as she had done when they had met in Trafalgar Square all those weeks before. Why? Was it her need or his? Did she need him more or less than he needed her? Did it matter? She could hear him thumping wearily down the carpeted staircase to the door. What was he thinking? Then it opened and without speaking he reached out to brush her cheek with his fingers.

Later she lay small and naked beside him in bed, the sweet smell of his sex on her body, the sheets and blankets hanging in shameless folds on the floor. And she tried to concentrate and hold those moments when past pain and fear and the future were lost in the strange stillness she felt in his arms. And she reached over to touch his hard shoulder and run her fingers lightly across his chest to his stomach. Then she rolled quickly on to her side and stretched down to the floor and felt in the darkness for where her jacket must have fallen. And when at last she found it she lifted it, crumpled, by the sleeve and reached into the pocket with two fingers.

'Here.'

'What is it?'

'What you want.'

He unfolded it carefully, then leant across to switch on the bedside light: *Admiralty issued warning of a U-boat* . . .

43

The bell rang in the grey half-world that was always his just before dawn, at the edge of consciousness when memories and images form and shift and dissipate like clouds at a front. An uncomfortable but familiar place, a rattling place, a place Jürgen Mohr could smell and taste in his sleep, and the faces always the same. Sometimes they were smiling, more often wide-eyed with fear and screaming, and then that tight grey world shuddered until it was lost in an impenetrable blackness. But at such times he was calm, he was careless, he knew that darkness so well, knew its deep, deep emptiness. Perhaps one day he would be caught and it would hold him for ever. Twice now he had been drawn from it by a small red light. Groping towards it, clutching at nothing, he had found himself between the smoking engines of his boat. And Heine's slight frame was bent over the starboard diesel with an oil can. He had reached out to touch his shoulder. The engineer had turned with a smile of recognition and pleasure. But his face was the beaten face of Lindsay's photograph, one eye closed, his cheeks purple and the weal about his neck scarlet and black. And then the roll-call bell had rung in the hall below, as it was ringing now, and there was the comfort of boots on the boards outside the room and the sharp knock of his batman at the door.

The men were gathering on the broad terrace at the back of Stapley Hall, chatting, yawning, lighting the first cigarette of the day, some in civvies, some in air-force or navy blue, most in a mixture of the two. It was cool in the shade of the house, even on a bright August morning, with a hint of vapour when they spoke. The prisoners were falling through habit into ragged lines, watched by the sentries at the wire and in the towers at the corners of the terrace.

'There seem to be more guards than usual, Herr Kap'tän.'

A tousled-looking Fischer was standing on the steps behind him.

'Perhaps the camp commander is going to pay us a visit.'

There were forty soldiers at least, twice the regular complement, and a good number of unfamiliar faces.

As they watched, a party of ten men under the command of Sergeant Harrison began marching along the wire to the gate. It opened and Harrison gave a sharp blast on his whistle, the signal for the parade to come to order. Mohr dropped his cigarette and walked round the prisoners – their lines orderly now – to stand at their head, Brand, the Luftwaffe major, to his right and Fischer to his left. The guards took up positions in front of him, bayonets fixed, backs to the wire, then on a command from Harrison the headcount began, a corporal and two men walking through the lines. Mohr glanced at his watch. It would be over in five minutes; everyone would be present and correct enough for the British and then he would breakfast in his room.

But Sergeant Harrison did not blow his whistle or bellow a shrill parade-ground 'Dismissed'. He put the piece of paper he had used to tot up the prisoners in his pocket and marched back to the gate. There was a rumble of surprise in the ranks and a Luftwaffe clown shouted something about breakfast that Mohr did not catch. He reached into his jacket for his cigarettes, to find there were only two left; he would buy more from the NAAFI at lunch-time. He took one and stroked it; half the cigarette, then he would dismiss the men himself. But as Fischer bent to light it for him, he saw out of the corner of his eye some British officers approaching the gate at the east end of the terrace.

'Thank you, Fischer.'

Four officers in khaki led by Benson with his – what was it they called it in the movies? – his 'posse' of guards. They took up positions at the gate, rifles at the ready. Benson and the other officers marched on towards him.

'Good morning, Captain.' There was a chilliness in the Major's voice Mohr had not heard before. 'This is Lieutenant Cox from the Military Police. He will be leading your escort. You and a number of your men are being taken to another camp.'

No, Benson could not say where, there were no further details and there would be no time to pack.

'I have the list here. Read it out, Harrison, would you.'

The sergeant took out his notepad, cleared his throat nervously, then began to read the names.

'May I?' Mohr asked with a dry smile and he took the pad. His name was at the top of the list, then Fischer, the officers of the 112 and the 500 and of course the propaganda reporter, Lange. No, they were not going to let it go.

'I'm sure it will only be a temporary arrangement,' said Benson uncomfortably.

Fischer read out the ten names to the parade. There was a murmur of concern as they stepped forward to be escorted to the gate.

'Dismissed.'

The other men stood at the wire to watch as their officers were led under close escort round the east wing and under the great monkey puzzle tree to the carriageway. A green military bus was waiting in front of the Hall, its engine grumbling, the windows painted black. As they approached the bus door, Mohr caught a glimpse of navy-blue uniform through the windscreen and his pulse beat faster.

'Wait here.' Cox left them there and crunched round the front of the bus but he was back a minute later with Lindsay at his side. They were together only a moment but there was something in his movements, in his face, his smile, that Mohr had not seen before, a stillness, a quiet assurance, and it was unnerving: 'You've come to escort us.'

Lindsay looked at him curiously for a few seconds and Mohr wondered if the composure in his voice had sounded a little studied.

'Where are we going?' he asked in German this time.

Still no reply. Then a guard prodded him sharply in the back with his rifle, forcing him to stumble on to the steps of the bus.

Mohr was woken by the cursing of the driver as the old military bus kangarooed to a halt. He yawned and glanced at his watch – they had been travelling for at least eight hours, with one brief stop for the lavatory and no food and now it was late evening. The military policeman opposite was sleeping, his rifle resting carelessly against the seat in front. Beyond the security partition he could hear someone climbing the steps and issuing orders to the driver. Fischer was snoring heartily across the aisle. Then the engine roared again and the bus began to roll forwards. He pressed his eye to a crack in the blackout paint on the window and hazy summer green seemed to flash by in the fading light, as if they were in a wood or a park. After a few minutes they began to slow down and then to crawl and there were more muffled orders before the driver lifted the heavy clutch and the bus shot forward, to stop seconds later. This time the engine coughed and died. The military policeman jerked upright and his gun clattered to the floor.

'I won't tell,' and Mohr gave him his sweetest smile.

The soldier blushed the colour of his cap badge and got stiffly to his feet. Boots clattered on the bus steps and the screen door slid back with a screech.

'All right, at the double.'

Another British sergeant stood squarely in the frame. The bus was close to the wire and it was a few seconds before Mohr realised with a start that it was parked in front of another great house, a finer house, its old bricks warm pink in the evening sunshine. It was elegant, handsome in an understated way, familiar – but it gave him no pleasure.

44

It was the same second-floor room at Trent Park he had shared with Heine three months before. That was deliberate, of course, and crude, but strangely affecting. And Helmut Lange had taken the same bed, the one on the right-hand side as you looked from door to barred window. There was a neat pile of brown blankets at the bottom of the other bed and the bucket with the broken handle they had been obliged to share. On the dirty white wall beyond it the tangled shadow of the cedar, just as he remembered it, twisting and turning interminably in even a light breeze. And his thoughts drifted with it to home, as they had before, but opaque, brittle memories and when he closed his eyes it was the kitchen at the camp that swam into focus and the swollen face of the little engineer. More than once he had tried to say his prayers but he could not shape the words, the old words of home, 'forgiveness', 'hope', 'salvation', empty and hollow in this place. And in the silent early hours he tried to bury the thought, no, the feeling, that they would never have meaning, never, unless he found the courage to do what he knew in the fibre of his being to be right.

They left him alone on the first day and he tried to prepare. He had lost control last time. This time he would say he had seen nothing, he knew nothing, he could say nothing more, nothing. Fischer had been sent to talk to him again at Stapley, a gentle reminder to keep his mouth shut. Bruns and Schmidt had visited too: no blows, only the thinly veiled threat of their broad shoulders and rolled-up sleeves. But he had known the matter would not rest. Lieutenant Lindsay was not going to let it rest.

It was after breakfast on the second day at the Park and he was taking a piss in the bucket. Footsteps in the corridor and he knew at once it was Lindsay.

'Helmut. How are you?'

The door closed on the guards and he pulled the chair from the table and sat down: 'You know why you're here, of course.'

Lange nodded.

'But I haven't come to talk to you about Heine, I've come as a friend,' and he reached into his jacket and drew out a small light blue envelope. Lange could see that it was from Germany, stamped by the Red Cross and the Military censor, the flap neatly cut.

'I'm afraid it's bad news, Helmut. Your mother . . . 'And he leant forward to offer him the letter.

Lange watched it trembling slightly in Lindsay's fingers and he wondered if he could refuse to accept it and the pain of what must be written inside. But it was insistent. He took it at last and drew out the thin pieces of paper covered in his father's neat hand:

. . . your mother is dead . . . an air raid . . . she was rushing for the shelter when she was hit by a car . . . she loved you so much . . . pray for her . . .

An accident, God, a stupid, stupid traffic accident of the sort you thought would never happen in a war and she was dead. He would never see her again, never be loved, never be scolded by her. And his father was alone after thirty years. He sat there, breathless, as if an iron band was being slowly tightened about his chest. One of the sheets of paper slipped from his hand and floated to the floor beneath Lindsay's chair. He bent to pick it up and, rising, placed it carefully on the bed. Then he reached across to Lange and gave his shoulder a gentle squeeze: 'Would you like to see a priest?'

He tried to say 'No' but could only manage to shape the word and shake his head a little.

'All right. I'll leave you now.'

Funeral steps across the floor and the door closed with a quiet click.

. . . your mother is dead . . . pray for her . . .

His father's words were softening, floating, drifting as his tears spattered on to the page, faster and faster. And when at last they stopped, the letter was impossible to read.

*

290

Lindsay was with the second officer of the *112* when a guard slipped the note on to the table. It was almost six o'clock in the evening and he had spent two fruitless hours with the silent, charmless Koch, persisting beyond reason with his questions. Koch was older than the rest, thirty-five, coarse in speech and looks, large calloused hands, small brown eyes that could narrow to a point. And always vigilant. Torture would break him, it broke everyone in the end, and there was something in Lindsay that almost wanted to try. He picked up the note and opened it carefully. It was from one of the other interrogators, Dick Graham, he needed to speak with him at once. Lindsay got to his feet and tidied his papers into a file.

'Is it over?'

Lindsay glanced at the prisoner, then turned to the door and walked out. He would instruct the guards to leave Koch at the table for another hour.

Lieutenant Graham was waiting at the end of the corridor. He looked impatiently at him over his pince-nez: 'It said "Urgent".'

'Well, is it?'

'The propaganda reporter wants to talk to you. Thought you ought to know.'

'Yes.'

Graham followed him through the door on to the broad landing of the main stair: 'We were surprised to see you again, Lindsay, after that business with Checkland.'

'It was the Director's decision.'

'Oh. And the prisoners? Why are they with us again?' Graham noticed his frown and held up his hands at once in surrender: 'Sorry, just conversation.'

'Well, thank you for letting me know,' and he turned towards to the stairs.

'You can't imagine how much we've missed you, Lindsay,' Graham shouted after him.

Lange was sitting at the edge of his bed much as Lindsay had left him that morning. His eyes were puffy and bloodshot and it was obvious to anyone that he had been crying, but he did not seem to care. He looked calm, if a little tired, his hands resting quietly in his lap. He did not get up when Lindsay came into the room but followed him with his eyes as he reached for the chair and sat down. And it was Lindsay who broke the silence in German:

'Are you all right? I'm very sorry.'

They were only an arm's length apart, Lange leaning forward on his elbows: 'I want to tell you about Heine.'

He was searching Lindsay's face, demanding eye contact: 'All I know at least. Can we walk, as we used to?'

Small groups of the park's staff in blue and khaki were chatting and walking on the terrace and the hard yellow August lawns, soaking in the evening sunshine, and it was not until they reached the trees at the edge of the lake that Lange felt free to speak.

'You see, they thought I was an informer and that I was working for you.'

'They?'

'He. Kapitän Mohr. He asked me lots of questions – he interrogated me. The British, you could learn from him.'

They stopped beneath a large willow tree on the north side of the lake and Lange reached up to draw a branch through his fist.

'What did he want to know?'

'He wanted to know about my visits to Dönitz and if I had visited the Naval Staff on the Tirpitzufer in Berlin, that sort of thing . . . and he wanted to know about you.'

Lindsay caught his eye and smiled.

'He wanted to know who told the British he'd served on the Staff at U-boat Headquarters and what else they, you, knew. He's trying to protect something and . . .'

Lange took a restless step away, head bent, his right hand pulling at the willow wand, stripping its narrow leaves.

'You see, he was convinced it was me. Sure it was me and I was afraid. Very afraid. And God forgive me, I told him.'

Lindsay could not see his face but he could hear his breath short and shaking with emotion and for such a broad man he had made himself very small. They stood together in silence beneath the veil of willow, an intense silence broken only by the distant splash of wild fowl on the lake and, from the lawn, a woman's voice calling to her friends. It was Lange who broke it at last. He

dropped the branch, his hand trailing at his side, his fingers plucking at the seam of his trousers. And his shoulders rose slowly as
he took a deep breath and turned to look at Lindsay: 'But you've
guessed.'

His face was white but strangely still: 'You know, don't you? I
told Mohr. I told him that it was Heine who spoke of it. I betrayed
him . . .' His voice was no more than a breathless whisper.

'And when Mohr questioned Heine he broke down?'

'Yes.' Lange reached up again to the willow and tore at another
branch: 'God forgive me because I know I'll never forgive myself.' He
wiped his eyes quickly with the back of his hand: 'Enough tears.'

Lindsay looked down at his shoes which were dusted with a fine
layer of light brown mud. Poor Lange.

'You know they tortured him, made him sign a confession. I was
there. What was he guilty of? A hidden microphone, a British interrogator – it could have happened to any of us. And it was a warning to
all of us. He was only nineteen. And you know, he looked at me and
he knew it was me, I'm sure he knew.'

'Was Mohr there?' Lindsay asked quietly.

Lange gasped and then laughed harshly: 'Which of you is worse?'
And he pulled the willow branch with such force that it came whip-
ping away from the tree.

'You want to know it all? All the sordid details?'

'Yes.'

'And if I end up hanging from a pipe too?'

'You won't. We'll . . . I'll protect you.'

Lange sighed and turned his head up to the arching canopy, golden
shafts of light dancing through the branches. After a few seconds he
closed his eyes and took another deep breath: 'Yes. I'll tell you, tell
you all I know.'

Lindsay smiled quietly to himself as he reached into his jacket for
his cigarettes: 'Here, take one, Helmut.'

It was dusk when they made their way back across the deserted lawn
and the shutters were already closed in the house. The first bats were
flitting in and out of the trees, caught black against the deep blue twi-
light. They walked in silence side by side. What more was there to say?

293

Lange had spoken of that night in the kitchen at the camp, every small detail, the blood on the engineer's nightshirt, the dirt beneath his fingernails, the scuffing of boots on the kitchen flags and the twisting, biting rope red raw about his neck. He had moved restlessly beneath the willow, tearing at its branches, the pain and disgust and remorse written in his face. The effort had left him drained but, it seemed to Lindsay, perhaps a little more at peace with himself.

At the bottom of the terrace steps, he stopped and turned his back on the house to gaze across the lawn to the lake and the hillside beyond, a crown of beech at its crest.

'And you will protect me?'

'I said so.'

Lange did not answer for a moment but kept his eyes fixed on the decaying sky, Venus bright yellow in the west. Then very quietly: 'I am glad I told you.'

'Why did you want to? Was it your mother?'

'If I told you, you would laugh. Your girlfriend, she would understand.'

'Try. Please.'

The expression on Lange's face was lost in the gloom but there was a moist light in his eyes.

'My mother. I couldn't pray for her.'

45

A night of cold thoughts and dreams, of Heine with his tormen-
tors, of Mohr and the ship – always the ship – and at first light
Lindsay left his camp bed to find some peace alone in the park.
Walking quickly, almost running, the freedom of movement, the
sun already warm on his face and a low mist rising from the dew-
covered grass. A soft summer haze – it was going to be a fine day
– on into the beechwood, fast short rasping breaths. At the top of
the hill he sat on a log to smoke a cigarette and watch the guard
changing at the wire below. Was it murder? Heine may have been
driven to commit suicide. Did it matter? No. He died because he
had helped Lindsay loosen the first threads. All that mattered to
Naval Intelligence, to him, was the unravelling of the rest, those
secrets locked so securely in Mohr's head. There was a way – it had
begun to take shape in his mind beneath the willow tree as Lange
was telling his story – a desperate way. It was with him through the
night, although he tried to bury it, and it was hovering in the back
of his mind there above the park. And as it pushed itself forward he
got to his feet again and, grinding his cigarette butt into the grass,
he began running, running as quickly as he could down the hill to
the house.

He washed in cold water and changed, then ate breakfast in
the mess canteen and it was there Lieutenant-Commander James
Henderson found him. His brisk manner suggested he had forgotten
nothing since their last meeting in June and was anxious to spend as
little time in Lindsay's company as possible.

'Fleming's telephoned. Says he will be here at ten. He wants to see
you in Colonel Checkland's office.'

But the Director's Assistant was late. Checkland was sitting alone in
his office.

'Come in,' and he pointed to a chair in front of his desk.

'You're back for the Director?'

'Yes, sir.'

The head of Section 11 stared at him for a few seconds, his face empty, then pushing his chair from the desk, he got up and walked a little stiffly to the window.

'Our codes,' he said thoughtfully. Then he turned to look at Lindsay and his face was almost lost against the window: 'You don't think much of me Lindsay, so you'll be surprised to hear that I think quite highly of you.'

'Thank you, sir.'

'I know what you've been through, you know. I saw people like you in the last war. I spent some time at the Front, did you know that?'

'No, sir.'

'It takes people in different ways. Some fall apart but others just draw into themselves – stand back from everyone.'

He paused for a moment, then turned back to the window, his face very white. When he spoke again his voice was tight with suppressed emotion: 'Sometimes you lose your compass. Guilt, anger, you distrust others, hate yourself. Believe me.'

'Yes . . .' It was difficult to know what to say. Lindsay knew he was speaking from the heart and he suddenly felt very sorry for the man. Sorry too for the things he had said about him.

'. . . And you need to seek help, guidance, it's not something that . . .'

But before he could finish Fleming was shown into the room. 'Help is at hand,' he said breezily. Checkland pursed his lips a little sourly and walked, head bent, back to his desk where he picked up the report he had been reading.

'Do you need me, Ian?' he asked with a nonchalance that sounded forced.

'No, sir.'

'Very good. Then I'll leave you.'

Fleming remained on his feet tapping a cigarette on the back of the packet until the door swung to, then flopped into the chair beside Lindsay.

'And do you need help?'

'Probably.'

'There are the interrogators here. Do you want that chap Samuels back?'

'Yes, that would be useful.'

Lighting his cigarette, Fleming inhaled deeply, his eyes narrowing a little as if preparing to throw a punch at Lindsay: 'The Director wants to know what progress you've made.'

'I know what happened to Heine before he died, and why. I can't be sure he didn't take his own life.'

'. . . But Mohr . . .'

'I was going to speak to him today.'

'There is a new urgency to this business. We can't wait six months, we can't wait six weeks. A lot of lives are at stake here. We need to know what he knows.' Fleming got to his feet and walked across the room to peer at a photograph of a battleship that had been cruelly nailed to the oak panelling.

'Can you do it?'

'. . . I think I can . . .'

Fleming turned to look at him, drawn by the hesitancy in his voice, searching his face for meaning. Checkland's secretary was clacking her typewriter in the outer office and a small carriage clock on the mantelpiece ticked away the seconds. Their eyes met for a moment. Fleming understood.

'Whatever you need to do.'

'Gilbert here.'

The line crackled and hissed as if the Colonel's office at MI5 was burning around him.

'Fleming from NID. Admiral Godfrey asked me to ring you, Colonel, about our man. He thinks it's time we called your chaps off.'

'Really? Would you mind explaining why?' Gilbert's voice was clipped and cool and sceptical.

'Of course we're grateful for their good work. They certainly seem to have made their presence felt . . .' Fleming smiled at the recollection of the punches traded in a London square. 'But they haven't come up with anything to suggest Lindsay's a spy or a security risk, have they? Nor has Duncan at the camp. Quite the contrary – he seems impressed.'

For a matter of seconds there was only the angry crackle of the line. Fleming slipped behind Checkland's desk and into his chair: 'So I'll let the Admiral know you're happy to let this thing drop now, shall I? . . .'

'I think you should let me question him again. Duncan says he was very upset about the death of his cousin – the U-boat commander . . .'

'Yes. I read that,' said Fleming drily. 'I think I'd be a little cut up about my cousin too. Wouldn't you?'

A few more hostile seconds crackled by until Fleming spoke again:

'I don't think you like Lindsay, Colonel . . . that's a pity because I was hoping Five would help him . . . help us out.'

'It's too soon to give him a clean bill of health.'

Fleming paused: 'Well, that's as may be but for now we're rather in his hands and we would appreciate some assistance – if you don't mind.'

Mit Käse fängt Mann Mause. Lindsay left the prisoners in the sticky heat of their rooms and walked with the thought all afternoon. Bait to catch the mouse. It was the only way. He stood for a while beneath Lange's willow tree throwing the occasional pebble into the lake, the ripples twinkling in an ever-widening circle until they were lost in the bright sunlight. Consequences, consequences. To risk one man's life for the many. It was at the edge of what he knew to be right but the thought had chased him all night, all day. 'Whatever you need to do.' Surely a conscience was a luxury in the war they were fighting. It needed to be an elastic conscience at least. But he wrestled with the thought that it was for more than the greater good, more than duty, it was his demon. A conviction – confused but firm – that in vanquishing it there would be some sort of release. Once the idea had taken hold of him, it held him in a breathless embrace, squeezing him tighter, tighter. 'Whatever you need to do': he needed to do this.

*

Jürgen Mohr was sitting at the table with a copy of yesterday's *Times*. Lindsay stood aside to let the guard remove the supper tray with its half-eaten meal of pork and potatoes and something that might have been gravy.

'This is how you hope to break me,' said Mohr in English and he pointed to the plate. The door closed behind Lindsay and he leant back against it.

'I don't need to break you.'

'Oh?'

'You and your officers are going back to the camp – for now. 'I have your old statement,' and he lifted the file he was holding. 'And fresh statements from the others.'

'May I have a cigarette?' Mohr sounded tired. Two days spent sitting, waiting, with only old English newspapers and a battered copy of Milton's *Paradise Lost* to relieve the boredom, and that special anxiety, the uncertainty of the prisoner, the frustration, the helplessness. Lindsay took out his cigarettes and tossed them on to the table.

'There is going to be a trial. We're preparing the papers. Two, perhaps three of your officers.'

Mohr took a cigarette and waved it at Lindsay, who stepped forward to hand him the lighter.

'Which ones?'

'And your part in the Council of Honour and the interrogation of Heine will be examined too.'

Mohr drew deeply on his cigarette. But for a small frown hovering at his brow, he looked calm, his chin in his hands, his elbows on the table.

'You're leaving tonight.'

Their eyes met for a moment, then Mohr looked away, the ghost of a smile on his face, and he picked up the Milton.

'This is hard for me, but I understand enough to admire.' And he opened the book at a small paper marker. 'The hell within. The mind is its own place, and in itself can make a Heaven of Hell, a Hell of Heaven.'

He raised his eyes slowly from the text to Lindsay's face. And Lindsay felt tense and uncomfortable for a moment. He turned to rap on the door. Heavy boots in the corridor, the drawing back of bolts, and as it began to swing open he looked again at Mohr.

'Keep the cigarettes.'

Rain brought the late summer smell of decay to the park on the following day, the horse chestnuts curling brown and the first fall of beechnuts and acorns. Helmut Lange was allowed to walk between showers, a guard at his heels. They walked in silence and he preferred it that way. Lindsay had sent a note with his apologies; did he want another book, what about cigarettes? Its warmth would have surprised the sergeant who delivered it if he had been able to read German. There were half a dozen prisoners with their escorts in the park and sometimes Lange was permitted to offer them a smoke. He did not see any of those who had travelled with him from Camp Number One. And it was the same the next day. No one seemed very interested in him any more and he spent hours on his camp bed day-dreaming of home, his mother never far from his thoughts. What would happen to him? He had never thought to ask. He had felt numb with exhaustion after the evening he had spoken of Heine, too full of grief to think of the future. Lindsay would come in time to tell him. There were other camps, perhaps they would send him to Canada. But in the stillness of early morning, as the rain beat against the shutters, a profound anxiety crept through him, penetrating every fibre until his nightshirt clung to him cold and wet. What, what, what was going to happen? Oh God, what was going to happen?

The breakfast tray was still on the table untouched when the guards came for him on the fifth day. Down the stairs at the double and through the fine civilised entrance hall, out to the forecourt and the old military bus, its engine idling roughly on the same note. The same, the same, everything the same. Where was Lindsay? There were other prisoners, officers, men in leather and Luftwaffe-blue chatting in hushed voices. Someone asked him a question but his mouth was sticky and dry and he could not think of an answer. Where was Lindsay? He tried to speak to the British Air Force officer in charge of the escort: 'Please, I must talk . . .'

But the guards were pressing the prisoners up the steps and on to the bus. Someone held his shoulder:

'Come on, Fritz. It's a long way.'

And in a daze, his heart sick, he was pushed to the door, tripping on the step, past the sour-faced soldier behind the wheel, and shaking to his seat.

46

It was Dietrich who noticed the short muscular figure in naval uniform shrinking at the back of the line. He looked frightened at six hundred yards. He was walking slowly towards the gate at the eastern end of the terrace, almost hidden by the new Luftwaffe officers shouting their greetings to friends behind the wire. But my God, he had a nerve. Kapitän Mohr was at the blackboard with his English class when Dietrich threw open the schoolroom door:

'He's back, Herr Kap'tän.'

Mohr looked at Dietrich for a moment, then calmly put down the chalk and walked over to the bay window. The class followed his example. The prisoners were parting like a river washing round a rock but for a few seconds he was lost behind their shoulders. Then Mohr saw him at the end of the line, white, unshaven, unkempt, clutching his sack to his chest like a tramp with a schnapps bottle. Shabby Lange, frightened Lange, one of the guardians of the German Navy's reputation. What would dapper Dr Goebbels have thought of his reporter? The British had held him for two additional days. Why? The camp was sure it knew; it was whispered a hundred times over lunch, on the touchline as the football pitch, and in the rooms after lights-out: 'Lange broken', 'Lange an informer', 'Lange', 'Lange', 'Lange'. Fresh evidence, statements, a trial. And yet here he was again shuffling into Stapley camp.

The new prisoners who knew nothing of Lange were speaking, laughing, shaking hands with comrades. But the rest were silent and some were turning away, presenting their backs to Lange in disgust. He was quite close to the window now and Mohr was surprised and struck by the stillness of his face, stiff, white, yes, but he seemed to have found a new strength from somewhere, an inner calm. But it was only a glimpse; the stocky frame of the 112's navigator, Bruns, had stepped in front of him, those intimidating shoulders blocking the view.

'Shall I ask Bruns to bring him here, Herr Kap'tän?' Dietrich was poisonous, a man who loved raw violence.

'No. I'll see him later,' said Mohr coldly.

Someone was pushing his way through the crowd towards the two of them – Fischer, the commander of the 500 – and he placed a warning hand on Bruns's shoulder. Strong words, an order and Bruns stepped smartly away. They spoke for a few seconds, then Fischer took Lange by the arm and began leading him across the terrace. As they passed the window he caught Mohr's eye but looked quickly away as if ashamed of his small kindness. They disappeared into the house but Mohr stayed at the schoolroom window for a moment longer. The same number of guards in the same places, the wire, the gate, the watchtowers, no, there was nothing that struck him as out of the ordinary.

'I want to see Kapitänleutnant Fischer and Major Brand in my room as soon as possible. And organise the Council for tonight.'

The expression on Lieutenant Duncan's face was eloquent testimony to the unpleasantness of the scene he had just witnessed.

'Of course he protested and asked to speak to you and then he wanted the camp commander. He was cold-shouldered by the prisoners. He was surprisingly brave and dignified. Poor sod.'

'Yes. It's tough.' Lindsay instantly felt ashamed of himself for uttering such a hopeless platitude. He was standing at the intelligence officer's desk, anxiously rolling a glass paperweight from hand to hand.

'How you got approval for this desperate enterprise I'll never know,' said Duncan hotly. 'Goodness, I hope you know what you're doing.'

He lifted a pot of tea on to a small filing cabinet beside his desk and began stirring it with a knife. 'And what if you get it wrong, time it badly? Lange could end up in the graveyard next to Heine.'

He stopped stirring the tea to fix Lindsay with a pulpit frown that a minister of the Free Kirk would have been proud of: 'Or don't you care?'

It was not worthy of a reply. There were listening devices in the old drawing room which the prisoners used as their mess, the kitchen and in the washroom, and a listening station in the west wing of the house.

They had also worked on night-time positions for a large detachment of military policemen. Lindsay had considered placing one of the park's German refugees among the new prisoners as a stool pigeon but that would have been even riskier. Yes, he was taking a risk, a terrible risk, but he had promised the camp commander he would pull the operation the moment Lange was in danger. There was just the doubt, the fear eating at him as he played restlessly with the paperweight: would he know when to take action?

'Mohr will deal with this at once so it will happen tonight,' he said with a certainty he did not feel. 'We need to keep the prisoners busy before supper and roll call. Guards in and out of the house.'

'It's organised.'

'And you've checked the microphones?'

'Yes.'

Lindsay spent the rest of the afternoon skulking in Duncan's office. It was important that none of the prisoners saw him but the time ticked too idly by and it was as much as he could do to control the old panic welling inside him. He was depending on Duncan and the Military Police for the arrangements. Major Benson visited him once to rumble anxiously about his 'mad scheme'; it should be a job for the Police not the Navy, his camp was being turned into 'a circus'. Then at eight o'clock Duncan returned to report on the evening roll call. Lange had stood a little apart, a lonely figure but in good health and calm, and surprisingly he had made no request to speak to the camp commander.

'I hear he's being ostracised by the camp. The Ältestenrat has let it be known that no one is to speak to him until he's cleared his name,' said Duncan, settling into his chair. 'But there is no news of an investigation or a Council of Honour.'

The men listening to the hidden microphones had heard only the cursing of the cooks in the kitchen, the songs and banter of the washroom.

'I don't expect anything to happen before lock-up,' said Lindsay, glancing at his watch.

Half an hour and then the game of cat and mouse would begin. The Military Police would move into position close to the west wing of the house ready to force their way in if called upon to do so. One group at the entrance to the old crew yard, the other close to the covered passage that offered direct access to kitchen and washroom. They would have to be discreet because Mohr would post his lookouts too. Could ordinary soldiers be discreet? Lindsay wondered. There were so many 'ifs' and 'buts', so many. A frisson of fear coursed through him from neck to toes. The more he thought about it, the more certain he was that it was going to be a disaster. Since the *Culloden* everything had been a disaster. Duncan was right, what if they were too late? Call it off now. He should call it off. But he knew he wouldn't.

Then, at half past nine, there was a sharp knock on the office door and without waiting for permission a corporal stepped smartly inside. His face was bright with excitement: compliments of Lieutenant Green, orders are being given in the prisoners' common room that suggest preparations are being made for the court. Lindsay was on his feet at once and without waiting for Duncan, he pushed past the corporal into the corridor, his heart pounding furiously. So, it was beginning.

Elsewhere in the house, Leutnant zur See Helmut Lange was placing one foot in front of the other very deliberately on the stairs. He felt strangely detached, as if he was floating above his body, marking everything from the escort at his back to the tiniest of stains on the rough strip of burgundy carpet. They turned right at the bottom and on through the hall, the armorial glass in the tall windows twinkling in the last of the light.

The lookout at the common-room door – a Luftwaffe officer he did not recognise – made a point of scowling at him before he stepped aside to let him pass. As Lange was reaching for the handle, it turned on the inside and the door swung open on a room full of faces. A little dazed, he stood there trying to focus on just one face until a hand pressed him firmly in the middle of the back and through the door. There were at least forty men, silent, watchful, hostile, leaning against the dark oak-panelled walls or draped over the common room's battered armchairs. It was gloomy, some bulbs had been removed from the chandelier and the corners were lost in shadow. On the side of the room opposite the door, two lookouts were standing at the bay window with an eye to chinks in the heavy blackout drapes.

The Council of Honour was sitting in front of the inglenook fire-place at a low trestle table, a yellow file and papers scattered across its green baize cover. Major Brand of the Ältestenrat was in the chair; to his right was Mohr, bent over pencil and paper; the third member was a fresh-faced captain of the Luftwaffe.

'Here, Herr Leutnant,' said Brand, pointing to a small wooden chair a short distance from the table. 'Sit down.'

Lange's right knee was trembling like a leaf in a gale and it was a comfort of sorts to sit down, to put the eyes of all but a few in the room behind him.

'This is Hauptmann Peters,' Brand turned his head a little to the Luftwaffe captain. 'He will be taking the place of your former commander on this council. Kapitänleutnant Fischer is indisposed.'

That was for the benefit of the room. It sounded like an excuse. Perhaps his old commander was refusing to play any part in the proceedings. And just the thought was enough for Lange to feel a surge of gratitude and warmth for Fischer, bawdy, drunken, decent Fischer. Try, try, try, he must try to draw strength from the thought.

'You know why you're here before this council?'

Lange nodded quietly. His left knee was beginning to tremble too. Why was his body letting him down? It was frustrating. Yet he felt an inner stillness he did not expect or understand. Brand began to read from a badly written charge sheet: . . . *that you gave aid to the enemy by providing him with intelligence on the disciplinary proceedings of a Court of Honour . . .*'

His voice was theatrically severe, almost comic, but there was also a note of pride, even of relish, that was entirely the man.

'. . . *that you have acted as informer on this and other matters of first importance to the Reich, endangering the security of fellow officers . . .*'

It was the same charge written a dozen different ways. Mohr was fidgeting impatiently with his pencil and Lange could hear coughs and the shuffling of feet behind him. At last Brand reached the end and, placing the sheet down, he leant across the table to glare at Lange: 'Can you answer these charges?'

'I would like to say . . .' He could hear himself as if at the end of a long tunnel. Was that his voice? It was a guilty voice. No. No. 'I

306

would like to answer, yes. There was a crime, a terrible crime, a man murdered for a moment of weakness. Heine murdered. And my fault . . .'

'That's enough,' snapped Brand. 'You're here to answer for yourself and . . .'

'I am at fault yes, yes. At fault for letting it happen and yes, perhaps helping it to happen.'

There was a rumble of surprise at the quiet but naked defiance, the steel in Lange's voice. No one expected it from the PK man.

'And to my eternal shame . . .'

'That's enough,' Brand shouted and he began rising from his chair, his face and neck an indignant pink. But a firm hand and a look from Mohr held him hovering over the table like a petulant schoolboy. And it was Mohr who now spoke to Lange:

'You've made your view known. But there is only one question we are here to answer: did you give intelligence to the British about the proceedings of this council and the disciplining of Leutnant Heine?'

There was an insistent cold purpose in his question. The room was still. Lange could hear his own short breaths and feel the eyes of many boring into the back of his head. He had resolved to say what was right, to condemn what had passed without fear but now, in that silence, Mohr's steady gaze upon him, he was afraid again, very, very afraid.

'I believe, I . . .' What could he say? What? 'It was a crime and . . .'

'The British are preparing a case. Did you provide them with intelligence? Did you speak of your comrades? Yes or no?'

Yes or no. Yes or no. It crackled distantly down the wire and through the small Bakelite headphones. Lindsay's stomach was churning with anxiety as he leant towards the volume control on the receiver. It was almost time, almost time. Silence, then something that sounded a little like a choking cough and then uproar. Shouting, the screech of chairs, hissing, and noises it was impossible to place.

And then the calm voice of Mohr cut through all: 'So to these charges against you, you plead guilty?'

Lange must have nodded because there were more hisses, shouts, an angry chorus of hate. And then silence. A complete empty silence. And a few seconds later a light buzzing. The line was dead. Lindsay spun round in his chair to look at Duncan: 'For God's sake. Can we get it back?'

'Well?' Duncan looked sharply at the young sergeant from Signals sitting at the receiver beside them.

'It may come back, sir,' he said weakly.

'Two minutes. Two minutes. We can't risk any more.' Lindsay got to his feet to stand shuffling anxiously behind the Signalman as he tinkered with the set.

'Let's go now,' said Duncan. 'Now.'

'No. We must see if . . .'

'It's back, sir.'

Lindsay snatched up his headphones and sat back at the table. Yes, yes. He could hear Brand, that pompous fool. Brand droning on about secrecy, the war being fought in the camp, the lives of their comrades, and the enemy's spies: but Lange, what of Lange? He glanced across at Duncan who was bent over the sergeant's shoulder, his hands pressing his headphones to his ears, a puzzled expression on his face. Why was Brand babbling on unchecked? He was addressing the room, not Lange. What was Mohr doing? The camp's intelligence officer caught his eye at last and scrunched up his face in concern. And he was right, yes. Lindsay could sense there was something very wrong. Was Lange even in the room?

'All right. That's enough.'

Duncan ripped off his headphones: 'Thank God yes. Let's go.'

A shrill blast on a whistle, then a distant heavy thumping like native drums, wood on wood, something atavistic. Lange heard it as they half marched, half dragged him along the corridor, dark, stumbling, like a primitive sacrifice. Every grunt, every movement, every colour and shape, a rough flashing pattern, familiar but opaque with a fear he could taste, sweet in his mouth. Twenty metres, prisoners' office on the right and the schoolroom, small pantry on the left, and at the end the heavy mahogany door to the servants' quarters. Closer, closer, every step closer and he could hear the short anxious breaths of the men about him, hands tight on his arms and the collar of his jacket, and Bruns's square head bobbing in front. And still the distant drumming, boom, boom, boom.

Hail Mary full of Grace, the Lord is with Thee . . .

Bruns was at the door and for a moment the hands loosened their grip as he was propelled through it into the servants' passage.

. . . pray for us sinners now and at the hour of our death.

And passed the kitchen and on, on to the washroom, a man in the shadows, blue on black. More banging, closer now, just a few metres down the passage. The door to the yard. The British. Lindsay. And why were they hammering on it?

Oh Mary be my strength.

Wet floor. White porcelain. A slash of violet light in the mirrors. A tap running. And more shadows, more men. Frightened faces but angry. They will stop now, they must. Arms tugged roughly back. The rope cutting into his wrists.

'No, stop, stop.'

'Fuck off, traitor.' Dietrich's saliva on his cheek. 'Quick. Quick.'

A chair. Another rope. Someone with large practised hands knotting the rope. Koch.

Shouting in the passage. English. German. 'Stop. Stop.' And he knew he should struggle. Time. He needed time. And the things he could have done. Words he should have spoken. To lose hope. Life. Love. And the greatest of these is love. *Hail Mary full of grace . . .*

The noose in Dietrich's hand too small and too stiff.

'Fuck. Koch, do something about this.'

Shaking hands on the rope. Faces lost in shadow then close and very white. And the banging. Banging at the washroom door now.

'There isn't time. We can't do it.' Dietrich frantically pushing at someone and screaming: 'Do it. That's a fucking order.'

The rope fraying at the knot. The noose in front of his face. Pulling his hair. Pulling his head back. And the rope rough on his neck. Burning his neck.

'The chair?'

'No. No. No. Pull him up.'

The knot hard. *Our Father, our Father . . .* The knot nudging the back of his head. Tight. Tight. Tighter. Tighter.

. . . and at the hour of our death.

Fuck, fuck, fuck, what a shambles. Banging on the bloody washroom door like buggers at a rowdy rugby club while a man's life was in the balance.

'For God's sake, hurry up,' Lindsay shouted.

The Military Police sergeant swung the sledgehammer again. Boom against the lock, bouncing up and down the dark passage, a dull hollow echo that resonated like the torpedo that sank the *Culloden*. Duncan was standing beside him touching an angry cut in his lip. They had fought their way to the washroom, trading punches with some of the prisoners. Yes, a shambles, close to a riot. Doors barred. Soldiers armed with rifles in corridors and crowded rooms. No one with authority. He had left the arrangements to the Military Police. A shambles.

'Get that fuckin' door open now, you lazy lummox,' Duncan bellowed, bank manager no longer but shipyard keelie. 'And put your back into it. Oh God, give it here,' and he snatched the sledgehammer from the soldier. Swinging his broad shoulders, he brought it down with such force that the lock burst, oak splintering, the hammer bouncing from his hands. It was as if a great cathedral bell had sounded only feet away. Only Duncan had enough presence to act, throwing his shoulder against the door: 'You after an invitation?'

It gave way and he stumbled headfirst into the washroom. Lindsay followed, the soldiers at his back.

'Stop it or we'll shoot.'

He could see Lange's twisted face and the rope in the light from a high washroom window. His body was shaking, his mouth open, gasping, gasping for air. But he was heavy and they were trying to lift his legs to tighten the rope. There were five, perhaps six men. Was that Dietrich?

'Stop it now or I'll shoot. Now.'

Dietrich turned to shout something to the others and they stepped back, their hands in the air. And now Lange was swinging, the rope creaking, taut, twisting, swinging free, a strange gurgling noise in his throat and his chest heaving for air. And Lindsay grabbed him and held his knees: 'For God's sake help me.'

Then a sharp crack above his head and a drenching spout of water and Lange's body slipped from the broken pipe. Hands helped to ease it to the wet stone floor. Strings of hair across his forehead, eyes half closed, and the water drumming against Lindsay's back as he bent to shelter him from its force.

'Please God . . . a doctor, a doctor now.'

The cold was seeping through his jacket and through his shirt and creeping through his body. What had he done? Lange was dead.

SEPTEMBER 1941

A single bad deed by one individual can jeopardise the
achievements of many others. The favourable reputation
of an entire fighter group can be wiped out by some
foolish or unnecessary act of violence by only one of its
members. This lapse of common sense actually gives
aid to the enemy, who will exploit the misdeed . . . the
guilty conscience alone will perform most of the work
advantageous to the inquisitor.

**Hanns Joachim Scharff, Interrogator, Luftwaffe
Interrogation Centre, Oberursel, Germany, 1943–45**

Raymond F. Tolliver, *The Interrogator:
The Story of Hanns Joachim Scharff,
Master Interrogator of the Luftwaffe*

47

The police van was careering through the streets at dusk like something from a Hollywood gangster picture. A railway arch, the broken front of a chemist's, sooty houses and the shell of a large department store, south London flashing by the small square grille in the rear door like images in a Rotoscope. And Mohr sliding about the seat handcuffed to a policeman who was clutching a helmet to his lap. It might have been comic but it was just demeaning. A large but simple church with fluted columns, more houses, then a sharp turn right to the gates and white stone towers of what could only be a prison.

'Where is this?'

The policeman glanced at him, then down at his helmet. The gates swung open on to yellow-black walls, a curious octagonal building flanked on either side by the four-storey wings of the prison. And it was here, in front of Prisoner Reception, that the van came to a halt.

'Strip.'

How had it come to this? To be treated like a criminal. He had fallen into a dark place.

'I am a naval officer.'

'Scales.'

Something was eating at his core, the loss of the boat, captivity, it was impossible to be quite sure, but he felt emptier and more uncertain. He had made mistakes.

'Uniform.'

Someone thrust a rough khaki shirt and trousers into his arms. There was a dark stain on the front of the shirt and the trousers were too large at the waist. One of the warders was turning Mohr's white cap over in his hands, then with a sly smile he placed it on the table and began prising the badge from the band.

'F' Wing at Brixton clattered like an empty dustbin. British fascists and Irish nationalists, spies and murderers, their shouts and groans in the night, their boots on the stairs and the landings, the rattle of keys in security gates and the heavy slamming of doors. A Victorian hell of steel and bare brick and chipped and dirty whitewash. His cell was four metres by two, a barred window high in the wall, a bucket and a bed. That night as he lay on his thin damp mattress, the cold echo of the prison shackling his mind, Mohr knew he was a prisoner in a way he had not been before.

At slopping-out the next morning he saw Dietrich and Schmidt further down the landing in the same prison browns, heads bent over their shit. And he felt a contempt for their stupidity that was matched only by the contempt he felt for himself. Then at eleven o'clock there were footsteps and voices outside his cell and someone pressed an eye to the slot in the door. A moment later it opened and Lindsay stood there, a prison warder at his back.

'I've brought you a newspaper,' he said in English and tossed the *Daily Mail* on to the bed. 'Now you're a celebrity here too.'

Mohr looked at it for a moment, then picked it up and opened it on his knee. His own picture was at the bottom of the front page beneath the latest news of the war in the Soviet Union. It must have been taken in Liverpool when the crew was escorted off the ship. And the bold headline beneath it:

U-boat Commander to be Charged with Murder

He flinched and closed his eyes for a moment as if someone had caught him hard in the stomach. It was public knowledge, perhaps in Germany too. Humiliating. The copy beneath the picture said that a man had been 'brutally' murdered at a camp for enemy officers in the north of England. A number of German prisoners were being held, including a 'senior Nazi U-boat Commander' and it mentioned him by name. And he was also to be 'charged' with conducting an 'illegal court-martial hearing'.

Mohr looked sideways at Lindsay: 'Have you read this?'

'Of course.'

'. . . *this ruthless Nazi officer is responsible for the deaths of many British seamen and now with equal ruthlessness he has turned against one of his own* . . .' Who is this person?'

'You, Mohr, you,' said Lindsay contemptuously. 'You will be brought before a court in the next few days. You and your lynch mob: Dietrich and Bruns and Schmidt and Koch and the others too. You will be found guilty and hanged.'

'You are the one who should be in court.' Mohr's voice shook with repressed fury.

Why had Lindsay done this to him? He was going to dress it up as a dirty little crime, Mohr the murderer, the mindless Nazi thug. It was more than just an intelligence trick, it felt personal in some way, an assault on his integrity, his reputation. But he was caught, a fly in a web.

He tried to collect himself: 'No one has taken a statement from me.'

'You look worried. We don't need a statement. We have witnesses. I heard you myself.'

'I want to give a statement.'

Lindsay shook his head, then; half turning to the prison warder behind him, said: 'Look after him. I don't want to give him the opportunity to make a complaint about his treatment to the court.'

The warder nodded.

Lindsay had reached the door and was on the point of closing it when he turned to look at Mohr again. There was something close to a sneer on his face: 'I would feel sorry for you but I saw Lange swinging there. The crimes of one man can bring dishonour to many. To think that man would be you, a hero of the Reich.'

The door slammed shut and the empty echo bounced round the hard walls of Mohr's cell and reverberated in his mind.

317

1500
14 September
King's Cross Station
London

Lieutenant Samuels was the sort of man it was easy to spot in a crowd, even in an undistinguished business suit. He arrived in a hissing cloud of steam and smoke on the three o'clock from Doncaster. It was half an hour late. Lindsay saw him at once rolling awkwardly along the platform, a space opening about him, head a little bent, his face pasty and earnest. He managed a warm smile when he saw Lindsay at the barrier, grateful no doubt to be back in 'the Smoke' and to the man who was making it possible.

'How was the racecourse, Charlie?' Lindsay asked, taking his bag.

'Heavy-going,' he said with another weak smile. 'I didn't expect you to be here to meet me.'

'We need to talk. We haven't got long. Admiral Godfrey wants this wrapped up in twenty-four hours. He's fending off a lot of people at the War Office who want to know about the riot at the camp.'

Lindsay's jeep was parked at the front of King's Cross Station. He did his best to brief Samuels as he ground up and down the gears through the London streets. If they could not break Mohr quickly, then the police would take him off their hands: 'And after the shambles at the camp, I will be hung out to dry somewhere.'

Samuels grunted: 'Again.'

'For good.'

They drew up at some lights in Fleet Street and Lindsay reached down for his cigarettes: 'I saw Mohr this morning and showed him his picture in the paper. I think he was upset. Very gratifying.'

'So the papers have it?' Samuels was surprised.

'No, no. We're trying to keep it from the papers. It was my own special edition of the *Daily Mail*. The tricks people at MI5 came up with the idea.'

The Security Service had tried the same thing on their prisoners. It was in the papers so it must be true. The *Daily Mail* had replaced a front-page story with the one that put Mohr on a murder charge, then run off half a dozen copies for Lindsay.

318

'And Five are helping us with three of their chaps.' He paused, then almost as an afterthought: 'Two of them work for a man called Colonel Gilbert. They look a little rough.'

Samuels frowned.

'. . . Oh and we've got Dick Graham from the Park.'

They stopped at a greasy-spoon café in Pimlico for precious eggs and some tomatoes, accompanied by bread and cups of tea. It was going to be a busy night. 'Our last chance, really,' said Lindsay, putting down his knife and fork and reaching for his cup.

'You seem quite calm.'

Did he feel calm? Perhaps something harder. Harder, yes. He knew he would risk anything. It felt almost as if life hung in the balance, hope and happiness, perhaps even his sanity in one scale and Kapitän Jürgen Mohr in the other. This was the time. There was no turning back.

'We'll try the Cross Ruff on all the prisoners but Mohr – play one off against another.' He put his cup back on the table, then caught the waiter's eye for the bill. 'Oh and congratulations. You've been promoted to Captain. Your new uniform is waiting for you at the prison.'

Samuels groaned, then laughed: 'Do you think it will work, a Jewish captain?'

'My God, it had better.'

1700
14 September
'F' Wing, Brixton Prison

It was their own little Court of Honour. A badly lit windowless room at the end of the wing with the necessary degree of discomfort. The new captain – Samuels – was in the chair. Nazi officers showed slavish respect for rank and Oberleutnant zur See Dietrich was one of the true believers. He seemed a hard case, the chief interrogator of Heine, the leader of the little washroom band, not afraid to take the rope in his own hands. But a man who needed things to be simple, easily led so easy to confuse, and brittle. And he was not one of Mohr's men but the first officer of the *U-500* and Lindsay sensed he had not been schooled to keep his mouth shut as well as some of the others. Above all, if anyone was going to hang it would be Dietrich and he knew it. His fear was transparent in his face the moment the prison warders led him into the room. He stood before the table, his chin raised, his lips pursed in a show of defiance that was compromised by a clownishly baggy prison uniform. Perhaps it was a deliberate attempt by the warders to undermine his sense of self-importance and dignity. The bottom of his trousers hung in rolls over his shoes and he was obliged to keep a firm hand on the waist to prevent them from falling down altogether.

Lindsay had asked one of Gilbert's MI5 officers to be the other member of their court, a large muscular man called Robbins who looked as if he would ask most of his questions with his fists. He sat at the table in his dark suit with the face of a hanging judge. It was Samuels who began the interrogation in German: 'You know why you're here, Dietrich. You've been charged with the murder of two men.'

There was a cold crisp authority in his voice that would not have been out of place on a parade ground: 'Tomorrow you will appear before a court. If convicted – and you will be – you will be taken to a prison like this and you will be hanged. Do you understand?'

Dietrich did not say anything but stared at a stretch of wall above Samuels' right shoulder. He was struggling to keep his composure.

'Do you understand? Answer me,' Samuels barked.

'Yes, Herr Kapitän.'

'Your only hope of seeing Germany and your family again is if you co-operate. I make no promises, will strike no bargains but there is a possibility, I put it at no more than that, if you answer our questions the court will take your attitude into account. Do you understand?'

Dietrich nodded.

'Do you understand?' asked Samuels sharply.

'Yes, Herr Kapitän.'

Samuels glanced across at Lindsay who, taking his cue, opened the file in front of him and pushed a sheet of paper across the table towards Dietrich.

'Was it your decision to interrogate Heine?'

'No.'

'Who gave the order?'

Silence. Dietrich shifting his weight awkwardly.

'Who?'

Still nothing.

'Who ordered you to interrogate Heine?'

'I am not sure . . .'

'Who?'

The hand Dietrich lifted to his mouth trembled a little.

'Your life may depend upon your answer. Who?'

His lips seemed to form the words but there was no sound.

'Who?'

'. . . I don't . . .'

'Who ordered you to interrogate Heine?'

'The Ältestenrat.' Barely more than a whisper but Lindsay pounced:

'Write this,' and he leant across the table to place his fountain pen on the paper.

'Write: "The Ältestenrat instructed me to interrogate Leutnant Heine." Write it now.'

Dietrich looked down at the paper. To speak it softly in a dark room was one thing; to commit it to paper in your own hand was an entirely different matter.

'Don't try our patience, Dietrich. We have the evidence to hang you.'

Dietrich's hand hovered above the paper for two, three, four seconds before he lifted it to cover his mouth once more.

Samuels cleared his throat and began gathering the papers into the file in front of him. 'All right, that's enough. We know the answers to these questions. This was your opportunity to do something to help yourself, Dietrich.'

And he lifted his hand to beckon the prison warders standing at the back of the room.

But the pen was in Dietrich's hand before they could take a step.

As his head bent over the paper, Samuels caught Lindsay's eye and gave a slight nod and a smile.

'Did Kapitän Mohr instruct you to extract a confession from Heine?'

Dietrich muttered something Lindsay did not catch: 'What did you say?'

'Yes.'

'Write it down.'

He wrote standing over the table, in an awkward schoolboy hand: the interrogation of Heine, the torture, his confession, the names of those who had played a part with him.

'And after that you strung Heine up from the pipe.'

'No. No.' It rang round the room and out to the landing. 'No.'

Dietrich denied murder. And he was not to be shaken. He was adamant that Heine took his own life.

'I was shocked.'

'You all but handed him the rope,' said Lindsay coldly. 'And then, Lange. Tell me, did Kapitän Mohr order you to execute him?'

Dietrich looked down at the paper and said nothing. The stuffing had been pulled from him, he was a sad figure, deluded, a weak man in the hands of the strong, a victim too in a way. And Lindsay could not help feeling some pity for him – a little. 'Well?'

He looked up at Lindsay and his eyes were a watery blue, then he shook his head slowly.

'You can't protect him. It's too late for that.'

'Kapitän Mohr gave no such order.'

'But that's what he wanted you to do.'

Again a slow shake of the head: 'No. We took the propaganda man.'

'You're protecting him.'

'No,' he said quietly. 'No. We only wanted to scare Lange. He was going to give evidence against us. Somehow it got out of hand when the soldiers, when you broke the door down.'

'I heard Kapitän Mohr give you the order myself.'

'No.'

Lindsay sat down at the table again and looked at Samuels who gave him a knowing look. Was he betraying his disappointment? But what difference if Mohr did give the order? His guilt or innocence was neither here nor there. It would have been neater, that's all.

'All right take him away,' said Samuels, signalling to the prison warders.

Dietrich looked surprised and a little distressed: 'And you will speak to the judge? It was an accident, a mistake. We didn't mean to hurt Lange. Just an accident. That's the truth.'

Samuels gave him a withering look and turned to one of the guards: 'Get him out of here.'

The door slammed behind them and Samuels got to his feet rubbing his hands with satisfaction, then leant across the table for the statement. Two sheets and Dietrich's signature.

'That went rather well. I like Captain Samuels, don't you? Who's next?'

'I think I'll see the navigator from Mohr's boat on my own,' said Lindsay, collecting his papers together. 'Why don't you take a break? There's a small hotel a few hundred yards from the prison.'

Samuels looked puzzled: 'But it worked well. Don't you want to try again?'

'Not with Bruns. I've spoken to him before. I want to see him alone in his cell. I think that will be better, Charlie.'

The MI5 man was on his feet and preparing to leave. He offered both men his large hand and a promise that he would be close by if needed again in the course of what was going to be a long night. Lindsay watched him leave, then turned to Samuels again: 'Can I have that?'

Samuels glanced down at the statement quivering slightly in his hand: 'This?'

'Yes.'

'Are you planning to do anything with it now?' Samuels sounded a little suspicious.

'Reference.'

'Ah.' He leant forward with the document and Lindsay clasped the top of it between the thumb and forefinger of his right hand. Samuels did not release the bottom. They stood holding the statement together and Samuels' soft brown eyes were searching his face:

'Don't do anything stupid, Lindsay.'

He said it softly and very deliberately.

'Please. Nothing stupid.'

2030
14 September
'F' Wing, Brixton Prison

Obersteuermann Bruns was pacing his little rectangle of floor like a bear in a cage. Three steps to the wall and a smart turn to the door. There was a dark frown on his face, more belligerent than anxious. The little disc slipped back over the viewing window and with a jangling of keys the door swung open. When he saw Lindsay he snapped smartly to attention.

'Easy, easy. How are you, Georg?' Lindsay asked in German.

Bruns raised his eyebrows in surprise. A friendly 'How are you?' was not at all what he was expecting. A moment later and his features settled into a stiff scowl and Lindsay could almost hear the cogs of his mind slowly turning over: it was a trick, it must be.

'Sit down, Georg.'

'I want to stand.'

'All right, if you feel more comfortable,' but Lindsay sat at the bottom of his bed. He leant down to take a file from his briefcase, conscious that Bruns's little brown eyes were following him closely. He had a curious face, long, with high cheek-bones and brown skin that would not have looked at all out of place in Zanzibar, his birthplace. But that was not an observation that would endear him to a devout Nazi like Bruns.

'You know you're in a great deal of trouble, Georg? Two charges of murder.'

Bruns was clenching and unclenching his hands as if he wanted to relieve his anxiety by taking a swing at something or someone.

'Well, Georg, what will you tell the court?' Lindsay asked him softly.

'I will say I am not guilty.' His voice shook a little. The defiant teenage scowl on his face was not enough to hide the fear growing deep inside him.

'I feel the court should know the full facts, Georg. Would you like to write a statement?'

'I have nothing to say.'

'Your comrade Oberleutnant Dietrich had plenty to say. I have his statement here,' and Lindsay opened the file to show him the confession written in a round childlike hand. 'Yes. Listen to this: *Bruns found the rope in the yard at the camp. It was his idea to use it on Heine . . .*

Oh and here's another bit: *we talked about what we should do. Bruns was for executing Lange as a traitor, he had confessed to betraying us . . .*

'You see. Oberleutnant Dietrich has been very frank with us.'

Bruns was biting his bottom lip nervously, his dark skin a shade paler. He was clearly at a loss to know what to say: was it possible that Dietrich had betrayed him to the enemy?

'Sit down here,' said Lindsay, patting the bed. 'It must be a shock. Yes, he has told us everything and not just about Heine and Lange. He's answered all our questions. He could see it was in his best interests.'

Bruns did not move but stood with his back to the wall, clenching and unclenching his big hands. Always at the edge. And schooled by Mohr to say nothing. A simple order. Duty and loyalty to the Fatherland. Yes, a simple order to be followed even if he was left swinging from a rope.

'Think about it,' said Lindsay, slipping Dietrich's confession back in the file. 'Help me and I can help you. Your life depends upon it.'

He got to his feet and rapped on the door. It opened at once. Standing outside was the Security Service man, Robbins, his muscular frame a little too snug in his dark suit, black shoes polished with military perfection. The door clanked shut and he stepped forward to shake Lindsay by the hand.

'We're ready for you. The room's on 'C' Wing where we keep the troublemakers.'

'Thank you, Captain. One by one, starting with Bruns. Leave them for half an hour before you fetch Dietrich.'

'And Lieutenant Samuels?'

Robbins' knowing smile brought the colour to Lindsay's face: 'No. Lieutenant Samuels doesn't need to be informed.'

There was a Sunday church hush in the Tracking Room and those not important enough to be at the table were bent over their desks in something very like prayer. The First Sea Lord was standing at the plot. His entourage was stirring the smoke into a restless pea-souper that lent mystery and a strange urgency to every small movement. Admiral Sir Dudley Pound did not visit the Citadel often. He preferred its product to drop into his in-tray on neatly typed sheets of yellow paper. But the Prime Minister was not as patient. The Admiral was expected in Downing Street with an explanation for the disaster within the hour. Winn was taking him through some lines at the plot, his arm planted just south of Iceland, gesturing at a cluster of black flags.

'Dönitz deployed a pack of fourteen U-boats here to the south-west of Iceland at the end of August . . .'

At her desk, Mary picked up a pencil and ran it down a report on something rather technical in an effort to appear busy.

'Of course we were tipped off by Bletchley. We knew their boats were in a search line somewhere here,' and Winn's hands swept across the flags again. 'We were able to use that intelligence to route our convoys away from the pack.'

But after a time Dönitz had drawn a new search line on the big wall chart at U-boat Headquarters. They had learnt that from the special intelligence too. The first little piece of rip-and-read with fresh orders to the U-boats had landed on Mary's desk.

'. . . unfortunately Slow Convoy 42 was forced south by a storm and the ice. It was picked up by the *U-85* five days ago. Of course, once contact was made Dönitz was able to direct the rest of his pack to the convoy and the rest is . . .' Winn did not feel he needed to say more. The details had already begun to appear in the papers. The pack had set upon the convoy and sunk twenty ships loaded with timber and steel, wheat and sugar and flour. A third of the convoy was lost and with it hundreds of seamen.

The awkward silence was filled with the shuffling of feet and the ringing of a telephone at the far end of the room. All heads were turned to Pound. He was standing on Winn's right, small, stooped and grey, resting on a stick, his eyes almost lost beneath his heavy brow. The clock ticked on and Mary began to wonder if he had fallen asleep on his feet. It was the Director, Admiral Godfrey, who came to his rescue: 'Perhaps, sir, Winn can tell us if there is anything to suggest the enemy knew of the convoy's movements from our signals?'

It was the question Mary knew Winn had been asking himself for the last four days.

'. . . I've spoken to Bletchley and it is not clear from the special intelligence,' said Winn cautiously. 'I don't think we can discount the possibility. I think the security of our codes is now the first priority.'

Admiral Pound's body gave a little jerk as if he was joining them again: 'Don't we have anything more? I can't tell the Prime Minister we think our own codes may be compromised but we're not certain how many or which ones.'

'Bletchley are doing some analysis of the enemy's signals traffic, sir,' said Godfrey, 'and we are still working on the one man we have who knows.'

Pound turned away from the plot to Godfrey: 'And when can I tell the Prime Minister we'll have news for him about this, John?'

'I can't be sure, sir.'

Pound made a noise between a grunt and a cough in his throat to indicate his displeasure.

'All right keep me informed.'

The smoke swirled again as Pound began to weave across the room like a balding enchanter, his Staff in close attendance. As he stepped through the door there was an audible sign of relief from those bent over their desks, phones began ringing, typewriters clattering; it was as if the stale air of crisis had disappeared with him. Admiral Godfrey was still standing with Winn at the plot, cigarette in hand.

'Thank God he didn't want to know who we're working on,' he said drily. 'He was impressed by Mohr, took tea with him in the Admiralty boardroom.'

Winn took off his glasses and began polishing the lenses with his handkerchief: 'I was more worried he would ask who is in charge of the interrogation.'

Mary could feel his eyes on her and she kept her head down over the report. It was already covered in small meaningless pencil marks.

'Don't you have faith in our man?' asked Godfrey with a short laugh. 'Half German, half mad, insubordinate, a little too ruthless I think – I've had the devil's own job clearing up the mess at the POW camp. Fleming had better be right about him and Lindsay had better be right about Mohr or the shit will stick to all . . .'

Winn must have pulled a face or touched the Director's arm to warn him to keep his voice down because he did not finish the sentence. Mary's face was hot with anger and she knew Godfrey was looking across at her. Slowly, she raised her eyes to meet his gaze, her lips pursed in naked disapproval. The Admiral gave her a half-smile, a don't-give-a-damn smile, then looked away.

A short time later, Winn flopped into a seat close to her desk. The Director had gone but his words were still ringing furiously in Mary's ears and she must have been wearing something close to a scowl.

'He was joking,' said Winn, leaning forward to pat her arm. 'He's trusting Lindsay with a lot. Have you spoken lately?'

'We keep missing each other, leaving messages. I haven't seen him for a while.'

The business with the convoy had kept her late at the Citadel and it was almost a week since she had found time to speak to him.

'What happened at the camp?'

Winn looked down for a moment, then reached into his uniform jacket pocket for his cigarettes. He took a thoughtful few seconds to light one.

'It was something close to a riot. A bad business. I think you'd better ask him yourself.'

'Isn't it an official secret?'

'Yes, it probably is, but you should ask him anyway,' and leaning awkwardly on the arms of the chair he levered himself back on to his feet.

'Ask him.' The stiffness, the coldness in his face and voice sent an unpleasant shiver down Mary's spine.

She left the Citadel a little after eleven and walked the short distance to Lindsay's flat in St James's Square. There was no answer. She did not expect there to be. She knew he was at Brixton Prison. But she was restless, she needed to walk, to move, to relieve the dull ache in her chest. It was more than the look Winn had given her. She was not sure how or why, it was a feeling, a strange instinctive feeling, that Lindsay was involved in something painful. Her mind was racing, turning dark corners. For a few wild seconds she considered walking to the prison and hammering on its gates. But she must have made an unconscious decision to go home because a short time later she found herself in Lord North Street. The house was empty and cold and she took an old fur coat of her mother's from the cloakroom and wrapped it tightly about herself. Then she lay on her bed and curled into a ball to breathe the comfort of her mother's perfume, the fur soft against her cheek. And she lay there sleepless until dawn.

0030
15 September
'C' Wing, Brixton Prison

Oberleutnant Dietrich was the senior officer in the room but the others were too afraid to care. The atmosphere crackled in the headphones like distant thunder. Bruns had remembered one of the lines from the first officer's confession perfectly.

'. . . *Bruns was for executing Lange as a traitor . . .*

What had the British promised Dietrich? What was the price?

'You're trying to blame us. You've made a deal,' Schmidt's voice was very shrill. 'You of all people.'

'What else did you say about me?' Bruns was close to the hidden microphone.

'I . . . but I think we should . . .'

Dietrich's voice was drowned by a screeching chair and a moment later Lindsay heard gasping, then a low moan. Someone had struck Dietrich hard, perhaps forcing him to the floor.

'Stop it, for God's sake.' It was the *U-112*'s second officer, Koch;

he sounded more composed than the others. 'Oberleutnant Dietrich, you must tell us. Help him up.'

'The British are going to hang us for murder,' said Dietrich thickly.

'You were frightened so you told them about us, you cunt. I'm going to kill you.'

'. . . they think we killed Heine and I tried to tell them . . . I explained we were only trying to frighten Lange. That's all, I swear.' Dietrich's voice was shaking with fear.

'I'm going to fucking kill you. You coward. You're no better than Lange. Betrayed your comrades and the Fatherland.'

'Shut up.' It was Koch again. 'Calm down.'

No one spoke for a few seconds. Heavy footsteps, short anxious breaths and one of them was obviously standing beneath the microphone hidden in the light fitting.

'Did they ask you about Kapitän Mohr?'

Koch must have been leaning close to Dietrich because he spoke in barely a whisper: 'His position at headquarters?'

'Yes, they asked me about his role but I told them I didn't know.'

'Good.'

'And the mission, the codes, did you tell him about the codes?'

'No . . . I . . .'

'Bastard.' Bruns must have taken his hesitation as an admission of guilt or perhaps he could not contain his anger for a second longer. But there was another sharp gasp of pain from Dietrich and the clatter of the chair falling sideways.

'Stop it,' shouted Koch, struggling breathlessly to restrain Bruns. 'That's an order.'

'I didn't tell them about the mission,' Dietrich gasped from the floor, 'or the B-Service . . . I've only heard a little, just a little . . .'

He cried out. Someone – Bruns – must have kicked him as he lay there. And again, and again. And there was the sound of scuffling feet. Perhaps Schmidt was wading in too. Both men were on a short fuse and Koch had given up trying to restrain them.

Lindsay pulled off his headphones and, half rising, leant across to touch the sleeve of the man beside him: 'Let's rescue him.'

Robbins pulled a face and shook his head vigorously. He bent towards the machine again, his hands clamped tightly over the earpieces.

'No, we must . . .'

But Robbins was waving him back into his chair, a wry smile on his face. Lindsay picked up the headphones again.

'. . . They don't know that we were intercepting their signals. I've said nothing about the captain's role, I swear I haven't.'

'Shut up . . .'

'But you've dropped us in the shit, you swine.'

There was a low moan that ended in a grunt of air as someone aimed another kick at the prone man.

'That's it, that's enough,' said Lindsay, pushing back his chair.

'Sure?' asked Robbins lazily. 'Chap's only getting what he deserves, you know. A few bruises.'

Lindsay did not answer but pushed past him to the cell door and on to the landing. It was only a few yards to the little interrogation room. He gathered guards in his wake.

'All right. Let me in. Prisoners back to their cells. Fetch the doctor.'

Dietrich was lying in a tight little ball beside the table, his hands over his head. The others stepped back at once. Koch was quicker than the rest. When he saw Lindsay at the door he looked surprised, then anxious as the truth began to dawn on him.

'Rabbit in the headlamps.' Robbins was standing at Lindsay's shoulder, a cigarette hanging from the corner of his mouth like an American gumshoe.

'You'd think they would ask themselves why they've suddenly been thrown together. They panic. Spill it all to each other. It's always the same. Especially at . . .' and he glanced at his watch, 'one o'clock in the morning.'

The doctor was bent over Dietrich who was uncurling slowly like a leaf in spring.

'You see, just a few bruises,' said Robbins. 'Did you get what you wanted?'

'Enough, I think.'

They watched as Dietrich was helped back to his feet. He swayed drunkenly, and there was a nasty cut high on his cheek that would certainly need stitches. The doctor took his arm and began leading him to the door. He was in his sixties with a shock of white hair and a heavy Old Testament brow, none too steady on his own feet. As they passed, he gave Robbins a sharp and knowing look that suggested it was not their first encounter in the interrogation room. If Robbins noticed, he was not at all concerned.

'And now?'

'Mohr.'

There was no choice. It was time to chance everything. The last throw. There was nothing more he could wring from the others tonight and he had promised the Director that he would have something by the morning. If he did not break Mohr then he would have failed and there would be nothing to show for the price he had made others pay. Nothing.

'Lindsay?' Samuels was walking along the landing towards him. 'What's happened to Dietrich?'

'Just bruises.'

'Bruises?' Samuels frowned, 'How?'

'He's fine.'

'Did you hit him?' Samuels looked shocked.

'No. I'm sorry, Charlie, I haven't got time', and he brushed past him to the stairs and began thumping down to the ground floor.

48

'It's almost a year to the day since my ship was sunk . . .'

'Is that why we're here?'

'No. We're here because you and your officers committed two despicable crimes.'

'Revenge?'

'War.'

'And your guilt?'

Lindsay leant across the table to offer him a cigarette. Mohr looked at it for a second or so then took it, rolling it thoughtfully between thumb and forefinger. He was a swarthy man but his skin had turned U-boat grey, as if he had spent weeks in the hull of his submarine, and there were dark rings about his eyes. It was a noisy landing at night with heavy-booted warders and the slamming of doors: that had been simple to arrange.

'Don't you want to smoke it?' Lindsay sent his lighter spinning across the table. 'There is more than one kind of death, don't you agree?'

Mohr snapped the lighter and held the long yellow flame to his cigarette. It flickered in the draught from the ventilation grille above, cutting sad lines in his face. Then he inhaled deeply and with obvious pleasure.

'Many men died on my ship,' said Lindsay quietly, 'Most of them. But their names will be remembered with pride and honour. That is one kind of death.' He paused to fold his arms comfortably on the table in front of him in a way that suggested he was reflecting on this thought.

'A man's reputation for a hundred years can depend on a single moment. To lose it is another kind of death.'

Mohr watched him closely through the haze of cigarette smoke that hung over the table, his face quite empty of emotion.

'What will people say about you and the others do you think? That you brought honour to your Navy and to your families in that washroom? Will your name be spoken in anything above a whisper?'

Still the quiet steady stare. Mohr's elbow was on the table, the side of his face in his hand, his shoulders hunched wearily over the ashtray, and there was ash on the sleeve of his shit-brown uniform. He seemed older and diminished, as if after slopping-out with the cons at Brixton there was nowhere further to fall. If that was what he was thinking, he was wrong.

'I've spoken to someone here and they say you're given your own clothes and a glass of brandy to steady your nerves – I would ask for the bottle. Then the hangman visits your cell to strap your hands behind your back. A "T" is chalked on the trap-door for your feet and there are warders on the boards on either side in case you faint. White cotton hood, the noose, the hangman's assistant straps your ankles.'

Lindsay paused to flick ash from the end of his cigarette.

'Then bang . . .'

And he wrapped his knuckles on the table.

'. . . the door opens and down you go. Very efficient. Twenty seconds from the condemned cell to the drop. I believe when they take you down they measure your neck and it's usually an inch or two longer. Then they bury you in an unmarked grave in the prison yard. Not a place of pilgrimage and a long way from the sea.'

Mohr sat there motionless still, his face stiff and white like a marble Buddha, as if determined to live up to the name he was known by in the U-boat messes.

'There is a choice you know,' said Lindsay slowly. 'An honourable one.'

'An honourable one?' Mohr laughed harshly.

'I think so.'

'I didn't want those men to die. You know that, don't you?' He lifted his right hand to his brow for a moment, a small troubled gesture. The mask was cracking a little. 'Heine took his own life. And with Lange, well, I let it be known that no one was to speak to him, he was to be isolated, ostracised, and that was all.'

For a few seconds Lindsay stared at him with an expression close to contempt, then he pushed back his chair and got to his feet. There was a yellow file on the table. He picked it up and took a few steps towards the door, his back to Mohr: 'That is for the court to decide but I am confident they have enough to reach the correct verdict.'

There was an early-morning chill and the corners of the cell were in shadow. It was the large one they had used for the interrogation of Dietrich, gloomy, lit by only a single bulb.

'Do you recognise the file? It's the one your men handed to Heine when he was forced to sign a confession.'

'I know nothing of that.'

'Well, I thought it was appropriate to use it again for the statements your officers have given to me. They all agree, you know. They're very clear that they were carrying out your wishes. Here, Dietrich: . . . *the Ältestenrat found him guilty of aiding the enemy . . . we were carrying out Kapitän Mohr's orders as senior officer . . .*'

Mohr shook his head but said nothing.

'Are you afraid of death, Mohr?'

'No.'

'And your family? Your lady friend, Marianne, isn't it? What are they going to think of you when they hear how you died?'

'Can I have another cigarette?' His strange high-pitched voice cracked a little.

Turning back to the table, Lindsay placed his silver cigarette case and lighter in front of him. Mohr picked up the case and turned it over in his hands thoughtfully. As he put it down again the small gold crown and letter 'M' on the face of Lindsay's watch caught his eye.

'My Grandfather's,' said Lindsay, drawn by his gaze. 'The cigarette case belonged to him too. He served in the Imperial Navy.'

'Your cousin Martin mentioned him to me once – he was on Admiral von Hipper's Staff?'

'He's of the old school. You know, he would think very poorly of what has been done in your name.'

The jibe found its mark, the colour rushing back to Mohr's face: 'That was an easy shot. I trusted people . . . and there was a certain madness. But what would he think of you?'

'That I was doing my job, I hope.'

'And if I told you what you want to know, if I betrayed the Reich, what would your grandfather say then?'

'He will never know.'

Mohr snorted and shook his head.

'If you tell me in confidence I guarantee there will be no record kept of the source. You and your men will be returned to the camp and in due course sent on to another in Canada. The charges will be dropped and a verdict of suicide recorded in both cases. These things are easy to arrange.'

'And my honour, my duty to the Fatherland?'

'Honour will mean nothing at the end of the rope. Disgraced. A murderer. And what about your officers?'

Lindsay dropped the yellow file and bent over the table on out-stretched arms so that his face was only a few feet from Mohr's and when he spoke it was no more than an earnest whisper:

'They trusted their commanding officer. Weeks in the U-boat, the hardships they endured for you, their commander, their captain, with their blind faith in your judgement. Are you going to desert them now? You are the one who has brought them here to this place. And their lives hang in the balance. It is your duty to return them some day to their families, to their loved ones.'

Slowly Lindsay stood up, his fingertips slipping across the tabletop: 'I want you to think about their families, about your family. No one will ever know, no one.'

Mohr's dark eyes were roving about Lindsay's face in search of some clue to his sincerity: 'Why should I believe you?'

'It has been cleared with those who are able to make these things happen.'

'Who?'

Lindsay picked up the file again and walked to the door. He knocked on it sharply and it opened almost at once. Then, turning quickly back for a moment, he asked: 'Would you like some tea?'

*

336

Ten minutes at most. A short time only for reflection but enough for the shadows in Mohr's mind to lengthen. Lindsay had sent for tea and was waiting on the landing, his hands on the rail. In the well below him, the squeak of a warder's shoes, someone shouting in his sleep, the restless echo of the prison, of confused, damaged people. And he was not so different. Perhaps Mohr was the same. Prisoners too, held by memories and guilt as securely as the men behind those heavy steel doors. Prisoners of war.

What would Mohr say when in a few minutes he stepped back into the cell? It was unreasonable, perverse, but he could not escape the thought that his own freedom was hanging in the balance too. Another condemned man in hope of a reprieve. They had met only a few times but he had lived with Mohr for months, rolling the man and the codes round and round in his mind like a stone until they were one and the same. A strange and dangerous obsession. And now the point of decision. He glanced at his watch, it was half past two and the warder was by the door with the tea. It was time.

Mohr was standing at the far wall, his face and shoulders in shadow. The door closed behind Lindsay and he stepped forward to place the mugs on the table. They were alone again, to dance, to fence, studying every word, every gesture.

'Sit down please. They give you two sugars here whether you like it or not.' Mohr did not move a muscle.

Lindsay pulled out his chair and sat, then reached across the table for the cigarette case. Two were missing. Two in ten minutes. He could sense that Mohr was watching him closely, like a cat, a cat in a shit-brown uniform. He took a cigarette and lit it.

'Sit down please.'

But Mohr stood there still.

The seconds passed in edgy silence. Mohr's chin slipped to his chest as if he was close to sleep. There was a loud metallic rattle on the landing outside, someone must have dropped a tray, footsteps, voices, then silence again.

'I was the Staff officer responsible for communications.'

Lindsay could feel the pulse thumping in his neck. He took a deep shaky breath to steady himself.

'Designation, A4.'

337

Silence again. More footsteps outside the door. Lindsay picked up his mug to sip the hard, tannic, sweet tea. Mohr was teetering on the edge. A small push would send him tumbling over. Slowly, he lowered the mug back to the table.

'Sit down, please, Herr Kapitän.'

And this time Mohr stepped forward to pull out the chair, his face white and drawn.

'How long were you on the staff at U-boat Headquarters?'

'Can I have another?' And he pointed to the cigarettes.

Lindsay nodded and pushed the cigarette case back to him.

'A little over six months.'

'And you joined?'

'For the second time, in the autumn of last year.'

'The second time?'

'Yes.'

'You are reading our signals?'

Mohr drew on his cigarette and looked away. Then, planting his elbow on the table, he bent his head to cover his face as if in prayer. A few seconds more and he muttered something that Lindsay did not catch.

'Are you reading our signals?'

'Yes. Yes, damn it.'

'How many?'

'Most of them.'

'Most of them?'

'Most of them.' He lifted his head from his hand and there was a small tight-lipped smile on his face. An involuntary smile, the pleasure of revealing a shocking secret.

'I will talk to you here and now in this room. That is all. And to no one else. Do you agree?'

'Yes.'

'Only in this cell.'

'And there will be no mention of the source?'

'No.'

Mohr gave a painfully heavy sigh and leant forward, his hands clasped in the middle of the table: 'You changed the Naval Cipher last summer. It didn't take the B-Dienst long to break into the new one. And the other one – the Naval Code – you introduced two basic books. We broke into those in just six weeks. Old habits. Too many short signals sent the same way. Your codes changed but the word patterns and most of the wording remained more or less the same. So it was simple.'

'And that means you know . . .'

'Convoy routes, lone ships, battleships, any kind of ship, times of arrival, times of departure. I expect we knew all about your convoy . . .'

Lindsay looked at him and for a desperate moment he wanted to cry. Madness. Why? He must take control of himself. He reached down to the briefcase at his feet to search for his notepad. As he lifted it to the table he noticed that his hand was trembling.

'All right. Let's start at the beginning.'

'Do you know why I'm telling you this?'

'Please tell me.'

'For my men. I don't care for myself. Believe me. I don't care. But they deserve better than to . . .' He swallowed hard, then coughed in an effort to disguise the emotion that was written plainly enough on his face. 'Heine is enough. A terrible, tragic mistake. But no more, I don't want any more deaths . . . and . . .'

Again he could not finish. For a few seconds they sat there in silence looking everywhere, anywhere but at each other. But in an hour, maybe less, Mohr might regret his decision. It was important not to give him the time to reconsider it : 'I want to start with the first code-breaks.'

'Your Merchant Navy Code was the easiest. We use it like a railway timetable, convoy departure and arrival times, call signs, and the routes.'

'How many Merchant Navy signals are you decrypting?'

'Sometimes two thousand a month with only a short delay.'

Lindsay wrote it down. Questions, then more questions. And notes in a small neat hand, the pace quickening as the minutes ticked by, sweet tea and cigarettes, and occasionally Mohr would push back his chair to walk about the cell. He spoke of code books captured from British submarines, and of the signals that had betrayed the Navy in Norway the year before, of Atlantic convoy traffic and lone ships tracked and sunk in African waters. At a little before four o'clock he was escorted to the lavatory and Lindsay stood by the door watching the second hand on his watch as if waiting for Cinderella to come home from the ball.

'And your mission to Freetown, what was its purpose?'

'It was my idea. Ha.' He shook his head ruefully. 'I've only myself to blame. I wanted to leave the Staff and return to my boat. So it was agreed I would co-ordinate attacks off Freetown. The wireless operators spoke English and were trained to intercept and decode the signals. I would then direct the nearest U-boat to attack, more than one if it could reach the convoy in time. It was happy hunting there.'

It was at a little before six o'clock when Lindsay put down his pencil. Doubt and fear were crystallising in Mohr like frost and for almost an hour he had refused to say much more than 'Yes' or 'No'. The emotional effort had left him exhausted, slumped on his chair like a sack of potatoes.

'You will honour your promise to release my men? And no one will know I've spoken to you?'

Lindsay picked up the pad and began slowly turning the pages of cream paper carefully covered with his pencil notes. Mohr had given much. One of the promises he had made to him would be easy to keep.

'Yes, your men will be sent back to the camp. They won't be charged with murder.'

'We aren't murderers, you know that.'

It was feeble-sounding from such a man.

Lindsay stared across the table at him. Why had he done it? Was it loyalty to the crew or vanity and a fear of disgrace and death? Perhaps a deep, deep weariness. It was impossible to be sure because there was often no answer to the difficult questions, the things that really mattered – duty, loyalty, love – only a confusing tangle of feelings and thoughts pulling in many different directions. Mohr would reflect on it for the rest of his life, the answer always different, changing year on year.

'No. You aren't murderers,' he said coolly. 'You won't be taken to court. You are not murderers because no one was murdered.'

Mohr frowned and leant forward a little to study his face: 'But Lange was . . .'

'Leutnant Lange is recovering in hospital.'

The nails of Mohr's right hand cut into the fist he had made of his left. He closed his eyes, his jaws were clenched, his face stiff with anger. Picking up the pad, Lindsay pushed back his chair and stepped over to rap once on the door: 'All right, take him away.'

Mohr was still sitting at the table, his head bent back a little, his eyes closed, breathing deeply. Keys tinkled in the lock and the door began to open.

'The two of us are the same, you know.' Mohr's eyes were still shut. 'You are a hunter.'

A prison warder was standing at the edge of the table waiting for him to get to his feet. He opened his eyes, the mask back in place, he was 'the Buddha' again.

'Come on.' The warder took his arm but he shook it free impatiently and, pushing his chair away, he got quickly to his feet.

At the door he stopped and turned to stare at Lindsay again, an outstretched arm apart. For a few seconds his dark eyes roved about Lindsay's face as if searching for some common feeling or warmth. He looked sad and tired and almost desperate. Then he was gone. And Lindsay listened to the disciplined beat of his footsteps retreating along the landing until they were lost in the echo of the prison.

And he was alone in the cell with the table and the chairs and an ashtray overflowing with cigarette butts. Triumph? No. A little quiet satisfaction, perhaps. Above all, bone-numbing exhaustion and a deep sadness. Pulling the door to, he walked over to the table and sat down. His eyes were swimming so he closed them and bent to rest his head on his arm. Almost at once he began to slip into that half-world between sleep and consciousness, to a place that was always the same, a cold place where the wind whistled and hissed and cut at the skin. And floating in darkness, a shape spinning and bobbing towards him, he touched it again and it turned its black burnt face to him, its eyes dull and empty. And as he pushed it away he wondered if it would ever be different.

'Oh sorry, sir.' A prison warder was standing at the door. 'I thought you'd finished in here.'

49

The Director wanted to be briefed before breakfast and the Admiralty's code and cipher people afterwards, headlines written for the First Sea Lord by mid-morning, the full report to be on his desk by 3 p.m. and then sent to Downing Street. Lindsay floated through the day, barely conscious of the compliments paid, the questions asked and the answers he gave. Objects and people began to soften at the edges, voices to reach him like the echo in a long tunnel. At five o'clock, Fleming took him by the elbow and led him from Room 39 to the doors of the Admiralty.

'Home. The rest can wait until morning. Can you make it on your own?'

'Yes, I'm capable of that but I was hoping to see Mary Henderson.'

Fleming frowned and looked away for a moment: 'Perhaps tomorrow. Or ring her, why don't you?'

Drunk with exhaustion, he collapsed on his bed fully clothed and slept a long and for once dreamless sleep until the early hours of the following morning. When he woke he lay on his back and stared at the ceiling, trying to bring the events of the previous day into focus. After a while the recollection of something small began to worry him. It was the slight frown on Fleming's face when he spoke of Mary. It was surely of no importance in itself but it unlocked troubling thoughts. 'A bad case of conscience, Doctor,' he muttered to himself. The early-morning blues. Swinging his legs from the bed, he padded through to the kitchen in search of bread and something to put on it. A few stale crusts and a pot of his mother's jam. He ate a little and drank some tea without milk, then took off his uniform and went back to bed. But he did not sleep again, turning restlessly until dawn. When the hour was civilised, he rang the house in Lord North Street but there was no reply.

For once he chose to breakfast in the Admiralty canteen, half in the hope of finding Mary there. But he did not see her and the food was as she described it – greasy and tasteless. Fleming had found a desk for him in a small office close to Room 39. It was little more than a cupboard with room for no more than the desk, two chairs, and a filing cabinet. No one was interested in his opinion of code security any more. And no one was interested in the opinion of the Code Security Section either. It was in the hands of the Staff and the cryptologists now. But there were some embarrassingly loose ends to tie up. Housekeeping. The Director wanted an account of the 'shambles' at Number One Camp and he had just begun to dictate excuses to a Wren when the door opened:

'You're not easy to find.' Samuels stepped into the room. He sounded very unfriendly.

Lindsay asked the Wren to leave them alone for a few minutes. The moment the door closed behind her Samuels said: 'You know, it was torture.'

'What?'

'Dietrich: the way you treated him, it was a kind of torture. The sort of thing the Nazis do.'

'I wouldn't have let it get out of hand.'

'He was badly beaten.'

'I'm sorry you're feeling squeamish.'

Samuels shook his head ruefully: 'I've heard about Lange. Was that necessary too?'

'Yes.'

'I don't think you would have thought so a few months ago . . .' but Samuels was interrupted by a knock at the door. It was a uniformed runner with a note from Fleming.

'Perhaps we could talk later, Charlie?'

'No, I don't think that will be necessary,' he replied coldly. 'Oh, I almost forgot – congratulations.'

Then he turned his back on Lindsay and walked out.

The door to Room 39 was slightly ajar and the murmur of voices from inside suggested that Fleming had just left a meeting. He must have noticed Lindsay approaching along the corridor out of the corner of his eye because he turned from the window with a question:

'The Director wants to know if there is any propaganda value to be had from Mohr. A radio broadcast.'

'No. He won't co-operate. I'm sure of it.'

And there was the same frown that had kept Lindsay awake half the night. Clearly Fleming was taken aback by the sharpness of his response: 'You're not expecting us to keep your promise?'

'Yes.'

Yes, he knew he was, yes. When he had made it to Mohr he had not cared one way or the other. It was not that he had spent hours regretting it, he had not given the matter any further thought, but now suddenly it seemed important. If asked, he would be at a loss to explain why. But Fleming just looked at him sceptically, then turned to the door. 'Wait across the corridor, Lindsay,' he said, and he stepped inside, closing it behind him.

The Director stood at the conference table, arms folded, head bent like an inquisitive bird, and thirty of his most senior officers were gathered in a semicircle about him. The head of Code and Cipher, a stout reserve commander in his late fifties, was addressing the room on the changes that were being considered to security. The stony faces about him suggested that difficult questions had not been answered to the satisfaction of those at the table. It would be a month before new code books were printed and distributed, he explained hesitantly, and a month more before wireless operators in the Navy and Merchant Service were able to use them properly. 'I'm afraid until then we will have to continue with the current code and cipher books.'

This information was met by awkward glances and some embarrassed shuffling of paper and feet.

'The Prime Minister exploded when he was told.' Admiral Godfrey glared about the table. 'It's a shambles. We'd better learn the lessons. All right. That's all.'

The meeting was over. The Director spoke briefly to his Assistant then picked up his papers and walked back through the green baize covered door into his office. The heads of section began to drift out of the room and after a few minutes only two men were left at the conference table. Half rising from his chair, Winn leant across the table with his cigarettes: 'Quite a coup, don't you think?'

344

'No thank you,' and Checkland held up his hand to refuse.

'Do you think Lindsay will be returning to you?'

Before Checkland was able to flannel an answer Fleming was ready to show them into the Director's office.

'It must be gratifying to know Dönitz thinks highly of your work, Winn.' Admiral Godfrey lifted the report on the desk in front of him and turned to a section he had marked in pencil:

Kapitän Mohr said the staff at U-boat Headquarters were often impressed by the accuracy of the daily intelligence summaries on U-boat dispositions that were produced for the Royal Navy's ships at sea by its Tracking Room . . .'

'Infuriating, sir,' said Winn who sounded anything but in complete control of his emotions. 'As you say, sir, a shambles. We're reading their signals and they're reading ours.'

'Not, I hope, for much longer. But God knows what Code Security was doing. And what sort of code is it that can be broken by the enemy after only a few months? It's cost us very dearly in ships.'

The Director dropped the report back on the desk: 'Lindsay's done a fine job. The cryptologists have been to Brixton to see Mohr and they've got nothing else from him.'

'They've probably got some scruples, sir,' said Checkland tartly.

'Then they should have left them at the prison gates.' Godfrey turned to glare at him: 'Yes, he's been insubordinate and a little unscrupulous but he's not training for the priesthood here. This intelligence may save thousands of lives.'

He sat back in his chair and looked to Fleming for agreement: 'Lindsay has a nose for this business. Finally, we've got something first-class from a prisoner.'

Fleming nodded vigorously.

'Don't you think it would be a good idea to have him back?'

It was not a question Checkland was expected to answer.

'There are going to be changes at Trent Park.' There was a coldness in Godfrey's manner that suggested the changes might involve the appointment of a new head of section. At least Checkland must have thought so because he flushed a deep shade of crimson.

There was an uncomfortable silence as the Director stared at each of them in turn like a hawk sizing up a meal. It was Winn who eventually spoke: 'Lindsay has done well, sir, but he's dangerous. He's a rule-breaker who encourages others to do the same.'

Winn balanced his copy of the report on the edge of the desk: 'I know Fleming has spoken to you about Mary Henderson. I've asked her to stand down.'

'Yes.'

'She was suited to the work, thoughtful and meticulous. It's a pity.'

'Yes.'

The Director pushed his chair away from the desk, then walked round it to the window. The first leaves of autumn were fluttering across Horse Guards.

'Was it necessary?'

The officers at the desk exchanged glances. The Director turned to look at them: 'Well?'

'Lindsay was very tired when he wrote his report, sir, he may not have realised he'd let it slip,' said Fleming.

'Let's not make excuses. It was a filthy thing to do,' said Winn coolly. 'But as you say, sir, he doesn't have to be a decent human being to be of service.'

Fleming frowned: 'You know, Rodger, I'm sure he's got no idea what he's done to Henderson.'

'I think perhaps he does. He's too clever. But tell him, to be sure. Didn't you say he was waiting outside?'

'Yes, you can tell him, Ian,' Godfrey said sharply. 'For God's sake let's move on from this.'

Lindsay had tired of the bustle and noise of the messengers' room and was pacing and cursing under his breath in the corridor outside. It was after eleven o'clock and he had been there for more than an hour. Everyone else seemed to move with purpose but he had spent the time smoking and brooding on his exchange with Samuels. You had to draw a line somewhere so it was worrying that someone whose opinion he respected thought he had drawn it in the wrong place. And Mary would surely think the same. She had helped him in so many ways, with support and understanding and confidence and love and, yes, with information too. And he should have thanked her, should have told her how much he felt for her. He knew he had always taken more than he had given in their relationship and had been cavalier with her trust. He must find her and tell her so. When Fleming had finished with him he would arrange for a note to be delivered to the Tracking Room.

He was about to scribble something on a scrap of paper when he saw Winn lumbering awkwardly towards him, file under one arm, head bent in contemplation like a monk in a cloister garden. He did not seem to notice Lindsay and it looked as if he might pass without a word but, an arm's length away from him and almost as an after thought, he turned and said: 'I suppose I should congratulate you.'

But I don't want you to, Lindsay thought, and the unspoken words seemed to hang in the air between them.

'Thank you, sir.'

Winn stared at him for a moment, his eyes lost behind the reflection in his glasses, then he turned and walked on without another word. Mary. He knew it was Mary and the little knot of anxiety he had been trying to ignore tightened in his stomach. He was on the point of following Winn but footsteps were echoing along the corridor towards him: 'Sorry to keep you.'

Fleming gave him a friendly slap on the arm: 'Let's stretch our legs, take some air, what do you say?'

The knot in Lindsay's stomach tightened even more.

'Is this something to do with Mary?'

Fleming took his arm: 'Come on, let's walk.'

It had rained heavily and yellow plane leaves were floating in the pools still forming in the gutters. A fitful sun was breaking through the grey, glinting in the fine spray thrown up by traffic sweeping up the Mall towards the Palace. They crossed Horse Guards and walked in uneasy silence until they reached the white stone memorial to those of the Household Division who had died in the Great War.

'I never tire of this view,' said Fleming, nodding towards the parade ground opposite, 'even the bloody balloons can't spoil it. Horse Guards, the Admiralty, Downing Street and Whitehall. Can you

347

imagine that lot goose-stepping here? I'd do anything to make sure it never happens.'

He reached into his jacket pocket for his cigarettes: 'Would you like to smoke one of these?'

Lindsay shook his head. Why was he taking so long to get to the point? A special torment. He watched as Fleming tried to protect his lighter flame from the stiff breeze. It was some time before he managed to light his cigarette and sensing Lindsay's impatience he held out a hand as if to steady him: 'You did well in the end. You took some chances and this time they were worth taking. But if you'd got it wrong the Director would have hung you out to dry. You know that, don't you?'

'Yes.'

'Mary took chances too. She got it wrong.'

'What do you mean?'

'Oh, please,' and Fleming gave a short cynical laugh. 'Please don't play the innocent. You know perfectly well that Mary told you we were reading the German Enigma ciphers. She also slipped you a piece of special intelligence that suggested at least one of our own codes was compromised. You're not going to deny it, are you?'

The answer was evident in Lindsay's face. It was one of the signs he never missed across a table from a prisoner. What was it American card players called it? 'A tell.' He felt hot with guilt.

'You betrayed her in your report, but you know that, don't you? And Winn has confronted her and she admitted it at once and told him she gave you help with our codes too. That little piece of paper?'

'For God's sake, what does it matter whether she helped me or not?' Lindsay made no attempt to disguise his anger. This was madness. Both of them had taken risks, yes, but they were worth taking, Fleming had just said as much: 'Mary broke the rules to help me and it was the right decision to take.'

'The Director and Winn don't agree,' he said with a little shake of the head. 'It was not information you needed to know. And she should have known better . . .'

'She wasn't handing it over to a spy . . .'

'Mary knows how precious special intelligence is to us, to this . . .' and Fleming gestured theatrically to the scene before them. 'She was

348

one of just a handful at the heart of our operations with access to the most secret intelligence. If we lose special intelligence we may lose the war at sea. Do you think Winn goes home and talks to his wife about it?'

'She doesn't work for Naval Intelligence.'

Fleming stepped forward to drop his cigarette in the gutter, then turned again to look at Lindsay: 'I'm fond of Mary but her position was impossible. She couldn't go back to the Tracking Room. She understood that perfectly.' He spoke sharply and quickly, clearly anxious to bring the conversation to a close. 'No one wants to take it further, thank God. Ah, you shake your head – people have been sent to prison for less.' He glanced at his watch: 'Look, I must be getting back.'

'So what will happen to Mary, sir?' Lindsay's voice cracked a little.

'She's left the Division.' He paused for a moment as if in two minds whether to say more. There was the distinctive little frown again: 'You know she feels badly let down.'

'Yes,' said Lindsay flatly. 'I expect she does.'

When Fleming left, the old panic gripped him again. Lindsay stood at the foot of the memorial breathing slowly and deeply, trying to clear his mind. What had possessed him to be so reckless with Mary's trust? Careless, careless, unnecessary words and Fleming was right, he could not play the innocent, he had understood the risk he was running. He had dictated his report to a Wren, short hard sentences, the brutal click of the typewriter keys, blind to any loyalty or feeling beyond duty to the war effort. At least, 'duty', 'the greater good' was how he chose to present it to others. But he knew it was guilt too. Guilt gnawing at him always, that desperate craving for release from the burden of being a man who was dragged from the Atlantic the night two hundred lives were lost. It distorted, warped his perspective like a fairground mirror. Mary could see that, understood and loved him none the less. He had to find her to try and explain and tell her he was so very sorry.

Nobody answered the bell at Lord North Street. The shutters were open and he wondered for a moment if Mary was in the house but had resolved not to see him. He pulled the bell again but no one came. But she was not the sort of woman who would skulk behind curtains to avoid a painful conversation. Perhaps she had left London for a few days. He would have to chase her by phone, and the nearest and most convenient place to begin was at the interrogators' office in Sanctuary Buildings. It was a short walk across Dean's Yard where builders were trying to salvage what they could of the Abbey's domestic range damaged in the Blitz.

Dick Graham was the only interrogator in the office. He had been sent to the prison but given nothing to do and it rankled.

'The hero of the hour,' and he glared at Lindsay over his pince-nez. 'I expect they'll give you another medal.'

Lindsay ignored him. First Mary's uncle. Settling at the desk by the window, he picked up the telephone and began chasing the number for Parliament round the dial. The operator put him through to a stiff assistant who refused to say when she would see Sir David next and only reluctantly promised to say he had called. He was about to try the house in Lord North Street again when Checkland's secretary presented herself at the edge of the desk: 'The Colonel said you would want to see this right away,' and she handed him a plain blue envelope. He took it and slit it open at once. There was a smaller envelope inside and a note in Checkland's own hand:

Enclosed a note from Leutnant Lange. He is making a good recovery and will be discharged from hospital in the coming week.

He held Lange's envelope in his right hand and stared at it for what must have been a minute. It was Graham who finally broke into his thoughts: 'A billet-doux from one of your many admirers in the Division?'

'Go to hell.'

'I probably will. And you'll be there too.'

It was not the time or the place. Lindsay dropped the little envelope into his pocket. There was still no reply from the house. Perhaps he should ring Mary's brother? It was surely a measure of his desperation that he was even prepared to consider it. What about her parents in Suffolk?

'Do we have a copy of *Debrett*?'

Graham was dictating interrogation notes to one of the clerical assistants. He looked up at Lindsay with a dry smile and stretched a hand over the typewriter to indicate that she should stop hammering the keys.

'I don't think they'll offer you a peerage, old boy.'

'Do we have a copy of *Debrett*?'

'Would you like some help choosing the title?'

Lindsay half turned to address the clerical assistant: 'Well?'

'I'll fetch it, sir.'

Charnes Hall, and yes, there was a number. An office shared with Graham was not the place to try it and he jotted it down on a piece of paper.

There was a telephone in the small registry down the corridor where the Section kept its records. It had a short flex and he had to stand beside the filing cabinet to use it. He had to dial the number of the exchange twice because on the first attempt, like a tongue-tied teenager, he hung up before the operator had a chance to put him through.

'Mrs Henderson? Douglas Lindsay here.'

A long uncertain silence.

'Yes?'

'May I speak to Mary please?'

'I don't know if she's in the house. Just a minute.'

Her voice was cut finer than her daughter's, very county. The telephone was probably in a stone-flagged hall because he could hear the long echo of her footsteps as she walked away.

Someone rattled the handle of the registry door. 'Go away, I'm on the telephone.'

His stomach was churning and the receiver felt damp and heavy in his right hand: 'Come on, *come on*.'

Twenty seconds from the condemned cell to the bottom of the scaffold. Every second an hour. But they would have buried him by now. At last he heard footsteps approaching the telephone again and the rattle as Mary picked up the receiver.

'Lindsay?'

His heart sank many fathoms. It was Mary's brother.

'Are you there?'

'Yes, I'm here, James.'

'I'm here, sir.'

'I'm here, sir.'

'I'll say this once and once only,' his voice was trembling with barely repressed fury. 'She has nothing to say to you. You shit. You used her. You betrayed her. Now leave her alone.'

Bang went the phone. The buzz of an empty line.

Lindsay replaced the receiver carefully, his mind very clear. How strange that the anger of another was calming. He knew what he must do.

It was some hours later that Mary heard he had called and spoken to her brother. If only her mother had dealt with it or her father. She was cross because she could not help feeling sorry for Lindsay and she did not want to.

'You should have told him to ring back,' she told her mother. 'He's going to think I haven't the guts to talk to him in person.'

'I doubt that, darling,' her mother replied.

But she knew he would not leave it there. He would come to see her, perhaps tomorrow, and she would say what she needed to say. She had rehearsed it all so very carefully – to distraction.

She did not have to wait for the next day. At a little before six o'clock her father called to her from the bottom of the stairs.

'A military-looking car. Mother thinks it might be your man.'

She had not discussed Lindsay with her parents but they seemed to know everything from James. By the time she had slipped into a mac and wellingtons the Humber was pulling up in front of the stable block. Lindsay jumped out of the car with the restless energy of one who has driven a long distance fast and with single-minded purpose. In spite of herself she could feel a warm rush of affection for him. Head bent a little, she began striding towards the car. Lindsay slammed the door and walked round the back of it to meet her. He was already fumbling for his cigarettes.

'You could have spoken to me on the telephone,' she said coolly.

'That wasn't the impression your brother gave me.'

She had reached the car now, hands in the pockets of her mac, only a few feet from him. He slipped the cigarettes back into his jacket without taking one.

'Can I kiss you?'

'No.'

'Can we talk?'

'Yes.'

'Here?' And he glanced towards the house.

'No. We can walk.'

She led him in silence round the stable block and through a brick arch into the walled garden where the roses had been replaced by vegetables and a flock of chickens.

'It's quite a house. Seventeenth century?'

She did not answer but walked on, conscious that he was watching her closely. At the far end, she opened a door in the wall and led him across the grass to the edge of a copse. It was already dark beneath the trees, the ground soft, and she could hear him stumbling and slipping and grabbing at branches for support. And she thought of his shiny black shoes and smiled with quiet satisfaction. It was not until they emerged on the other side of the wood that she stopped and turned, arms tightly folded: 'Well?'

'Well, I'm very sorry. Very, very sorry. No excuses. Can you ever forgive me?'

'Can I forgive you?'

'Yes. I love you. You know I love you very much. I didn't want to hurt you,' and he stepped forward to touch her.

'No, Douglas,' she said firmly and held up a hand. 'No, don't. I can't forgive you.'

He took half a step back again and looked away, as if uncertain what he should say next. Did he really think 'sorry' would be enough? Did he think it would be that easy? And she could feel the anger she had been so determined to control rising inside her.

'It was unforgivable and I can't explain it,' he said. 'At least I can't explain it better than you when you called it a dangerous obsession.'

He was gazing across the patchwork of stubble and recently turned fields that dipped gently westwards away from them. The sky was heavy with blue-grey cloud too thick for any sort of sunset.

'I can't understand when we both work for the Division why . . .'

'Aah,' Mary grabbed her hair with both hands and pulled at it in exasperation. 'You don't understand, do you? It's you. It's not the Navy,

353

it's not me. It's you.' And she swung away from him in exasperation. 'What have you become?'

'It's over now. Believe me,' he was almost pleading with her. 'I'm sorry I dragged you into this but I was trying to do my duty, trying to make some sort of amends. You know that.'

'It's not about me. Yes, it was disloyal and unnecessary but I half expected you to let the cat out of the bag. It's what you put that poor man through when he trusted you. Helmut Lange almost died. I don't think you'd have cared if he had.'

And now she had said it the anger began to ebb and there was just the deep heart-breaking sadness of it all. And she knew she would have to be careful or she would cry and she did not want that to happen.

'I didn't want to hurt him but it was the only way I could think of to trap Mohr.' He was looking at her now and his voice was hard and defensive as if surer of his ground. 'The Director wanted me to do all I could to break Mohr. The national interest – it will save lives. You know what was at stake.'

'It was in your interests and you've admitted as much.'

'They were one and the same.'

'Lange was your friend, you promised to protect him.'

'He was never a friend but of course I'm sorry I had to drag him into it. Look, is this getting us anywhere? I'm sorry I messed things up for you, really I am.'

He didn't sound that sorry now. He sounded irritated and she wondered if he was thinking, Why is this woman so unreasonable?

'You can dress it up as your duty and in the national interest if you like but I don't think I can love someone who is so ruthless with his friends, someone who lies and will betray anyone.'

'You lied to Winn.'

'Yes, for you, God forgive me,' she said bitterly.

'We're fighting a war.'

'But what's the point of winning it if we don't have something better to fight for? You behaved like a Nazi.'

He flinched and looked away. And she was pleased because now she wanted to hurt him. 'You've been trying to prove something too. What? Your loyalty?'

'That's rubbish. I don't have to do that. Lives will be saved. You know that.'

'It's all about you.'

He stepped forward to look at her intently and she was struck as always by the light blue of his eyes.

'Gosh, how you love the moral high ground,' he said sharply. 'It must be very lonely up there.'

That was cruel. She knew she was close to tears and that he knew it too. And it was too much. The frustration and the resentment and the anger burst from her. She slapped him. She slapped him hard on the cheek. It happened so quickly that for a moment she was not quite sure she had done it. But he had flinched and was reaching up to touch his cheek with his fingertips. And it looked hot and very red and her hand felt hot. His blue eyes were moist with tears. She wanted to reach out and stroke his cheek but she turned away instead, her hands at her mouth. For a few seconds, he stood there, his breath shaking, then she heard him push through the branches into the wood. She listened to him stumbling awkwardly on until she could hear him no more and she knew she was alone. A thin mist was rising from the land and, in the dying light, the hedges and trees and the sharp little stubble stalks at her feet were shapes in an almost colourless landscape. It was closing in on her, changing by the minute, by the second, into a cold and unfamiliar place. And it was so desperately sad. She brushed a tear from her cheek, and another, and another, and then she stopped trying. And she leant forward with her head bent and her hands on her knees for support and she sobbed, sobbed so hard her body began to shake uncontrollably and it was impossible to breathe.

How long did she cry for? It was dark when she stopped and she could barely see her hand in front of her face. She was tired and cold and empty. She did not want to go back to the house but knew she would have to or her father would come looking for her. The short walk through the wood was difficult and slow in the dark and she scratched her face and then her hand on a thick bramble. Through the walled garden and into the stables where she slipped out of her boots and into a pair of old shoes. Cook had gone home and the kitchen was empty, the pans and supper dishes washed and tidied away. There would be something for Mary in the range. She did not feel hungry. She wanted to slip quietly upstairs to bed but she knew she would have to speak to someone first. Her father was standing in the large stone-flagged entrance hall with a copy of *The Times*.

'Are you all right? You've been crying,' and he folded his newspaper and took half a step towards her as if to put a protective arm around her shoulders.

'No, honestly, I'm fine. Tired, that's all. I'm going to have a bath.'

'Not yet you're not,' he said with a dry smile. 'You've got to deal with him first,' and he waved the paper in the general direction of the door. 'I've had the devil's own job restraining your brother. Your man's sitting in his car.'

How foolish of her to have missed the Humber. It was still parked in front of the stable block. She could see Lindsay behind the wheel and the pinprick of light from his cigarette. She was sorry she had slapped him and she would say so but nothing more. Short, businesslike, no mention of Lange or the Division. A brief goodbye. She turned the handle of the passenger door and slipped on to the red leather seat.

'I'm very sorry I struck you. It was unforgivable,' she said quickly.

There was his small, slightly supercilious smile, the one she had marked at their first meeting and so often since.

'So many things seem to be unforgivable. Actually I deserved it. You can do it again if you like,' and he turned his head to offer the other cheek.

And she could not help but smile: 'Please. Christ-like isn't you at all.'

'No?'

He looked exhausted and the car's ashtray was overflowing with cigarette butts.

'Here,' and she leant across to brush a little mud from his jacket. 'I thought you'd gone.'

'I can't go.'

They sat there in silence for a moment. He was trying to catch her eye but she looked away.

'Do you want me to go?'

'Yes.'

'Here,' and he picked a sheet of blue writing paper from the dashboard and offered it to her. It was a handwritten note in German from Helmut Lange. Just four short lines.

'Read it to me,' and she handed it back to him.

'It says: *"Dear Lieutenant. The doctors say I am well enough to be transferred to a camp in Scotland. Will you visit me . . ."'*

His voice choked with emotion and he paused for a few seconds to regain some composure.

'And he says: *"You know it's strange but after all that has happened to me I feel at peace with myself and happier. Please come and visit me before I go. Your friend, Helmut."'*

He folded it slowly and slipped it into his jacket pocket.

'And will you visit him?'

'Yes.'

She gave a slight nod of the head, then looked away. There was nothing more to say. She should leave. And she leant towards the handle of the door.

'You've cut your face.'

'I must be quite a sight.'

'Yes. You are,' and he reached for her hand, opening her fingers, kissing her palm, small tender kisses. And then he pressed her hand against his cheek. Her bottom lip began to tremble. It was impossible. And without thought she pulled her hand away and opened the car door.

'Mary, please.'

The driver's door opened too.

'Mary.'

He was standing on the other side of the car. 'I'm so sorry, really I am.'

'No, Douglas,' and she began to walk away. 'Please go home. It's over. It's over.'

PART THREE

50

Dahlem
Berlin
December 1990

The little boy at the gate was blowing into his hands, trying to capture the warm vapour in a tight ball of fingers and thumbs. Even in his best coat and hat and scarf he was beginning to shiver. Grandfather's friend was late. The street was white with a hard frost and the old man opposite was scraping the ice from the windscreen of his Mercedes. The boy glanced over his shoulder to the house. His grandfather was at the study window, his head turning up and down the street. And a few seconds later, with a broad smile, he began gesturing frantically to the boy's right. An elderly but tall and upright man in a long black coat was walking carefully along the icy pavement towards him. Tears of frustration and disappointment welled inside the little boy and he ran towards the house. The door was already open and Herr Hans-Günther Gretschel was standing on the steps, leaning heavily on an ebony stick.

'Come here, Karl. Wait with me.'

But the little boy slipped past his grandfather's outstretched arm and disappeared inside the house. It was an imposing villa with a yellow and cream façade and sweeping red-tile roof, set back a little from the road in a mature garden. The little boy's great-great-grandfather had built it when Dahlem was just a village.

'Herr Lindsay. So very good to see you,' and Gretschel dropped a step to offer his hand in greeting. 'And looking so well.'

In the years since the war Gretschel had perfected the English he had begun to learn as a prisoner.

'My grandson Karl was watching for you. I'm afraid he's a little upset you surprised him.'

'Are you well, Herr Gretschel?'

'Old and tired and fat.'

And it was true he had put on a great deal of weight since Lindsay had last seen him a few years before. His black flannel trousers looked as if they were under enormous strain. Arthritis had left him much less mobile: 'My wife says I am turning into a large grey ball.'

He led Lindsay through the hall into the drawing room where Frau Gretschel had left a tray of coffee and cakes. Karl was sitting on the couch in his coat, his cheeks stained with tears. It was a light and modern room quite out of keeping with the imperial character of the façade. The house had been reduced to a shell in the battle for Berlin. Lindsay had visited it for the first time just a fortnight after the city had fallen, drunken Soviet troops roaming the streets, and he had found Gretschel's elderly parents and sister living in the cellar.

'Have you seen this?' Gretschel held out a framed photo to Lindsay. 'It's me with your Prime Minister. What a wonderful lady. I admire her so much.'

'And did you tell her you were the first officer of a U-boat that sank twenty British ships?'

'Of course not,' said Gretschel impatiently. 'It was a happy occasion. The Berlin Chamber of Commerce. Poor Lange was there too.' He put the photograph back on the shelf alongside a large collection of family pictures.

'Lange's daughters have made all the arrangements for today.'

They had moved in different social circles but they had always kept in touch. Lange had worked in the city's information bureau until a newspaper article forced him to retire. A young hack anxious to make his name wrote a story with the headline, 'Nazi PK Man Briefing the Press'. Gretschel had used his business contacts to find him another job in public relations.

'May I smoke?'

'Karl, please fetch our guest an ashtray. Shouldn't you give up at your age?'

Lindsay's wife was still badgering him to stop. After the Navy he had become a journalist and many of his colleagues on Fleet Street were unrepentant smokers too. Now in his seventies he was too old and too impatient to try. He woke each morning with a hacking cough, he was wrinkled and grey and a little short-sighted but a source of wonder to his friends – or so they said – and the doctors considered him fit for his age.

'I saw Admiral Mohr last month.' Gretschel reached across to hand Lindsay a cup of tea.

'Oh?'

'A reunion of the old comrades in Kiel. Fewer and fewer of us now. There were veterans from HMS *White* there as our guests. The Admiral made a generous speech. He's in good health and sends his regards.' He paused for a moment, then: 'I did sense he was a little troubled. Did you read the profile of him in *Spiegel*?'

'No,' Lindsay lied.

'It suggested he gave vital intelligence to the British during the war. No one believes it.'

'No.'

They did not speak for a moment but sipped their coffee, the silence broken only by the tinkle of the china cups and by Karl who was crunching a biscuit and showering crumbs on his coat and the couch.

'Do you think of the war, Herr Lindsay?'

'Sometimes.'

'I've begun to think of it again. I tell Karl stories of our boat. His mother does not like me talking of those times but . . . I've told him a little about the camp too.' He chuckled and leant forward as if to share a confidence: 'He knows you did something very secret. He thinks you're James Bond.'

Lindsay smiled and looked across at the little boy: 'Does he know we were enemies?'

Gretschel put down his cup and folded his arms slowly over his stomach in a way that suggested he had something of substance to impart: 'I've tried to explain to Karl that sometimes those who appear to be enemies become friends and our friends become our enemies. War is a confusing business. And the battles we fight are often with ourselves – in here,' and he tapped his head with his forefinger. 'Of course he doesn't understand. It was only at the camp in Canada that I began to understand it myself. Perhaps I didn't dare to before. It was the business with Lange, the night he almost died, that made me wonder what I should render to Caesar. My conscience. Do you understand?'

Lindsay nodded quietly. Gretschel looked at him for a moment, then frowned: 'You know, it was hard for Lange. Some of the veterans refused to speak to him because he helped the British. And the most ridiculous thing; the young – his own daughters – accused him of being a Nazi propagandist. Can you believe it? After all he went through.'

He glanced at his watch: 'But we should be going. And your wife will meet us there?'

It was a short drive in Herr Gretschel's large silver car. Karl came too. A bleak red-brick church and the nave less than a quarter full, the pine coffin before the altar covered with white chrysanthemums. Lindsay found Mary on her knees in prayer and settled into the seat beside her.

'You've got ash on your coat,' she said as she rose to sit beside him. 'His daughters are there,' and she nodded towards two short, very well-built women to the right of the aisle. Two large men were sitting behind with children. The organ was rumbling through some gentle counterpoint.

'Dr Henderson,' Gretschel had leant forward from the chair behind to shake Mary's hand. 'You look well if I may say so.'

'You may, Herr Gretschel. You may.'

And she did look well, Lindsay thought, very well, straight-backed and trim and her face still youthful, her green eyes as light and bright as that first day in the Citadel.

The tinkle of a handbell and the priest and his two servers stepped up to the altar. A young priest almost lost in his heavy funeral vestments, his head bent slightly in reverence, his voice soft, a little soapy. And he began with a few words about the dead man. Helmut Lange was a loyal and much loved member of this church who had fought a courageous battle against cancer until it took him from us, missed by family, missed by friends. Funeral words, trite, anonymous words and Lindsay's thoughts drifted to another place, smoky, half lit, and Lange's eyes shining, his fingers drumming on the table to the rhythm of the band.

He leant across to whisper to Mary: 'Do you think he made it to New York?'

She turned slowly to look at him and she was smiling but there were tears in her eyes: 'You're thinking of the evening at Hatchett's. You know, he was a much better dancer than you.'

'But not as good a lover.' She pushed his shoulder in rebuke then looked away to hide her smile. In a way it was Lange who had brought them together as lovers again in those weeks after the attempt on his life in the camp. Lindsay remembered it as a sort of healing, scars inside and out – poor Lange carried the marks on his neck always but as a reminder of distant pain.

'Stand up for this bit,' and Mary pulled him to his feet.

A short time later and the first snow of winter was swirling lightly through the forest cemetery as they gathered beside the grave. It had been dug between tall pine trees and their roots scratched and rattled the coffin as it was lowered slowly into the hard ground.

Mary squeezed Lindsay's arm tightly and he reached round her shoulders to hold her closer, her coat flecked with drops of melting snow. Only fifteen people had made the journey from the church to the cemetery. Most of them were Lange's family, his daughters calm and their husbands indifferent, but there was also a young man shivering in a dark suit, with large brown eyes and long, rather greasy hair. A student, perhaps, without the means for a decent coat. Lindsay had not noticed him in the church but he seemed to be the most affected of those at the graveside. And there was something in his manner, his thin face and dark looks, that rang a distant bell.

The coffin slipped from the pall-bearers' straps with a clunk and the priest stepped forward with his aspersorium to sprinkle it with holy water. And then he invited them to throw earth into the grave. Lindsay bent to pick up a frozen nugget from the mound for Mary, something to rattle the lid.

'Make sure he knows we're here,' he whispered.

She smiled and squeezed his hand.

As the family began to make its way back to the cars Lindsay stepped up to the grave again and stood staring into the trench, his thoughts full of those few months fifty years before. He was dying for a cigarette. Lange would forgive him but the priest was still talking to the funeral director close by and there was something in his manner and voice, a righteous fervour, that reminded him of the men he used to meet in the interrogation room at Trent Park. Break expectation. As he slipped his hand into his coat pocket for a cigarette, someone touched his elbow.

'Herr Lindsay.'

It was the young man with the greasy brown hair.

'Yes?'

'Herr Lange told me you would be here.'

'Did he?'

'My name's Franz Lehmann,' and he offered his bony hand. 'I'm here on behalf of my family.'

'Oh?'

'My mother's a little unwell and couldn't make the journey.'

One of the cemetery men cleared his throat impatiently and gave them a 'talk somewhere else' glance. Three of them were standing ready with their spades. Fifteen minutes of mourning, get the job done, on to the next, order, efficiency, death by timetable.

'Can we walk a little way?' Lehmann asked. 'Just to the chapel.'

Gretschel was hobbling slowly towards the cemetery gates with Mary at his side, their heads bent close in conversation.

'All right, Herr Lehmann.'

The chapel was a short walk in the opposite direction, half hidden by trees, simple, wooden, windowless, like a pagan longhouse. Beneath the open porch at the west end there was a bench and Lehmann dropped on to his knee to wipe it dry with the sleeve of his jacket. Lindsay sat down and reached for his silver cigarette case: 'Do you smoke?'

Lehmann pulled a face.

'So, Herr Lehmann,' and he bent to light his cigarette. 'What do you want?'

'Herr Lange was like a grandfather to me. He helped my father when he was too ill to work, helped me through school and paid for me to come to university here. He was a friend to the family. Excuse me.'

He stopped to blow his nose on a grubby handkerchief. Lindsay looked away until he was calm enough to continue. It was a friendship of more than forty years, that had begun at the end of the war when Lange had found Lehmann's grandmother and her two children in a hostel for the homeless in Hamburg. Her husband had been killed in the British blitz of the city, her elder son lost on a U-boat, no money, no friends, no hope, two children to feed and care for, one of them Lehmann's mother.

'It was a small miracle. He spent weeks searching for my grand-mother. He said he owed it to an old comrade, a friend from the U-boat service, my uncle.'

'Your uncle?'

'He served on one of the most successful U-boats of the war.' Lehmann's voice rang with a pride that would have been a cause of comment in his student hall.

'The *112*?'

'Yes. Did you know . . .'

'Yes. I did know him.'

'Uncle August. He was only nineteen.'

Yes, they had the same eyes. He could see the little engineer rocking on the chair on the other side of the table, his eyes large and frightened and close to tears. Nineteen. God. So many years lost to him, a terrible waste, a terrible and pointless crime. Black and white and as sharp in his mind as it was fifty years ago, the picture of Heine dangling inches from the washroom floor. It brought a hard lump to his throat.

'I found out recently that he took his own life in the camp,' said Lehmann. 'Do you remember him? Herr Lange said you would.'

'I didn't know him well.'

'No one seems to know why he killed himself. I asked his commander, Admiral Mohr – he spoke of combat fatigue. He said my uncle's death hit all the survivors of the *112* very badly.'

'Yes. It was sad and senseless.'

And he thought of Gretschel tapping his finger against his temple. He was right, of course. Every hour, every day, guilt, fear, conflict-ing loyalties pulling first one way and then the other. Millions of small battles. Fought long after the parades and the bunting and the speeches. Scarred. Victor and vanquished the same. Lange, Mohr, Lindsay, he was sure they were the same. A secret history beyond the numbers and the dates and the shifting of borders. Someone had asked him to do an interview for a radio programme, just his memories of the war, but he declined. Some memories should be buried.

Lindsay leant down to extinguish his cigarette in a puddle, then got stiffly to his feet. A sharp wind was gusting powdery snow from the pines into the chapel porch where it swirled in a fine mist, dropping wet crystals on their clothes and in their hair. It felt colder – perhaps that was the memories – and the sky was a filthy Berlin grey.

'I think we'd better go back. My wife will be waiting for me.'

They did not speak and the graveyard was silent but for the crunch of their shoes, figures in a monochrome landscape like something from a piece of forgotten archive film. Picking their way slowly between the stones, they found the main path and a few minutes later reached Lange's grave. The cemetery workers were beating the hard ground between the pines flat with their spades, the rhythm like the ticking of a lazy clock. When it was level they loaded their tools into a handcart and left without a word, rattling down the gravel path to the gate. And Lindsay stood alone at the foot of the grave. He stood there until the raw earth was lost beneath the snow.

HISTORICAL NOTE ON CODES

In the autumn of 1945 Commander Tighe of the Admiralty Signals Division submitted a secret report on German code-breaking efforts during the Second World War to the Director of Naval Intelligence. The report was considered 'so disturbing and important' that only three copies were made. In it, Tighe detailed the success of German cryptographers in repeatedly breaking both Royal and Merchant Navy codes and suggested that their efforts were responsible for many of the U-boat's greatest successes in the Battle of the Atlantic. The Royal Navy's codes were changed a number of times but the German B-Dienst was able to break into them again and again, often within a few weeks. The Admiralty was slow to recognise and interpret evidence that its codes were compromised and carry out the necessary investigation.

After the war, the success of the cryptographers at Bletchley Park in breaking the German Enigma ciphers helped to shield the Royal Navy from critical scrutiny over the failure of its own codes. In his report, Commander Tighe concluded that British code security was so disastrously lax that it cost the country dearly in men and ships and 'very nearly lost us the war'.

NOTE ON SOURCES

Many of the characters are based on real people although most of the events described are fictional.

Admiral John Godfrey was the Director of Naval Intelligence until 1942 and Ian Fleming, the author of the James Bond books, was his assistant. Fleming was instrumental in recruiting people to the Division and those who worked with him often remarked on his love of cloak-and-dagger operations. The man charged with responsibility for tracking German U-boat operations from the Citadel was Rodger Winn and while none of the duty officers in Room 41 were women, a Margaret Stewart held this position across the corridor in Room 30 where the movements of the enemy's surface fleet were plotted. Her confidential memoir of life in the Citadel is in the National Archive in London (ADM 223/286).

For further details of the Citadel and the work of the Combined Services Detailed Interrogation Centre (CSDIC) I quarried written sources but also the memories of those who visited and worked there. I am particularly grateful to the late Colin McFadyean who served as a naval interrogator and at the end of the war became head of the section. Transcripts of the secret recordings (SR reports) made of German prisoners at CSDIC, notes on the detailed interrogation of U-boat crews, and intelligence assessments written by the interrogators exist in the National Archive (Record groups ADM 223 and WO 208). They provide an invaluable insight into the work of Section 11 and the views of U-boat prisoners. Occasionally I have quoted from these documents, for instance, the observation made in 1941 by the then head of Section 11 that it was a mistake to use Jewish interrogators or men of 'Jewish appearance' (ADM 223/475). I have also drawn on authentic pieces of special intelligence, including some of the Enigma decrypts from Bletchley Park that suggested British codes might be compromised in the spring and summer of 1941 (ADM

223/2). Evidence that prisoners let slip valuable intelligence on the work of the B-Dienst can be found in CSDIC secret recordings made in March 1941 (WO 208/4141).

Although there were three U-boat commanders with the name Mohr, none of them served on Admiral Dönitz's Staff or fell into British hands. One of Admiral Dönitz's most senior Staff officers was the distinguished U-boat commander Günther Hessler, who sank fourteen ships off the coast of West Africa in May and June of 1941. The official history he wrote for the Ministry of Defence after the war was an important source for the German Staff perspective on the Battle of the Atlantic.

The most successful commander of the war, Otto Kretschmer of *U-99*, was captured in March 1941, brought ashore in Liverpool and taken to Trent Park for interrogation. The officers of *U-99* were then transferred to Grizedale POW camp in the Lake District. His first officer, Hans-Jochen von Knebel Doeberitz, had served for a time on the Staff as Dönitz's adjutant. During Kretschmer's time as the senior German prisoner at Grizedale, a secret Council of Honour was held to question and judge the First Officer of the ill-fated *U-570*. In August 1941 the inexperienced commander and crew of the boat had panicked and surrendered to a British aircraft at sea. The first officer was found guilty of cowardice by the Court of Honour for his part in the affair and ostracised by the other prisoners, but he was not beaten. In an effort to regain his good name, he attempted to escape and was shot while on the run in the Lake District. There were two investigations into the Court of Honour but no charges were brought against Kretschmer or any of the other prisoners at the camp. After the war, Otto Kretschmer served as an Admiral in the West German Navy. A more disturbing example of a kangaroo court took place at a POW camp in Scotland in December 1944 when a prisoner called Wolfgang Rosterg was wrongly accused of giving information to the British. He was brutally beaten and hanged by some of the SS prisoners in the camp. Five men were eventually tried and executed for the crime, although many more had played a part.

Camp 020 was MI5's secret centre at Ham Common, London, where spies were interrogated and broken by the formidable Colonel

Stephens and his team of interrogators. There is no evidence to suggest that physical torture was used by the Security Service but a senior officer in one branch of Military Intelligence [MI 19] who spent time at the camp is known to have used excessive force. A number of secret reports were written by Naval Intelligence, MI5 and Military Intelligence personnel after the war describing their interrogation techniques in some detail and I have made use of these. The memories of the master Luftwaffe interrogator Hanns Joachim Scharff, quoted in *The Interrogator* by Raymond F. Tolliver (Schiffer 1997), were also useful, as were more contemporary British and American police sources. It was not unusual for POWs to be taken to bars and theatres in London in an effort to win their confidence and a special fund existed for this purpose.

The Royal Navy lost a number of escorts like the *Culloden* on convoy duty in the course of the war but particularly shocking was the sinking of HMS *Firedrake*. The destroyer, *Firedrake*, was cut in half by a torpedo while on convoy duty in the Atlantic in December 1942 and all but twenty six of her crew of 194 men were lost. A secret Admiralty report was critical of decisions made by her captain (ADM 199/165). No official Board of Inquiry was held into the loss of the ship. For the effects of Post-Traumatic Stress Disorder on war veterans, I spoke to both Merchant and Royal Navy seamen and was able to draw on a number of recent medical studies. Of particular valve were J. P. Wilson, B. Drożdek, and S. Turkovic: 'Post-traumatic shame and guilt', *Trauma, Violence and Abuse*, vol. 7, no. 2, April 2006, 122–141, and R. E. Opp and A. Y. Samson, 'Taxonomy of guilt for combat veterans', *Professional Psychology: Research and Practice*, 20, 1989, 159–165.

Of the many books, papers and people I have consulted in researching the story, I would especially like to thank Volmar König for his memories of life behind the wire as a prisoner. Admiral John Adams helped me with his recollections of life aboard an old V and W Class destroyer in the first years of the war and of the dark days of the Liverpool blitz. I am grateful to Sarah Baring for her insight into life in the Citadel and on the home front and to Dr Iain Hamilton of the University of Witwatersrand in Johannesburg for sharing his knowledge of the Naval Intelligence Division. Donald Coombes spoke to me of the night HMS *Firedrake* was lost. I interviewed Colin McFadyean more than once about his work as an interrogator and the late Sir Charles Wheeler also shared his memories of the Naval Intelligence division with me.

I would also like to acknowledge my debt to the following sources: The Admiralty's *A Seaman's Pocket-Book* (June 1943); Patrick Beesley, *Very Special Intelligence – The Story of the Admiralty's Operational Intelligence Centre 1939–45* and *Very Special Admiral: The Life of Admiral J. H. Godfrey*; Clay Blair, *Hitler's U-boat Wars 1939–45* (2 vols); Kendal Burt and James Leasor, *The One That Got Away*; Patrick Campbell, *Trent Park: A History*; Simon Crump, *They Call it 'U-boat Hotel'*; Roderick De Norman, *For Führer and Fatherland: SS Murder and Mayhem in Wartime Britain*; Karl Dönitz, *Memoirs: Ten Years and Twenty Days*; Günther Hessler, *German Naval History of the U-boat War in the Atlantic* (3 vols); Chris Howard, *The Battle of the Atlantic – The Corvettes and Their Crews*; Major H. R. Jordan, unpublished memoir in the Imperial War Museum of Major H. R. Jordan of Military Counter Intelligence; David Kahn, *Seizing the Enigma: The Race to Break the German U-boat Codes 1939–43*; General Raymond E. Lee, *The Journal of General Raymond E. Lee 1940–41*; Andrew Lycett, *Ian Fleming*; Donald Macintyre, *U-boat Killer*; Donald MacLachlan, *Room 39: Naval Intelligence in Action 1939–45*; Jak P. Mallmann Showell, *German Naval Code Breakers*; Timothy P. Mulligan, *Neither Sharks Nor Wolves: The Men of the Nazi U-boat Arm 1939–45*; Axel Niestlé, *German U-boat Losses During World War II*; James Owen and Guy Walters, *The Voice of War*; Léonce Peillard, *U-boats to the Rescue: The Laconia Incident*; Graham Rhys-Jones, 'The German System: A Staff Perspective' in *The Battle of the Atlantic: The 50th Anniversary International Naval Conference*; Phil Richards and John Banigan, *How to Abandon Ship* (1942); Terence Robertson, *The Golden Horseshoe*; Jürgen Rohwer, *Axis Submarine Success of World War II*; Captain S. W. Roskill, *The War at Sea* (4 vols); Stephen Sansom, *Westminster at War*; Hanns Joachim Scharff and Raymond F. Tolliver, *The Interrogator: The Story of Hanns Joachim Scharff – Master Interrogator of the Luftwaffe*; Lt Col A. P. Scotland, *The London Cage*; Simon Sebag Montefiore, *Enigma: The Battle for the Codes*; Lt Col R. W. G.

Stephens and Oliver Hoare, *Camp 020: MI5 and the Nazi Spies*; John Strachey, *Post D*; David Syrett, *The Battle of the Atlantic and Signals Intelligence U-boat Situations and Trends 1941–45*; Eric Topp, *Odyssey of a U-boat Commander*; Colin Warwick, *Really Not Required*; Herbert A. Werner, *Iron Coffins*; Derek M. Whale, *The Liners of Liverpool*; Richard Whittington-Egan, *The Great Liverpool Blitz*; Joan Wyndham, *Love is Blue* and *Love Lessons*.

Finally, I would like to thank my agent Julian Alexander and my editor, Kate Parkin and all those who helped me with advice and encouragement. I hope they find enough of the spirit of the times in the story to forgive the liberties I have taken with the history.